PRAISE FOR AMANDA PROWSE

'Amanda Prowse is the queen of family drama'

Daily Mail

'A deeply emotional, unputdownable read'

Red

'Heartbreaking and heartwarming in equal measure'

The Lady

'Amanda Prowse is the queen of heartbreak fiction'

The Mail Online

'Captivating, heartbreaking and superbly written'

Closer

'Uplifting and positive but you may still need a box of tissues'

Cosmopolitan

'You'll fall in love with this'

Cosmopolitan

'Powerful and emotional drama that packs a real punch'

Heat

'Warmly accessible but subtle . . . moving and inspiring'

Daily Mail

'Magical'

Now

Very
Very
Lucky

ALSO BY AMANDA PROWSE

Novels

Very Very Lucky

Amanda Prowse

LAKE UNION
PUBLISHING

Text copyright © 2024 by Lionhead Media Ltd.

Published by Lake Union Publishing, Seattle

www.apub.com

Amazon, the Amazon logo, and Lake Union Publishing are trademarks of Amazon.com, Inc., or its affiliates.

ISBN-13: 9781542024860
eISBN: 9781542024853

Cover design by Emma Rogers
Cover image: ©Elena Istomina and Net Vector / Shutterstock

Printed in the United States of America

I had only written two chapters of this story when my beloved brother Simon Ward Smith died suddenly. He was young, vibrant, and so very funny; my family and I will miss him every day we live. We are felled by sadness, yet still standing. It's odd to me that I had chosen to write about life and particularly death – the one thing we are all guaranteed to experience and yet the one thing that shocks us most. Sorrow has wrapped every word, and yet I am beyond thankful that I knew Simon and his lust for life. I hope this joy shines from the page! This one small life is all we have. Love it, live it and, to quote my brother, 'It's important to make yourself laugh, every day!' I promise to try, Simon, I promise to try . . .

CHAPTER ONE

Emma Fountain

All was calm in Emma Fountain's world as the breath left her lips in a soft purr. It was the kind of breathing that occurs only when you slip from that glorious state of dozy into deep and restful sleep, leaving the real world behind. She felt her mouth fall open, yielding against the smooth pillowcase. It was as if her muscles softened, falling, weighted into the mattress, sinking right into it and taking comfort from it. Any sounds were tuned out, as her world grew smaller. With the duvet pulled up under her chin, she was warm, happy and extremely grateful for the chance to rest. Because Emma was tired. In fact, she was more than tired; she was weary, fatigued with a bone-deep ache of exhaustion that meant rare moments like this were so very much appreciated.

These were the seconds of bliss, when her mother and her many ailments, her kids and their demands, even the financial struggles she and her husband, Brendan, faced – they all disappeared, and she was lost entirely to the blissful escape of slumber . . .

'Emma?'

She vaguely knew the man's voice but couldn't immediately place it. Whoever it was, she wished they'd shut up.

'Emma!'

The voice was a little louder now, almost forceful, and one she now recognised as belonging to Mr Blundesthorpe, her mother's neighbour, who lived next door to her childhood home. A kind enough man with a bulbous nose, who always seemed to be a little more involved than he should be, offering opinions and dropping in, mowing the front lawn after her mother became a widow and generally being helpful to the point of irritation. She was sure this said much more about her than him. The man who, during the summer months, traipsed the half-mile from his street to hers with heavily laden cardboard boxes. Gifting her with more figs, courgettes and tomatoes than she knew what to do with. It was a sad fact that after a couple of tarts, a few batches of soup and several jars of chutney, she quickly ran out of recipes and enthusiasm for his home-grown wares. Those first boxes groaning under the weight of free organic produce were admired and received with gratitude, especially by her son Reggie, who, when the mood took him, liked to whip up fancy suppers with the stuff; but by the end of the season she sometimes considered hiding beneath the kitchen table to dodge having to take it off his hands, thus avoiding the huge dollop of guilt that accompanied the action of tipping the spoiling fruit and veg straight on to the compost. But how to avoid it? She was certain that refusal of his generosity would only cause offence.

It was odd, having him enter her dream. Typical of her luck though – not for her the arrival of Liam Neeson in his underwear with a big bag of prawn crackers or Pierce Brosnan with a bottle of champers and a slab of chocolate to share. There was no beach, no massage, no warm heat of the sun on her skin . . . skin that would of course be taut over young, healthy bones that didn't creak when she overdid it at Zumba. Skin that didn't sit over a snug layer of fat that meant her skinny jeans could only be worn with the zip undone and an oversized sweatshirt that dropped down to her thighs. I mean, crikey, of all the fantasies she might have pondered while idling in the car waiting for the lights to change, before she drifted off or even as she joined the longest, slowest queue at the supermarket checkout, as was her knack – she could categorically state that none of them had ever, ever involved the aged Mr Blundesthorpe.

And yet here he was.

Only this felt different. It wasn't only that she could hear him, but, as bizarre as it sounded, she could *sense* him too. Surely he wasn't in their bedroom, was he? Had her alarm gone off? She couldn't remember. Her heart raced a little at the prospect, but still with her eyes tightly shut, sleep-thought and reality fused to fill her mind with mental fog; was she decent? Please don't say she'd hopped into bed in just her bra and knick-knacks again, or worse, that one cotton nightie that allowed her boob to escape through the neck hole and come to rest at her throat – good Lord, she'd never be able to face the man again! And who had let him in? One of the boys? Were they late for school? Or was Brendan home? And why did he think it okay to let the man wander upstairs? She wasn't being rude, but decided to lie very, very still and keep quiet, hoping he might take the hint and leave her alone to sleep . . .

'Mrs Fountain!'

This time it was a shout, a very definite, very real and very obvious shout. Emma felt herself jolt, in the same way she had when dreaming she'd jumped off a building and shook on the mattress as she landed, waking at the supposed point of impact. Opening one eye, she stared at Mr Blundesthorpe.

'Mr Blundesthorpe! What . . . what are you doing in my bedroom?' she asked, clutching the duvet under her chin in case there *was* a need to preserve her modesty. 'Is . . . is my mum okay, is that why you're here?' she pressed. Why had Lorraine, her mum's carer, not contacted her directly? It was the only thing that made sense and her sense of impending panic rose accordingly.

3

Finally, she opened both eyes and as Mr Blundesthorpe spoke, the reality of her situation hit her like an ice pick in the chest.

'Your mum? No, no.' The older man shook his head. 'My niece drove me in. I came to get some novelty ice-cube makers' – he held up a lurid lime-green mould – 'and to have my breakfast. I do like a cooked breakfast midweek. And it's very good value, even when I have beans as a menu add-on.'

Shit!

A vague titter of amusement rippled like a gentle sound wave around her as she threw back the duvet and swung her legs around until she was standing. She kept her gaze on the floor, not wanting to catch the eye of any of the gawping onlookers clutching their big blue plastic bags, as they too prepared for their early-morning saunter around Ikea.

'And I'm not in your bedroom, Emma.' The old man spoke kindly. 'And neither are you.'

'Yes, thank you for that. I'm well aware.'

'Are you okay, dear?' he asked softly, his concern touching but doing nothing to alleviate her embarrassment.

'I'm great, thank you, Mr Blundesthorpe. Just great!'

It felt only right to make the bed that she must have slipped into, pulling the duvet straight and plumping the pillows before smoothing any obvious creases with the flat of her hand.

With her bag hitched on to her shoulder and her dark wavy hair tucked behind her ears, she made her way along the floor, walking as fast as her navy Skechers allowed, following the small arrows on the floor, and almost jogging with intent until she reached the escalator that took her to the lift that meant escape.

Having retrieved her car keys from the confines of her small blue backpack, she had never been so happy to slide into the driver's seat of her Ford Focus. With her head on the steering wheel, she closed her eyes and breathed slowly.

The truth was she didn't remember getting into the bed but could clearly recall arriving at the store and climbing the escalator and then feeling overwhelmed. So much to do, *always* so much to do, thoughts racing, the clock ticking, and her worries over the smallest of details sitting like tiny needles that lanced her thoughts. *Reggie . . . was Reggie okay?* He was so quiet, often detached; should they seek expert help, and how would that conversation start? Or would the involvement of a meddling professional only make things worse?

And then she'd woken in the bed . . .

'Emma. What on earth were you thinking?' she whispered as her phone rang, making her start.

'What're you up to?' This was how Rosalind began their calls.

Having known each other since primary school, very best friends since the age of five, there was no need for the formality of 'Hello!' or 'It's me, Roz!' or even 'How are you today?'

'I'm . . . what am I up to? God, Roz. I can't even tell you.' She cringed, her eyes once again tightly closed, trying in vain to erase the memory of the last twenty minutes of her life.

'Well, this sounds interesting. Do I need to guess?'

'You couldn't if you tried.'

She scratched at the small blob of dried egg yolk on the thigh of her jeans. It came away in tiny crystal-like flakes under her nail, which she rolled and dropped to the floor. A reminder that while she'd cooked the boys fried egg on toast before school, she was yet to have her own breakfast. Her stomach rolled with hunger. It was like this on her days off, her routine thrown into chaos as she rushed to complete all the tasks set by her family like she was on some shite quest, but instead of a prize if she succeeded, they simply set more tasks. She made the decision to grab a coffee and some toast when she got home.

'Challenge accepted.' She heard her friend take a deep breath. 'Well, infidelity is out of the question as I know you're still smitten with that dickhead you married.'

'True.' She smiled at the thought of her husband. 'As in true, "infidelity is out of the question", and not that he's a dickhead.'

'Let's agree to disagree.'

Emma laughed. Roz and Brendan had been squabbling and putting each other down for nearly thirty years. It was a bickering with strong admiration – indeed, affection – at its foundation. The fact was they both loved her, and she loved them, and this was enough to run a thread of loyalty and connection right through their verbal jousting.

'Okay, let's see. You've gone out with odd shoes again? Bumped into Mackenzie McTeeth?'

Emma sprayed the car with laughter; it still had the power to do that to her, the nickname Roz had given Mackenzie Baverstock, the girl in their class at secondary school who had the neatest, whitest teeth they'd ever seen at a time when both teens were rather ashamed of their own less than pearly whites. A time when their tongues probed the grey amalgam fillings that cluttered up their gobs, and they cringed at the sight of the chipped and slightly ochre-tinged enamel that was far from the Hollywood smile they both craved. Emma knew Mackenzie's nickname was based on nothing more than pure, sour-tasting envy.

'No, my shoes are matching. And I'd like to remind you that the only reason I had odd shoes on that one time was that you were rushing me, you said we'd miss the bus, and it was dark, the bulb had gone in my bedroom. I grabbed what I thought were matching pumps from the bottom of my wardrobe. They felt the same.'

'One was red and one was black, you dipstick!'

Again, Emma laughed – *dipstick!* This too had been funny when they were kids and was still funny now. They shared many a private joke, many moments where just one word could send them into fits. Their laughter nearly always floored them at the most inappropriate moment, almost as if the more solemn or inopportune the occasion, the funnier they found it.

'Yes, but do you remember the following week we saw Tiffany and her mates all wearing odd shoes? I was a bloody trendsetter!' Emma chuckled at the memory.

'You keep telling yourself that, darling.'

'I will. And actually, I feel a bit sorry for Mackenzie McTeeth, still trying so hard to be perfect. It must be exhausting. The last time I saw her, she was keen to tell me that her son was at university *in* Oxford, which is categorically not the same as being *at* Oxford. And I wanted to say, "You don't need to do that, no one really cares which university your kid is at, chill out, woman!"'

'But I bet you didn't,' Roz sniped.

'Of course I didn't. I'm not mean.'

'You are a bit,' her friend countered. 'You're mean enough to say it to me, but not brave enough to say it to her.'

'You don't count.' She meant it; Roz was like her other half, her delinquent twin, they had no secrets. To talk to her friend like this was therapy, a respite from her towering to-do list, which felt insurmountable. This was what Roz did: distracted her, allowed her to breathe, provided moments of unbridled joy!

'Well, I think she's an arsehole.' Roz gave her succinct appraisal and this time they both laughed. 'So come on, what have you been up to?'

Emma paused for a beat, knowing it would heighten the impact.

'I fell asleep in Ikea.' It was amazing how after a short chat with her mate, and the passage of very little time, even she could now see the funny side. 'It can't have been open ten minutes and people were wandering in, grabbing their blue plastic bags, and I was snoozing away like a baby.'

'Are you joking?' Roz squealed.

'I wish I was. If they've got me on CCTV, they are definitely showing that at the Christmas party.'

'Where exactly did you fall asleep in Ikea?'

'Where do you think? On a kitchen display – I just hoicked up my leg and curled up on a cooker! In a bed, of course! I got into a bed and fell asleep. I'm dying just thinking about it. I'd only gone in to grab a couple of white plates because Martha's new boyfriend is coming for supper, and she said under no circumstances are we to use the green plate. Said it was humiliating that we didn't have a matching set.'

'Priceless! Absolutely priceless!' Roz howled. 'Only you.'

'And that's not the worst of it.' She swallowed.

'Oh God, you didn't wet the bed like you did at Brownie camp?'

'I told you it was water! My flask wasn't done up properly.'

'Of course, Em.'

'And no, I didn't, but I was woken up by Mr Blundesthorpe.'

'Overly keen courgette guy?'

'The very same,' she confirmed.

'Okay, I need all the details and besides, I called to say I need to talk to you, so come over. I'll put the kettle on. I'm not going into work today.'

'Sure.' This wasn't unusual; Roz often needed advice on the latest unattainable or disinterested man she had a fancy for, or conversely one she was keen to shake off but who clung on like a limpet. Actually, 'advice' was a bit rich – Emma knew she was more of a silent sounding board while her friend verbally explored her options. They often caught up on her day off. 'I've got a few bits and bobs to do – can I come later, after tea? Are you going to be in? I'll get the kids sorted and pop over. I'll bring Brucie.' She grinned.

'Don't you dare bring that filthy, stinking animal anywhere near my cream sofa.'

'But he loves you.'

'Well, I don't love him!' Roz snapped. 'And yes, I'll be in. I'll cancel my date with the sexy Hemsworth brother.'

'Which one?'

'Em, does anyone know which one is which, and frankly does it matter? To be honest, any of them would do.'

'I hear ya! See you later.' She noted Roz's affection for the Australian actors and decided it might be time to update her dream fantasy men. Goodbye Mr Neeson with prawn crackers and Pierce with champagne and chocolate, and hello Hemsworths . . . she'd have to think about it.

CHAPTER TWO

Thurston Brancher

Thurston Brancher sat at the wooden table, littered with the witness marks of a hundred thousand cups of tea, and looked out through the kitchen window at the greying sky. Rhubarb, 'Barb' or 'Barbie' for short, his faithful Jack Russell, was curled in his basket by the range, but with his eyes firmly on his master.

A bruise of a day . . .

That's what Mary would say. He'd done this a lot recently, in the last two weeks to be precise, heard her voice in a way that made her present, like he was talking to her in his mind. And more interestingly, like she was talking to him. He wondered if it was real, wondered how long it might last and wondered if people would think he was mad if he shared the fact. Not that he planned on telling anyone, not that he told anyone much. His reputation was, he knew, as a private man. A quiet man. He was indeed both of these things and yet there was a side only she had known. His wife of sixty-two years.

I told you when we first met, didn't I? When you were all shy and stuttery and we danced at the Young Farmers, I told you then when you first asked if we could go courting, that if a marriage was good then I'd be content to have twenty, thirty, forty or fifty years of it, rain or shine, that'd be enough. But we got even luckier, Thurston, we had sixty-two years. Rain and shine . . . and that should make you glad.

Yes, Mary knew all sides of him, knew he was a man prone to silliness when the opportunity arose, a man who was quite adept at singing the hymns he'd learned by rote as a child, and only when his throat, tongue and larynx were lubricated with God's golden nectar. This referring to cider and not honey, lest there be any doubt, and with a love of classical music that when played well, played live, or played loudly or rarely, could make him weep. He was also a poet. Him – Thurston Brancher with his gnarled, hammer-bashed, frostbitten, wire-cut, grafting hands with fingers that knew the bite of cold and the sting of fire – he could also wield a pen with such grace he scarcely believed it himself.

You old dafty . . .

That's what she called him. Often.

You old dafty . . .

And it made him happy, because it meant she knew him like no other and that when, after a day on the land, he hung up his waxed coat that had gone shiny on the arms, and his cap with a repair on the brim, he stepped into a different world. At that very moment, along with the garments he wore in all weathers, he could hang up the worry over cattle, grain, oil prices, tractor repairs, shrinking subsidies, inflated insurance premiums, broken fences, litter, climate change and all the other concerns that were like a thousand mental paper cuts.

Yes, when he closed the door of the boot room behind him, he stepped into another world. The boot room: where she liked to leave a lamp on, casting a warm glow over the flagstone floor and the old butler sink where his mother and grandmother had skinned rabbits, washed spuds and scrubbed clothes on the washboard with a bar of carbolic, the smell of which he could still sense if he breathed deeply enough. He stepped into the world Mary had created for him, and it was a warm world of love, poetry and hot tea drunk by the hearth in favoured earthenware cups. A world of soft cake and crumbly biscuits, of thick lavish gravies and buttery golden-crusted pies. A world of clean sheets, plump eiderdowns, and her trimming his hair every so often in the kitchen, with a frilly plastic cape that he believed had once belonged to his sister, June, tied around his neck and shoulders. And no matter that it had been the case for decades, the donning of the pink garment and the sight of it next to his coarse beard sent her into fits of laughter that folded her double. Every single time.

And each time she laughed like this, while not wanting to put a dent in her joy, he'd say 'Be careful with them scissors' as she bent low, and her face neared the pointy end that sat sharp and to attention between her fingers. Because it was always this way. Him worrying about any harm, any sadness, any dark cloud, or any danger that might bring shadow or hurt to her life. He wanted her to walk in nothing but sunshine. Sunshine and good things. That was it. This had been his wish.

Very best of all about the world they made was night-time, when they sought out each other's arms. A place in which they found comfort and solace. Home. He always thought the *real* world was the one that lurked behind the door of that boot room. *Him and her. She and him. You and me. Thurston and Mary. Mary and Thurston . . .*

'Thurston!' his sister June shouted, and she banged the table. It made him jump, only realising by the jolt and the set of her mouth that this was not the first time she'd hollered. 'You're miles away!' Her tone was accusatory.

I wish . . .

'I said, where's the big teapot? Grandma Brancher's teapot?' She pointed at the clock, as if to emphasise that time was of the essence.

He stared at her, knowing the teapot she meant. It was enamelled, green and chipped around the lid, and had always been in the house, like most things. This state of affairs made him feel more like the custodian of the farmhouse, its buildings, the ornaments, and the heavy, dark furniture that came with it, rather than the owner. Not that it mattered now; it was only a building and in it only things.

Mary had never asked for anything to be replaced. Never requested fancy pale carpets or the latest this or that, as if she knew that the soft touch of the bread board with its dip in the middle was more valuable, more precious because of the Brancher history that went with it. He'd worried when they'd started courting with a view to marriage that she might think it awful to live among the relics placed by generations of women before her, items both pretty and functional chosen by his mother and gran, but she hadn't.

Their honeymoon was two blissful, barefoot, sleeves-rolled days in Lyme Regis, where they'd stayed in a boarding house and laughed as the bed springs creaked under their combined weight. The youngsters, in love and excited for the future, had coupled, and all his nerves and any hesitation, any sliver of doubt, had gone in an instant.

He had been worried, terrified even. Try finding a boy who before his first time isn't. Anticipation of the act itself so heavy with expectation, and not for him, as you might suspect, whipped up into a frenzy by the ribbing of his mates or the nudges of his peers. He had always been his own man. No, for him it was the expectation he placed on himself. A pressure of sorts. Thinking, hoping, praying it might be something as wonderful and life-affirming as he had hoped, as he imagined. Unsure if he could stand the disappointment if it turned out to be no more than . . . okay. He wanted it to be life-changing.

And it was.

What words best describe the glorious union that bound them heart, soul and body? *Heavenly, new and exciting.* That'd do. An act that had left them both a little dazed, a little breathless not only at the physical exertion, always greater on his part than hers, but also at the sheer surprise and pure, pure joy of it! It was wondrous, addictive and, dare he say, divine. An act of which he wanted more and more . . .

When they'd arrived here at Merrydown Farm, she'd simply and quietly hung her coat on the peg rack and reached for his mother's apron, tying it about her tiny waist, satisfied and humming as she opened cupboards and let her fingers dance over the contents. Sweeping dusty corners, polishing brass and silver, washing curtains, opening windows and beating the heavy rugs woven in a foreign land and brought back by his Great-uncle Booth, a travelling man. She arranged flowers into vases, swapped pictures around and shone mirrors until they gleamed. She tended the small but pretty garden, planted anything that was deep or wide enough to hold a bloom and tacked a wooden lattice trellis up around the front door, to which a climbing rose still clung. The house sang to a new rhythm, learned a new life, and welcomed in a new era.

And Thurston knew happiness – the level of which he had been unable to imagine!

He liked to know she was around. Liked the sound of her singing, the knock of wood on wood as cupboard doors opened and closed, was thrilled by the noise of the electric mixer whirring, the wooden spoon hitting the side of the china bowl, the burst of water from the pipe, filling the kettle, the vacuum cleaner humming above his head. Her laughter, as she listened to a play on the radio, or watched her beloved *Only Fools and Horses* on TV, knowing every joke, every plot, every episode and every cue, yet still laughing like a girl as if it was the first time she'd seen it. She was his background noise, his music, confirmation that his was a life lived as part of a couple. A life in harmony.

It had been in this happy state that they'd idled the years, working like dogs during the day but always, always breathing long and deep as night fell. In the summer they'd lie upon an old tartan blanket in the paddock and stare at the sun as it sank. And in the cooler months, with the fire lit, he'd take up his place on the saggy sofa, where she slipped her hand into his. Or their legs lolled thigh to thigh as she knitted jumpers and scarves, sewed patches on to sheets or tablecloths by way of repair, or crocheted baby hats, donating them to the neonatal unit for couples who had got luckier than them.

> *Tis all I ever yearn for,*
> *this evening touch from you.*
> *As our wintering years beckon,*
> *I am as warmed now as I ever was,*
> *by the feel of your hand in mine . . .*

How he loved her, his Mary. How he missed her and how unthinkable it was to imagine a life without her.

Entirely unthinkable *and* impossible. It really was that simple. A world without Mary was a world in which he had no desire to be. None at all. This in part was how he had reached the conclusion that he wanted out. He was cashing in his chips. Packing for his final voyage. Cancelling the milk and waving goodbye to life with no more than a brief 'Adieu!' over his shoulder as he left.

And with very little by way of expectation, his decision was cemented by the fact that if there was even the smallest sliver of a possibility that in death they might be reunited, then that was what he wanted, what he wished for, and what he would plan . . . To die. And soon. What was the point in lingering?

CHAPTER THREE

EMMA

Still sitting in the Ikea car park, no sooner had Emma ended the call to Roz than her phone rang immediately. It was her older son, and middle child.

'Hello, Reggie. Everything okay, love?'

She braced herself, waiting for the familiar request or moan that didn't get any less draining, no matter that she now expected it. Wishing, wishing that just once he might be calling to say he was having a blast and not to pick him up after school as he was going out with friends . . . her heart flexed with longing for this very thing.

'Can you pick me up?'

This is what he did, cut straight to the chase when he was agitated. It was no surprise. He hated school. Well, that wasn't strictly true, he liked the learning bit, loved some lessons even, but hated every social aspect, every interaction with his classmates, hated not feeling like he fitted in and found sports . . . challenging.

'I, I spoke to Mrs Bauer, she said I could call you to come and collect me, like the counsellor said, if it gets too much . . .'

Well versed in what the counsellor had said, she glanced at the clock on the dashboard and struggled with the mental maths. She had to be at her mum's in forty minutes to sit with her, so she'd eat her lunch. Quickly, she did the sums to see if she had time to collect her son from school.

'Mum,' he prompted, 'you said you'd pick me up if ever I needed you to, you agreed, and I need you to now.' His words were at once a rebuke and a reminder.

'Okay, okay love. Of course. I'm on my way.'

She refrained from admitting that she hadn't realised when she made the statement that he might 'need' her to pick him up thrice weekly. Personally, she felt the routine of school might be the best place for him, but as Mrs Bauer had pressed, *The fact that he comes in at all is to be lauded and he works well at home on set tasks, never misses a deadline . . .*

That, thought Emma, was because he wasn't trying to fit so much into his day he felt as if his head might explode!

'Come as quickly as you can, Mum!'

At the singular note of rising panic in his voice, her pulse quickened. She had devoured enough articles, books and podcasts to know that sixteen was a tricky age for boys and that he was suffering with anxiety, stress and mild depression. It was like walking a tightrope, a fine and fragile gossamer line between supporting their oldest boy, letting him know they would always provide a safety net, and giving him carte blanche to slide out of any chores he didn't fancy, or school days that were no more than a little tricky. How was she to know if at that particular moment he was simply having an 'off' day and didn't fancy triple geography, or was about to find a place from which to jump? The thought of the latter was enough to make her turn the key quickly and pump the accelerator.

She'd asked him once on a dark, dark day, when he lay beneath his duvet, gazing at the ceiling and so withdrawn she couldn't sleep for worry, drawing on her courage as the words stuck like sticks in her throat, her tongue dry, her heart hammering, *Do you ever think about, do you ever think about taking your life, darling? Have you ever thought about that?* His smile was slow and lopsided, his eyes wide as he swallowed and shook his head. There was no relief or consolation to be found in his response. She hadn't believed him then and she didn't believe him now.

'I'm on my way, love, just leaving Ikea car park, be there as soon as I can.'

'Hurry up, Mum.'

He ended the call.

Hurry up! Hurry up! Hurry up!

Emma dumped her phone on the passenger seat and threw the car into reverse. It shot backwards. The crash was loud and followed by the sound of glass or similar hitting the floor.

'Oh no!' Emma tugged on her seat belt too quickly and it snapped back, trapping her. She took a beat, ran her hand over her face, and did her best to calm her own rising tide of panic as the clock ticked. Jumping out, she ran to the back of the car, only to see that what she'd hit was the concrete edge of a post in the car park. Her rear light was smashed and the back bumper had an ungainly crack along it. She stared at the damage and her first thought was that it looked expensive to fix. Just what they needed.

'I saw what happened. You were on your phone and then there was a loud bang! Are you okay?' a woman called out across the car park, pausing in her task of shoving fake plants into her cramped boot.

'Yes, thank you. I'm fine.' She shook her head with hands on hips and sighed at the bloody inconvenience of it all. 'And actually, I wasn't on my phone.'

'Oh right, no. I just meant . . . I suppose it could have been worse,' the woman added, before continuing without waiting for a response. 'I mean, a child could have been standing by the post, or an old lady, and they'd have been totally squished—'

Emma cut the woman short. 'Thankfully they weren't, though, were they? Neither of them. As far as I can see, the only damage is to my car and a scrape of paint on the bollard, which, if I look closely' – she did just this, bending low to examine the post – 'there are several shades of paint on it, mine being merely the most recent. And so, I shall head off now, as I have' – she wondered why she was about to regale the stranger with her long list of chores – 'stuff to do.'

'Yes, but if you look . . .'

'Sorry?' Emma felt the throb of a vein in her temple, again denying her the chance to speak.

'I was going to say, if you look—' The woman pointed at the post. Her words were accompanied by a gesture that looked very much like she was practising her backhand.

'I'm just going to stop you there!' Emma yelled. 'I was looking! And who are you, the car park police? Is this what you do, hang around offering sage advice after the fact? And not that it's any business of yours, but I'd finished the call. The phone was on the front seat, where it still is!' She couldn't help it; the words had left her mouth before her filter had kicked in.

'There's no need to be so rude!' the woman fired. 'Why are you shouting at me?'

'And there's no need for you to be so interfering and . . . and gloomy! The world is shitty enough right now, so busy, so . . . demanding, without you reminding me I could have squished kids or elderly people. Trust me, when it comes to kids and old people – I have experience! Good God, I bet you're fun on pub quiz night, a right old ray of sunshine. I bet everyone is desperate to have you on their team!'

'I don't go to pub quizzes.'

19

'Well, maybe you should, maybe that's your problem! Maybe you need more quiz nights in your life!' She couldn't help herself, hating this anger, this tension that spilled from her mouth, as she made her way back to the driver's seat. Doing her best to ignore the woman, who stared after her, like an extra in a horror movie, lurking . . .

Pulling away carefully, she looked in the rear-view mirror at her accuser, who now stood with her palms upturned, arms tucked in at the elbows, close to her body. Her expression was one of dismay and Emma instantly wished she hadn't been so sarcastic, so tense. If she didn't have to dash off to pick up Reggie, she would have doubled back around and apologised. But there was no time for that, not today.

The A-road was busy, of course it was. Her car stuttered along, navigating through road works, crawling behind wheezing buses and coming to a stop at junctions to allow other road users to jump ahead of her in the queue. The lack of urgency in her fellow drivers was infuriating. Her fingers drummed the steering wheel and her foot danced against the mat in the footwell. Her mental metronome sped up. All she wanted to do was get Reggie in the car, drop him home and get to Church Street in time to encourage her mum to eat her lunch. It didn't seem like too much to ask.

Catching sight of her face in the rear-view mirror, she wiped the smudge of mascara from beneath her eyes with a spit-covered finger. *Falling asleep in Ikea!* What state was she in if this was even possible?

She hadn't always been this way, this frazzled. When Alex had started school, some eight years ago, she'd taken a job at a local architects' as the office manager, organising the couriering of plans, setting up interviews, booking meetings, welcoming clients, holding the calendar for the four partners, and even helping pull together estimates and quotes for jobs. It had been a role she loved;

but when eighteen months ago her dad had died suddenly, it had fallen to her, their only child, to be on hand for her mother, and so a job with fewer hours, less pressure and sadly less pay had been the solution. Not that she didn't enjoy working at the greengrocer's a few days a week – she did, but any idea of enhanced responsibility in the architects' office had been left behind the day she handed back the keys and grabbed her spare tights and toothbrush from the top drawer of her desk.

Finally, finally, with a green light guiding her towards the school gates and a break in the traffic, she swung the car sharply into the lay-by . . . but there was no sign of Reggie in the spot where she always picked him up.

With her phone in her hand, she was about to punch the number into it – remembering to keep her voice steady so as not to add to any anxiety he might already be feeling while asking in the most subtle way possible, *Where the bloody hell are you?* – when Reggie loped into view. She felt her jaw tense and instantly reprimanded herself. This was her son, her boy. His slow pace was torturous.

He ambled, pausing to rearrange the bag over his shoulder and then to reach into his pocket for his phone. She focused instead on the clock on the dashboard, again doing mental sums, searching for a way to magic another minute here or there so she wouldn't be late. Maybe she'd skip going to the loo when she dropped Reggie home, despite beginning to feel a little desperate. No, that wasn't going to work, she'd never be able to hang on that long. Her need to visit the loo had increased along with every year of her forties – and she was now at the point where she planned trips, walks and outings with one eye on where and when she could dash into a bathroom. Maybe she'd nip to the loo but not wash her hands.

Sweet Mother of Betsy what is wrong with you, Emma Fountain? Not wash your hands?

The fact was, she hated being late, hated others being late and knew without a doubt that her mum hated it too. The cup of coffee and slice of toast she'd promised herself were also struck from the schedule.

A gentle wave, she decided, was maybe a good way to encourage Reggie, alert him to her need to get going without being too obvious, too confrontational. But Reggie actually stopped walking and looked over his shoulder.

Emma bit the thumbnail of her left hand. Chewed it until it hurt a little and had gone soft. Running the pad of her index finger over the tip and liking the feel of the soft, bumpy skin at the tip of the thumb where the nail used to lurk, she felt satisfied, and her pulse calmed a little.

Eventually, Reggie made it to the car, opened the passenger door, and just as she felt the beginnings of sweet relief, he left it open and walked slowly towards the back.

'Can you open the boot?' He held up his school bag.

'Just lob it on the back seat, love. Don't worry about the boot, haven't got time, just shove it on the seat, jump in and let's go!' She clapped, swallowing the temptation to yell *Chop chop!*

'Oh my God, Mum! Someone's bashed your car!' He spoke with urgency.

'Yep, it's okay, I know, love. I mean it's not okay, but I do know about it. Happened in the Ikea car park this morning. Jump in, Reg!'

He disappeared from view, no doubt dropping down to survey the damage.

Again, she ran her hand over her face. 'Reg, please, love, don't worry about it now, just hop in!'

'Someone's reversed into you!'

'No, no, it's fine, Reg. They didn't. I reversed into them, entirely my fault.' She thought about the car park police woman and felt the hot flush of shame. 'And actually, it wasn't a "them", it was a post, thankfully. Could have been a child or an old person, of course, but it wasn't. Just a post.'

'Does Dad know?' Reggie's face, eyes wide, popped up in the rear-view mirror.

'Not yet,' she sang, irritated, as his question suggested that he, very much like his younger brother Alex and older sister Martha, believed she was in some way answerable to Brendan. 'Get in and I'll tell you all about it.'

'He's not going to be happy.' Reggie sucked air through his teeth, and she felt the grip in her gut of alarm at the thought of the expense she had incurred when every penny of their monthly budget was accounted for.

'Probably not, but just get in, lovey, I really, really need to get going. Need to . . . need to get to Nanny Marge, you know what she's like about her lunch.' Her dad had, after his retirement, made a point of eating his lunch with his wife, the two of them sitting with small plates on their laps and cups of tea within reach. She felt it was the least she could do in his absence; one small thing to alleviate her mother's loneliness.

Reggie's general demeanour when it came to most tasks could at best be described as slapdash. The lid was always left off the butter dish, cereal bowls were abandoned in the sink instead of washed, damp towels carelessly flung wherever he happened to be drying off. It irritated her, all of it, but today there was nothing slapdash about any of it. Oh no, today, when she would quite like him to shove his bloody bag on the seat and slam the door, he worked precisely, taking his time to position the bag carefully like it was a large tray of eggs.

Entirely without urgency, he climbed into the car and moved the seat back and forth before deciding on the perfect point to give himself more leg room, and finally he buckled up, before checking on the long fringe he was carefully cultivating over one eye in the sun-visor mirror.

'Come on then, what're you waiting for?' He spoke with a slight shake of his head, and more than a whiff of impatience. 'I need to get back.'

She nodded and, with the beginnings of a headache, pulled out into the traffic.

CHAPTER FOUR

THURSTON

Yes, that was his desire, his plan, and his enduring thought: to take his life, end the pain of his longing and either sleep for eternity or be reunited with his beloved. Either or. The only question now was how . . .

'Thurston!' His sister's shout drew him; even the dog looked up. 'For the love of God, get a grip. I asked you where's Grandma Brancher's big teapot?' Louder now; her thin mouth, he noticed, was the opposite of his wife's, whose lips had been full, her face smiling, always.

'I don't . . . I don't know.' He rubbed his nose.

'You don't know?' she asked with such incredulity it made him doubt the truth of his answer.

He shook his head, unable to voice how he couldn't quite think straight.

'God only knows how you're going to cope if you can't so much as locate Grandma's big teapot!' she spat, opening cupboard doors and slamming them shut. He found the din excruciating. 'This is where a daughter would have come in handy.' Her words were like a punch to the throat, and he wondered, not for the first time, if having a daughter in Mary's image would make this moment easier or harder to deal with.

A daughter . . . He couldn't imagine the comfort it would bring, and yet to be so powerfully reminded of the woman, her mother . . . he feared that might be too much. It wasn't a proud admission, but his sister's tone, her words, her actions, stirred in him something very close to hatred.

'And you can't just sit here moping,' she continued. 'Folk have come from far and wide to celebrate Mary's life, to pay their respects. You can't hide in here. It's rude.'

Not as rude as June borrowing your mother's pearls for her Nancy's wedding and never returning them. Your mother told me she was too embarrassed to ask for their return. That's not only rude, Thurston, that's theft. Not that we should get involved. Least said, soonest mended . . .

He acknowledged his wife's wise counsel, hearing her voice loud and clear.

'I'll go say hello in a bit.' He offered the concession to his sister, hoping it was enough for her to leave him alone.

'In a bit?' she fired, and he noticed the tiny tributaries of unhappiness that snaked from her top lip up to her nose and down in deep gorges from the sides of her mouth. Grooves that could no doubt carry her sour tainted words from her mouth upward, where she could sniff them and turn her nose up at the sound, and down her chin, to pull her bottom lip into a gurn of disapproval.

'How long is "a bit"?' she pushed. 'Mr and Mrs Mulvaney have already left. I made your apologies as best I could, but they looked miffed. And the Reverend Dunster is on his third whisky and making a beeline for Mrs Blackstock-Hughes, most inappropriate as her Michael is only cold in his grave for the last three months. *In a bit?* What would Mary say?'

What would Mary say?

'I think she'd say . . .' He took his time, figuring out how to navigate the boulder of grief that sat at the base of his throat and made talking, swallowing and eating nigh on impossible. Finally, he remembered where he had seen it. 'I think she'd say the big teapot is on the shelf at the back of the broom cupboard.'

June huffed and took off for the boot room with a shake of her head. The broom cupboard . . . He pictured the bottles of cleaning fluids, drain unblockers and bleach that clustered on the shelves. What would ingestion of these noxious chemicals mean? Could that be his method? How bad would it be to administer? I mean, yes, he wanted out, but was keen to find the least painful, least messy and most expeditious method. Swallowing something so toxic felt risky – slow and grim, and what if he didn't succeed? What kind of life would that mean, severely damaged and still cloaked in this sorrow?

'Mr Brancher?'

Thurston, his train of thought broken, looked up at the Reverend Dunster himself as he poked his head into the kitchen, quickly followed by his lanky body. Dunster clicked his tongue on the roof of his mouth, like any other drunk who was making small talk. Rhubarb bared his teeth in the way he did on rare occasions at anyone he held in low regard.

'Yes.' Thurston sat up straight. Old habits die hard. Sitting up straight in church. Removing your hat when speaking to any member of the De Ganier family, the once ruling elite of the county whose crest had sat above the church since the first timbers were hewn from ships to construct the roof beams. To always congratulate anyone who beat you in any sporting situation, as losing sorely left a mark that was more permanent and memorable than a win. And – *You are not to cry. Boys don't do that. Not ever.* He could hear his father repeating these very words.

'Not disturbing you, am I?' the man quickly continued, without waiting for a response. 'I thought it was a smashing service. Quite sure Mary would have been overjoyed at the turnout, and the flowers were first class.' He winked and made the okay symbol with his forefinger and thumb.

'Yes.' Thurston nodded, not wanting to talk about it, not wanting to be reminded that it was real, not wanting to think that she was gone. Not wanting to talk to the vicar, who his father would have described as one over the eight. He took it as a mark of the utmost disrespect that the man had the glow of whisky on his nose and an alcohol-fuelled twinkle in his eye that was unfitting for the day.

'I know it was Mary who was a regular at St Isaac's, but please know that our doors are always open. Except when they are not, because of the risk of pilfering. Little bastards. They swiped the door knocker last week; can you believe that? I'll be watching out for that on eBay. But if you call the number on the door, someone can let you in. If you needed to. For any reason.'

'Yes.' Thurston tried to think of any reason he might want to gain access to the church.

For praying, you silly thing! For taking time to quietly contemplate life, or for doing some of that pilfering the vicar's talking about. I've always rather liked the two big brass candlesticks that the verger polishes on a regular basis. They'd look lovely on our dining table . . .

'And remember, Thurston . . .' The man spoke slowly. 'Mary might not be here, but she is not gone.' He made a sweeping movement with his arm like a panto magician, faltering on his feet before steadying himself on the door frame. 'She has eternal life. Eternal,' he stressed. 'And you can talk to her any time you choose, with God as your conduit.'

Thurston stared, remembering something else his father told him: *If you can't say anything civil then don't say anything at all.*

'Right then.' Reverend Dunster clapped, and this too made him jump. These loud bangs jarring, as if he were made of glass. 'I'll be pushing off. Thank you for your, for your' – the word seemed to elude him – 'hostipality. Yes, hostipality. See you soon, Thurston.'

'Yes.'

The vicar left, but Thurston continued to stare at the space he'd occupied with a peculiar numbness to his spirit.

He watched the clock, aware of June's regular interruptions, her close proximity, clattering objects in the sink, her huffs of irritation no doubt at the fact that he refused to mingle. He cared not.

The neighbours left.

Then the farmers and their rosy-faced wives, who had travelled from all over the county, left.

Then the wider family left and finally, thank God, so did his sister, June, and her grown daughter Nancy. Nancy who he still thought of as a good kid, even though she was nearly forty. Nancy's husband, Andrew, had recently undergone minor surgery and was therefore not in attendance. Mary wouldn't have minded either way, understanding that Andrew would do what he needed to do and any fuss over her funeral would be secondary.

Thurston threw the bolts on the heavy iron-latched wooden front door, lest anyone should think of returning, and switched off the lights. Ignoring the cling-filmed platters of soggy ham and tomato and cheese and tomato sandwiches and halved Scotch eggs cluttering the table, which collectively gave off the pungent scent of cold food gone warm, along with the rectangular slabs of fruit cake.

His faithful hound was in his basket, head on paws, eyes downcast. Thurston knew how he felt. Bending low, he rubbed his ears. 'It's all right, Barbie old boy. You sleep well. I promise—' He stopped and swallowed the catch in his throat. 'I promise that whatever I decide and when I decide it, you will be loved and cared for.' This was one of his primary concerns. But no matter how much he loved his little dog, his yearning for escape was greater.

Stepping out of his shoes, he paired them to carry up the stairs in his forked fingers. Ready to return them to the bottom of the wardrobe, where they had sat for the last six years, only seeing the light of day for weddings, funerals and the visit from Prince Charles, as he was then. An auspicious day when the prince had graced the county show, had shaken Thurston's hand vigorously and complimented Mary on her apricot jam. That had made her so happy! He smiled at the memory of her gabbling away, retelling the detail to anyone she encountered for weeks after.

And blow me down, he only went and shook my hand!

He said my jam was delicious and didn't just say delicious, but you know when someone really enjoys something, and they say deeeelishus! He said it just like that!

I ain't never washing this hand! Never! Prince Charles shook it. He loved my jam. My apricot jam. It's an old family recipe . . .

He unknotted his black tie and hung it over the wire he'd stretched between two hooks inside the wardrobe door, home to six ties and two belts, one black, one brown. He unbuttoned his starched shirt, laundered by Mary's fair hand, and balled it. Along with his vest, he put them inside the old wicker laundry basket that sat in the corner of the room. Next, he peeled his socks from his white, white feet and stood to undo the hook of his trouser waistband and to unzip his fly. His trousers fell to the floor in a dark cotton pool around his feet. In his pale grey boxer shorts, he sank down on to the bed and tried not to look at her pillows, still unwashed, still with the odd stray curl of grey hair lingering in the fibres, still with her scent upon them.

Reaching for her quilted dressing gown, the colour of fresh lavender, he held the insubstantial fabric to his chest before falling on to his side, longing, longing for one more night with his wife in his arms. Thurston Brancher cried great gulping tears that he feared might choke him with their ferocity.

'Maaaary . . .' he managed through his sorrow. 'Mary . . .'

It was only as he quieted, calming his pulse until he was able to breathe normally again, that he lifted his head from the mattress, listening, and realised for the first time in weeks he could not hear her reply in his thoughts.

Nothing.

The silence rang out like a note of mourning, the ding of a sorrowful bell inside his head. Thurston jumped with a jolt that was as frightening as it was sobering, understanding that he was alone.

She had gone.

He also knew that she had been wrong, his beloved wife, when she'd said, *We had sixty-two years. Rain and shine . . . and that should make you glad.* He was not glad. He was the very opposite of glad. Sixty years, indeed sixty-two years, was not nearly enough. Not even close.

CHAPTER FIVE

EMMA

Emma put her key in the door and called out as she entered, 'Only me, Mum!'

Slipping off her sky-blue lightweight jacket, she hung it on the newel post and fixed a grin as she made her way into the spacious kitchen, which had been knocked through to incorporate the dining room, largely redundant after her dad had died. Victor had insisted they have a dining room, liking the tradition and status it afforded – even though the family only made full use of it for Christmas lunch and the odd Sunday when her mother's grey roast lamb and undercooked or overcooked spuds were served with much aplomb.

It was now a light, airy space with enough room for a bed in the corner and providing easy access to the loo and shower in the hallway, for the time when the stairs became too much of a challenge. For now, though, her mother insisted on slowly making her way up and down them each morning and evening to sleep in her marital bed, surrounded by all that was familiar and only ever lying on the right-hand side, as if she still fully expected her husband to climb in next to her. While Emma looked forward to the convenience of having her mother in the one space, able to quash the worry of all that might befall her, moving around when no one was on hand, she also knew that it would signify the beginning of the end and so dreaded it too. Her dad might have died eighteen months ago, but the loss of him sat at the base of her throat like something freshly drunk. The thought of losing her mum too . . . she was not and probably never would be ready.

'You're late. I mean, I don't mind,' her mother said in a tone that suggested otherwise. 'I've told you before there's absolutely no need to come and sit with me. None at all. I'm perfectly capable of eating my lunch alone as and when I feel like it.'

Emma doubted this was true but was moved by how her mother tried to be stoic, unwilling to burden her daughter with just how achingly alone she was.

'I mean it, Emma, I'm fine! But if you are going to come then do come when you say you are. Being late or just popping in upsets my routine, messes with my plans . . .'

Emma smiled, undaunted, knowing her mother had a routine that was dull, fixed and certainly without any plans to speak of. As ever, she sat in the pale green and lilac tweed checked chair with the winged back, angled towards the television that sat on a blanket box in the corner. A tray of lunch – sandwiches, and small squares of cake, foil-wrapped – was within reach on a side table. Lorraine, the care nurse, always left her lunch, but her mother seemingly refused to eat without company.

'Yes, sorry I was late, Mum. Reggie called and needed me to pick him up. Traffic's a nightmare.'

'What's wrong with him now then?'

Her mother's turn of phrase bothered her.

'Do you want soup with your sandwiches?' Emma opened a kitchen cupboard and moved tins to see what was on offer. 'You've got a lot of tomato, and there's a couple of broccoli and Stilton.'

'No.' Her mother shook her head. 'I don't want any soup. So, what's wrong with the boy now then? Still fed up?'

Clearly her mum was not going to let it drop.

Emma shut the cupboard doors and took the twin chair next to her mother's, before removing the foil from the little plate of sandwiches.

'He's more than fed up, Mum. He's not well.'

This, she knew, was a watery catch-all that hopefully might satisfy her mother. Emma didn't want to transfer any worries to her. Since Reggie had hit his teens and started to display unhappiness at the world, expressing anxiety, losing interest in the things that used to spark joy for him, like cooking and hiking, she had felt helpless. Perhaps the less she mentioned it, the fewer details she gave, the more likely it was to simply go away. Least said, soonest mended, wasn't that the phrase?

'Pffww.' Her mother's meaning was easily decipherable. 'When your father was his age, he was a member of the Royal Navy, about to sail the seas! About to meet me, but he was *busy*, that's the thing. No time to be fed up about anything, too busy "doing". That's the trouble nowadays. The world and his wife are depressed. It's all you hear about. Endless celebrities and people on the telly with their big houses and even bigger bank balances, depressed? They don't know hard times! They just need to be occupied instead of all this self-obsession, pouting in mirrors and putting pictures of their dinner on the Intergram. No one was depressed when I was young, we were all too busy. It's a fashion, like the gay thing.'

'You think being gay is a fashion?' Her mother's often draconian views and commentary still had the power to shock her, no matter how often she heard them voiced.

'You know what I mean. No one was gay before the eighties, no one! Even Elton John got married to that lady. I remember reading about it in a magazine in the hairdresser's. Then suddenly one person says, "Oh hello, I'm gay!" and the next thing we know, *everyone* is gay. And it's the same with depression. People just need to be busier.'

'Yes, so you've said, too busy to be depressed. I get it.' Emma ground her teeth. 'So just to be clear – do you think people wouldn't be gay if they were busier too? Like if Graham Norton had a cleaning job of an evening as well as doing all that interviewing, he'd be married to a woman and living a hetero life?'

'I know you're being sarcastic, Emma-Jane, and so I'm not going to rise to it. I'm just saying, there were no gay people when we were growing up, none, and now there are. Fact.'

Her mother sat back and chewed the inside of her cheek, as was her habit. She did this: used the word 'fact' at the end of a sentence as if this was enough to make it so. How Emma wished it were that simple.

I am a size 10. Fact.
There are thirty hours in the day. Fact.
Reggie is loving life. Fact.
We have spare money in the bank. Fact.
I have a large set of matching dinner plates. Fact.
I got to my dad in time. I did CPR. He lived. Fact . . .

She let the atmosphere settle and stared at the TV, which had the sound down and the subtitles on. It was a property programme where a couple, who in her view wore inappropriately flimsy footwear, were being trawled around a humble Spanish villa by a perky presenter in an orange frock. Judging by the couple's sour-faced expressions, she suspected they were without any intention to purchase, but were happy to have the free trip and to get their smug faces on the telly.

'What have you been up to today? Brendan said you'd gone *shopping*?'

The way her mother said the last word made it sound like something unsavoury or illegal.

'Only to Ikea.' She decided in that instant not to invite criticism by detailing how she'd hopped into a bed and fallen asleep.

'*Ikeeeeaa?*' This too her mum managed to make sound like of den of iniquity. Emma ignored her. 'Your dad would have sorted Reggie out.' They were back to this. 'He'd have had him in the garage, sorting boxes, building stuff, a project. Your dad always knew what to do to make things right.'

The conversation was familiar, a reminder like a thorn in her foot of just how much better everyone's life would be if her dad were still around, not that Emma found it any less upsetting for that.

CPR . . . She'd locked in the method, studying it in the aftermath of his death: *Heel of your hand on the middle of their chest. Put your other hand on top of the first and interlock your fingers. Keep your arms straight and lean over the casualty. Press down hard, to a depth of about five to six centimetres, before releasing the pressure, allowing the chest to come back up.* If only she'd got to him sooner, been closer when he'd called . . .

'Yeah, I know. Dad was remarkable.' This was the truth.

'I miss him.' Her mother's bottom lip trembled. This sudden switch from high judgement to high emotion, part of the rollercoaster of their day, was familiar but no less wearying for that.

'I know you do.'

'It's *her* night off, isn't it?'

Her mother's carer came in twice daily but had Wednesday afternoons and evenings off. When her mum was calm, Emma was more than glad of the chance to sit and chat while they watched repeats on TV together and she encouraged her mum to eat. In truth, it was a break from the mayhem of home, but on days like this . . .

'Yes, it's Wednesday, so Lorraine will be back in the morning.'

'I'd rather she wasn't! She's awful. Don't know why I need such round-the-clock monitoring. I shake a little, my balance is off, and my muscles get stiff, I've got MS, but it doesn't mean I need to be babied. I can take care of myself. And if I can't, I'll holler for help! I've told you this over and over.'

Just the thought of a rerun of this conversation made Emma's heart sink. She admired her mother's desire for independence but knew she was only putting on a brave face. Her dad had done many of the chores that kept the wheels of their life oiled. He'd been on hand in case his wife tumbled and had made sure her drug regimen was adhered to. Emma had taken on that role, with the help of Lorraine. It was unspoken and what he would have wanted.

'I've told you, Mum, it's not as simple as hollering for help; someone needs to be close by. Lorraine is bright, early and reliable, and with me coming in every day, we've got you covered. I don't want you to worry.'

'I worry I don't get a minute to myself! That's what I worry about!'

Emma ignored her. She, Lorraine and Brendan had established a routine. Working at the greengrocer's three days a week meant Emma might not arrive till mid-afternoon, but her mind was at rest, knowing the carer was in place and with Brendan always making time to pick up the slack.

'I know you joke,' she placated, 'but we've got you covered. I always come in every day, every single day.'

'No one makes you!' her mother fired.

'No, that's right, I want to. I do. I like seeing you.'

'God knows why. Sitting here all day with my useless legs and my weak old arms, what's the point? You must find it very boring. Do something else! I'm not going anywhere.'

Emma was in no mood for her mother's self-pitying soliloquy, not when she knew it by heart. She decided against suggesting her mother might feel better if she ignored her physical impairments and maybe got a little busier. Had she ever considered going out into the garage to sort boxes or build something? – wasn't that the cure for everything?

Placing the top of the index finger of her left hand between her teeth, she pulled and ripped until as much of her nail as possible splintered away, rubbing her thumb over the nubbly soft skin that remained and chewing the tiny fragments that clumped in her mouth.

'You'll get worms if you bite your nails. It's disgusting. How many times do I have to tell you that?'

Obviously a few more, she thought.

Emma felt the pink flush of shame and ignored her mother, staring at the perky presenter on TV who was now pointing out the sea view – ah yes, there it was, if you squinted, twisted your head, and looked towards the gap between hotels and motorway bridge on the curve of the coast.

Her phone pinged. It was a text from Reggie:

We've run out of pizza

'What does he need now?' Her mother smirked.

'Nothing. It's Roz,' she lied. 'She wants to talk to me about something.'

'Tarty piece.'

She ignored her mother's distasteful slur as she had been doing ever since Roz, aged fifteen, had turned up at their house braless, in a ra-ra skirt and an off-the-shoulder number that left very little to the imagination. This one act clouded her mother's opinion, it would seem, forever. The fact that her friend, now in her late forties, was a nurse, a successful nurse, single, driven, funny and fabulous seemed not to register, or impress, Margery Nicholson.

Emma rattled off a reply.

There's some in the freezer

'Just letting her know I'll pop round later,' she lied again.

'Is she still single?'

Why did this question from her mother's lips sound so accusatory, and so much like her best friend's unmarried state was a failure? Emma knew that for her mother, nabbing a husband and having matching china and a warming hostess trolley from which to serve adequate, repetitive suppers to the neighbours had been the sole extent of her ambition.

Emma had wanted different, her sights set on living in a big city, earning decent money, driving a nice car . . . but then she'd met Brendan, fallen in love and her ovaries had plotted to get her pregnant and keep her local. Not that she resented her life, not a bit, knowing how lucky she was. But that wasn't to say Emma didn't sometimes envy Roz her freedom: living life at her own pace, having to please only herself, keeping her house as neat as a pin without stinky sports kit littering the bathroom floor, fridge raids where its entire contents were devoured by hungry teens with locust-like intent, and she was master of her own remote control. Not to mention owning a wardrobe to die for, or the fact that Roz had the time and means to go to the gym. And as for her sex life – hooking up with good-looking colleagues and breaking hearts rather than let hers get broken. It didn't sound too shabby. Only last year Emma had tried to explain to her friend how she and Brendan had to arrange to have sex.

'So let me get this straight . . .' Roz had shaken her head as if still trying to digest the idea. 'You have to *schedule* in sex night?'

'You make it sound abnormal, but I think it's just what it's like when you're married.'

'Or maybe it's just what it's like in your marriage?'

'Possibly,' she conceded with a flicker of irritation.

'I mean, did you have to schedule sex before you waltzed up the aisle?'

'Well, no, of course not, because we didn't have kids and my mum wasn't poorly and we were younger and had more energy and it used to just happen . . .' She hardly remembered what it had felt like in those carefree early days.

'When did it stop just happening?'

'I guess when Martha was little, and I was feeding her and knackered.'

'Martha who is now twenty-two.'

Emma had nodded and sipped her tea, as her reasoning was exposed as no more than an outdated excuse. So what if their sex life wasn't perfect? Did it really matter if they'd rather choose sleep?

'I know you are making a point, Roz, but I can't work out what it is.'

'The point, my lovely, is that you need to have sex! It's important!'

'Did Brendan tell you to say that?'

'I'm serious. It's the glue, Em, it's always the glue.'

'So, remind me again why you're single?'

'Because I refuse to settle for someone who I might end up living with who feels like a brother. I want that spark, forever!'

'Spark? Listen to yourself! We used to think the mark of a good partner was one who'd hold your handbag while you went to the bathroom or stopped to tie your laces or had to vomit in the kerb, the kind of man who'd just have that bag hanging on his shoulder without a second thought.'

'I'm older, wiser, and now I know I want a bag carrier plus the sexy spark!' Roz had boomed.

'And good luck finding that man. It's a great thought, but it's not reality, is it? I mean, we all want to carry on like we are still teenagers, but life has a funny way of catching up with you. I never could have imagined when I first met Brendan that I'd pick an early night in my comfies and a hot-water bottle over passion with him. But then I never thought I'd end up wiping my own mum's arse on occasion and feeding her porridge while she waffles on about her late husband. I never thought I'd be working in a greengrocer's and counting every penny that comes in and out while our kids live like we have a large money tree in the back garden.'

'We all have choices, Em. You just choose not to put yourself first, not ever. You don't make yourself a priority and you should!'

She used to think this was true, but the deeper she dived into marriage and family life, the less true it felt. The chore cycle never ended while other people's needs took up her emotional and physical reserves. And when it came to her and Brendan, they might not be as sexually adventurous as they once were, falling into bed more often than not too tired to get physical, but there was comfort in the familiar and their love, she knew, ran deep. Or was this just how she felt, unable to recall the last time they'd discussed it?

'Anyway, I'm off to get my bits waxed. One of us has a night of passion to look forward to . . .' Roz grinned.

'I thought you were working?'

'And since when did that stop me?' Roz winked. 'The one thing there are a lot of in hospitals, Em, is big cupboards . . . big cupboards with locks on the inside.'

'Eeuuw, cupboard sex!' Emma had laughed like the teen she missed being. A teen who was unaware of the rather predictable and linear course her life would take. And while she didn't hanker for those days, there was no denying she had loved it, pondering what lay ahead and the endless possibilities of where she might end up and with whom . . .

The tarty piece.

Maybe Emma envied her best mate a little, but only sometimes.

'How about you have some lunch, Mum?'

'I'm not a child.'

'I know, but you need to eat.' Reaching for the plate, she picked up a sandwich and held it out.

'What's in it?'

'Ham and cheese with a little bit of pickle.'

'Is it the fat, chunky pickle? I don't like that.' Her mother pulled a face.

'No, it's the thin little pickle that's easy to digest. The pickle you like. Sandwich pickle.'

'I'll try it.' Margery took the crustless triangle into her less than nimble fingers and took a small bite. 'Bread's a bit dry.'

'Sure you don't want soup? Won't take me a mo.'

Her mother shook her head and stuck out her bottom lip petulantly and again Emma felt a flare of irritation, reminding herself to be nice. The first half of the sandwich was eaten slowly, each bite, each chew deliberate and accompanied with sighs of dislike even though she readily accepted the second half, and that too was similarly disposed of.

'Right then, Mum. I'll make you a quick cuppa and then I'd better get back to Reg, take Bruce out for a quick once around the block and I've got to pick Alex up. It's sports this afternoon and he's up at Marton Weir.'

The expensive private school her younger son attended on a full scholarship had a sports facility on the other side of town. Acres of wide-open space with neat green grass and a coffee shop serving overpriced flat whites to shiny-haired women who didn't work, ordered carrot cake, joked about the vegetable content and only ate a forkful, and young dads with fat, heavy watches who'd retired young after making a killing in a tech boom. Here, Alex received expert instruction on everything from soccer to rackets. She still had no idea what 'rackets' was.

'All that money!' her mother tutted.

Emma bit at a tiny edge of nail that had escaped her earlier assault.

'I've told you – it *would* be a lot of money, but Alex gets a full scholarship so all we have to pay for is his extras.'

'Extras!' her mother shouted as if this was in some way amusing.

'Let's get you that cuppa.'

As she rinsed her mother's sandwich plate under the tap and popped it in the drying rack, she stared at the kettle, waiting for it to boil. *Extras* . . . Yes, his fees of nearly eight thousand pounds per term were taken care of, but the extras like sports kit, uniform, trips, tuck money, clubs, this was their responsibility and a commitment they had improperly factored when they'd opened a bottle of Prosecco and toasted the wonderful opportunity being offered to their bright little boy.

His peers' parents, she noticed, barely blinked as they signed the forms for hobby night and agreed to pay six months up front for materials. But for her and Brendan, the cost of Alex's education kept them awake at night, chasing the maths, trying to make it all add up. *And on top of that I've gone and bashed the bloody car!*

As if in tune with her musings, a text arrived from Brendan.

Pricing up a job near Marton Weir so I can collect Alex X

Emma smiled; he was a good, good man and a good, good dad.

Thank you love, see you later. I'll take Bruce for a wee – Reggie home X

His reply of a single down-in-the-mouth emoji said it all. She shared the weight of his disappointment. When Reggie was in school, there was the slim chance that he was living his best life, happy even, laughing with mates, head down, devouring knowledge. A fantasy that enabled her to crack on with her day, but knowing he was at home, either lying on the sofa or lying in his bed after foraging for pizza – well, it only confirmed the fact that *Houston, we have a problem . . .* As a family, they didn't analyse it, but rather went with the flow, almost as if it was too scary a discussion, and again that darned phrase 'least said, soonest mended' leaped into her mind.

The kettle whistled.

'She's only gone and left me mini Battenberg again!' Her mother's shout pulled her from her musings. 'Emma!' she called again over the sound of the kettle's crescendo. 'I said, she's given me Battenberg! Can you believe it? She knows I don't like it!'

God, what a catastrophe! I'll alert the media . . . Emma thought as she bit at the skin around her nail, still soft, still sore, momentarily distracted by the short, sharp pain.

CHAPTER SIX

Thurston

Up with the lark and what a joy!

That was the phrase his father had cited each morning of every season, and it still rang true. It was how Thurston had always started the day, whistling or singing as he went.

Today he lay on the mattress, reluctant to open his eyes. Especially now his life was on a timer, the buzzer about to ring. Even waking felt a little pointless. Not that he had much choice about it. Not yet. Knowing he was on this countdown, however, certainly made him focus and appreciate the beauty of small things, a goodbye of sorts to the place he so loved.

Sitting now on the side of the bed, he took a moment to listen to the birdsong. It was, he had always thought, one of the most beautiful sounds. The language was poetic, the sound melodic, and no matter how indecipherable to his ears, the crescendo, response and call left him in no doubt that this was the morning meeting for all his feathered guests. A roll call for the ones that popped by on the lookout for breakfast. The ones who made unscheduled stops, having happened upon his land. And those for whom it was their home, whether it be the wrens who built nests in the hedgerow, the tits and sparrows who took advantage of the birdboxes he had tacked up hither and thither or the swallows, who liked to build a home on the dark ledges, nooks and crannies of the barn roof or the tractor shed. All were welcome, as were the bigger birds – his chickens, ducks and even the gang of geese who liked to holler at newcomers and make a big show of claiming the farm as their own. He loved them all. And in truth, it was nice to wake to some sort of noise. He glanced at the empty side of the bed and ran his hand over his wife's dressing gown, which he had now folded neatly and placed on the silky counterpane.

His shower was brief. The water tepid. As part of an ageing duo, and with Mary by his side, his decaying body hadn't bothered him too much. His fall from youth and the inevitable decline mirrored in his wife's made it somehow bearable, normalised. But alone, his sagging muscles, aching bones and all associated frailty disgusted him, as he gave attention to his physical self for the first time in decades. His findings were not pleasant and did little to bring relief to the melancholic state that wrapped him.

His underwear and clothing for the day were plucked without thought in the half-light. He took his time, however, pulling on his socks and using the silver-backed brush that had been a wedding gift, along with a matching comb, to ease his hair over his forehead, where it would stay put under his cap. The one with the repairs on the brim that Mary had hand-stitched over the years. He took his time because the simple truth was, he didn't want to go downstairs. Didn't want to do anything, just wanted everything to stop. Everything. It motivated him to put his plan into action, to take the necessary steps to end his life. He drew breath and put his best foot forward.

Thurston knew it was ridiculous, just as he knew others managed to get over such events, but knowing it and telling his heart were two very different things. Leaving the bedroom meant facing what was beyond the door. It meant walking along the narrow landing and down the creaky old wooden stairs, which would lead him to a quiet, dark hallway. A corridor where his wife had not walked in advance and put on the lamp by the front door, throwing soft light in an arc until the sun rose when, mid-morning, it would be switched off. A vestibule without the lingering scent of her floral shower gel or her sweet perfume. He'd then make the turn into the kitchen, the room that most echoed with her absence. The Aga warm, but the air cold. No amount of heat from the old range could compensate for the energy of her presence, the soft hum of their favoured hymns on her lips, the questioning over what they might have for supper. The kettle cold to the touch, with no residual warmth from her first or second cup of tea. No bacon crisping in the old skillet, filling the room with a smell so rich it made his mouth water. No toast popping with such vigour it made them chuckle when it caught them unawares. No chattering to the dog, no reading aloud headlines from the local paper, no mixing of flour and butter, cracking in fresh eggs, whipping up a cake for mid-afternoon to be taken with tea. No baking of bread. No filling the washing machine with dirty laundry. No ironing everything from underwear to bedsheets while listening to a play. No smiling at him across the slightly wonky table, no standing at the sink with her hands in suds, laughing as she recounted something she'd heard on the radio or had read in one of her novels. No loving him like no other soul on earth ever would or ever could.

Keeping his eyes low, he trod the stairs, concentrating on his footfall, doing what he'd done since he was a small boy and trying to stand only on the side of the wooden tread where the central strip of floral carpet left a gap. A habit, a quirk. The hallway was, as expected, dark; the kitchen, as he had pictured, flat and impersonal. Platters of sandwiches cluttered the table here too, and Grandma Brancher's big teapot was in the sink, full of suds. Without appetite, it was more than he could face. One quick, sharp whistle and

Rhubarb climbed from his basket, put his two front paws on the flagstones and lifted his bottom, stretching his back in a low, elegant curve that looked like it felt good. The little dog gave a grin of a yawn that Thurston always found comical; his yawn, he always said, was wider than his head.

Gathering his cap from the boot room and stepping into his steel-toe-capped work boots, he made his way out into the yard with his little Jack Russell keeping pace. He decided to think about what needed to be done, the final clear-up, wanting to leave his affairs in order as it were, and it was so much more than packing a case, closing the door, turning off the light and cancelling the paper delivery. Rhubarb barked and Thurston knew this was the first thing he needed to put in place – someone to care for his beloved pup when he was no longer around to do so. It wasn't as if the list of potential candidates was exhaustive; only three names came to mind: Loftus, his younger brother, his sister June, and his niece Nancy. Each had their merits, but disadvantages too. Loftus, a farmer through and through, lived in Cumbria, quite a journey for a dog already having to face so many changes. June was nearby, but bossy, barking instruction at her own dogs. Thurston worried her methods might not suit a rather independent little adventurer like Barbie. That only left Nancy, who was kind and patient, but worked long hours – would she take him along to work? He felt the weight of pressure at the enormity of the decision.

He looked up into the blue-sky day with no more than wisps of cloud that floated along on the horizon, far different from yesterday's mauve clouds and light drizzle. The cold air hit his face and filled his lungs and it felt good. Stooping to pick up a dropped ball of blue twine, he rolled the end until it fitted neatly into the hole in the middle of the ball and carried it to the small barn, where he would put it on a shelf along with various bales of string and twine that were part of his essential kit. He swept the floor and gathered up the dust, the brown leaves that had blown in and various bits of twig and bark, depositing the lot in the old cinder box, which he would then throw on the bonfire the next time he built one.

Having noticed that one of the fence posts at the edge of the driveway seemed to be listing slightly, it made sense for him to spend whatever time he had left completing chores, wanting to leave things in the best order possible, shipshape. He grabbed the large mallet from the tool shed and made his way outside. There was always some small job that required his attention. Rhubarb disappeared head first under a leggy shrub; he'd clearly caught a scent.

'You'll be okay, little dog. I'll figure it out. I won't make the decision in haste, you're far too important to me to do that.'

He wondered how to ask the right questions without revealing his plan to those close to him. Small talk he guessed was the answer, something at which he was less than adept. June, if he had to guess, would give him short shrift, but Nancy, he knew from chats with Mary, had many a maternal instinct and yet no babber had materialised. This was a private sadness he understood very well. He watched the dog's tail appear between the branches. No matter how coolly he could speak the idea of passing him on, his heart twisted for the coming goodbye to his best four-legged friend.

Standing now in front of the post, Thurston gripped the handle and, paying no heed to his ancient shoulder injury, his ageing back or his present physical state, weakened through grief and lack of sustenance, he wielded the heavy mallet with force. His skin broke into an instant and satisfying sweat as his stomach muscles bunched and something very close to fury flared in his veins. All these people: idiots, murderers, warmongers, none half as good or kind as his wife, how come they still walked the earth while she did not? He knew this was a ridiculous rabbit hole down which to tumble, but it felt good to reconcile his anger at least partially.

He brought the hammer down several times, each accompanied by a bovine grunt as the post sank lower and lower. It went past being level, the issue corrected, and still Thurston kept hitting it. The sound was harsh and jarring and a new thought occurred: to hit something hard with his soft head, that'd do it. But what? A wall? That was obvious, *and* how to hit it hard enough – maybe in a car. Trouble was, his sturdy pickup was made for such eventualities and knowing his luck he'd just end up with a hefty repair bill and a busted wall . . . no, that wouldn't do.

Eventually, with his energy spent, his spirit flagging and the post truly sunk to the point of useless, he sat down on the grass and leaned against the stump, waiting for his heart to stop racing and his breathing to return to its normal rhythm.

Scanning the wide expanse of green that was their land, his family farm where now very little farming took place, he looked up to the blue skies and closed his eyes.

'I can't get to you quickly enough, Mary, that's the truth of it. But wait I must, leave things . . . neat, for June, for Nancy. No loose ends.'

'What on God's green earth are you doing?' June's voice cracked the air, and he felt his jaw tense. That was all he needed. Her shrill hectoring when he was feeling so low.

'What does it look like? I'm having a sit-down.' He looked across to the lane where she walked briskly towards him, flanked by her two black Labradors, Fern and Flora, sisters who were excruciatingly well trained. Rhubarb, as if alerted by the arrival of his cousins, emerged from his shrub with fox shit on his face. *Perfect.* June pulled a face of disgust.

'I wish I had time for a sit-down!' she bellowed. 'Aren't you going to cut the hedging along the back lane? It's hard to see to turn left when you're coming out of Reedley Wood. I was going to mention it a while back. I took an age edging out the other night at rush hour. It's dangerous.'

This made him smile a little. Rush hour? They lived on the outskirts of town, among farms and fields. It was quiet. What rush hour was she referring to? A couple of cyclists? A few dog walkers driving out this way in their battered Golfs or off-roaders to hike the trails? Jon up the road carting his rare breed sheep in his clattering old trailer up and down the lane? Or God forbid, a bloody caravan tottering along, carrying chatty city folk who were looking for a place to holiday . . .

She came to a stop in front of him and the dogs sat accordingly. He had to admire her fitness; she hadn't so much as a hair out of place beneath her headscarf and her breathing was even, despite the long walk along the rugged lane from her house to his.

'I'll get to it, June.'

'Get to it?' She wrinkled her nose. 'And while you're "getting to it", the hedge will be flourishing – making it treacherous for horses and cars going around the bend. Tell you what, if it's beyond you, and you prefer to have a "sit-down", go fetch me the tractor keys, fit the flail and I'll do it myself.'

He stared at her.

'Look at your face!' she laughed. 'That bloody old tractor, worth more than diamonds to you and Dad! God forbid a mere slip of a girl like me might be given the chance to drive her!'

Despite her humour, there was truth in it; the old workhorse was worth more to him than he could say . . .

While he was still able to plant his feet on this earth, he would stop June getting her hands on his tractor keys. She was clumsy with anything mechanical, cavalier with the processes that kept them in tip-top condition. He pictured her rusting bike abandoned on its side as a teen and, in later years, the way her arrival home was heralded by the crunch of a gearbox and the sound of a handbrake being ratcheted beyond its comfortable point.

That old tractor was his pride and joy. He still recalled the day his dad had turned up in it. The man had seen his children born, grandchildren too; he'd celebrated a long and happy marriage to Granny Brancher with a fancy barn dance topped off with a waltz. He'd even buried his own parents. Yet the only time Thurston had seen his old man close to tears was at the sheer beauty of the red Massey Ferguson, newly parked in the yard. He blinked away the moment of clarity, wondering who would recall his defining moments when he'd gone. He also made a note to make sure his sister was left the tractor in his will.

'I'll do it.' He stood slowly and wiped the sweat from his top lip and the damp from the seat of his trousers.

'Good.' She exhaled as though it was a victory. 'Have you eaten?' she asked as she made her way towards the farmhouse. It was always this way. It might have been his and Mary's marital home but as it was the house of her childhood, where June had grown up, she therefore didn't feel the need to be polite when it came to arriving unannounced or indeed digging in cupboards to find Grandma Brancher's big teapot.

He followed her a few paces behind, irritated by the swish of her kilt, the tread of her walking boots, her very presence, knowing that soon enough the house and all that came with it would be hers and hers alone. She'd more than handle it. He had to give her that, she was a strong and adaptable woman.

'I'm not hungry,' he mumbled.

'Of course you're hungry! I'll fry up some of the leftover ham sandwiches and put a fried egg on top. No different to fried bread and bacon, come on! Walk with me!'

He stopped on the lane, wondering why on earth she wanted him to walk with her and feeling the flare of resentment at the way she was instructing him, when he realised she was of course talking to Fern and Flora.

He couldn't wait to tell Mary.

I honestly thought she was calling me to heel – can you imagine if I'd run up and taken a position! Good job she didn't say roll over or I might have dropped to the ground there and then – oh Mary, you'd have laughed.

A huge gulp of breath lodged in his throat as yet again his thoughts stuttered over the fact that he wouldn't be telling his wife anything. Not until he shuffled off this mortal coil . . . This confirmed his intention to die was the right one. A flare of energy, verging on excitement, flooded his veins at the thought.

CHAPTER SEVEN

EMMA

From the kitchen, Emma heard the front door slam shut and then the sound of Brendan's keys hitting the wide blue ceramic bowl on the whitewashed sideboard she'd painstakingly renovated after finding it in her dad's garage. Its top had been cluttered with half-empty bottles of turpentine and paint pots with a rainbow of drips running down the outsides. Not only did she like the fact it was recycled, and that it looked so smart in their square hallway, but also that her dad had touched it. The sight of it took her back to Saturday afternoons at his workbench, watching him tinker with bits of engine and craft things from scraps of wood, the smell of turps, the paint sticky on his sleeves, his weekend beard, and the way he'd immerse himself in the project before coming inside for a warm supper and a snooze in front of the telly. Happy, happy memories of the man she had idolised.

'Hello Brucie! Hello mate! Here he is! Here's the boy!'

She heard her husband give their Border terrier the usual greeting, with more enthusiasm and energy than he ever did a human member of the family. Bruce adored him for it.

'Great timing, dinner's ready!' Emma hollered from the stove, where peas bobbed in the saucepan of boiling water and the smell of cottage pie crisping under the grill wafted into the room that was her pride and joy. The house in Station Avenue had been a wreck when she and Brendan, as newlyweds, had taken out a hefty mortgage, borrowed from her parents, and scrimped and saved to make their dream of home ownership possible. It was in the built-up part of this market town where houses for families were affordable, the streets too narrow to cope with the level of traffic, and it was easy to walk to a shop if the need arose.

The day they had been handed the keys to the red-brick Edwardian terrace, her mother, declining a seat on a battered crate, had turned her nose up at the rotten floorboards, the overgrown back garden and the layers and layers of wallpaper, chosen by previous owners who all shared not only the address, but also, it seemed, the same chronic taste in interior design.

'Good Lord! I reckon it'll take you a lifetime to get it all looking nice! It'll be like decorating the Forth Bridge!' her succinct commentary. Brendan had pulled a face behind his mother-in-law's back and Emma had had to suck her cheeks in to stop herself from laughing.

'Well, I think it's got good bones.' Her dad, ever practical, had knocked on the walls, listening for what she wasn't quite sure. Drawing on his cigarette, he had nodded and winked at his new son-in-law with something close to approval. Brendan and her dad had been great friends, and this had been one of the great joys of her life, doubling her feeling of security as the two men she loved most formed an alliance of sorts. Another reason she now carried the sharp edge of his loss in her throat.

'Stayin' Alive' . . . having a song in mind if and when you need to perform CPR will help you maintain a steady rhythm of 100 to 120

BPM (beats per minute). And while the rhythm is very important, so is the quality of the compressions . . . This too she had learned by rote.

Many was the time, with thoughts laced with guilt, that Emma wondered how different her life would have been if it had been her mum who had popped her clogs suddenly one Tuesday afternoon after a good lunch and a glass of red. Not that she'd ever dare voice such a thing, of course not. But if her mum had a knack of making even the simplest of situations about as stressful as they could be, her dad was the opposite. What was it he always said? – 'Nothing is ever as bad as you think it will be. Nothing.' And she loved him for it. Loved his wisdom, his nature, and his ability to make her believe this. Losing him had set her adrift and keeping occupied was how she held on, fearful that if she stopped for long enough, she just might sink.

Two years ago, after much scrimping and saving, she and Brendan had installed her dream kitchen. It was sleek. Grey with brass accents and faux white marble countertops. Her heart still lifted every time she opened the door or walked down the stairs each morning. Only the ropey, dated bathroom to tackle and they'd be nearly home and dry . . . except by then the hallways would need doing again. Maybe her mother was right.

'Just going to wash my hands!' Alex called before thundering up the stairs, one of the only thirteen-year-old boys she knew who would think of this before being prompted, but that was Alex all over. Smart.

Brendan slipped behind her and kissed the back of her neck.

'Something smells good.' He inhaled deeply.

'Not sure if you're referring to me or the supper?' She wriggled free to grab her oven gloves and pulled the heavy cottage pie from the top oven, twisting to place it on the wooden trivet on the island where Brendan was now leaning.

'You might be on to something, Em. For anyone like me who loves their grub, how great to have their missus smell of eau de bacon, essence of beer or parfum de garlic bread.' His attempt at a French accent was terrible.

'Oh Bren, I'd be so happy to unwrap any of those on Christmas morning. What a lovely thought!' She stared at him; yes, he loved his grub but was still spare, with small defined muscles. A runner.

'Would you?'

'No!' She curled her top lip. 'What is wrong with you! Stick to my White Company candles and then we shall all have a peaceful day.'

'Reckon we'll get that job up near Marton Weir. They were nice people.'

'Oh good, what is it?' She took an interest in his company, a partnership with his brother Cormac, supporting her man who worked so hard for his family.

'Wrap-around patio and a retaining wall for a sloping front lawn. It'll look nice once it's done. I need to email the quote and give them dates. Can you check it before I send it off?'

'Course.' She winked at him.

'It's a good job I'm handsome, isn't it?' he laughed.

'Bloody is.' She glanced at his face and yes, he was still handsome, even with the greying temples of age and the lines of life that criss-crossed his forehead.

'How's your mum?' He reached into the wide American fridge for a bottle of beer, removing the lid with his teeth, which always made her cringe. She pictured a tooth or two crumbling away with the bottle top. It made her think of her chat with Roz earlier, *Mackenzie McTeeth* . . . reminding herself she'd promised to pop round to her friend's later. Looking forward to hearing about the latest shenanigans in Roz's life. Emma wanted her to meet someone nice and settle down, no matter how much Roz railed against it, worried that the freedoms she enjoyed in her forties might not be so attractive when she was elderly and a little hard of hearing, with grey hair and a slack bladder. She wanted Roz to find someone to grow old with, knowing the comfort she took from having Brendan to snuggle up to on a cold night.

'How's my mum? Annoying.' She drained the peas and gathered the plates, three white and one green, from the pile on the shelf, and placed them on the counter. Brendan took a seat at the breakfast bar that adjoined the island, where they sat on wide leather stools that fitted snugly underneath when not in use.

'No change there then.' He swigged from the bottle.

'She was on form today, even suggested that depression was only a thing because people weren't busy enough and that there were no gay people before the nineteen-eighties.'

He spat beer and laughter over the breakfast bar.

'It's not funny!' She glared at him.

'I know it's not,' he countered. 'It just amazes me that she even has the gall to say such things.'

'I know.' She reached for the big spoon to serve supper. 'It's like she throws these hand grenades of controversy and bigotry out to see where they explode, and as ever my philosophy is not to rise to it. Hoping she'll come to see that it's pointless and stop altogether.'

'Yeah, let's see how that works out. And talking of controversy, green plate alert! My wife is living on the edge!'

'The others are in the dishwasher.'

It was daft, really, and had become a comical yet irritating thing. She couldn't remember who had started it, but someone had pushed the plate away, and with an expression of disgust flatly refused to eat off the odd china – and now, no one wanted the bloody plate. But when there were only three matching ones left on the shelf, that was just too bad.

'Reggie, Alex, dinner is *actually* on the table!' she called through the open door towards the hallway, hoping her words might drift up the stairs.

Brendan stared at the empty table and shook his head.

'What?' She stared at her husband. 'I have to say that, or they never come down on time.'

'They never come down on time because you always say that when it's not true.'

She ignored him. This had not occurred to her.

'So, what happened with Reggie today?' he asked, his voice a little quieter, his eyes darting to the door, knowing they'd change the topic when their older boy appeared.

'The usual.' She dolloped large helpings of cottage pie on to the plates and then tipped small pea mountains next to it. 'Called me late morning and said he needed to come home and that was that.'

Shit! She remembered that she'd bashed the car, and how rude she'd been to the interfering woman in the car park.

She heard him sigh and hated that she was about to add to his emotional burden.

'Well, I've had a right old carry-on with Alex.' He took a deep breath, robbing her of the moment, for which she felt a small amount of relief. A reprieve of sorts.

'What d'you mean?' She halted the serving of supper and waited for him to speak; the words 'right old carry-on' and 'Alex' were rarely used in the same sentence.

Brendan took his time, mentally ordering his words, as he often did. 'I drove to the school playing field and parked up on the main strip alongside the Range Rovers and sports cars. I could see groups of boys coming down from the pitches and to be honest, Em, they all look the same in their hooped tops and shorts, especially at a distance. So, I was peering into them, smiling at any who got close in case one was Alex.'

'Oh my God, you didn't shove the wrong child in the back of the van *again*?' she joked. 'How long did we have that boy here, three weeks, wasn't it? Mind you, he was a lot tidier than Alex, so . . . I was sorry to hand him back.'

'No.' His expression told her it was not a cause for humour. 'But one kid, can't think of his name, the one whose dad owns the bank—'

'Adedayo.' She liked the boy, always smiling, always happy. Mind you, it must be easy to smile all the time if your dad owned a bank.

'Yes, lovely lad, he waved, and they all filed past, heading to the changing rooms or to pick up their bags or whatever from the locker room, and then out of the corner of my eye I saw Alex and I know he was looking at me, I could sense it. You know how you can feel someone looking at you. I was about to call out or wind the window down and say, take your time, son, no rush, Mum will only lie about when dinner is on the table.'

'Very funny.' She chuckled in spite of his sarcasm.

'And blow me, Em, he looked at the ground and marched forward as if he hadn't seen me. He cut me dead. Ignored me.'

She held his gaze for a moment. Maybe Brendan was mistaken. She hoped Brendan was mistaken.

'Are you sure he saw you?'

'No doubt about it.' He took another deep breath. 'I had it out with him in the van. Not arguing or anything like that.'

She knew this wasn't her husband's way.

'I asked him outright, "What was all that about? I know you saw me."' She noticed the crease of either hurt or confusion at the top of his nose and didn't like it one bit.

'What did he say?'

'He said he wished I wouldn't go and get him in the van.' He swallowed, letting this dire fact land. 'Then kept his face shielded with his hand until we'd cleared the car park and got out on to the main road.'

'Bren . . .'

'I know. I felt really small.'

'I'm sure he didn't mean it in that way.' She was sifting the emotional breadcrumbs that littered her thoughts, trying to use words that were both a balm to her husband's upset and didn't validate or excuse her son's actions, as was her instinct, when Reggie loped in. He was still wearing his uniform, which looked crumpled and had a slick of tomato sauce, no doubt from his earlier pizza, streaking the front of his white polo shirt. She ground her teeth; why did he not consider hanging it up, putting his sweatpants on, or even pjs – saving her the job of laundering them.

'Hi, Dad.'

'All right, mate?' Brendan picked up his fork and tucked in, speaking with his mouth full of cottage pie. 'Mum said you had to come home again?'

Her son sat opposite his father. 'Thought my dinner was on the table?'

'It's here! Right here!' She grabbed the green plate from the counter – mere feet away from her boy – and plonked the plate in front of him. 'Although it's probably freezing cold now.'

She put the other two plates of food in the spaces on the breakfast bar and went to fetch the salt and ketchup, which she knew at least one of them would want to douse their supper with.

'No, it's lovely and hot,' Brendan encouraged. She shot him a look – was he unaware that she was trying to prove a point? 'So why did you come home?' he tried again.

'Just . . .' Reggie swapped the green plate for one of the white ones and took his time, forming a response and forking peas one by one on to the tines.

She felt the tick of irritation before hollering again towards the hallway, 'Alex! Dinner! Now!' She sat on one of the spare stools to the sound of his feet thundering down the stairs.

Alex sat and placed his iPad on the tabletop next to him. He looked a little flushed, a little self-conscious, as if his behaviour and subsequent discussion with Brendan was on his mind. As it jolly well should be.

'You can put that away, mate.' Brendan spoke softly. 'Your mum's cooked supper. You know the rules, no games at the table.'

Alex adjusted his glasses and stared at his dad. 'It's not a game, it's homework.'

Brendan laughed out loud. 'Sure it is! Do you think I was born yesterday?'

Alex held up the tablet, so the page of quadratic equations was visible to all.

'Well, I don't care what it is, smart-arse, no tech at the table. It's family time.'

Alex made the screen go blank before swapping the green plate for the white one, smiling coyly as he pushed the green one until it was in front of Emma, who grabbed her fork.

'Sorry, Reggie, did you say what happened today?' Brendan, like her, couldn't quite recall.

'I just needed to come home.' He double-blinked.

'What's up, pal?' Brendan reached over and held his son's forearm.

Emma's appetite disappeared.

'Same as always, Dad.' Reggie looked up with eyes misty with tears that tore at her heart. She felt the stab of guilt at her impatience, her earlier irritation with her gentle boy. 'I can be in a lesson or talking to someone and I suddenly feel like . . . like everything is too much, like I can't breathe.' She watched as he rubbed his throat, as if just the thought was enough to cause him discomfort. 'I just wanted to come home and be quiet here, on my own.'

'Okay. Okay, pal.'

Her husband's nails turned white, squeezing Reggie's arm as if this physical affirmation might take away some of his son's anxiety. She understood; she'd do anything and everything to try to make it all go away, to try to make him happy. They exchanged a brief but knowing look before all four stared at the plates in front of them. It happened like this sometimes, moments of limbo when none of them knew the right thing to do or say. It might have been Reggie who suffered with poor mental health, but the ripples were felt by them all. As if his depression threw a dark veil over them. It was Alex who broke the impasse.

'I've, I've been having a think, Dad, and I'm sorry I didn't like you picking me up in the van.'

Emma smiled at him and then Brendan, happy that he'd thought it through. He was a good kid. A young, naïve and impressionable kid, but ultimately good.

'S'okay, mate. And I get it a bit.' Brendan pointed at him with his knife. 'At that school you're surrounded by all that cash, all those fancy motors, holiday homes and swanky watches, but that's not normal. None of it is. It's a rare and privileged world and just because you see it up close and are immersed in it, I don't want you to think that's how most people live because it isn't, far from it.'

'I know.' Alex nodded and reached for the ketchup.

'That van and the work Uncle Cormac and I do, and Mum working at the greengrocer's, is what keeps the roof over our heads and puts food like this on the table. And we have a nice life, a very, very nice life.'

'We do indeed.' She echoed the truth, even though at times she wished it could all be a little bit easier. She didn't hanker for the fancy motors, holiday homes and swanky watches her husband had mentioned, but she certainly wouldn't have said no to a bit of extra cash.

Brendan wasn't done. 'Don't ever be ashamed of the life you have outside of those school walls, because I tell you now, some of those kids whose families use fifty-pound notes to wipe their arses—'

She tutted at the use of arse and his example.

'Well, I bet you a pound to a pinch of shite they'd give their left nut to be sat here with a mum and dad who love them as much as we love you. Parents who give them their time instead of palming them off with the nanny every chance they get so they can go and play golf or go get more Botox.'

This time she refrained from tutting – not that she wasn't irked by 'shite' and 'left nut', but he was absolutely right. This was the way they parented, learned from their own experience. Brendan's mum was attentive and kind, and Emma's dad had had all the time in the world and had only ever supported her choices.

'Pass me that iPad.' Brendan took the device and tip-tapped away with more dexterity than she could ever master. 'I want to show you something.'

He pulled up on the screen. It was a green, green expanse.

'This is where I lived in rural Kent when I was little and this' – he whizzed along with his finger until he stopped at a point – 'is where my school was. It was three miles away. Three miles. And Nanny Breda didn't have a car and there was no bus.'

'And your dad had done a runner.' Alex filled in the gap and with his rounded vowels it sounded comical to hear the phrase, but she didn't laugh, knowing Brendan was making his point.

'That's right. He was shacked up with Big Shirl from the pub. But that's another story for another day. The reason for showing you this is that Nanny Breda walked Cormac and me there in all weathers, rain, shine and snow, three miles there and then three miles back and then in the afternoon she walked three miles there and then three miles back. That's—'

'Twelve miles a day!' Alex jumped in with the maths.

'That's right.' Brendan put the iPad down. 'And when she died, all I could think about were the chats we used to have on the way and what we saw en route, the dark nights with brilliant stars, the sunny mornings that were quiet and golden, but most of all . . .' He swallowed the catch in his voice. 'I remembered how she spent the best part of her day, for years and years, walking. Walking – just for us.'

'I'm sorry, Dad.' She watched two high spots of colour rise on their little boy's cheeks.

'That's okay. Every day's a school day, right?' Brendan winked.

''Tis for us because we're still at school. Worse luck.' Reggie sighed.

'I've had a think about it, and you can come anytime and pick me up in the van. I don't mind.' Alex brightened.

Brendan gave a dry laugh and ruffled Alex's hair. 'Thanks for your apology, son, but what I am trying to say is . . . It's your turn to walk to and from school: two miles there and two miles back. What am I, a bloody mug?'

Alex looked a little startled, a little horrified. 'But . . . but Dad . . .'

Brendan held his nerve. 'Or I tell you what, if you don't fancy the walk – you could maybe get one of your mates' dads in their four-by-four to drop you off? Only at the end of the street, of course – you wouldn't want them to know you lived in Station Road, right?'

Brendan, she knew, might be soft and kind, but he was no pushover.

'He's teasing you, Alex. We'll always come and get you. Always come and get both of you.' She looked at Reggie, who was tackling some mashed potato. 'I'm going to Mum's after dinner to put her to bed, then I promised Roz I'd nip in if that's okay?'

'Course, love. I'll be watching the football, with anyone who wants to join me?' Brendan looked towards the boys, who flatly ignored him. 'How is it I can have football running through my veins and yet my sons couldn't give a fig!'

'I like rugby!' Alex offered, as if this might be some consolation.

'And I like sleeping.' Reggie yawned on cue.

'Martha likes football,' Emma reminded him. 'And don't forget she's coming for supper on Friday with her new boyfriend. I'm going to do a big lasagne. We'll set the table in the dining room, which means, Alex, you'll have to move your Lego, and Brendan, can you shove your fishing gear that's propped up against the wall into the garage.'

'He's not new, we've met Carlo before, he took me bowling.' Alex pushed peas on to his fork with his finger.

'Ah, yes . . .' She exchanged a brief look with Brendan, who stared with a raise of his eyebrows that she interpreted as 'This one's over to you . . .'

'Martha and Carlos broke up and she's bringing her new new boyfriend, who's called Sergio.'

'Is he Spanish too?' Reggie asked, chasing the remnants of his cottage pie around the plate.

'No, not Spanish, he's Italian. From Italy.'

'I know what Italian means.' Reggie pulled a face.

'So do I!' Alex was not to be outdone.

'Course you do, you go to that fancy school, after all.'

'Reggie.' Brendan shook his head at their older son. Alex winning a full scholarship to Reynard's College often caused Reggie's issues to flare, as if he felt somehow lacking in the face of his little brother's achievement.

Emma's phone rang. She jumped up.

'Emma, Emma . . .' Her mother's breathless stutter filled her ear and her heart leaped accordingly, the memory so powerful it made her tremble.

Emma . . . get the . . . get the doctor. I can't . . . I can't . . .
Dad? Dad?

'It's okay, calm down, Mum! I'm on my way. Hang on, I'm on my way!' She hung up. *Oh God! Oh God! Oh God!* She spoke as she stood, trying to hurry while keeping calm; her breath came in shallow pants and her mouth went dry.

. . . having a song in mind if and when you need to perform CPR will help you maintain a steady rhythm of 100 to 120 BPM. Press down hard, to a depth of about five to six centimetres, before releasing the pressure, allowing the chest to come back up . . .

'Want me to take you?' Brendan abandoned his supper and stood too. Her sons sat with cutlery poised.

'Just see to the boys. You guys finish supper, there's, there's yoghurt and—' She spoke while mentally locating her jacket, phone and keys.

'Don't worry about us, just go! Call when you get there, let me know what's what and what you need me to do.'

She grabbed her car keys. This was not the first time her mum had made such a call, not the first time she'd scared the wits out of them all with the grim possibilities of what might lie ahead in the coming hours.

But as Emma raced out of the front door, she was acutely aware that one day it would be the last.

CHAPTER EIGHT

Thurston

Thurston heard the delicate sound of her laughter. He opened his eyes and there was her face, her beautiful face, smiling as she leaned over him. Her long fine hair danced across his bare chest. The curve of her shoulder, the pale, perfect nature of her porcelain skin. He wanted to touch her, stare at her for eternity.

'I like watching you sleep,' she whispered.

'Do you?' He was in awe at the wonder of her.

'I do. And I like sleeping next to you, knowing that if I need anything in the night or want a chat, you're right there! I don't think I've ever slept so soundly. It feels very safe.'

'I would never let anything or anyone harm a hair on your head.'

'I love you.'

'And I love you. We have two whole days, Mrs Brancher, two whole days of bliss.'

'I love being here with you, but also I can't wait to get to Merrydown and get started.'

'Get started with what?' he laughed.

'Being your wife. Making our home lovely. Making babies!' She blushed.

He reached out and hooked his big palm behind her neck and pulled her face down to meet his, wanting nothing more than to kiss that mouth. Mary pulled free.

'Do you think we should maybe go and explore the coastline? We might find fossils.'

'Fossils, you say?' He propped himself up on his elbows, his eyes wide.

'Yes!' She didn't realise he was being sarcastic, and he loved her lack of guile. 'My cousin Bernard was here in Lyme Regis during the war, and he has a fine collection.'

'Well, why didn't I think of that, yes! Let's do that, let's go looking for fossils.' He slumped back on the pillows and ran his hand over her arm. 'Or we could stay in this bed, this very comfortable bed, and only leave it later, to go and find an inn that serves a decent hot supper and a good beer, and then we can rush straight back here . . . I don't want to waste a second.'

'Aren't we the bohemian young things.' She straddled him and bent low to kiss him again. 'Do you think anyone has ever loved each other as much I love you and you love me, ever, in the whole history of the world?' she asked earnestly.

Thurston shook his head, quite overcome at the beauty and truth of her words.

'I don't think they ever have, Mary. I surely don't.'

A gate banged outside, followed by Rhubarb's bark, and he sat up straight. The shock of waking to find himself old and in his chair was harsh. His heart raced. Immediately, he closed his eyes, concentrating, trying his very hardest to go back to that dream, the sweet memory of their honeymoon when they had made promises that sustained them for sixty-two years. Sixty-two wonderful years . . .

With a shaking hand, he reached for the glass of water from the side table where he kept his clutter – a book or two, the most recent paper, the TV remote and the manicure set with nail scissors that he'd placed there some while since. *To cut* . . . Yes, that might be it. To find a sharp blade and cut. Where exactly he wasn't sure, or how, but he'd figure it out. His stomach bunched with nausea.

How would he manage the act? Could he do it drunk? That might help. A good slug of whisky and he'd get going. In what room? Not in the bedroom, too messy. The bathroom? Might be best. The linoleum floor easier to clean. And who would that woeful task fall to? June? He closed his eyes, feeling remorse in advance for all that he might bring to her door. It would most likely be June that found him. Should he leave a note? Probably. A note saying don't go into the bathroom, possibly – would that work?

And what about Rhubarb? How long before June came over and fed the little chap, let him out for a pee . . . His decision to check out was not without complications and details that he had hitherto not considered. With the memory of his dream lurking, he decided to think carefully about the details and take the necessary steps. *A blade* . . . Supposing he chickened out, found the task too involved. Was there a more remote method that might require less activity on his part? There must be.

On unsteady legs, he walked to the telephone table in the hallway and sat on the embroidered prayer chair that had always been there. Opening the red leather-bound address book, whose gold lettering on the front had long since faded, he let the grease-thumbed pages fall open and slowly dialled the number for Mr Shackleton.

'Shackleton and Shackleton.' The woman answered confidently, and Thurston wondered at the loveliness of having a namesake to hand on the business to, his life's work in steady, willing hands.

'Mr Claymore Shackleton, please. It's Thurston Brancher.'

'One second, Mr Brancher.'

He held the phone close to his ear, wondering if he was still connected, and just as he was considering hanging up . . .

'Thurston!' the solicitor boomed.

He and Claymore had been at Reynard's College together and the man was as affable now as he always had been.

'I expect you heard, Clay, about Mrs Brancher?'

'I did. I did indeed and was very sorry. Mrs Shackleton and I sent flowers.'

'Well, thank you. That was very kind.' His lawyer had sounded defensive. It was to Thurston's embarrassment that he'd paid little heed to the bouquets and wreaths that had clustered forlornly on the grass at the church, resenting their very presence.

'How are you bearing up?'

How to answer?

'As you'd expect.' Felt adequate. 'Reason for the call, I'd like to talk to you about my will.'

'Of course.' The man's tone now serious.

'I left everything to Mary and she to me.'

'I remember. Quite standard.'

'Well, now I need to have a think and get the thing rewritten or amended or whatever needs to happen.'

'Of course, Thurston. It's very straightforward, you just let me know who is or are to be the beneficiaries and I can draft the changes, then you pop in to the office and sign to approve, and that's pretty much it. We could go for a pint at the Old Fox afterwards if you time it right.'

'Yes.' He was in no mood for pints and was unsure why they would, now in their eighties, start this.

'As I say, Thurston, let me have it in writing. An email will do.'

Email? He rolled his eyes; he wouldn't know how to send an email!

'And I can make the necessary amendments and give you a shout.'

'How long do you think it will take to get it done?'

'As soon as I have the details, bearing in mind we're approaching the Christmas period and my diary is a little busy to say the least, we should be able to get it tucked up over the next few weeks.'

'Could you be more specific?' He did, after all, have a suicide to plan. This vagueness didn't suit him at all.

'More specific?'

'In reference to the time it will take.'

'Five and a half weeks, maybe six.'

He got the feeling the man had plucked the figure from thin air only to placate him.

'Thank you, Clay, I shall be in touch.'

He ended the call and stared at Rhubarb, who looked a little fed up, as if aware of the topic. 'What's that face for? You think I should leave it all to you, Barb? What would you buy? A lifetime's supply of biscuits and an automatic tummy scratcher?' He smiled at the hound, but his heart was heavy. 'Nancy will love you very much. And I want you to know that I am sorry, little one, but I know you'll understand. I know you will.' He cursed the crack to his voice as his dog stared at him with his eyes wide and ears down.

CHAPTER NINE

Emma

The car was parked haphazardly, to put it mildly, abandoned almost on the road outside her mother's house, when with her heart pounding and her fingers trembling Emma put her key in the door. The hallway was dark, and her stomach dropped at this fact alone. All the lamps were on timers, meaning her mum's world was bathed in a golden glow as dusk fell. And if she woke in the night, she was not scared of the darkness, but soothed by at least one lamp, reminding her that the sun would rise again.

'Mum? Mum, I'm here. It's me!' She felt her way along the hallway and flicked the light switch. Nothing. She did her best to keep calm, knowing a clear head was important for whatever might come next.

. . . heel of your hand on the middle of their chest. Put your other hand on top of the first and interlock your fingers. Keep your arms straight and lean over the casualty.

'I'm in the dark!' came her mother's steady reply.

Emma closed her eyes and felt nothing but sweet relief. Her mum was talking, with more than a hint of impatience in her tone. All was well.

'Yep, I can see. Well, I can't, but you know what I mean. Are you okay?' Swallowing her previous fear as her pulse settled, she followed the sound of her mother's voice into the kitchen, where she found her in the chair.

'I'm fine. I fell asleep and woke in the dark and it startled me. I went to stand but I'm more than a little wobbly today, didn't want to risk it. Luckily I had my phone. It's never dark. Never *this* dark. You said you'd put those switch things on so the lamps would always come on.'

'Yes, I did, and they do, but I think something might have tripped the switch. The other houses in the street have light. Let me go check the fuse box.'

'Don't be long!'

'Mum, you have a lovely home but it's not that huge. I will be in the hallway – you'll be able to hear me. Let me put your phone on to torch.' She did just that. 'I need mine to see the switches. Hang on.'

Leaving her mum with a beam of light thrown eerily across the room, Emma made her way back to the front door and sure enough, a quick glance inside the white-painted cupboard in the corner of the hallway and she could see that one had tripped. With a quick flick of her finger, the house jumped to life.

The lamps came on, the TV started chattering and the clock on the cooker beeped in an attempt to get someone to set it to the right time.

'There we go. Not sure why it happened – maybe a bulb blew somewhere, I'll get Brendan to have a look tomorrow. Have you had your supper?'

'I'm not hungry. I did get up for a pee though, about an hour ago. I just took it slowly. I'm not too fussed about being wobbly in the light, but in the dark . . .'

'I understand, Mum. And you're right, always go slowly, and hold on to the handles and bits and bobs along the way to keep you steady. It's good for you to get up, flex those muscles.'

'If you say so.' Her mother sighed. Emma bit the nail of her middle finger on her left hand and ripped it between her teeth.

'It's not me that says so, it's Dr Burton.'

'She's an idiot! Look what happened with your dad! I'll never forgive the woman. Never.'

Emma took her time, not only unwilling to have the conversation again, feeling the echo of it long after they'd exhausted the topic, but also not wanting to stoke the fires of a row. Not when her head was already full of a rather hectic day, and it wasn't done yet. The thought of her conversation later with Roz, and the inevitable laughter, lifted her mood.

'Do you remember, Mum, that they said even though Dr Burton saw Dad a couple of days before for that routine appointment, no one – not even she – could have had any clue that his heart was going to just give up the ghost. Even he had very little warning.'

'I know that's what they say, but I'm not so sure,' her mother spat, then came a loud, visceral sob that was heart-rending to hear. 'I miss him!'

Me too! Oh God, me too!

'I know you do.' Emma was quite sure that in other mother/daughter relationships, this was the point where she'd hold her mum's hand or hold her tight, but they had never been that kind of mother/daughter. Awkwardness cloaked her. So, she did what she always did and made herself busy, grabbing a discarded teacup and a crumb-dotted plate to wash while she chatted, trying to drown out the sound of her dad rasping on the phone as his last call played loudly in her memory.

'I was thinking . . .' Her mother sniffed, and wiped her eyes on the sleeve of her cardigan. 'I'd quite like to make your dad's favourite pie.'

'His favourite what?' She thought she might have misheard.

'Pie, Emma! I'd like to make his pie!' She banged the arm of the chair. 'I miss making the pastry and knowing he was coming home to tuck into a minced beef and onion. It'll take me back and I'd like to do it. Plus it's the kind of skill that if you don't practise, you might lose. And you never know when you might be called upon to whip up supper for a gentleman. The way to a man's heart and all that . . .'

'Oh God, Mum, as if!' The thought of her mum dating at her age and in her situation was as funny as it was unlikely.

'Would it be that shocking if I were to meet someone? I'm not dead yet, Emma-Jane!'

'Yes, yes it would be that shocking!' she laughed. 'But also you're highly unlikely to meet someone sitting here night after night. Did you and Dad—' She didn't know how to phrase it. 'Did you and Dad talk about the idea of either of you meeting someone else?'

'No.' Her mum bit her lip.

Emma regretted asking.

'But, you know what? If you want to make Dad's pie' – it sounded bizarre, but who was she to judge, having spent more time than she would care to admit preparing for and mentally practising the CPR that she feared might have saved her dad, had she only been on hand – 'and it brings you some comfort, I can understand it. I'll get the ingredients together in the week and we can—'

'I've got the ingredients, help me up!'

'Oh! You want to do it now?' She felt the twin pull of fatigue and disappointment in her bones. This was the last thing she felt like doing, keen as she was to see Roz, which would, she knew, be the highlight of her day.

'Haven't you somewhere you need to be? Don't let me stop you! I can manage.' Her mother shuffled forward in her chair and took deep breaths. 'I can manage perfectly if I take my time – you go home! I'll be fine.'

'No, no, I'll stay and help.' Her mother looked frail, her hair needed a brush, her wrists were thin, and it tore at Emma's heart. 'I'll just call Brendan and let him know what's happening.'

'Emma, seriously, I can manage, please go home!' She raised her voice.

Ignoring her, Emma took her phone into the front hallway. Brendan answered immediately.

'All okay?'

'Yep, she's fine. It was a power cut thingy, but all sorted. I'll be a little while longer, just going to help her with a chore or two.'

'Course you are.'

'What does that mean?' she whispered, but her tone was sharp.

'Don't bark at me, Em! I'm the good guy! It's just that I bet the boys a Magnum ice cream that there'd be something you'd get stuck doing and that's our whole evening gone.'

'Well, congratulations, you were right. Enjoy your Magnums!' She ended the call. Instantly she regretted it, but hearing his very accurate prediction was a needle in her side. On a cold, dark night like this she wanted nothing more than to slouch on her friend's sofa in her socks with a cup of tea, as they put the world to rights.

'Right, Mum, I'll get the scales out and you grab the butter from the fridge.' She washed her hands as she issued instructions, watching as her mother gripped the countertop to steady herself.

'First, don't give me instructions in my own kitchen, I've already told you I can manage without you, and second, since when did I need scales? Any woman who doesn't know the correct flour and fat ratios for a good pastry wants shooting.'

'I'll go get the gun . . .'

'What did you mumble?' her mum shouted.

'I said, I'm glad we've begun! Fun times!' She grinned.

'Are you being funny?'

'No, Mum, please—' She bit the skin around her nail and sighed. 'Can we just make the bloody pie?'

'I thought you were coming over?' her friend asked down the phone.

Emma put the key into the ignition and sat back, rubbing her tired face. Roz: her reward at the end of a hectic day and now her mum had eaten up her time. Margery might have said 'Go home' but Emma knew she didn't mean it. Not that it made it any easier, knowing she'd let her mate down and Brendan and the kids. Cloning was probably the answer – three of her, to be in all the places her presence was required.

The night was dark and there was the smell of smoke in the atmosphere. It was a scent she loved. It spoke of autumn and real fires, warm stews, soft blankets and Sunday afternoons curled up on the sofa watching movies with full stomachs and Brucie snoozing between them. The way it used to be when her dad was alive, and she didn't feel the pull of responsibility that meant she was permanently on call.

'Honest to God, I was going to come over, Roz, but I ended up going over to Mum's and stayed to help her make a pie for my dad. I've just put her to bed.'

'Sorry, did you say a pie for your dad, who died eighteen months ago? Victor, that dad? – who used to let me steal his cigarettes and turned a blind eye to us swigging out of his cherry brandy bottle? The dead one.'

'Yes, as he's the only one I have. Had,' she corrected; the image of her dad being so lovely to them when they were teens caused a lump to rise in her throat.

'Okaaaay, so how does she plan on getting this pie to him? I mean, I know the Royal Mail is great 'n' all, but even they might struggle.'

'I think it was more symbolic. A symbolic pie for her dead husband.' Her mouth twitched in amusement at the utter absurdity of it all.

'Could she not just put flowers somewhere and say a Hail Mary?'

'We're not Catholic. Plus, I think a symbolic pie is more fitting in many ways.' She tried to explain. 'I guess it helps her pretend for a little while that he's on his way home to come and eat it.'

'Jesus, that's so depressing.' Her friend was clearly not in the mood for sentimentality.

'Isn't it just?'

'What you doing now?'

Emma glanced at the clock. It was a quarter to nine. Her desolation complete. Too tired to venture anywhere but home, defeated by chores and utterly spent.

'I think I might just go home and sit in the bath. Take a bottle of plonk in with me and roll up a towel like a pillow and do a face pack and everything.' The idea formed as she spoke. 'An hour by myself in the bath with wine, I'd like to do that. Does that make me a bad friend?' She felt guilty at not nipping to Roz's house, which was only a short stroll from hers, but she was honestly knackered. Plus, she thought it best to get home to Brendan before inviting more scorn about her being MIA.

'No, it makes you a lightweight one, which I am entirely used to. And when you say sit in the bath, you mean that thing where you don't actually put water in it, but just use it to hide in?'

'Yes, but it's not hiding.' She coughed to clear her throat of the lie.

'What is it then?'

'What it is, Roz' – Emma had to think fast – 'is taking a moment from the stresses of family life to be alone and think a little.'

'Okay, I don't want to disagree with you, but that sounds very much like hiding.'

'Whatever. Shut up.'

'Mew mew, mew mew mew!' her friend squeaked.

It was something they did, imitated the other with this non-word if they thought the other was talking crap or being overly moany. Emma ignored her.

'What do you need to talk about anyway? Tell me now, in brief?' She yawned, knowing she'd rather have the gist of the discussion to ponder and guessing it was probably man-related. A new man, a previous man, an unattainable man, a man Roz liked who didn't like her or a man that liked Roz who she didn't like . . .

'Nah, it'll keep. Night, tart.'

'Night, tart.'

She looked up at her mother's house before pulling away, feeling a little mean for mocking her wanting to make a pie. Who was she to tell the old lady how to grieve, how to feel or – worse – what she could and couldn't do to celebrate the husband she so missed. She thought of Brendan and how she would feel if she lost him. It was unthinkable and her heart went out to her mother. Mr Blundesthorpe's lounge curtain swished; had he been watching her? The thought was a little unnerving.

'Night, Mum,' she whispered into the ether as she headed off.

Their house in Station Road was lit up like Blackpool Illuminations. She winced at the thought of the cost of all those lights and all those lamps burning away.

'Only me!' she called as she entered the square hallway and threw her keys in the ceramic bowl to join Brendan's.

He was in the lounge, leaning far back on the sofa with his feet, in their orange socks, up on the old pine coffee table and Bruce nestled in a gap that looked impossible for him to fit into between the arm of the couch and Brendan's thigh.

'How's your mum?' He turned his head to face her.

'Asleep, I hope. Kids all right?' The room was hot, and she unzipped her thin blue fleece before slipping her arms out of it and lobbing it on to the armchair. Keen to get to her bath, she knew the nice thing to do was chat for at least a second or two.

'Haven't seen much of Reggie, but Alex has been doing his level best to talk my ear off instead of letting me watch the football. He was jabbering away when Rashford scored from the eighteen-yard line – I only caught it on the replay.'

'Isn't chatting to your son more important than watching grown men kick a little ball around a pitch?' She had never understood the appeal. Her dad had been a cricket man.

'Erm.' He paused. 'I never want to lie to you, so can I say "pass"?'

'It's not *Mastermind*, Bren, it's real life!' She stared at the man she loved, feeling slightly aggrieved that his choice was between watching football with his feet up and chatting to Alex with his feet up. She'd happily take either. This was followed by the self-rebuke that her time was in her control, she was a grown woman. A grown woman who needed to learn how to prioritise a little better. The fact was, her mum needed her and it wasn't her husband's fault. Emma had, after all, done the very thing she was nagging him about: abandoned her kids, her family, and focused her attention elsewhere.

'Thank goodness it's not *Mastermind*, because my specialist subject would be the goals of Marcus Rashford and I'd have a big bloody hole in my knowledge because our youngest can't keep his trap shut for five minutes. I swear we've covered everything from the melting of the polar ice caps to whether Dr Seuss was a real doctor.'

'Don't you start with doctors; I've had enough of that topic tonight.'

'Let me guess, *If that Dr Burton had done her job . . .*' He pulled a face.

'Something like that.' She sank down next to him on the sofa, and he reached for her hand; their fingers lay entwined on the cushion, and she liked the feel of his warm skin against hers. It calmed and centred her.

'Anyway, good job you're sitting down,' he began.

'Oh, I don't like the sound of that.' She sat up a little straighter.

'Nothing to panic about, but one of the reasons Alex was so keen to chat was that he had news.'

'A girlfriend?' She smiled. Alex's school had joint socials with the local girls' grammar school, and she liked the thought of this co-ed interaction.

'Nope. A ski trip.'

'A what?'

'The biennial ski trip to France. End of February.' He pinched his nose, and she knew that, like her, he would be thinking of the expense.

'What did you say to him?' She kept her voice low in case their discussion travelled up the stairs.

'Well, he didn't exactly ask permission, just assumed he'd be going. Kind of like, "Guess what, Dad, I'm going to France!" and then he did a little happy dance, fists in the air, hopping around in his slippers. It's not his fault, is it? It sounded like his mates went straight into planning mode, talking about who's sharing a room with who, what sweets they'll take for the plane, who will sit next to each other and what computer games they'll play. The level of detail was breathtaking, considering they only had the news this afternoon.'

'Oh no!' She closed her eyes and knew it would be just as hard to burst his bubble as it would be to find the money for a bloody ski trip.

'Honestly, Em, I was so taken aback, I didn't sugar-coat anything but just blurted that it was out of the question, nipped it in the bud. And now he's definitely not going to want to travel with me in the van. I have literally crushed his ski dream, as well as driving a shite car.'

'I can't stand the thought of all his friends going and him being left out.'

'Me too, of course, but we can't afford it and I figured if I let him run away with plans to go on the trip, the worse it'd be to have to let him down.'

'I know, but—'

'There's no but, Em, we can't afford it!' He spoke slowly, as if to emphasise the point.

'How much is the trip?' She wondered if there was any way . . .

'One thousand two hundred.'

'*One thousand two hundred?* What the flippin' 'eck?' She stared at her husband, again keeping her voice low.

'I know. Skiing in France . . .' He squeezed her hand. 'Don't think I even knew where France was when I was his age. His world is a lot smaller than ours. Everything feels within reach.'

'And for the right price, it is – over a thousand quid.' She let the sum float around her mind. 'I'd love him to go.'

'Yes, I'd like us all to go! I'd like a villa in Portugal and a ski lodge in some fancy resort, I'd like both of those things, but the reality is, every penny is accounted for. You know this.'

'Yes, I do know this.' His sarcasm irritated her. 'But don't get angry with me because I can't stand the thought of how much it must hurt to be the only kid not going in your friendship group. Let's see if we can figure something out.'

'Figure something out? Are you being serious? It's the same as we'd pay for a week's family holiday, if we ever took one!' He gave a wry laugh.

'You think I don't know that? But what's the alternative – tell him we're running on empty? The cupboard is bare! He doesn't need to know that. None of the kids do. It's our job to worry about how we keep all the plates spinning, not theirs.'

'Well, that's certainly what you do, keep all the plates spinning!' He snorted.

'What's that supposed to mean?' She raised her voice while looking at the door to check the kids were still ensconced upstairs, not wanting this to reach their ears.

'I mean you never stop, Em! Always rushing to the next chore, the next task. I just wish you'd slow down, take a minute.'

'I have a lot to do, Bren.'

'We all have a lot to do, but I think you could slow down. Your mum is fine, the kids are fine, Brucie is fed and watered. Dishes are washed, kitchen tidy. You can afford to relax.'

'Nice to know I can afford something,' she countered.

'You always sound so defensive when we talk about money, but it's not your problem, it's *our* problem. I hate letting Alex down as much as you do, but if we don't have the money . . . it really is that simple.' He raised his hands and let them fall into his lap.

'I guess so, but it makes me wonder if we did the right thing by agreeing to let him go to that bloody school,' she mused. 'I don't mean that!' She rubbed her forehead. 'It's a wonderful opportunity for him, everyone says so.'

'Do they? Maybe we should let them pay for it then,' he huffed.

They both let the air settle and she squeezed his hand. They weren't angry with each other, they were angry with the injustice of it all, at how hard they worked and how despite trying to do the right thing for Alex, he was going to be gutted.

'I love you.' She leaned her head on his shoulder.

'And I love you.' He kissed the top of her head. 'I just worry sometimes that we're delaying the kick in the teeth he's going to get when he realises he can't keep up with the other boys. Boys who have names like Dimitri and Piers – because we don't have yachts, second homes and a spare bloody grand lying around for a school trip. Is it unfair on him?' His question was genuine.

'I don't think so. I guess it's about balance, letting him benefit from all that his school offers while keeping him grounded at home. No one said it was going to be easy.' She yawned again. 'But there are worse problems to have.'

'There are indeed, like how to stop him talking so I don't miss a goal!' He gave a sharp snort of wry laughter before leaning over and kissing her cheek and then her neck. It made her squirm; he knew it tickled her when he went anywhere near her neck. She hated it. 'Any chance of a cuddle?' he breathed.

'Well, anything is possible, Brendan, as long as you don't want me to take this opportunity to rest.' Her whole body sagged with exhaustion.

He kissed her hard. 'Your rest can definitely wait.'

'Thought so. I mean, I'm tired, running on empty, and it's not only our finances that are scarce – my sex cupboard is definitely bare!' She did this, used humour to defuse the incendiary topic. Her heart was not in it right now, her body tired, her mind busy;

sex was at the bottom of her agenda, not that understanding the root of her reluctance to indulge made her feel any less guilty.

Brendan pulled away, laughing loudly with his head thrown back. 'Did you say "sex cupboard"?'

'I might have done.' She laughed, without any clue where the words had come from.

They both giggled until they became raucous and, jumping up, he dived on top of her, nuzzling her with his stubbled chin and kissing her face all over. 'Sex cupboard!' he wheezed.

'Shhhh . . . get off! The boys will hear you! And look, you're upsetting Brucie!' The dog was staring at them quizzically with eyes wide, ears back.

He climbed off her and beamed at her. 'Reckon I could wake you up a bit. I even think if I dug deep enough into that cupboard, I might find a little crumb!'

'Maybe you will.' She knew she had to make more effort; it would be good for them both. 'But first I need to spend time in the bath. Alone. Clear my head.' She rubbed at her eyes, which were misty with tiredness.

At the sound of Alex coming down the stairs, they sat up straight. Brendan folded his arms and pulled a serious expression.

'Can I have some crisps?' he asked with his little nose shoved through the door.

'It's a bit late.' She yawned. 'But I guess so.'

Without taking the risk to see if she changed her mind, he raced into the kitchen. She could hear the sound of rustling. It was a lot easier to let him have crisps than it was a ski trip.

'Jesus, Em – first you'd prefer to bankrupt us rather than admit the kid can't go skiing, and now crisps at bedtime? You need to learn to say no.' His sharpness spoke of frustration.

'You're right, Bren.' She stood up. 'No, I don't fancy a cuddle. I fancy a sit in the bath and an early night.'

He stared at her with his mouth open.

Emma waited until Alex was ensconced in his room before sneaking into the bathroom with the chilled bottle of white New Zealand wine she'd squirrelled from the fridge and up the stairs. Her breathing slowed. This was her place of refuge and she'd never been so happy to lock the door behind her and slip off her blue sneakers.

CHAPTER TEN

THURSTON

Having made the necessary call to Claymore, and unable to get back to sleep and recapture his glorious dream, Thurston sat on the sofa and picked up the remote control. He didn't like the idea of watching TV without Mary but liked even less the idea of sitting in silence. The clock on the mantelpiece seemed especially loud.

It ticked.

And it ticked.

'It's a strange time.' He spoke softly into the darkness. 'I watched you get weaker and frailer over your last months. I was there when you passed away, holding your hand. I was at your funeral. I watched the curtains close as your coffin was lowered. And pretty soon, I'll have your ashes in a box on a shelf in the broom cupboard. I feel the loss of you every second of every day and yet I don't believe you're gone, I just don't believe it, does that make any sense?' He swallowed, and this too was loud in his ears. 'I keep thinking you might pop your head around the door and tell me it's all been a very cruel joke. But I wouldn't mind, love. I wouldn't mind how bad taste or misjudged your plan, if you would just come back to me now.' His head dropped to his chest as his tears once again fell. It happened like this, taking him by surprise and robbing him of composure, lost entirely to his sorrow in the stillness. 'Please . . .' he managed, 'please come back to me now. Let me wake up from this nightmare. I miss you. I miss you so much!'

Rhubarb, aware of his distress, pawed at his leg, enough of a distraction for Thurston to gain composure.

'You want a treat, boy? Why not.'

With the dog crunching enthusiastically on a bone-shaped, gravy-flavoured biscuit, Thurston took a seat at the table and set about writing to Claymore, making it all official and hastening the moment of his demise. He knew that once his affairs were all in order, there would be nothing left to sort, meaning he could slip away at his convenience. His body gave an involuntary shudder at the thought.

It felt formal, official, and he chose an appropriate tone, writing slowly with the chunky ink pen that had been his father's, wondering what the man himself would make of his present state of mind.

Dear Claymore,

As per our discussion on the telephone, I am writing to confirm that I would like to make the following amendments to my last will and testament.

Merrydown Farm, the house, associated land, and all contents of the house are to be left to my sister, June Armitage. Some shares, which I shall list separately, antique farming implements and other farming memorabilia, details of which I will also attach on a separate sheet, that have been in the family longer than I've been here, are to go to my brother, Loftus Brancher. A cash amount of fifty

thousand pounds is to go to my nephew, Peter Brancher.
One hundred thousand pounds is to be given to my niece,
Nancy Finnigan, to cover any expenses she might incur
in caring for my little dog, a nice amount for her and her
husband, just to see them right.

Thurston remembered his conversation with June as he sat by the fence post.

And I'd like to leave my old tractor, the red Massey
Ferguson, to my sister, June . . .

He put the pen down and tried to imagine his sister when in receipt of this news. 'I have no doubt, Barbie, that none of the family will understand or approve of my actions, but I reckon when she's over the shock, that sister of mine will be chuffed as chips to get her hands on them tractor keys.'

The phone in the hallway rang. He jumped up, raking his hair over his head with his fingertips as he answered the call in the steadiest voice he could muster.

'Hello?' He kept his voice level.

'Nancy's car's kaput,' his sister began her breathless rant. 'She could have had her father's car but stuck with that old banger, now she's carless, I knew this would happen! She can't drive Andrew's because it's an automatic and she's anxious about no gear stick.' June tutted at the ridiculousness of it. 'Andrew can't take her as he still can't drive after his varicose vein surgery. Can you take her in, in the morning? I'd do it but Fern's got the runs and I'm taking her up to the vet's for a once-over. Think she might have been scrumping in the orchard, eating the rotten apple falls, her farts would honestly kill a bear, but can't be too sure – so can you pick

Nancy up at half five? And then collect her at the end of the day? She should be right for the day after if her car gets fixed.'

'Yes.' He nodded.

'Good.' His sister sighed. 'Is that it then? Nothing else to add apart from "*Yes*"?'

'What would you like me to add?' He stared at his reflection in the glass of the framed floral print above the telephone table. He looked faded, smudged and a little lost.

'Nothing, Thurston. Absolutely nothing. I have better chats with the dogs.'

And with that, June ended the call. He didn't mind picking Nancy up, not one bit, it would be the perfect opportunity to sound her out about looking after Rhubarb; but his sister he felt to be a right pain in the bum.

A quick glance up the stairs confirmed it was too early for bed, knowing if he succumbed to the temptation, he'd likely be wide awake in the early hours and that was a prospect worse than having to fill the lonely evening ahead. Decision made, he went back to the sofa and pressed the button. The TV roared to life and there were people on a stage dancing around, dressed as . . . he couldn't quite make out what it was meant to be, a bottle of tomato sauce? Surely not. This was where Mary came in handy, filling him in on the detail he missed and explaining the plot twists he had dozed through. But a bottle of tomato sauce, dancing on a stage? He was sure that even she might be a little stumped. What was the world coming to? Not that he'd have to worry about any of it for too much longer. He closed his eyes. This thought alone was like a safety net. He could get through any day, any minute – safe in the knowledge that pretty soon he could disappear.

Rhubarb yawned and whined at the same time.

'I should also have mentioned that Nancy will likely feed you sausages and before you know it, you'll forget all about your mum and me here.'

His little dog blinked at him, and Thurston could only look away, hoping beyond hope that this was true. Staring back at the dancing bottle of ketchup, he thought of blood and wondered how much of it there might be when he cut himself and leaked to death. It wasn't a pleasant thought.

Maybe taking a blade to his body was not the answer. He scratched his scalp. There had to be a neater, less messy way . . . It was as he looked up at the big barn through the window that the solution came to him. A building away from the main house with sturdy beams, good lengths of strong rope and a door that he could lock from the inside – with a note pinned to the outside. Yes, that was it. June or whomever could simply call the police and go tend to Rhubarb, leaving the mess, the horror and the husk of the man who had chosen the timing of his own exit in the solid old barn. Having now identified the location and method of his passing, he felt something close to peace. All he need do now was tie up loose ends, sort his finances, end various contracts and make sure everything was in order, not wanting June or Nancy to be lumbered with the hassle that could arise from a lack of clear administration. Looking again up at the big barn, he thought it very fitting; the building that had been so central to his life – his youth club, his hobby room, the space in which he had learned farming craft and mechanics from his father, his office, workshop, shelter, haven . . . and now his final resting place. Perfect.

CHAPTER ELEVEN

Emma

Emma locked the door and opened the bathroom's sash window to let the cool night air into the room, then lit her large three-wick candle, which almost instantly filled the air with a soft glow of light and the glorious, heady scent of sandalwood. It felt almost spa-like, if she ignored the missing tiles, exposed plaster, gurgling toilet and wobbly sink. Taking the fluffy bath towel from the rack, she folded it into a pillow, placing it carefully over the end of the bath. How she hated the thought of Alex not being able to keep up with his mates, picturing the excited planning of what sweets to take on the coach, only for his little dream to be quashed. Still, she kept the flame alive of how to make his trip possible.

A headache began to drum on her skull. She inhaled deeply, hoping to calm both her worries and her pounding head. Was Brendan right? Did she make herself busier than was necessary? And to what end? The answer came quickly: to stop her from having time to think about all the things she couldn't fix, couldn't control. It was a hard habit to break. And as if to prove her point, she shook the thought from her head. Climbing in, she lay back and closed her eyes, taking deep breaths through her nose and out through her mouth, the way Paddy at work had taught her to.

Nancy, the owner of the greengrocer's, had discovered them a couple of months ago, sitting cross-legged out the back while he instructed her to breathe in . . . and breathe out . . . before they both collapsed in fits of giggles.

'Are you . . . are you both okay?' their boss had asked in her nervous voice, which Paddy could imitate to perfection.

'Yes, Nancy, just finishing up our break. I'm trying to stop Emma from doing something stupid, she's a woman on the edge.' He stared at their boss. 'And she just needs to take a second.'

'Oh, Emma! I . . . I didn't realise.' Nancy had looked quite flustered. She was a sweet woman who seemed ill at ease, as if expecting at any moment to receive a tap on the shoulder and be asked to leave the premises. Even though she owned the place.

'I'm really not, Nancy. Ignore him. I'm not on the edge, I just mentioned to Paddy that my home life is a little stressful. But please ignore him.'

'I do understand. Please take as long as you need.'

'Bless you, Nancy,' Paddy had offered as she crept backwards into the storeroom.

The moment the woman had disappeared, he had pulled a squashed Mars bar from his pocket and got stuck in to it.

'Did you just say "bless you"?' She had stifled her hysteria.

'I might have.' He bit his bottom lip.

How she loved Paddy, who made even the direst of tasks, like sorting trays of mushrooms or lugging heavy mud-smeared sacks of spuds on the darkest of mornings, seem almost fun.

She thought of him now as she lay in her bath, hiding. Once more, she practised her breathing and was certainly more relaxed than she had been; she decided that sex, even on a school night and even if she was a little sleepy, might be nice after all. With the bottle balanced between her legs, she unscrewed the lid.

The bathroom window flew upwards.

Only seconds away from letting out a bloodcurdling scream as her whole being jolted, she heard a voice she recognised.

'Don't freak out!' Roz's instruction cut through the air.

'What the hell are you doing?' Emma asked, her pulse settling a little, staring in disbelief as her best friend poked her head and arm in through the window.

'Can I come in?'

'What do you mean, can you come in! Are you on a ladder?'

'No. No, I'm not. I suddenly got very, very tall. Of course I'm on a bloody ladder! It's the one Brendan leaves at the back of the shed and hopes no burglar finds it. The idiot. Help me in!'

Emma put her bottle of wine on the floor and levered herself out of the bath as all calmness left the room. Pulling the window up as far as it would go, she watched as Roz slithered in across the windowsill like a snake – a snake wearing jeans, a hoodie and cow-boy boots – before landing in a crumpled heap on the rug in front of the basin. Roz stood slowly and dusted off her bottom. The two women stood face to face.

'Why are you looking at me like that?' Roz questioned.

'What do you mean? I have every right to look at you like that – you've just climbed through the bloody bathroom window!' She pointed. 'Why didn't you knock on the front door like any normal human?'

'Because I am not a normal human and if I was a normal human you would never have wanted to be my best friend.'

'True.'

Emma could have sat anywhere she wanted on that first day of school but chose to sit next to the blonde girl who was taking small plastic dinosaurs out of a tub and placing them in her mouth until her cheeks bulged.

'Plus . . .' Roz sidled past her, pulled off her cowboy boots and grabbed the wine. 'I knew that if I did knock on the front door, you'd come down and we'd sit in your fancy-pants kitchen and have a nice cup of tea, whereas now . . .' She climbed into the bath and sat down with her legs to one side. Emma followed suit and once again placed her head on the rolled-up towel. 'We get to lie here in peace and drink!'

'I was much comfier in here on my own. I should never have told you that I'm a secret bathroom drinker,' she joked, moving her foot to a better position. Beyond happy to be in her friend's company.

'I'm glad you did. It made me love you more, Em. I like that you are outwardly such a goody two-shoes, but you have this dark side. Locking the door and necking booze in secret!'

'Hardly necking! One glass, possibly two. Then I put the rest in the fridge till next time. And actually, I resent that. I'm not a goody two-shoes.'

'You are though.'

'I'm not.' She felt affronted.

'Em, I've known you for a hundred years and you definitely are.' Roz swigged wine from the bottle and handed it to her.

'But I'm not.' She didn't like the implication. It sounded dull.

'Okay, tell me this – have you ever been arrested?'

'You know I haven't!'

'Do you cross on the red man or the green man?'

Emma tutted. 'Green every time. Sets a bad example otherwise. Kids might be watching.'

'Have you ever killed a man?' Roz stared her down.

'Not intentionally.' She giggled and took a drink.

'Ever cheated the "weigh your own veg" counter by bagging up your courgettes and then adding another after you've printed the label?'

'God! No! Who does that? And besides, I get most of my veg free from work.'

'What do you think of people who walk on the grass when there's a "Don't walk on the grass" sign?'

'I think there's a special place in hell for them.'

'Worst crime you can picture that deserves a public flogging?' Roz pulled a serious face.

'That would be folding the corner of a page over in a book to mark your place. Spoils the page.'

Her friend smirked. 'I rest my case.'

The two lay quietly, as if it was perfectly normal to be lying in the bath, fully clothed, on a Wednesday night with your bestie. Their breathing in sync. Joy restored.

Emma closed her eyes. 'Do you know, this is the only room I get any peace. The only door with a lock on it and the only place I can sit quietly and think for a minute without someone asking me to do something.'

'And now I'm intruding.' Roz kicked her in the shoulder.

'Yes, you are. What are you doing here anyway? I thought you said that whatever fascinating snippet of gossip you have could wait until tomorrow?'

'I lied. Plus, I wanted some company. And some wine.'

Emma opened her eyes. 'Rough day, honey?'

'Yeah. I found out one of my patients died yesterday. Only young. It's weird – I deal with death every day and just sometimes it knocks the breath out of my throat. And I can't say why. I can deal with losing a hundred people and then bang! The hundred and first goes and it floors me.'

'That's probably a good thing, isn't it? Shows you're still human inside that sexy, cynical shell?'

'Spose. It was a woman in her thirties, and she had two kids and a husband, and it made me feel . . .'

'Sorry for them?' Emma prompted.

'No, it made me feel jealous! Why have I not been able to sort my life out, find a man, have kids . . . someone who might be bothered if I died.'

'Don't say that. You have sorted your life out; you don't live with my level of chaos. Anyway, I thought you didn't want kids, ever.' Emma reminded her of her viewpoint, which had been unwavering since their twenties.

'I don't . . . but then sometimes I think that I don't not want them.' Roz drank long and slow from the bottle.

Emma tried to read her expression, wondering where this change of heart had come from, refraining from pointing out that now, in their late forties, that ship might well have sailed.

'I mean, everyone says they're the best thing that can happen to you, don't they?'

Emma exhaled through bloated cheeks, considering the pros and cons and all the stresses that being mum to three kids brought her.

'I'd say they're not *not* the best thing,' she conceded.

'So, if you had to choose something memorable, a happy thing about being a mum – what's the first thing that comes to mind? Don't overthink it!'

It was easy; the first thing that popped into her head was vivid and wonderful.

'School nativities when they were little, oh goodness . . .' She placed her hand at her throat. 'The first sight of baby Jesus being manhandled by Mary and Joseph with tea towels on their heads, all the kids waving to their families in the rows behind me the moment they walked on to the stage. I was off, sobbing, and that was before either Martha, Reggie or Alex made an appearance and, depending on the year, had to utter, and fluff, their one line.' She giggled. 'Martha's was "We have no room here for people like you!", Reggie's, "Is this your donkey, my friend?" And Alex, spoken with more enthusiasm than either Bren or I were comfortable with, suggesting a future career as a debt collector: "If you can't pay, you can't stay!"'

'Oh God, I can actually hear Alex saying that!' Roz closed her eyes briefly.

'Ah, they were marvellous, Roz.' She still had the programmes somewhere with their names in and the parts they had played. Martha, innkeeper's wife. Reggie, kind traveller. And Alex, shepherd number four. She felt warmed by the memory; shepherd number four had always been her favourite shepherd.

Roz opened her eyes. She looked a little nervous, which was odd; nerves had no place at this stage of their relationship. Point being, they were top to tail in a shared bathtub. 'Before we get further distracted, the reason I wanted to talk to you is that I want to tell you something.' Her smile was faltering.

'Go on then.' Emma's own nerves started to flare.

Roz took a deep breath. 'I've given up my job. I've stopped working. I'm almost a lady of leisure.' She lifted the bottle and grinned.

'What?' Roz, she knew, loved her job; this was out of character, to say the least. 'Is this a joke? Have you won the lottery?' She kicked her friend in the shoulder.

'It's not a joke and I haven't won the lottery.'

'Bloody hell! What are you going to do instead? Don't say go travelling, please don't say that! I'd miss you way too much! Although I could come and visit if maybe you were in Cornwall or Devon, but not anywhere exotic, we don't have the cash for travel—'

'Em,' Roz interrupted, and held her eyeline. Her voice stern, commanding.

Emma shut up and something told her that whatever her friend was about to say was not necessarily something she wanted to hear.

'I'm not going travelling. But I do need to tell you . . . I need to tell you . . .' Roz took her time, and the air seemed to leave the room. 'That my cancer's back. That's why I've stopped working. My cancer came back.'

Emma was aware that Roz was speaking but her words would not land. She shook her head. It felt as if her heart had dropped into her stomach and the room spun.

'What? *What do you mean?*' Her voice sounded small in her ears, and she wondered if she'd spoken out loud.

'My cancer's back, doll.'

'No.' Emma shook her head, as if this denial could in some way make it all go away.

'Yes. It's back and that's what I wanted to tell you. What I'm ready to tell you, *needed* to tell you tonight, while I have the courage.'

'No, that's not . . .' She felt a tightening in her chest as her heart raced. 'That's not right.' Her voice was no more than a whisper. 'It can't be! They said, they said you had the all-clear! You were fixed! It's not right.'

'I know it's not right, but it's the truth.' Roz stared at her, her voice low and steady. 'I thought it could wait until tomorrow, but it can't. I wasn't comfortable, me knowing and joking with you as if everything was normal when it's not. And I need to be able to talk to you about it. Who else am I going to talk to?'

There was the briefest flash of distress in her friend's eye, and it made Emma order her thoughts, calm down. She was needed. Roz needed her.

'Same, same place?' she managed to ask, and watched as Roz's hand flew to her breast, no doubt to feel the thick rind of scar where her left breast and then her right had been lifted from her body.

'No. A different place,' she whispered. 'Lots of different places, in fact.' Her voice broke as she voiced the devastating truth.

'Rozzie.' Emma wanted to howl, wanted to sob, but knew it was important to match her friend's stance. The news was like a hammer blow to her chest. Selfishly, she remembered the horror of nursing her bestie through her last illness, but far, far worse was the fact that her beloved one and only true friend was going to have to go through it all again. It was a prospect as galling as it was unfair. She sat forward and took Roz's hand, at a loss for what to do, what to say.

'Nope! Stop!' Roz pulled her hand free. 'I honestly can't cope if you're nice to me. I can only deal with this and talk to you because you are an arsehole who isn't going to sob and suggest I go for an aromatherapy massage or take up Tai Chi. I need normal life.'

'Even if you aren't normal,' she responded, doing her very best to keep her utterly desolate thoughts suppressed.

'Even if I'm not normal.'

Emma coughed, trying to clear the distress from her throat. 'I can be an arsehole. I can do that. Like Mackenzie McTeeth. You called her an arsehole earlier too.'

'Because she is!' Roz grabbed the bottle. There was a beat or two of silence.

'I don't know what to say, Roz. I can't believe it.'

'You and me both.'

Emma fought the temptation to give in to the sadness that welled inside her, knowing that if Roz was keeping it together then she must too.

'How long have you known?' She stared directly at her, looking for a lie.

'A little while.' And there it was, the double-blink and jut of her chin, suggesting she might have known for more than 'a little while'.

'When are you starting your treatment?'

Emma's voice shook as she asked the question, thinking of the last time, only six months after her dad had died, when they'd driven there and driven back on more days than she cared to count with a bucket in the footwell of the car to catch Roz's vomit, and she'd sat with her until the early hours when sleep finally came and Emma felt able to slip off home for a bit. Hard times. Harder still for Roz. Her beloved, beautiful, impetuous Roz.

When they'd got the all-clear she felt elated, vindicated somehow, as if they'd cheated death, and while she might not have been able to get to her dad on time, she had devoted herself to Roz's recovery and they had made it! This news undermined all of that and she felt a deep quake of fear in the base of her gut, understanding that once again she was on shaky ground. If they had fought a battle, she had thrown down her sword and shield, confident the job was done, and now she mentally scrabbled for both.

'Not sure exactly.' Roz took a deep breath.

There was a sharp knock on the door that this time made them both jump.

It was Reggie. 'Mu-um – I need a poo.' And they both laughed, as much with the hiatus from the topic as her son's request.

'Can't you use the loo downstairs?' She pulled a face as her friend scrambled from the bath and pulled on her cowboy boots, and felt the pang of fear that her friend was leaving, not wanting her to leave, to go away, not ever . . .

'I can't, there's no loo roll! I can't believe we only have one bathroom and you're hogging it!' Reggie kicked the door.

'And how is that helpful when I can't exactly build a new bathroom in time for you to poo! Just go and find loo roll! Look in the airing cupboard!'

'I did, but I can't see it and now it's an emergency so I can't go downstairs, I wouldn't . . . wouldn't make it!'

Then came a firmer knock.

'Jesus Christ!' she muttered, rubbing her face as she tried to steady her breathing. Their exchange a current of pure fear. 'Just a second, Reg! Please, please, give me a minute!' Louder now.

They then heard Alex's voice.

'Mum, have you washed my swimming kit, I need it for tomorrow! We're practising for the inter-house gala!'

Shit!

She pictured the wet stinky towel with swim shorts no doubt wrapped inside, shoved inside the plastic bag in the laundry bin.

'Inter-house gala, what the actual?' Roz whispered, pulling a face that under other circumstances would have been hilarious. Emma resisted the temptation to pull her into a close hug and never let her go.

'Erm, just give me a sec, Alex, and I'll come and sort it out.' She spoke softly now to her friend as she headed for the window. 'Why don't you stay, just for . . . just for a bit longer.'

'I should get going.'

'Well, why don't you, why don't you go out the front door?' And here it was, the beginning of worry, of mothering, of protecting her and trying to figure out what was for the best, should she be climbing a ladder? Going out in the cold? Drinking?

'I will climb up and down this bloody ladder until I can't. Okay?' She was direct.

'Okay.' Emma felt her gut fold with an icy fear. Everything was far, far from okay.

'Besides, using the front door, where's the fun in that?' Roz laughed.

As her mate climbed out of the window, Brendan could be heard calling up the stairs.

'Emma, Em? Sorry, love, but Martha's on the phone, wants to know if you can get the double cream, and do you have any chocolate sprinkles. What shall I tell her?'

'Tell her . . .' Emma's mind went blank. She considered shimmying down the ladder and going home with Roz, not only to see her returned safely but to escape her family, who were closing in with their demands.

Roz leaned back in through the window. Her tone was pure love.

'I think you're Wonder Woman, Em, I really do.'

Emma looked around the room, her head still full of her best friend's news and only just keeping her distress tamped down. Her fingers shook. 'I'm not. It's not like I have any choice.'

'Oh, but you do! You could tell them all to sod off and do something for yourself! Put yourself first.'

'Like what?' She held the window open.

There was another knock on the door, as Reggie yelled, 'Mum! Hurry!'

'I don't know, mate.' Roz smiled. 'What would you do if you had a whole undisturbed hour to yourself? Or what one thing would you change about your life?'

Roz began to descend the ladder until only her face was comically visible through the window.

Emma looked at her and took a deep breath. 'If I had a whole undisturbed hour I'd lie in the bath with a glass of wine, a towel pillow and a scented candle, top to toe with my best friend in the whole wide world . . . and I'd make out everything was okay. And what one thing would I change about my life? I'd be happy to get the green plate every day, every meal, if it meant you were better.' Her voice cracked.

'That's some sacrifice,' her friend acknowledged.

'What are we going to do, Roz? What are we going to do?' Her plea was sincere as tears rushed into her throat, and she swallowed them.

'We'll get through it, like we always do!' Her friend's echoing reply. 'I love you.'

'And I love you.' She watched her friend's head getting lower as she climbed down, barely able to watch as she disappeared.

With a sense of urgency, she opened the bathroom door and Reggie rushed in, his trousers already undone as he held them closed at the waist. He sat on the loo as she stepped out on to the landing and shut the bathroom door behind her.

'Bloody hell, Mum! There's someone on a ladder outside the window!' he screeched.

'Calm down, Reg, it's only Auntie Roz.'

'I don't care who it is,' he yelled. 'I don't want her to see my bum!'

She heard her best friend shout, 'I'm a nurse, Reg, I've seen lots of bums!'

'Mu-um! I still can't find my trunks!' Alex yelled.

'Emma, sorry, love, what shall I say to Martha? She's being pushy,' Brendan called.

Without warning, the strength left her legs and she sank down on the landing floor. Tipping her head back, she took deep breaths through her nose and out through her mouth . . . just as Paddy had taught her, taking a second.

'Are you okay, my love? I told Martha you'd text her later.'

She hadn't heard Brendan come back up the stairs. He reached out and took her hands, pulling her upright and into him. Emma rested there for a second with her eyes closed. It felt easier to talk this way.

'I fell asleep in Ikea today. I was woken up by Mr Blundesthorpe, who'd gone in for a novelty ice-cube maker.'

She felt him titter. 'You daft thing.'

'And I'm so sorry, love, but I bashed the car. I did it in the car park. I've cracked the back light and the bumper too.' Brendan stopped laughing. Her stomach folded.

'I forgot to wash Alex's swimming kit and he needs it in the morning. And now I've got to go and search the cupboard for chocolate bloody sprinkles and remember to buy double cream, and I'm tired.'

It was then that her tears came.

'It's okay, Em. It will all be okay. It's late. Things will feel better in the morning. I promise. I can get Alex's swimming stuff ready.'

She clung to him, unable to believe that things would 'all be okay' ever again. How could they, if she lost Roz?

'It's okay, I can do it. I know where everything is.'

'But why don't you just let me—'

'Roz's cancer is back.' She cut him short. 'Her cancer's back, Bren, and it's spread.' She wiped her mouth, as if having tasted something toxic.

'Oh no. No,' she felt him say, 'that's the worst news. I'm so sorry. Poor old Roz, and poor old you.'

'Look!' Alex came running up the stairs with his iPad and on it was a large, impressive mountain whose white summit fractured a bright and beautiful big blue sky. 'This is where my friends are going skiing. Val d'Isère! Doesn't it look ace?'

'It does look ace.' She sniffed her tears and pulled away from Brendan, tucking her hair behind her ears. 'And we need to try and find a way to get you there too, my little love.'

'Really, Mum, do you mean it?' He danced on the spot.

'Emma,' Brendan tried to interject, but she knew it was important.

'I mean it.' Avoiding both her son's celebration and her husband's disapproving stance, she trod the stairs, off on her chocolate sprinkle hunt. 'Because life's too bloody short not to grab every opportunity. It's just too bloody short.'

CHAPTER TWELVE

THURSTON

As a farmer, Thurston was not unused to early starts in all weathers, working in the dark, the cold and sometimes both. But since they'd sold off most of their acreage nearly a decade ago and stopped rearing cattle, he had got out of the habit. Not that he was complaining; he and his sister and younger brother, Loftus, lived off the healthy bounty paid by the building company who'd bought the land. He slept without the financial worries that had dogged his father and was no longer beholden to his alarm. To hear it pip-pipping at this hour was a shock to his system.

He sat up straight, unsure at first if it was fire, flood, or simply the radio alarm clock, which had been functioning with accuracy since the 1970s. Mary used to joke that if ever they popped the radio on, it would be the Radio One breakfast show with Noel Edmonds, playing Tony Christie. He'd quite like that. To turn the dial and slip back to then. A time when the music felt slower, and he understood the lyrics. A time when he got the jokes and felt more certain about life, unskilled in and ignorant of most of the technology that in his eighties seemed to have passed him by; ithis and ithat . . . he wouldn't have a clue where to start.

Not to mention the fact that he felt baffled by the constant need to be connected to the rest of the world at every second of every day. What was wrong with living in the moment, ignoring the news occasionally, breathing good air, looking at the shifting skies and marvelling at an ancient tree? Oh yes, he'd go back to the seventies in a heartbeat, when he and Mary, in their early thirties, would lie in bed wondering if they were going to get lucky and hear the pitter-patter of tiny feet. And even though by that point they'd been more than a decade wed, they were still hopeful that their time would come and that one day they'd look out of the bedroom window to see a large family gathered in the field, old and young, to do what? Play sport? Have a picnic? Not that it would matter. It was all about being together. They'd imagine it often, the burble of chatter, bursts of laughter, shared food, ribbing in the way that families did. Life . . . Life right there in their backyard.

And singing, oh yes, lots of singing. Not that he could imagine, in his present state of melancholy, ever singing again. His throat was narrow, vocal cords tight, and lyrics of hope and love were no more than lies on his tongue. This another facet of his loss. Another strand to the blanket of sorrow woven in a unique way for whoever wore it. And another justification for his planned early exit.

The dream he'd had of them on their honeymoon still hovered around the edges of his consciousness. It had been wonderful and devastating in equal measure, so very glorious to feel her, see her and hold her, and yet the emptiness following the realisation that it was just a dream had knocked back any progress he had made emotionally. It was a cruel trick, and he was unsure if to dream so vividly was worth it if this was the consequence.

His grief, he decided, was like a game of snakes and ladders. He might crawl up a rung or two, holding on, trying to gain ground, make progress, but one small thing, like a dream, a memory, a scent, and he would be quite undone, hurtling back to square one. At least today was one that started with a purpose that had been lacking. His mission: to get Nancy to work and to ask her, as directly as he was able, about her taking care of Rhubarb, should the need ever arise.

Standing, he stretched and yawned, looking out over the skyline where just out of sight, along the road that went into town, on fields that used to be his, sat the new builds. Eighty-five red-brick houses, some no bigger than rabbit hutches, all squashed together and in newly formed streets, which, in their naming, tried to capture the very thing their presence had erased: Willow Fields, The Brackens, Marsh Fields and Oak Leaze. Unlike some in the community, who had railed against the change to their landscape, he liked the sound of children playing as he drove past into town. He thought it quite marvellous that young families were building lives and creating futures in affordable homes where once had stood the old tractor shed. He wondered what his old dad would have made of it all, hoping that as someone who was always keen to secure his family's finances, he would have understood that the offer was just too good to turn down. An offer that arrived as Thurston was about to enter his eighth decade, meaning he could slow down, sleep a full eight hours a night, not work on Christmas Day, and most crucially it meant he got to spend time with his beloved wife in what turned out to be her last years on the planet.

He had no regrets and neither, it seemed, did June, who had forked out for a brand-new Range Rover. What their brother Loftus did with his share he could only guess at; probably invested in more sheep or a shiny bauble to add to his wife's collection of such things. His sister's flash car was a source of amusement. It was the very kind she had always lambasted when they hurtled past her on the lanes. Only hers had every bell and whistle going. A shiny grille and a growling engine.

Still keen to avoid the kitchen until the morning had passed, he slipped out into the cold backyard, in shadow before sun-up. He could hear Rhubarb, who, for a small dog, could sure snore loudly! With his cap firmly on his head and the wool scarf Mary had knitted wound at his neck, he started his truck and made his way out towards Nancy and Andrew's smart single-storey cottage, which was built in the grounds of his sister's house, cleverly converted from an old pigsty and added to over the years. There was a room that in his view had been decorated like a nursery, not that he mentioned it and neither did anyone else; who knew what heartache that little room with its pastel-coloured walls represented?

He felt a little sorry for his niece, who had never left her mother's shadow. Nancy wasn't a bad person, but was a little naïve, a tad shaky in new company and sometimes sharp around the edges, a little odd. Mary used to say it was nothing spending time with a good friend wouldn't cure, and that what Nancy needed was to laugh more and worry less. Maybe she was right. He doubted she laughed much, not living with the hapless Andrew Finnigan, who had been 'very, very ill' over the last couple of years.

Andrew hadn't always been this way; Thurston pictured him as a rather robust young man who worked in insurance and who'd had somewhat of a spring in his step. But to see him in recent years . . . It was a miracle really that he was still going. His saving grace, and surely the reason for his longevity of life with such a frail constitution, was that his ailment seemed to travel. One day it was a weak heart, on another a bad back, sometimes migraines, often 'biliousness', and most recently: suspected Lyme disease. He was sure there'd been other afflictions he'd forgotten. Thurston used to cruelly joke to his wife that if the lad had been a wounded creature, they'd have put him out of his misery long ago . . . But considering his latest plans for self-annihilation, it didn't seem quite so funny now.

With his headlights picking up the twists and turns of the lanes, Thurston trundled along in his truck without complaint. He had to admit it was quite nice being up at this hour once again, watching as the dark, silent sky split on the horizon – allowing a tiny crack of golden light to peep through as if it was taking a look at the day before it arrived slowly, slowly, to bring light and warmth, this glimpse of nature's beauty a reminder of the farming life he'd given up. A life lived in harmony with the seasons, in tune with the hours of the day. And one that, despite the arduous nature of it, he would forever be grateful for. A life well lived. He felt a flicker of regret at all that he might miss. The sights of the changing landscape that had been his daily routine for as long as he could remember.

Many was the time he was asked by his peers, who he happened upon at the market or the petrol station, how he'd cope with not getting up at 4 a.m. and would he have trouble sleeping for longer? It had taken two nights. Just two, after all those years, before his body got into the new, glorious habit and he woke at a little after 6 a.m. – a lie-in by his standards. He more than understood their expressions of envy when in receipt of this news, knowing that when he had been beholden to the needs of animals who cared little whether it be day or night, he didn't have time to appreciate the creeping light of day or the sun setting on the horizon. It was all about focusing on and planning for the next timely task and the next.

'Yes,' he thought aloud, his old dad would certainly have understood. And as to what the man would make of Thurston planning his own exit from this beautiful earth? Well, that he'd prefer not to contemplate.

CHAPTER THIRTEEN

EMMA

Emma woke to the sound of her alarm. Remnants of last night's headache still lingered, along with a sense of impending panic. It didn't take long to remember why.

Same, same place?

Lots of different places.

The brief, impactful exchange played over and over in her mind like a song that had got stuck, only able to repeat the short burst, not knowing what came next.

Ain't that the truth . . .

It was twenty-five minutes to six, five minutes before she needed to get up. The theory being she had five minutes to come to, open her eyes and let her mind process and plan for the day ahead without having to leap into action. She wasn't someone who hated mornings but today could have quite happily turned over and closed her eyes, yearning not only for more sleep but also the escape of slumber.

'Morning.' Brendan spoke with eyes closed, head still sunk into his pillow and his body spread like the starfish he liked to emulate on their less than spacious mattress. She'd spent every night since their wedding day coiled around his recumbent limbs. 'Did you sleep okay?'

There was something in his tone that she detected, in the way that only someone who knew every nuance of another's voice and manner could, that was a little . . . off. It didn't take a genius to figure out what. She had bashed the car. She had undermined him in front of Alex, given in to her desire to please her youngest rather than consider the practicalities of their finances and show solidarity with the man she loved. And at some level, maybe even subconsciously, he knew that Roz's diagnosis meant he, and at times the kids, would be sidelined in the face of the treatment that loomed.

'I took an age to nod off.' Troubled as she was by thoughts of Roz and what lay ahead, tumbling in her mind in so many variants. 'Then I hit a rich seam of sleep about five and here we are.' She rubbed her eyes.

'Why does it happen like that? Always the best sleep just before the alarm, and why is it that when you don't have to set an alarm, you wake up early, fresh as a daisy?'

She shrugged; it was too early for lots of talking. This was, after all, supposed to be her five minutes of slow, quiet time. That, and it irked her, the whiff of deceit that framed their encounter. Both holding back on what needed to be said, performing, aware that they were not only almost out of time before the day got started, but also that neither was in the right state of mind to address the specifics. It was what they did, how they ran, and the kinks always worked themselves out, kind of.

'I'm worried about you, Em.'

She felt him twist on the mattress until he was facing her.

'I'm okay.'

'I think you have a lot going on, what with your mum, Roz, work, the kids.'

'We've always had a lot going on.' She pointed out this truth, having long since given up saying, *When things are quieter, I will read more. When I have more time, I'd like to tackle the garden.* And *When we can, let's go walking, just you, me and Brucie, out for rambles* . . . Realisation had dawned some years ago that things were never going to be quieter, and she was always going to be short on time. The treadmill of family life ran quickly and relentlessly. It was just how it was, and she felt a little clueless as to how to fix it.

'You can talk to me any time. You know that, and you can rely on me. I'll do whatever you need to make things easier. I'm here for you.'

She turned to face him, her hands in a prayer pose under her cheek.

'I do know that. Thank you.' Words were easy and would ordinarily ease her worries, but not this morning. Not with the news that Roz was sick and the knowledge that no words could fix that.

Her phone beeped. A text from Martha. Emma sat up and read it aloud.

Thanks for getting cream etc Mum. You're a star! Call me when you can, not urgent, but call me. Not urgent but give me a shout when you can. Love you. Not urgent! X

'Well, that's clear. Not urgent but call her. I think that's the message.' Brendan laughed and the air around them softened. It was the Martha effect. Their daughter was beautiful, smart, hard-working, yet light of spirit, concerned with frippery and a desire to sprinkle the world with fairy dust. Often overly obsessed with the detail, she strived to make even the smallest of events feel like a celebration. She had always been this way and no matter how they lovingly mocked her preoccupations, their lives were undoubtedly richer because of them. 'And if she's run out of money, tell her the bank of Mum and Dad is on strike, as we are now trying to figure out ways to fund a bloody ski holiday in Val de Doodah or whatever it's called.'

His words were, she knew, a compromise, and she felt the love in it, knowing she might have spoken too soon, said the wrong thing, but that he understood where it came from.

'A ski trip feels very low on my list of priorities right now and I'm sorry.' Her words tasted of guilt.

'I know.' There was tension in his jaw. 'But here we are. To tell him he now can't go would feel cruel and like we were toying with him.' He clicked his tongue against his teeth and pulled a face, a reminder that this was not his doing. This was a mess of her own creation.

Roz's news was a wide broom that had swept other worries out of the way. It was hard to focus on anything, but her friend's face as she gave her the news . . .

Same, same place?

Lots of different places.

Pulling back the duvet, she took a deep breath as she climbed from the warmth of their bed, ready to face the day.

'How bad's the car exactly?' he asked, scratching his chin.

She cringed. 'Broken light and a nasty crack along the bumper. I can live with it though; we can shove some tape on it or something, can't we?' She rummaged in the chest of drawers for clean pants, bra and a navy hoodie that was warm and comfortable for work over her jeans.

'Depends.' He sat up. 'It's illegal not to have your lights working. I'll have a look tonight when you get back.'

'I am sorry, Bren.' She reached for her towel, which was hanging on the back of the bedroom door. 'It was a split-second thing. I got off the phone to Reggie, whacked the car in reverse and didn't think, didn't look properly, didn't see it.'

'At least you weren't hurt. It could have been worse.' He gave one of his forced smiles, his platitude predictable. The awkward politeness where words were selected and scrubbed was unsettling.

'I'd better get going.' She nodded towards the door.

'Yep, don't worry about the boys, I'll get them sorted for school and make sure they've had breakfast, drop them off. And I'll let Brucie out for a wee.'

It was childlike, the way he wanted extra points, or a special mention. There was also an uncomfortable note of truth in the silent admission that she liked doing all the chores, being responsible for the running of the house and everyone's well-being. It made her feel secure, knowing every little thing was done in the way she wanted it.

'Thanks,' she cast over her shoulder as she headed for the bathroom.

With a hot cup of tea warming her from the inside out, and restored a little by her shallow bath, Emma jumped in the car and put her phone in the hands-free bracket that was linked to her Bluetooth before heading towards the high street of this small market town where they lived. The best thing about the early starts was that she finished mid-afternoon, meaning she could collect the boys from school and be home in time to make supper before going to sit with her mother.

She punched in a call to her daughter, who was living in Bristol, only an hour or so away.

'Morning, early bird!' She dug deep to find a voice that was enthused and happy, an illusion at best.

'Morning, Mum!'

'Ooh, you sound out of breath.' Emma pulled a face, hoping she hadn't called at an inopportune moment.

'Yeah, just been for a run!'

Oh, thank God! Emma smiled.

'Where did you go?' She liked to picture her girl.

'Just around the Downs, up over the suspension bridge and back again. I'm knackered.'

'Just thinking about it makes me knackered,' Emma admitted. 'But then I haven't really run since nineteen eighty-seven and that was for a bus.'

Martha ignored her attempt at humour.

'So, I wanted to talk to you about Friday. Sergio is really looking forward to seeing you all.'

'Well, that's because he's never met us. Once he has, his enthusiasm for visiting will probably fade, so we'd better make the most of it.'

'I hope not. I really, really like him, Mum. I mean, *really* like him.'

Mum, his name is Rico, I really, really like him . . .

Mum, his name is Costas, I really, really like him . . .

Mum, his name is Janus, I really, really like him . . .

Mum, his name is Carlos, I really, really like him . . .

And now they were about to meet Sergio . . .

'Do you though, Martha?' Her question was genuine, and another paper cut of worry. Martha worked for a travel company and met eligible young European men with whom she could share all the joys of the wonderful city, but was she making good choices, walking a path to happiness, putting plans in place for a great life? 'I mean, I want you . . . I want you to find the real deal. I want you to be with someone who makes you feel the way your dad does me.'

'How does he make you feel?'

'Safe.' The word came instantly and without forethought. 'He makes me feel safe. Like no matter what's going on, he's got my back and I've got his. It's nice.'

She pictured her and Roz sitting in the bath and her friend's fake expression of calm as she spoke the unthinkable. A boulder of distress grew in her throat, which she swallowed. No time for that right now, and not something she'd share with Martha while she was away from home, not wanting to unsettle her and not be there to comfort her. Besides, she had to get to work.

'I know what you're saying, and it's different with Sergio. Different this time. It really is.'

She listened to the note of excitement in her daughter's voice. It was a step change from the slightly manic verbal list of tasks and demands she usually reeled off.

'Well, I'm looking forward to meeting him, love.'

And just as she was about to comment on how different her daughter sounded, calmer . . . the old Martha popped up, and Emma could only smile at her fast-talking, go-getting strong daughter, who she and Brendan had raised by total fluke. A swell of happiness rose in her gut.

'Anyway, Mum, apart from to chit-chat, the reason I called is to go through a few things for Friday.'

'Right.' Emma sat up straight in the seat and slowed the car. This was what Martha did – made her feel like she was being instructed and had to pay attention in case there was a test later.

'Sergio is obviously of Italian descent and so please, I beg you, no pasta – no pasta! Don't whip up one of your lasagnes.'

'You like my lasagne! It's a Jamie Oliver recipe!'

'I do, but not for Friday. Remember, Sergio is *Italian*.'

'Is he? Why have you never mentioned it?'

Again, Martha ignored her.

'Imagine, Mum, he's probably spent hours at a farmhouse table in the sunshine, watching his nonna create masterpieces with no more than a simple dough and a splash of olive oil, and so anything vaguely pasta-related would be an absolute cringe-fest. And he'd be forced to say it was lovely, and I'd know he was just being polite, and I'd probably die.'

'Got it. No pasta. I don't want you to cringe and I definitely don't want you to die.' She pictured the ingredients for her planned lasagne nestling on the shelf in the fridge and instantly thought of spag bol instead – before realising that this too was pasta!

'And tell Reggie and Alex absolutely no fart jokes, nothing vulgar.'

'I can't guarantee, but I'll try.' She didn't want to mention that by suggesting to the boys this might be an unsavoury topic, it might actually give them the idea to discuss the very thing.

'Tell Dad not to talk about the wine as if he *knows* about wine, in the way that he does – "Oh, this is a fruity little number!" What does that even mean? And we all know that whatever plonk he's serving, he chose based on how much he liked the label and what was on special offer in Tesco.'

'I think you should tell him that yourself.' There was no way she was going to further dent her husband's lack of confidence when it came to wine choosing and serving. 'In fact, no, don't worry, I'll have a word.' As long as Martha *thought* she had said something to him, then all was good.

'And I'm making pudding. That's why I need the double cream and chocolate sprinkles. In fact, I was thinking of making two puddings – home-made vanilla ice cream and chocolate brownies? We can have a warmed brownie with a curl of ice cream on it – what do you think?'

'I think it sounds delicious.' Emma was not about to protest. One less chore in an already compressed diary. 'But how are you going to transport ice cream? It's a long drive even if the roads are kind.'

'Ah, we have a metal container that we put inside a cool box packed with ice blocks, done it before and it works a treat. If it softens, a quick whizz in your freezer and it'll be fine.'

'That's clever.' Her turning loomed ahead. 'Right, so no pasta, no fart jokes, don't forget he's Italian, tell Dad not to bang on about wine, you're making puds. Have I missed anything?'

'No, that's good.' Martha missed her sarcasm. 'Oh, one more thing, Mum.'

'Yes?'

'Did you pick up the white plate from Ikea like you said you would? Can't stand the thought of everyone tussling to avoid the green plate. It's nuts you don't have enough!'

'Well, as you know, we used to have eight, and there are only five of us, so in theory that's three in the dishwasher, spare. But then Reggie trod on one that he'd left on his bedroom floor and had got covered up with a wet towel, meaning we were down to seven, and then your dad made out to frisbee one instead of washing it up to make me laugh, but accidentally let go. It shattered against the fridge, and it did not, incidentally, make me laugh. So, we were down to six. More often than not there's one or two lurking somewhere waiting for a wash, and so when needed, I grab the green one, which I think Auntie Norma brought a cake over on when Grandad died, and we never gave it back.'

'Just tell me you got another couple of white plates, Mum! It's not that hard! I thought you were going to Ikea, that's what you said?' She hated her daughter's underlying huff at her assumed ineptitude.

'I did.'

'Oh good! Great! I can breathe again.'

'No, I mean I did go to Ikea, but I didn't get the plates.' She felt her cheeks colour at the memory. 'It's all a bit complicated, but in simple terms, I . . . I bumped into Mr Blundesthorpe and then had to leave.' This wasn't entirely untrue.

'Are you *kidding* me right now? You went all the way there, but didn't get the plates? How does that even happen!'

'Actually, Martha, if I was kidding, I'd be a lot funnier. I can be funny, I used to be funny.'

'You know what, Mum – I'll get the plates. I'll go online, just order a dinner service and get it delivered to home.'

It always amazed her how Martha made things sound so easy, as if it was a case of simply picking a colour, a design, and pressing a button, with no mention of how she was supposed to afford the dinner service. Nope, the best she could offer had been three new white, scratch-free plates from Ikea – and even that hadn't happened. Her daughter's haranguing made her feel less than capable and this on top of her sorrow-laden thoughts about her dear, dear friend, another situation she couldn't fix.

'If I'm being honest, Martha, I think you're giving way too much credence to the state of our crockery. I'm sure Carlos is not coming to look at my mismatched plates.'

'Oh my God! Mother! I am literally on the floor, I'm *literally* on the floor! You said Carlos! You actually said Carlos! I can't believe you did that!'

'Did I? I meant . . .' And in that second, the name of her daughter's latest beau slipped clean out of her thoughts.

'Sergio!' Martha shouted, far more loudly than Emma was comfortable hearing at that hour of the day.

'Of course, Sergio. Sergio the Italian!'

'Mum, listen to me, this is serious.' Martha took a sharp breath. 'I was with Carlos when I met Sergio and there might have been a small amount of overlap, like a week or so, maybe a fortnight, but nothing really and it doesn't matter now. Not at all.' The way she verbally flapped suggested it might not be 'nothing', and might actually matter a little bit. 'Anyway, Sergio is a little sensitive as they played in the same softball team and they'd been out for drinks and stuff, and were kind of friends, so please, please don't mention Carlos or under any circumstances call him Carlos. I beg you.'

'I won't! Goodness me, one slip of the tongue.' She yawned. 'And going back to plates, I saw a programme with Nigella doing her thing and none of her crockery matched, and she licked the spoon with cake mix on. So, I think what we can take from that is that we all need to relax a little, and when I say "we" I mean you, Martha. It's only a Friday night supper around ours. Not an audition or an interview. Just supper. It will be fine.'

'Honestly, Mum, you are so not Nigella.'

'None taken.' She smiled.

'And I'm begging you, don't lick the cutlery in front of Sergio.'

'I wasn't going to lick it in *front* of him, I'm not an animal!'

Martha's laughter was warming, momentarily diluting her own distress.

'Told you I was funny. Speak soon, sweet girl.'

'Funny weird more like. I love you.'

'And I love you.'

CHAPTER FOURTEEN

THURSTON

Thurston parked on the gravel and the light above the front door of his niece's house came on. Staring up at the house, looking for signs of life along the old piggery, he jumped when there was a sudden bang on the passenger window.

'Jesus!' he yelled, placing his hand over his heart as if this was where he felt the full effect of his startling.

'What's the matter with you?' June barked as he opened the window.

'What's the matter is that you scared me! It's dark and I was looking the other way!'

'Oh, don't be such a baby.' She tutted her irritation and handed him a Thermos. 'Tea.'

'Thanks.' He took the flask and placed it upright in the central console. He'd have that later.

The front door opened and out crept Nancy, her tongue between her lips, her manner exaggerated and comedic, like a cartoon character tiptoeing past a slumbering baddie, suggesting she was doing her best not to wake her sickly husband. Who, as far as

Thurston knew, was not a baddie, but he certainly thought he was a lame duck.

'Good morning, dear!' June yelled, and Thurston laughed quietly to himself, knowing her well enough to realise that she cared little if she woke her son-in-law, or even that it might be her sole intention.

'Morning, Mum.' Nancy brushed past her and hopped up into the cab. 'Thank you, Thurston. Sorry it's so early. I really appreciate you doing this.'

'No bother at all.' He meant it and felt the smallest lift to his heart to be appreciated.

June gave a deafening whistle, and the two Labradors followed her back into the house, Fern loping a little behind as if she felt sorry for herself. *Must be all those rotten apples,* he thought.

'So, how . . . how have you been?' Nancy asked softly, as they turned out of the driveway and up Foxhole Lane. Her tone suggested she was a little unsure of the convention – was it okay to mention his grief?

'Oh, you know, as you'd expect really.' The second time this catch-all had popped from his mouth. Aware of the mealy-mouthed inadequacy of his response, he kept his eyes on the road, the hedgerows lit by his headlights on full beam. He had no desire to speak of the reality to Nancy, to burden her with the weighted truth, add to her worry or share his intentions. He was far too fond of her for that.

'I thought the funeral was beautiful. Well attended, and it was good that the rain held off.'

Bless her, he could tell she was trying her hardest.

'Yes.'

There was a pause where the engine seemed to knock and the indicator tick sounded louder than it really was, a background tympany that only emphasised their silence.

'And I . . . I just wanted to say that, that I really liked Auntie Mary. I liked her very, very much,' his niece stuttered. 'She was always so kind to me. And I shall miss her. I shall miss her greatly.'

'Yes.' If he started to talk about her, there was the very real danger of becoming emotional and that was more than he could cope with.

. . . *You are not to cry. Boys don't do that. Not ever.*

'I keep thinking about the prom when I was in my final year at school. Mum wanted me to wear one of her old evening dresses, said it was a waste of money to spend on something impractical that I was only going to wear once. But her dresses were awful, ancient!' She made a 'tsk' noise and he pictured June some decades ago in an oversized, drab, mustard-coloured chintz number. He didn't know much about fashion but could concur in this instance. 'I think she'd made them out of Granny Brancher's old curtains in the first place. I decided I'd rather not go at all than have to wear one of hers. Auntie Mary knew I was upset and so she took me shopping and bought me a beautiful dress. I couldn't believe it was mine. It was really grown-up – black taffeta with a tulle underskirt, and you had to lace the bodice up at the front. I put it on in the changing room and stared at myself in the mirror. I wasn't shy, boring old Nancy who found it hard to make friends, Nancy who felt like she had nothing to say. I looked like someone else. I *felt* like someone else! Like one of those girls who has the whole world in her hands, and everything is possible. I loved it. I've still got it. I walked into school and felt like I'd burst out of a chrysalis, transformed. That was the night Andrew asked me to dance and the rest is history.'

He glanced over to see she was beaming, her face lit by the memory, and it quite changed her whole demeanour. It seemed she, unlike he and his sister, was still rather enamoured with Andrew, and he decided for that reason alone to cut the man a bit of slack.

He knew they had been at school together but had no idea about the prom and the magic of her special dress, bought by Mary.

'We ripped all the labels off and told Mum we'd found it in the charity shop, so she approved, but it wasn't.' She raised her shoulders and wrinkled her nose as if still a little giddy at the subterfuge. 'It was brand new, and it cost seventy pounds, *seventy pounds*, Uncle Thurston! Which was so much money! But Auntie Mary said it was worth every penny. I've never forgotten it. She was wonderful.'

'Yes,' he whispered; *she really was.* 'I know she was fond of you, Nancy, we both are.' He coughed away the bloom of embarrassment at the rare admission. 'Rhubarb, too.' He felt his throat tighten at the forced segue. 'And I was thinking . . .' He paused and was suddenly stuck for words at the enormity of what lay ahead for him. 'I was thinking . . .' he tried again, to no avail.

'What?' Nancy asked softly.

He drew breath to continue. '. . . that if anything should happen to me, would you consider taking Rhubarb? It's on my mind and I'd like to know that in the event of, of . . .' It was his turn to stutter. 'You might take him on and look after the little fella.' His voice cracked.

'First, nothing is going to happen to you,' Nancy stated with false authority. 'But if it did, of course I'd take Barbie. He loves me and I him. Of course I'd take him. No question.'

He felt his whole body flop with relief, not sure what plan B might have been and able now to tick the most pressing issue from his mental to-do list. His little dog was going to be just fine.

'And also, Nancy . . .' He took his time, wanting to get his phrasing right. 'I just wanted to say' – he licked his dry lips – 'that you *are* one of those girls who has the whole world in her hands, and everything is possible. That's how Mary and I have always seen you. You do have something to say, you're kind, a good and *tolerant* daughter,' – she chuckled at this emphasis – 'you've done your grandparents proud, running the shop and making it successful. You've done us proud too. And you should be proud of yourself. You've never been and could never be shy, boring Nancy. You're an amazing person who deserves friends, friends who'd be lucky to have you in their corner, and I think it's time you saw yourself in that way.'

'Thank you, Uncle Thurston.' Her voice no more than a whisper.

'No, thank you,' he whispered back, and stared at the road.

They drove the rest of the way in silence, and he guessed that his niece, like him, was digesting every element of their exchange. He also guessed that Mary would have got as much joy from buying Nancy that dress as she got from it herself. That was her all over. It warmed him to know, in that moment, that he was not alone in his grief.

Street lamps lit the way as the country lanes gave way to roads and fields to houses. The town was quiet. A few cars travelled slowly down the high street, no doubt heading towards the motorway or one of the out-of-town business parks that had bumped up employment in the area. The bakery – run now by the fourth generation of the Clarke family – was well lit. Already, fat crusty cobs lined trays in the window along with flaky sausage rolls, a row of crimped pasties and the generously iced finger buns that were his weakness. On market days, back when he was bringing livestock in, he'd sometimes snaffle a couple with his morning coffee and deny all knowledge when he turned up at home and Mary had prepared him a good lunch. He wore the effects of this snaffling around his midriff for years, until he'd retired, cut out the tempting snacks and, miraculously, his waist had shrunk by an inch.

Indicating now, he turned into the cobbled side alley and reversed the truck up at the back of the greengrocer's that Nancy had inherited from her grandad, Thurston's father. In truth, she did a great job, adding a fancy range of jams and chutneys, pickles, plants and hand-cut locally grown flowers, farm-fresh eggs and a range of specialist organic fruit and veg. She certainly worked hard at it, although he sometimes wondered if this was owing to an interest in the business and growing the bottom line or whether it was her haven, a way to escape the company and proximity of her mother.

'Deliveries will be here any minute. Thank you for dropping me in.' She spoke softly as she climbed out of the truck and reached in her bag for the keys to the back door.

'Six o'clock pick-up?'

'If it's not too much trouble.' She smiled at him.

'No trouble at all, Nancy.' He meant it. Feeling a new energy, enthusiasm almost, for the task that awaited him, giving his day some purpose.

He watched as she disappeared inside the building, confident all was well when the lights went on and she rolled the rear shutter of the small delivery bay that led straight into the storeroom, a clever conversion his father had put in way back in the eighties. To have had the conversation about Rhubarb placed pearls of poison on his tongue. It was one vital step closer to saying goodbye to this wearying world, possibly one step closer to reunion with his beloved, but also one step closer to abandoning his faithful boy, and while he relished the prospect, at this latter point his heart felt a little heavy.

He was about to reverse when a blue Ford Focus whizzed into the snicket and tried to turn into the small space, coming to an abrupt halt when the driver saw his headlights. He sat and waited for them to reverse, giving him the space to manoeuvre. He waited . . . and he waited . . .

CHAPTER FIFTEEN

EMMA

Emma was surprised to see a big old flatbed truck blocking the small parking spot that she usually slipped into behind Nancy's Polo. Possibly an early-morning delivery, she'd wait it out, with neither the energy nor inclination to move. She was early anyway, but dipped her lights so as not to dazzle the driver. She pondered the call with Martha. She loved her daughter, of course she did, yet these conversations left her feeling spent. It was not the start to the day she had envisaged, already exhausted and emotionally fraught. She gripped the steering wheel and stared at the big monster truck, still blocking her way.

'What *is* he doing?' She killed her engine and left her lights on dim before jumping out.

As she approached, she could see an older man in the driving seat. Not wanting to make him jump, she walked with caution, waving as she did so. She stopped alongside the passenger's window, and he wound it down.

'Good morning.' A lovely face, wide-mouthed and shy. He was wearing a cap and had a big burgundy woolly scarf around his neck. His eyes looked a little misty and to see someone of his age brimming with emotion was almost more than she could bear.

'Good morning,' he replied.

'I can't . . .' She pointed at her car, sitting feet away. 'I can't get into the space, and I've waited as I thought you might be making a delivery. I usually park behind Nancy's Polo.'

'Ah, yes.' He gave a small nod and scratched his chin. 'Her car's not working. I'm delivering her to work, but I can't move forward, as you're blocking the road.' It was his turn to point.

'Right. Yes, of course.' She looked back at her car and wondered why she hadn't considered this. 'I'm sorry. I'm usually more, more on it. But, erm, everything is a bit—' She felt her heart rate increase.

'Are you okay, dear?'

His tone was warm, his voice soft, measured, and this alone was enough to invite the distress that she was trying so very hard to keep at bay.

'Not really.' Her voice faltered and her tears pooled. He had a kind face and in that moment it was as if the dam had been pulled up on her worries, and they all came tumbling out. 'My best friend had cancer, nearly two years ago now, but she got better.'

'Oh?' She could see him trying to figure out why she was telling him this and why she was so distressed at this seemingly good news story.

'They *told* us she'd got better. We went out for dinner, drank three cocktails and we laughed and laughed because it felt like a second chance, like she'd won!' She remembered that night, they had raised a toast to *Long life and happiness!* 'But it's come back. She got *better*, that's what they said, and then just like that, it's back and I don't understand. And I'm not ready. And I'm tired, and I do my best to keep my mum company, fill the gap my dad left, but she keeps going on about bloody Battenberg cake and my kids are—' She stopped talking and stared at the man, who held her eyeline, his manner unhurried, as if he was willing to hear her babble of thoughts. Words and sadness trickled from her, and she felt weakened, leaning on his vehicle. 'My kids are not always great, especially my son Reggie. He struggles a bit.'

He looked at her as if her speech was not exactly what he was expecting at this early hour and with a complete stranger. He didn't speak immediately, or loudly, but when he did, she listened.

'It sounds like you have a lot to deal with, but you will be stronger than you think, and nothing is ever as *bad* as you think it will be. Nothing.'

'Oh, my goodness!'

And just those words, uttered regularly by her dad as a balm, were enough to unlock her sadness, her fatigue, and the worry that she could not stop her best friend being so sick, could not afford a ski trip for Alex, could not seem to fix her lovely Reggie, and couldn't even manage to buy enough white plates so as not to embarrass Martha in front of ~~Carlos~~ Sergio! Oh my God! *Sergio!*

There was a crack of thunder in the air and raindrops began to fall.

Without overthinking it or even asking permission, she opened the passenger door and climbed in. The man stared at her, his eyes wide.

'I'm Emma, Emma Fountain, I work here.' She pointed over her shoulder.

'Oh, I see. And I'm Thurston. Thurston Brancher. I'm Nancy's uncle.' He settled back in the seat.

Any flicker of concern at being in a vehicle with a stranger evaporated. 'It's nice to meet you, Thurston.'

'And you, Emma.'

'Sorry for venting at you. It's just that sometimes it all feels like too much, you know?' She sniffed and watched as the rain lashed the windscreen.

'I do indeed.' He took a long, slow breath. 'My wife passed away. Her funeral was earlier this week.'

'Oh, I'm so sorry.' The mention of a funeral and she felt the punch of grief in her throat, remembering her dad's and the one she would inevitably have to attend for Roz. Shaking her head, she tried to exorcise the thought. 'And there's me wittering away when you are in the midst of grief! I'm sorry. It's hard, isn't it. I lost my dad and of course that's the natural order of things, if you're very, very lucky, but my goodness, how I miss him. And, and—' She felt the lump of distress in her throat, the one that appeared whenever her own sadness flared. 'I kind of think it's my fault he died.' This was the first time she had said this aloud to anyone and it felt as frightening as it was freeing. Shaped by the enormity of the admission, her breathing was irregular.

Thurston turned to face her. 'Your fault how?'

She took her time forming a response; her fingers twitched with nerves. 'He . . . he called me. He called me as he lay on the floor. He felt ill, he collapsed, and he called *me*.'

Emma . . . get the . . . get the doctor. I can't . . . I can't . . .

Dad? Dad?

'Then what happened?'

She got the feeling he was asking as much to give her the chance to clarify events as to inform him. This kindly stranger in whose truck she sat as the rain lashed the windows, and with whom she felt inexplicably comfortable. So much so that she was able to tell him the details she had kept to herself.

'I was at home. It's not far from where my parents live, only a short walk and—' She swallowed, mindful of the story as she saw it. 'I didn't have my phone on me, but I could hear it ringing. I thought it might be one of the kids.' She shook her head – what did it matter who she thought it might be? It was her dad and he had needed her. 'I put my coffee down quite slowly, in no rush. Didn't know I had to rush. Picked up my phone from the hall table and my dad said . . .' She felt the wobble to her bottom lip. 'My dad said, "Emma . . . get the . . . get the doctor. I can't . . . I can't . . ." And then he went quiet. I think I told him to hang on and that I was coming, and I ran. I ran to their house, I don't remember the journey, don't remember what or who I saw . . . but when I got there he was on the kitchen floor, he wasn't moving. I called the ambulance. My mum was at the hairdresser's, and I didn't know what to do, I froze. I now know that if you can start CPR or get them to a defibrillator, lots of things . . . but I didn't do any of them. He called me because he thought I might be the one who could help him, but I didn't. I couldn't.' She felt her mouth twist with the torturous gurn that was familiar whenever she felt a sob building.

Thurston's expression was one that resembled something very close to pity.

'Or maybe he called you to say goodbye or so that you were the last one to hear his voice or to say *I can't* thank you enough or *I can't* tell you how proud of you I am or . . .' He raised his hands and let them fall.

His words were warmth, and she felt her mouth relax. 'Your kids are very lucky.' She knew it was the sort of thing her dad himself would have said and it helped, a little.

'We didn't have children, but we do have a little dog, always had dogs. My latest companion is a Jack Russell called Rhubarb.'

She felt embarrassed to have mentioned children in light of his response. 'Well, the way you react when you talk about Rhubarb reminds me very much of my husband, who is in love with our Border terrier, Bruce. It's quite mutual.'

'They certainly know how to steal your heart.' He spoke with obvious emotion.

'And they keep us going even if we don't feel like it.' She recalled the moments Brucie had pawed at her for a walk or some grub, paying no heed to her sadness or fatigue.

Thurston nodded and looked towards the window and coughed, as if trying to contain his own emotion.

'What was your wife's name?'

'Her name was, erm . . .' He swallowed. 'Her name was Mary. We were married sixty-two years.'

'Sixty-two years.' She couldn't imagine being without Bren, couldn't contemplate what her mother must feel every single day. 'That really is something. I think it's hard when you've built a life with someone. I know it's the same for my mum. I try to be on hand to fill the void left by my dad. She just can't get used to it, doesn't know how to deal with it, she even made him a pie the other night, just because for an hour or so she could make out he was coming home to eat it. She says she doesn't want me at the house all the time and that she's fine on her own, but I know that's not true. She's lonely, she must be. And she's so angry. Very angry. At me, at the world, at everything.'

'I understand that. I was angry when Mary first got diagnosed. Cancer.' He looked at her briefly, a look of understanding, and she nodded. 'Then I felt panicked about losing her and now I just feel . . .' His mouth moved but no words came, as if he didn't have the vocabulary to adequately describe his loss. 'Sorrowful.'

This was the word he settled on, and she thought it perfect. Sorrow was one thing she more than understood. Right now, it filled her up entirely, sadness from her head to her toes, an ache, a jitter, a feeling of something dark lurking in her peripheral vision.

'I think the sorrow eases, but never goes entirely. If that helps at all.' She declined to mention how it could come flooding back in a heartbeat, as it had when Roz had shared her news.

'It does.' He stared at the rain-soaked windscreen.

135

'I don't think we fully understand the devastation and hurt we cause when we leave those behind who love us, do we?'

'I don't suppose we do.' He nodded.

Emma noted the way he looked into the middle distance, thoughtful, and she felt affection for him, no doubt due to his age and his nature, like her father's. It made it easier to open up.

'I keep all the plates spinning but just sometimes I want to curl up and hide somewhere dark and warm.'

'Well, I understand that. I can't go into the kitchen in the morning.' His breath caught as if it might be a forerunner to distress, but instead he rubbed his hands together and gained control.

'Why not?' She got the distinct impression, based on the man's hesitancy, that to talk this freely was not second nature.

He turned his face to the side window, where tiny rivulets of water raced down the pane. 'Mary would always be up before me, and she'd pop the lamps on in the winter, set the kettle to boil, hum and laugh as she made our breakfast.'

'That sounds so lovely.' He made it easy to picture.

'It was.' His expression softened, as if the memory alone was enough to thaw some of that icy sorrow. 'Trouble is, the room is in such contrast now, it seems so . . . quiet . . . that I can't stand to go in and see it, don't want to feel it. So, I potter anywhere until it's light. I make out she's in there and if I don't open the door, I don't shatter the illusion until I have to.'

'I do that a lot. Not the room avoidance, that'd be hard in our house, always something going on. Instead, I tend not to look up, not to acknowledge a lot of the chaos while running on the spot, working hard to keep everything oiled and running. Our youngest, Alex, is at Reynard's College.'

'Well I never did! I went to Reynard's College!' He looked chuffed by the connection.

'Did you?' She smiled at the man.

'Yes, all the farmers' sons did back then. Trying to turn us into gentlemen I think was the idea.'

'How did that work out?' she teased, and the man laughed, instantly putting his hand over his mouth as if he had no right to be laughing, no right at all. Emma remembered the first time she laughed after her dad had died and the tide of guilt that carried her laughter away, how *could* she be laughing when she had lost her dad . . .

'Let's just say,' he began, a little more composed, 'that I am a dab hand with a cricket bat. I can probably still recite the periodic table and, believe it or not, some of my accent was boxed out of me.'

'You must have been proper broad before then!'

'I were that!' he joined in the joke. There was a beat of silence before he spoke again. 'But other than that? I think it was a nice place to spend my schooling, beautiful buildings and top-notch facilities even then. I was never going to go into the professions and so for me and many boys like me, it was all about treading water till we could get home and get in the tractor. Get out on the land. That's all I ever wanted to do.'

'Are you still farming?' She looked at the mud gathered in the footwell of his truck and the general battered state of his waxed jacket and hat. Big clues.

'Still got the farm, or most of it, but not farming these days, not so much. But it's still the only place I want to be, or it was. In recent times I want to be somewhere else entirely.' He sighed and she couldn't quite decipher his expression, but it was at once both resigned and afraid. Had they been better acquainted, she'd have asked him outright, *Where do you want to be?*

'My Alex is on a full scholarship.'

'Clever boy then.'

'Yes, he was super bright at his primary school and his head teacher told us about an open day with entrance exams for the scholar's award. We never thought in a million years Alex would get it, but knew it would be good experience for him to see the school, and understand that if he steered right there was this whole world outside of his horizon that he could reach for.'

'And he got it.' Thurston filled in the blanks.

'Yup.' She nodded. 'And even though he's smart in some ways, flies through his exams, a proper little professor, he still can't manage to make his own bed or put his stinky little socks in the laundry bin. You know what boys are like.'

It was nice, chatting so easily to this man who was not judging, not aware, not involved, probably not even interested, and it was for precisely these reasons that her tongue was loose in her head. Therapy of sorts.

'I vaguely remember being a boy. Don't remember helping my mother either, always in a rush to get somewhere or start or finish something. Always too busy.'

His words a reminder that he had no son himself, nor daughter. The same as Roz. Snippets of her conversation with Martha came back to her now. *I must sort the plates out . . . and figure out what to make for supper . . . ooh, chilli! Would that work? I've got the mince and an onion, tomatoes, I'll grab some of those fresh chillies that Paddy said he'd used before – that might give it a kick.*

She huffed; invasive thoughts of all that needed doing, her own hectic agenda, were robbing her of this moment of peace in the cab of this man's truck. 'My mum thinks that's the cure for everything, keeping them busy.'

'Well, I've been busy most of my life and it's kept me out of trouble.' He looked up above his head, as if picturing another time.

'It's a bit more than that. My older boy, Reggie, as I mentioned, he's—' She paused, overly aware how easy she found it to talk to this man, a stranger, and yet to have the same conversations with those close to her felt harder. 'He's not very happy and I worry

138

about him so much, all the time really. He has anxiety and would rather be at home than out in the real world. The truth is, I don't know how much I should worry. I don't know if it's just normal teen behaviour or a bit of rebellion or whether I should wrap him in cotton wool and feed him soup. I worry he might do something, something stupid. Something irrevocable.' She could not use the word suicide. Tried not even to think it, as the thought alone was enough to make her shudder. And was reluctant to mention it to Brendan or even Roz, not wanting to burden them with the same level of worry she carried, especially now her beloved friend was sick. A fact that was still a bitter lie of disbelief on her tongue.

'How old is he?'

'Sixteen, physically. Socially, he's a little way behind, not exactly worldly. But lovely, so lovely. He seems only to want to be at home, hiding almost.' She noted the parallel of her bathroom escape . . .

'I can relate to that. We lived a quiet, farm life while other boys were heading up to Bristol to race around with the Clifton College boys.'

'Where do you live?'

'Do you know Merrydown Lane?'

'Oh, yes, where the new housing estate is? It's pretty, isn't it? All those houses in that lovely red brick, with cobbled roads. I think it's smashing up there.'

'Yes, that's right.' He brightened, as if taking her compliment about the houses personally. 'Well, we're at Merrydown Farm – the end of the lane almost. And you?'

'Station Road.'

He nodded as if he knew it; most people did.

'It's a busy life inside our house, chaotic in many ways, it swallows me up.' She glanced at the man, who nodded as if he understood the concept.

'My grief has done just that, swallowed me up, and I don't mind telling you I feel great shame in that, my inability to cope, to look ahead, see through the fog and plough on.'

'That's so sad.' Her heart gripped at his honesty; she more than related to his words.

'It is.'

'It won't always feel that way.'

His eyebrows lifted in a way that suggested he didn't quite believe it.

As their chat slowed, so the rain stopped.

'I'd better get inside.' She thumbed in the direction of the greengrocer's, reluctant to leave him, cosy inside this bubble of truth as the rain ran down the windows.

'Of course.' He smiled, his slow tone still a little hypnotic, a stark contrast to her thoughts, which whirred at a thousand miles an hour. 'And I meant what I said, nothing is ever as bad as you think it will be. You'll survive, life goes on, no matter what happens with your friend, because you have no choice. You're *young*, so young,' he offered stoically. 'The best advice I could give you, Emma, would be don't waste a second of this little life . . . It goes by so quickly.'

'Yes.' She swallowed, aware of how quickly Roz's time was ticking by, and how abruptly time had stopped for her dad. 'And also, and I hope you don't think I'm speaking out of turn, but I think your wife wouldn't want you avoiding the kitchen. I think she'd say, get in there when you wake up and you put the lamps on and make the tea, enjoy the home you shared and all the memories you both made there. I never knew her, of course, but having spent this brief time with you, I think she might say something like that. And I think the strength of your grief is only really a mark of how much you loved her, the other side of the coin – sorrow at their loss and deep love, they're closely aligned, I believe.'

'I think you're probably right.' His smile crinkled his whole face and was quite moving.

'Yes, I think I am—'

'What the bloody hell is going on here?' Paddy, her boisterous colleague, shouted through the dwindling rain.

Emma, startled, opened the door a little to confront the man who had shattered their peace.

'Em! Are you being kidnapped, held against your will? You've abandoned your bloody car in the middle of the road. I couldn't find you! I was worried sick. I thought you'd been abducted by aliens for probing. I've seen programmes about it on Channel 5.'

'No! I'm not kidnapped.' She looked awkwardly at the lovely man who had given her shelter and advice. 'We're just chatting.'

Paddy bent low and poked his soggy head through the gap in the door. 'Hi, I'm Paddy. I work here with nervous Nancy and this reprobate.'

'Thurston. Pleased to meet you.' She noted the change to his tone, as if Paddy had offended him.

She rolled her eyes and wiped her face. 'It's been so nice talking to you, and I'll remember what you said.'

'If you reverse, Emma, I can go around the back and you can drive into the space.'

'I will, and thank you.'

'My pleasure.' Thurston bent down to speak directly to Paddy, his tone one of paternal protection. 'And could you please tell Nancy that her uncle will be here at six o'clock to fetch her home. And for your information, son, there's nothing nervous about her. She's smart as a whip and as kind as you can get. Remember that, young man.'

Considering his big gob and the fact that he always had a lot to say, Paddy had gone a little quiet. With her car manoeuvred into the space and Thurston freed from where she had boxed him in,

Emma jumped out, turned to her colleague and they both started laughing.

'Abducted by aliens? Probed? What in the world were you thinking?' She doubled over as Paddy leaned on the wall, chuckling.

'He scared me!' Paddy pointed at the cobbled lane down which Thurston had driven.

'Good, you deserved it!'

'I was trying to strike a balance between my very real fear that something had happened to you, having found your abandoned car, and keeping it light in case he was an acquaintance of yours!'

'Well, I think you failed at both of those!'

'Made you laugh though, and that's always a win.'

'God, Paddy, I need a laugh at the moment.'

'Well, you're in luck! Come with me, doll.'

'Where are you taking me?'

'You'll see!' He shouted his laughter in anticipation of whatever the big reveal was going to be. Grabbing her hand, he dragged her to the storeroom.

She had taken the job eighteen months ago based on no more than the convenience of the hours after her dad had died, the freedom it gave her to spend more time with her mother, and the above average hourly rate. The fact that she liked the job, enjoyed sorting the displays of fruit and veg, serving customers and sweeping up, made it a good decision, and meeting Paddy was a bonus.

The smell of the storeroom was one that lived in her nose. It was an earthy scent, a mixture of all the vegetables and the soil in which they had grown, the pungent mushroom and the fragrant asparagus. In summer, the sugary aroma of the various fruits at the exact point of ripeness made her mouth water, none more so than the zing of vibrant lemons and the punnets of fat, glossy red strawberries, piled high and smelling so inviting it took all of her willpower not to dive right into them.

'You're going to love this! I spent an age yesterday preparing them for you.'

'What is it?' She couldn't imagine.

'Ta-da!' Paddy stretched out his arms as if revealing a magic trick and pointed towards a dusty wooden shelf where she spied a whole row of potatoes. Nothing extraordinary about that, except that these potatoes, carefully curated by her colleague and arranged in height order, were all shaped like bottoms. Her laughter burst from her; they were delightful!

'Look, Em! Eight arses! Isn't it the best thing you've ever seen!' he howled.

'It's certainly up there!' she had to agree. They wheezed until they leaned on each other for support, a welcome chance to momentarily shrug off her cloak of sorrow.

'I don't know what I find funnier,' she managed, 'the fact that you found them or bothered getting them ready, all lined up for me!'

Paddy straightened up. 'I think it's a new variety,' he said, 'called Anuspud.'

'Anuspud?' she tittered. 'I can see them on every menu in every Michelin-starred establishment this side of Texas.'

'Roasted Anuspud!' he yelled.

'Anuspud rosti!' she called out.

'Spanish omelette . . . with Anuspud!' Paddy was laughing so hard he had tears on his cheeks.

'Everything all right?' Nancy's voice came from the doorway behind them.

'Nancy!' Emma swung around to face her; it felt mean to leave her out of the joke. 'You have to come and see this. Paddy has been hunting out bottom-shaped spuds.' She pointed to the shelf, watching as the woman put on her spectacles and zipped up her gilet, as she drew close and bent down to study the rather comical collection. It was an uncomfortable second or two before her boss reacted and Emma hoped she hadn't made a misstep or, God forbid, offended the woman.

'I think,' Nancy said as she prodded one, 'that this could really catch on. How do we market them?' She stared at them, asking without cracking a laugh or missing a beat, which only made it funnier. Nancy was usually reticent to join in.

'I rather liked Anuspud.' Paddy kept a straight face.

'Hmm, no, Paddy, no. Too anatomical to be appetising.' Nancy spoke with authority. 'How about bum bums for baking?'

'I like it!' Paddy clapped. 'Bum bums for baking!'

Nancy wasn't done. 'Or rear-end roasties?'

'Also good,' Emma nodded.

'Derrières for deep frying?' Nancy was on a roll. 'Posterior Parmentier? Cracks for crinkle cut? Booties for boiling?'

'Nancy, you're a genius!' Paddy looked genuinely impressed and Emma had to admit it was nice to see the more relaxed side of the woman she worked for.

'I actually am.' Nancy removed her specs.

'I had a lovely chat with your uncle earlier.'

'He's one in a million.' Nancy gave a rare and confident smile; it quite changed her. 'I've got it!' She clicked her fingers. 'It's nearly December – and quite obviously anyone who is anyone will want a "Christmarse" – perfect with turkey and gravy!'

'Christmarse!' Emma had to agree, it was indeed perfect. 'I know I want one.'

'God, me too!' Paddy added with just enough lasciviousness to make them all roar with laughter once again. Emma felt a lightness to her spirit that she knew had come from unloading her story to Thurston. She felt a pull of connection to the man and, for that reason alone, sincerely hoped she might see him again.

CHAPTER SIXTEEN

THURSTON

Two things had bothered Thurston: hearing Nancy describe her own lack of self-worth when he knew the very opposite to be true, and seeing young Emma so upset. He hoped his niece might pay heed to his words and he decided to write to her before he passed, pressing the message and hoping it might help having the affirmation written down for future reference. He decided then that it might also be a good idea to write to everyone he cared about; there weren't many, and wasn't that the done thing, to leave notes?

Emma's predicament was not so easily addressed. It was one thing for Mary to fall ill and his grief for her was, of course, all-consuming, but he was wise enough to know that while it was a tragedy for him, to the world she might be considered fortunate. His wife had lived a warm and happy life and had achieved old age. Not that he ever saw her as anything other than in her prime. But Emma's friend, how old must she be, or rather how young? Her forties? No age at all. It was startling how easy he had found it to talk openly to a stranger when with his own sister he could barely conjure a full sentence. And as for feeling responsible for her father's passing, he too understood how impotence in the face of a loved one's death could masquerade as guilt.

It also bothered him that there seemed to be some kind of epidemic when it came to teens and anxiety and depression. He'd read that suicide rates among men were three times higher than among women, and that young men were more likely to die by their own hand than any other age group, and the thought alone horrified him. How must Emma feel? Living with that constant source of worry, it couldn't be easy. The irony wasn't lost on him that this was precisely his intention. There was, however, a certain justification that came with his age, a right to choose that he felt he deserved after a life well served.

He wondered what the cause of her son's anxiety and depression might be. Thurston had always had a good life and yes, there had been moments of sadness – his and Mary's battle to become parents, for one, and of course the sorrow that now cloaked him – but suicide? It had never occurred to him in his youth, not once. In fact, he could only recall one of his peers who had taken this, the saddest form of action. He'd been a young farmer whose family hit hard times financially and the lad had to leave his course at Cirencester agricultural college. His father needed him to get straight to work and help ease their burden. He'd died a week shy of his twentieth birthday and Thurston, of a similar age at the time, remembered how his own parents had beaten themselves up over all they could have or should have done. A terrible business that left a mournful legacy. His own decision felt like no more than a running towards the inevitable, but doing so on his terms and therefore quite different.

It was a hard thing to explain, but he felt a connection to the young woman with whom he'd chatted so candidly.

'Come on, Barb.' Clicking his fingers, he watched as the little Jack Russell hopped out of his basket by the Aga and made his way over to his master. 'My little shadow, aren't you, boy?' Not that he minded. Holding the dog's head in his wide palms, he rubbed the little fella's ears with his thumbs and liked the warmth of the touch. 'You are a good boy, the best.'

Rhubarb followed him into the study and nestled at his feet as Thurston rummaged in the drawers of his desk, retrieving sheets of paper from various foolscap files that now formed a pile in front of him. Methodically, he went through each one before dialling the first number, knowing that to call the phone company, the bank, the internet people, his car insurance, was going to take some time. The first call was protracted, laborious, yet necessary. It took an age of button-pressing and listening to awful lift music before he finally spoke to a human being. A disinterested human being at that.

'Yes, that's right, I want to cancel my phone contract. I'm quite sure, thank you. The date?' He stared at the wildlife calendar his wife had tacked up on the wall in front of him. The whole year reduced to two-inch-square blocks of numbers with the month written above. Nesting birds stared at him from the accompanying photograph. This was the last calendar he would ever need, ever look at or ever buy, his last year on earth. It was as sobering as it was comforting. Letting his eyes fall momentarily to the photograph of him and Mary on honeymoon in Lyme Regis, both laughing, skin sun-kissed, eyes bright and their youth so dazzling and apparent, he looked back to the calendar. 'The date, right, yes, erm . . .' What had Claymore said, a few weeks to get it all sorted? He'd add an extra week for good measure. 'If you could end it on December the twenty-second, that would be great.'

December the twenty-second, six weeks away. It was an odd sensation. A date chosen almost at random; the best he could offer was that his eye was drawn to the symmetry of the line in which the number sat and that he could not contemplate a Christmas without Mary. This way, he would never have to. A Christmas that

June, Nancy and his family would already approach with a little subtlety, in the wake of Mary's loss. He felt it easier for them to lose him then too, get it all over and done with in one ghastly year that would become no more than a footnote in his family's history. It was an odd feeling; he, unlike most people, knew the date he would die. It was powerful, moving, and filled him with immense relief. With an agreement in place, he ended the call and instantly picked the phone up again, his bank this time.

It was an arduous hour and a half of phone calls, but at the end of it, he felt a certain peace in his heart, partly at the fact he'd got the ball rolling, relieved that Nancy would, he knew, take great care of his little dog when the time came, hoping his words of encouragement and support would have an impact on her, but also because he had a plan and a date.

Now it was simply a matter of executing it. Literally.

Having set off to pick his niece up from work, Thurston arrived at the back of the shop a little before six o'clock. He could hear Nancy singing as she rolled the shutters and locked the doors of her little empire. It was unusual to hear her in such a buoyant mood and he welcomed it. It gave his old heart a lift.

'Thank you for coming to get me, Thurston.' She spoke as she entered his truck. 'I believe you had a good chat with Emma?'

'I did. It was odd, really.' He recounted the morning. 'It was raining, and she was a little out of sorts I'd say, which obviously so am I—' He glanced at his niece's face, to see her nodding in understanding. 'And maybe because we were here in the cab of the truck, which felt small and safe, or whatever the reason, we had a lovely chat. And I felt a bit better after I'd spoken to her, if that makes any sense.'

'It does. She's like that, Emma, very practical. Everyone likes her, the customers warm to her, and I get the feeling she has a lot going on, but has the capacity to cope, you know? What's the old phrase, if you want something doing, give the task to a busy person? She's like that.'

'She's a nice friend for you to have.'

'She's not my friend, not really.' Nancy, he noticed, had something hidden in her palm. 'I mean, she works for me, so as Mum always says, best to keep a margin of distance.'

Thurston hated the parroting nature of his niece's response and the words themselves, which sounded odd from her lips. He took his time in forming a response. He would, if he could, like to think that when he was no longer around, his niece might be able to cut some of the apron strings that kept her tethered to her mother.

'I meant what I said earlier, that you are an amazing person who deserves friends, and you could do a lot worse than someone like Emma, the little that I know of her. But she certainly seemed pleasant to me, and you speak highly of her. And' – he drew breath – 'your mother is a good woman. A good sister.' Despite her rather forthright manner, he knew this to be true. 'But sometimes I think her advice was learned at the knee of Granny Brancher, who was a Victorian, don't forget. And the world has moved on quite significantly since Granny Brancher's day. There is no "them" and "us" any more, no more separate dinner tables at Christmas, one for the help and one for the family, and thank the Lord for that! There's only the people who surround you, who hopefully make your life a little easier, a little better, and those that don't. I divide people into two camps, those I like and choose to spend time with and those I avoid. Money, class, position, career, none of that comes into it and neither should it. You could do a lot worse than have a friend who is as warm and reliable, as you say.'

Nancy was quiet, as if pondering this thought.

'You should ask her over to the farm for a coffee or whatever, see her in a non-work setting. That's how you build friendships.'

'Are you trying to organise me a play date?' Nancy laughed.

'Well, I never thought of it like that, but maybe I am!'

'That's funny.'

Again, he noticed she was clutching something, running her fingers over it.

'What's that you've got there?' He stared at the curious shape, recognising it as a potato.

'It's a spud shaped like a bum!' She held it up for his scrutiny, a wide smile splitting her face.

'So it is!' He pulled a face. They both chortled at the absurdity of it. 'And what do you intend to do with it, if I may ask?'

'I've got a few of them actually.' She pulled another from her pocket. 'Paddy found them, we had a bit of a hoot earlier.' She beamed as if this was a real find. 'I thought it might make Andrew laugh. I mean, God only knows I love the man, I do. But he needs to cheer up!'

'You do love him, don't you?'

'Yes, and it's a good job, being as we are married and all.' She pulled a funny face. It was the most relaxed he'd seen her in the longest time.

'What I mean, Nancy, is that all relationships hit bumps in the road or have hard times, obstacles to overcome and moments of regret.'

'Did you and Auntie Mary have moments of regret?' she asked softly. 'Because I can't imagine you did. You always seemed so, so . . .' Clearly, she struggled to find the word. 'So taken with each other.'

It was a phrase that lifted his heart. 'Yes, we were. And no, we didn't have regrets, or at least I didn't. But bumps in the road, obstacles to overcome, yes, of course.'

He pictured finding her on the kitchen floor, his beautiful young wife, weeping as she clutched her stomach. *I got my p . . . period, Thurston . . . I really thought this time . . .*

'It made us stronger, that adversity, and I suppose what I'm saying is, it would be good to get to the root of what ails Andrew and to help him find solutions. I can get involved, if you like,' he offered, knowing he only had six weeks to make a difference, but also that it would feel like success if he could.

'The trouble is, he doesn't feel very good about himself,' Nancy confessed. 'He lost his confidence when he lost his job and it's kind of spiralled from there. He says he feels ill, but I think he uses that as an excuse not to go outside. It breaks my heart, because I do love him. We're two odd socks, he and I.'

It hadn't occurred to him before that Andrew's issues might not be solely physical, and knowing how his own mental health had fractured in the wake of his loss, he felt sympathy for the man.

'Would being busier help? And I don't mean to sound crass' – he remembered Emma's words – 'but could he come and work on Merrydown with me for the occasional day? At least it'd get him out of the house.'

'I could ask him if he feels up to it.' She turned to face him. 'And if he's not keen, I'll cheer him up with this.' She held up the potato. 'We have a lot to look forward to, we really, really do, he just doesn't know it yet.'

'That's the spirit, Nancy.'

He smiled as he indicated and eased the truck out on to the high street. The sight of his niece smiling and her buoyant mood were warming coals that helped thaw the icy kernel of his sorrow. It had been, if not a good day, then certainly a better one. This, he was certain, was in part down to the fact that he had his date fixed.

Pulling up on to his sister's driveway, he noted Nancy's car sitting forlornly in its usual spot. This only seconds before the booming voice of his sister carried along in the shifting light of dusk.

'Bloody car! Needs a new whatnot and will be at least a few days before Otis can get the part delivered!' June shook her head as if it was the end of the world.

'I don't mind driving you up in the morning, Nancy, running you in. And picking you up, it's no bother for me.'

He welcomed the thought of spending a little time with her, to tell her exactly what Rhubarb liked and disliked, his preference for chicken and his dislike of the vicar. How he preferred his tummy tickled but was wary of anyone touching his ears. That kind of thing. He knew it would make what came next easier, when he took his final walk out to the big barn.

'Well, I can do it, Thurston, if it's putting you out?' June spoke gruffly, indicating she was more than a little miffed at the prospect of the added hassle.

'I just said, June, happy to do it. See you in the morning, Nancy.'

'Yep, thank you.' She nodded at him sweetly. 'See you in the morning.'

'Night, June.'

She raised her hand over her head in a wave as the back of her disappeared inside her house.

As he swung the truck on to the lane, he noticed his niece had left him a bum-shaped spud on the passenger seat. It made him chuckle. Instantly, he wished he could share it with Mary, make her laugh. How he'd loved her laugh; it was light, sweet, and reminded him of spring and all good things ahead.

His own laughter halted as he approached home and his head-lights picked up the outline of a character in the yard, and he could hear Rhubarb barking in the boot room. His heart rate increased, and he looked towards the tool shed, where his old axe handle lurked. It was a sturdy piece of shaped wood that, living remotely, he had over the years taken comfort from, knowing it was close to hand. Not that he'd ever had to fetch it in all the time he'd lived out here, man and boy. And not that he had the strength to fend off any attacker in his present physical and mental state, axe handle or not.

His sigh was one of both relief and irritation when he realised it was none other than the Reverend Dunster standing in the yard. No wonder Rhubarb was barking. Standing tall, the vicar waved both his arms as if he was on the deck of an aircraft carrier. He was a man Thurston's father would have described as 'a total ornament', suggesting that other than as something nice to put on the shelf, he was pretty useless. He rubbed Thurston up the wrong way, that was for sure.

Thurston killed the engine and took his time climbing down from the cab.

'Evening, vicar.'

'Good evening, Thurston, good to see you. I seem to have rather upset your hound!' The man laughed as though it was funny and not, as Thurston saw it, unfair to so disturb poor Barb from his slumber.

'I'll let him out.'

Ignoring the man, he opened the boot room door, watching as his faithful Jack Russell circled the yard, sniffing out potential intruders and staring over his shoulder at the vicar, who, he could tell, the little dog wasn't entirely sure of.

'Attaboy,' he calmly encouraged, while putting on the outside lights that lit the yard from all angles. 'What can I do for you, vicar?' He cut to the chase, wanting nothing more than to get inside and set a fire on this chilly evening.

'I really just wanted to see how you were faring after the funeral. I know these first few days can be tricky.'

Thurston felt bad for thinking negatively about the man and looked him in the eye. 'That's very kind of you, Mr Dunster, and I appreciate it. I'm doing okay.' This felt easiest – to give the expected response so the man could be on his way, saving them both the pretence.

The vicar nodded. 'I find that in the immediate aftermath of someone passing, people aplenty are around to offer support and share their shock, as well as their memories. Funerals often feel like closure for those in attendance. Then the attention on the bereaved dwindles accordingly. Becomes less exciting for those on the periphery. But very often for the loved ones left alone, this is when the quiet hits, realisation that this is the new normal, and it's hard.'

'It is hard, but someone said to me today that my grief is only really a mark of how much I loved her, the other side of the coin, and that makes sense to me. I've been thinking about that.' It was true; the suggestion had helped him better understand his sorrow.

'Yes. Absolutely.' The Reverend Dunster nodded sagely and took a breath. 'That aside for a minute,' he began, and Thurston felt a flicker of irritation at how quickly he wanted to move on from the subject of his grief, making his previous enquiry feel most insincere, 'what I wanted to say was . . . what I wanted to say was . . . actually, I'm rather distracted. What is that in your hand, Thurston?'

'This?' He held up the spud. 'It's a potato, vicar, in the shape of a bottom.'

'I see.' The man coughed. 'Where was I?'

'You were saying that we were to set aside my grief for a minute.'

'Yes, quite.' He smiled briefly. 'Mary was a wonderful and much appreciated member of our congregation, who will be so missed by us all. And she always gave so *generously* to our appeals.'

Thurston stared at him with the sole intention of unnerving him, guessing what might come next.

'I did discuss with her the hope to fund a retreat for myself and other members of the ecclesiast to travel to Brazil later in the year for a refresh, if you like, a . . . a . . . holiday, yes, but also a chance – nay, an *opportunity* – to understand different learnings about the faith . . . Will you . . . will you be making a donation, do you think, to this trip of which your wife was very much in favour?'

Thurston thought of how happy the seventy-pound frock had made Nancy when Mary bought her the dress of her dreams, and he looked the man squarely in the eyes.

'You can rest assured, vicar, that any provision Mary has made in her last will and testament will, of course, be honoured. Anyone and anything she felt strongly about will be given a little something, as per her wishes, all written down to the letter of the law. Witnessed and sealed by Mr Claymore Shackleton, the lawyer in the high street.'

The man positively beamed. 'Yes, yes, I know Mr Shackleton.' He licked his top lip. 'And did she, *Mary*, did Mary feel strongly about us at St Isaac's?'

Thurston took his time in answering, liking how the man seemed to stew on the spot, his face puce with the delightful possibility of getting his mitts on Mary's cash.

'I honestly don't know, vicar.'

'Oh.' The reverend's demeanour seemed to sag.

'But you're the one who told me she isn't really gone, and that communication is possible with the Lord as a conduit, so I suggest the best thing would be to ask her yourself.'

The vicar swallowed and toyed nervously with his car keys.

'And if you do manage to get through, can you ask her how to set the timer on the television? She used to do it so it would switch itself off if we fell asleep, but I'm darned if I can figure it out!'

'I'll let you get on.' The vicar spoke sharply as he made his way to his car.

'Yep.' Thurston held the man's eyeline before picking up Rhubarb and keeping him tucked under his arm. The little dog growled as the vicar made his retreat.

He walked into the kitchen and popped the dog in his basket, setting his uniquely shaped spud on the table, where he took a seat. 'Bloody cheek of it! A retreat in Brazil, I should be so lucky! We told him though, didn't we? It's made me think, mind. I need to get the letters sent to Claymore as soon as possible and get this will sorted. The thought of the farm and all we've worked hard for falling into the wrong hands is more than I can stand.' Shaking his head, he rubbed his face. 'Look at me, Mary, I'm sitting here talking to a potato. Is this what I've come to?'

Rhubarb barked and the spud toppled over.

CHAPTER SEVENTEEN

Emma

'What're you up to?' It was astounding to Emma that Roz sounded her usual calm self.

What am I up to? Rushing, trying to fit everything into the day that needs to happen as the hands on the clock move too quickly. Worrying, I'm beside myself with dread of what your illness might mean. The treatment the first time around was hard; to see you so low, so broken, was unbearable, and the thought of going through it all over again but with the added factor that I know what to expect now and won't be fooled by the platitudes. At least before I was unaware of all the rubbish side effects, so yes, dreading that. And I'm sad because my kids have their own set of demands, Brendan and I are running around trying to put out a thousand tiny fires, and I blurted my life story to a complete stranger today because it felt easier than telling it to those I love.

'Not much.' Her succinct response, as she stood on the pavement, now resting the phone in the crook of her neck as she fished in her bag for her mum's house keys. 'Just outside Mum's.'

'Any thoughts on our conversation last night?' It was so casually asked that she tried to reply in kind.

'Apart from the fact you invaded my privacy and arrived in my bathroom on a ladder?' The words they'd shared had wrapped her, as Thurston had so eloquently put it, in sorrow . . .

'Yes, that conversation.'

'Actually, I can't stop thinking about it.' Aware of her horror-struck expression, she forced a smile. 'I thought you had it beaten. I mean, Jesus, I even took you out for dinner! You had a starter and a dessert, even though I was paying! We had three cocktails, broke our golden rule of never more than one drink on a school night. That was to celebrate the end of the bloody nightmare and now what?'

This was the truth. Emma thought she had worked hard, paid attention and done everything she could to 'fix it'!

'You want me to refund you the cost of the starter? It was about seven quid, if I remember rightly, and to be honest it wasn't that great. The melted Brie was a little frozen in the middle. But I didn't want to say anything as you were paying, and I also seem to remember the waiter was a little disinterested. And the third cocktail was suspiciously less boozy. You know the old trick, only to give a mere splash of alcohol when the recipients are too sloshed to notice.'

They were silent for a second.

'Roz, I mean it, what are we going to do? I can't . . .' She held the phone close to her face with shaking fingers. It was easy to joke, to mask the concern, bury the reality under a fog of love and friend-ship, but the truth was her heart hurt for all that she suspected was coming her friend's way. Unable to even contemplate the very worst scenario, because that was more than she could take.

'I know.' She heard her best friend take a deep breath. 'It's a shitstorm, but I've weathered it before. *We've* weathered it before. One day at a time, I guess.'

'When does your treatment start? Brendan has of course said just do what we need to do, he'll pick up the slack at home. I'll have a word with Nancy, she'll let me work suitable hours, she's a good person.' The image of their bum-shaped potato shenanigans flew in and out of her mind. 'I can trade days with Paddy, he—'

'No, Em, that's . . .' Her cool friend sounded uncharacteristically flustered. 'That's okay. You don't need to do that.'

'I know I don't *need* to, but I want to. As if I'd let you go through it without me to catch your sick in a bucket, get you ice pops when you have mouth ulcers, and tell you that you look perky when you look like you've just crawled out of a crypt.'

'No, Em, I mean there's no need because I won't be having any treatment.'

'Oh.' This was good news! The best! 'I thought it was inevitable. How are they going to treat it then? I guess whatever it is, it has to be better than what happened before.' But as she spoke, she realised there might be a very different admission behind her friend's words. It felt as if the ground was rushing up to meet her and simultaneously like the breath had been knocked from her lungs. 'They, they are going to treat it though, aren't they?' She was aware she was whispering, almost as if she believed that if she spoke very softly, then Roz might answer very slowly and then there was the smallest chance that she might not have to hear what she had to say.

'I can't,' her friend began, and Emma leaned on the car so she didn't fall over. 'I can't do it again, Em. I just can't.'

'What do you mean?' Emma asked, and then denied Roz the chance to respond as her thoughts rushed faster than she could sort through them. 'Don't, don't say that. That's not what's going to happen, Roz, no way. Don't be ridiculous! You can and you will do whatever is necessary and I will be there to support you through it and Brendan too, who I know you call a dickhead but he loves you too, we all do, even Brucie.' She cursed the crack to her voice, her tongue sticking to her dry mouth. 'And when, when you get the all-clear, I'll take you back to that shitty restaurant and you can have a starter and a pudding and I'll tell the waiter to be better and we can, we can . . .'

'No, Em. Not this time.'

'No. Roz. You are not *listening* to me!' Now she raised her voice, caring less who heard, anything to get her message across.

'No, Em, you're not listening to *me*! I'm not being ridiculous! I don't want to do it again. I won't.'

'That's not . . .' She did her best to fight her rising sense of panic. 'That's not okay. It's not. That's not what is going to happen. You can't just, you can't. No.' She shook her head emphatically and let out a noise that was almost a growl, guttural and a visceral manifestation of her frustration and hurt.

'God, you are so boringly and predictably bossy. And besides, my darling Emma, the greatest, greatest friend I could ever have wished for. My person and my best ever love. There's no point. There's just no point.'

'There is a point! Of course there is!' Her voice squeaked through a throat that felt narrowed with distress. 'Don't say that! There is a point and I'm going to make you, I'm going to . . . I'm going to . . .' She ran out of steam.

'It's everywhere, Em. Everywhere.'

Emma listened as her friend took her time, swallowing and doing her best to keep her breathing on an even keel. This was her worst nightmare come true. Her very worst, and she wanted to lie on the floor and weep.

'Don't forget I'm a nurse. I know how this plays out. Trust me, it's not a decision I've made lightly. I've given it a lot of thought, for a while now.'

'How, how long have you known? And why didn't you tell me sooner?' It hurt her that Roz had not confided in her, included her, allowed her to share her burden and, worst of all, not given her the chance to try and change her mind . . . and therein, she realised, was the reason.

'I had to get my head around it first. I needed to figure it out.' Roz paused. Her words, when they came, sounded slightly rehearsed. 'Treatment, which we know might be horrible, would weaken me, make me miserable and only give me a little bit more time – or not. They can't really say. And so, if it's okay with you, I would much, much rather spend my last few days, weeks, months laughing as much as I can, drinking gin, going for walks, and making the most of every single second of every single day, rather than let invasive treatment – which won't make that much difference in the grand scheme of things – make me sick and miserable.'

'It's not okay with me,' Emma managed from a mouth twisted with distress, 'it's absolutely *not* okay with me.'

Days, weeks, months? Was that all they had?

'Well, that's too bad because my mind is made up.'

'You're an arsehole!' Anger and distress whirled like a potent and paralysing tornado in her mind.

'I know you are, but what am I?' Roz fired back, and ordinarily this would leave them in fits of laughter, but not tonight.

'I am not joking, Roz. You can't give up, you can't. That's not you. You fight, we fight. I can't . . . I can't do this without you.'

'Do what?' Roz barked.

'Life! I can't do life without you!' And there it was, the admission that made her blood run cool. Roz was the person she turned to for each and every life eventuality and she had been since they were small. She was Emma's anchor, her sounding board, her roots . . .

'Well, you're just going to have to figure out how, and for the record, Emma, this is not your battle. It's mine and I'm done. I'm done.'

'Don't . . . don't make a decision without talking to me first, we need to talk about it more, we need to, we need to—'

'I've made the decision and I need to go now – I have a date. Speak later.'

And just like that, she was gone.

Emma took a moment to compose herself, folding her trembling hands tightly and fixing her jaw as she stared up at the cloudy night, wondering why the universe would pick Roz. It was as unfair as it was devastating. She sniffed, knowing she had to keep it together until she could fall into Brendan's arms.

'Only me, Mum!' With shaking fingers and a desire to vomit, she found her happy voice, put her key in the door and called out as she entered. 'Hi Lorraine, how are things?' she asked cautiously, glancing at her mum, who had an expression like a smacked arse and was sitting with her arms folded tightly across her chest, looking every bit like a disgruntled toddler. Just the sight of her was enough to make Emma's heart sink with anticipation of her mood. She really was without the reserves to handle any ranting this evening.

Lorraine stood, folded her novel on to the arm of the chair and spoke tartly.

'Things are . . .' It was as the woman's mouth moved, like she was searching for words, that her mother took up the mantle.

'Things are terrible! Absolutely terrible. She just sits there in silence, reading.' Nanny Marge pointed at Lorraine, lest there be any doubt as to whom the 'she' in question was. 'She doesn't listen to a word I say! She hurt me this morning, pinched my skin when she got me up, hurt my arm, she's rough with me. And the more I yell, the rougher she is! She's a horrible person!'

Lorraine looked mortified and bit her bottom lip, whether to stop any potential tears or to stop any ill-advised words it was hard to tell. Either way, Emma felt more than a modicum of sympathy for the woman.

'I'm sure she didn't mean to hurt you.' She tried to calm her mother's ire, knowing in advance that it would only do the opposite, but was at a loss for what to say in front of her carer, on whom they as a family relied.

'Why do you never listen to me? Why do you not hear what I'm telling you, Emma? She hurts me and she calls me names!' The wobble to her mum's voice was undeniable and it cut her to the quick. 'And I know you don't believe me! And that's hard for me because you're the only person I can tell! And if you don't believe me then what am I supposed to do? There's no one else. Not really, only old Mr B next door, but it's not his place to sort this out, is it?'

It was a disturbing and terrible statement of truth. Emma turned her head in time to see Lorraine roll her eyes and twist her mouth, and there was something in the small, almost instinctive response from the woman that fired a bolt of concern right through her.

'What names does she call you?' Emma bent down in front of her mother, her heartbeat faster, her jaw tensed.

Lorraine exhaled in a deep breath of disapproval, which she ignored.

'I'd rather not say.' Her mother looked into her lap, staring at her fingers, which anxiously shredded a square of kitchen roll, rolling it into skinny worms that dropped on to her legs.

'I need you to say,' she coaxed, bending down until she was low on the floor but was able to look up into her mother's bloodshot and tear-filled eyes.

'I haven't called her names, Emma – this is just another of her—'

'Give us a minute, Lorraine.' Lorraine shifted from foot to foot, as if a little uncomfortable. 'What names, Mum? You can tell me; you *have* to tell me. What names does she call you?'

'Emma, I—'

'Please, Lorraine, just don't say anything for a second.' She felt the rising tide of anger at the possibility that her mother might have been misspoken to or mistreated by the woman they trusted. The woman they paid with her dad's savings. 'Go ahead, Mum.' Emma laid her hand on her mum's narrow knee, encased in fawn elasticated-waist trousers.

'She calls me Mrs . . . Mrs P.I.S.S. Pants.' Her words were clear and heartrending. Emma saw her mother's eyes dart in the direction of her carer and knew that to speak out like this took immense courage. Lorraine let out a nasal snicker that was incendiary. 'And S.H.I.T. breath. And Dog Face.'

The way her mother spelled out the words, which echoed with shame, and used the phrase 'Dog Face', not words she'd ever heard her say before, was something Emma knew she would never forget. And as she stood to turn and face Lorraine, her mother pushed up the arm of her thin turtleneck sweater and, to her horror, Emma saw the dark purple and black spread of a bruise. A large bruise.

'And she gives me Battenberg. Whenever she can, she gets Battenberg, and I tell her I don't like it! That piece of cake is the one thing I look forward to in the day, I might feel low or a bit bored, but I perk up when I think about a little piece of cake and a cup of tea and I know it seems like a small thing, but it's a big thing to me. And she says that's too bad, and she smirks. I've always hated it. My mother-in-law used to give it me when your dad was away at sea, and I missed him more than I can ever say. My heart felt ripped in two and the smell of it is enough to take me right back.'

'Oh, Mum.' Emma ran her hand over her slender shoulders as she stood, hating that she had not listened when her mother had raised concerns over the woman. How was she to make it up to her? First, however, she had to deal with Lorraine. Keeping her voice as level as she could, Emma stared at her, doing her best not to give in to the volcano of pressure that built inside her as her gut burbled and her mouth went dry. 'I suggest you get your things together and get out before I *really* lose my temper.'

The woman had the smallest suggestion of a smile around her lips. Emma felt her blood begin to boil and took a step closer to her.

'I'm wary of saying something I might regret without further investigation, but I promise you, Lorraine, that if you ever set foot anywhere near me or my family again, you will wish you hadn't.'

'Well.' Lorraine picked up her book and popped it into her bag before grabbing her coat from the back of the chair at the breakfast bar and her keys from the countertop. 'I wish I hadn't taken the bloody job in the first place. All she does is moan and go on about bloody cake and how hard done by she is while she sits on her skinny arse, and I wait on her.'

Emma fought hard to control the rage that rose inside her, knowing it would do no one any good if she were to unleash all that lay coiled in her gut. 'I'll be speaking to your employers. I need to make sure that someone like you is not allowed to go near vulnerable people. You should be ashamed of yourself.'

'Did you say something?' Lorraine stopped still, her head on a slant, and stared at Emma. 'Just that I wasn't listening, I was thinking about the fact that I work for myself and can and will work anywhere I bloody well choose!'

'We'll see about that.' Emma took a step towards her as Lorraine turned on her heel and headed along the hallway with Emma chasing her. Lorraine reached the front door first and shot out of it like a rat out of a drainpipe. Emma yanked the open door and stood on the pathway, yelling now at the top of her voice as Lorraine jumped into her Corsa, 'She hates fucking Battenberg! She fucking hates it! And I fucking hate you! How dare you treat my mum like that! Fuck off and don't ever, ever come back here!'

Lorraine sped off in her car, flipping the bird at Emma as she did so. Emma felt very real tears of frustration in her eyes and a gripping sensation in her stomach like she wanted to punch a wall, as guilt, anger and the helplessness she felt in the face of Roz's illness rose in her like lava. A voice behind her spoke and she turned to see Mr Blundesthorpe by his gate, holding an Aldi Bag for Life.

'Are you okay, dear?' he asked quietly, his concern touching.

'I'm great, thank you, Mr Blundesthorpe. Just great!'

Taking her time, she walked back inside her childhood home, feeling weary.

'Mum.' She dropped down into the chair only recently vacated by Lorraine, the seat still warm and carrying the imprint of her wicked arse. 'I'm so sorry. I don't know what to say to make it better. I guess I thought you were just . . .'

'Moaning?' Her mum filled in the gap.

Emma nodded, her mother's accurate summation ladling guilt on to her already broken spirit. 'I feel terrible that she wasn't being kind to you.'

'The thing is, Emma, I could've handled someone like her when I was younger and fitter, but ageing and illness make you feel frail, make you dependent on people, and I think that's the worst thing about it. Apart from the wonderful partnership I had with your dad, I've always been independent, and to sit in this chair, walk around on wobbly legs and have the likes of Lorraine talk to me that way and mishandle me, it made me feel . . .'

'Made you feel what?' she asked softly.

'Made me feel old. And I never, ever want to feel that way.'

'No matter that you're in your eighties?' She admired her mother's pluck.

'Even when I'm in my nineties and beyond!' she countered. 'While we're on it, I really don't need you coming over every five minutes. Popping in all the time. I like to see you, of course I do,

166

appreciate all you do, but please live your own life and stop feeling so responsible for mine. There's not enough of you to go around.'

'I . . .' It felt confusing, equal amounts of hurt that her company might not be required, but also relief at the prospect of letting go the reins of worry a little when it came to her mum's well-being.

'And in case you're thinking about what happens in my next chapter, I will not go into a home to sit with a load of elderly pensioners. If you think that, you've got another think coming . . . those places are death's waiting room! I won't go! No way!'

'No one is suggesting that, or even thinking of it!' She did her best to calm her mum.

It came over her suddenly, the thought that Roz would not make old bones and that old age was indeed a privilege. Her tears fell thick and fast, and her actions were almost instinctive. Dropping to her knees, she let her head rest on her mother's lap and closed her eyes to savour the rare contact, the feel of her mother's palm running over her scalp. They had never been this duo, not huggy and physical, but more awkward and businesslike. Her dad had been the hugger.

'There there,' her mum cooed in a way that was uncommon yet immensely comforting. For a second, she could pretend she was little, her daddy was upstairs, Roz was coming over later to play . . .

'Did you really just shout the F word four times in the street, Emma-Jane?'

'I might have,' she managed through her tears.

'Well, here's hoping that my immediate neighbours are as deaf as me and none of them heard you.' Her mother sighed. 'You don't think anyone heard you, do you?'

'No, Mum.' She pictured Mr Blundesthorpe's shocked expression. 'I don't think anyone heard. I'm full of sorrow, Mum.'

'Well, that sounds dramatic! Don't be, I'll get over it. Dealt with worse than the likes of Miss Lorraine!'

'It's not only that.' She sat up straight and looked her mother in the eye. 'Roz's cancer is back and she's not having any treatment.' She let the enormity of her words sink in.

'Well, your dad bore old age with fortitude, and I manage my illness, so it can be done.'

Her mother's words, verging on the dismissive, were like a match to tinder and Emma flared. 'Are you serious? Dad was old and didn't know he had heart disease until it was too late! And you have a good life, limited in some ways, yes, but, but Roz is young, vibrant, with a whole lot of life left to live!'

'Are *you* serious? Are you saying your dad's life or mine, for that matter, is worth less than your friend's because we've got more years under our belts? Is that how you rate those who die?'

'I suppose a bit, yes,' she admitted, knowing it felt impossible to understand the death of babies, children, teens who were denied the chance of life. Yet someone very old – their passing would, in time, feel more like a celebration of the inevitable. This despite the fact that the loss of her dad had felled her and there was no denying the desolation Thurston had expressed, despite his long and happy marriage.

'Well, what a horrible person you are!'

Her mother's words felt like a physical slap.

'I'm not a horrible person!' She cursed the huskiness of her voice. 'But I do think it's different when an older person dies because it is kind of the natural order of things, if you're very, very lucky, but someone so young like Roz—'

'But he was your dad!' Her mother wiped away her tears with the tip of her fingers. 'And I am your mother!'

'And I love you! Of course I do, and I loved him! I loved him so much!' She pointed at her chest, her heart specifically, where pain lurked, her breath coming fast and her thoughts a knotty jumble that was quite overwhelming. 'And I know he'd say the same. He'd say he was an old fart, make a joke, but young Roz, he'd be gutted by it.'

'I'm gutted by it, of course I am! Poor Roz.' Her mother sat forward in her chair.

'You are? You're doing a good job of hiding it.'

'There you go again, being so mean to me!'

'And dismissing my best friend's demise by saying she needs to bear it with fortitude, that's not mean?'

Her mother opened her mouth, eyes narrowed, and Emma realised her expression was similar. The two women stared at each other, as if each trying to figure how to make the other understand how she felt, what she meant; why was it so hard?

Emma decided to say nothing else for the time being, to do what they always did and let the residual dust of their words settle around them, leaving a fine uncomfortable mist of hurt that filled her lungs and stung her eyes. Because what was the alternative? Argue around and around in an exhausting spiral until one or both of them left the room, left the conversation, and retreated to lick her wounds? It had always been this way, not that this fact made it any easier to bear. Quite the opposite; it was saddening how this had become their dance of choice.

'I think it's time for bed.' Her mother spoke plainly and folded her arms across her chest.

◆　◆　◆

Emma sat in the car and stared down the street, looking at the houses she had known her whole life along with many of the families who still lived in them. Memories of childhood that provided a moment of calm and made her heart soar. She could see herself walking along the street with her mittened hand inside her dad's on a wintry night at dusk, and waking on a summer's morning with a bubble of excitement in her stomach at the thought of the hot, sunny day ahead when she and Roz planned on spending most of it running in and out of the sprinkler in the back garden. How she missed her dad and as for Roz . . . her beloved Roz . . . had they really rowed?

What a dreadful thing.

She bit the nail of her ring finger on her left hand and tore it down to the quick. It hurt and she took a little bit of comfort from it. Mrs Tate opposite came outside in her slippers and placed her milk bottles at the front door, and Emma felt a fondness for the old lady, based on nothing else than she knew she liked to natter to her parents when they happened upon each other in the street. Part of her history. Mrs Tate looked happy enough and she wondered if the lives of her mother's neighbours were as complicated and as tiring as her own. Trying as she was to figure out how she would manage her mother's care while they either found a new carer to come in each day or came up with plan B.

She, Brendan and her mother had decided a while back, when her mum's health had deteriorated, that it was best to have someone come in and wash and dress her for the day, take her to the bath-room and all the other things that meant her mother kept a little dignity. It also meant Emma retained a little separation from the chores that she felt would overstep the line in the sand her mum had drawn when she was little. Unlike her husband, Margery was never a toucher or a hugger, and Emma felt it would be odd to start now. Although getting stuck in and helping more with the physical stuff was looking more and more likely, in the short term at least. When her mum had quibbled that to hire a carer might not be the best use of the nest egg Victor had built up over his life, Emma had argued that it was for this very purpose, to keep his wife safe, happy and comfortable in her dotage.

'So, how's that working out, Em?' she asked her reflection, still with shards of fury pricking her throat when she thought of the way Lorraine had tricked her and, worse still, that she had disbelieved her mother, thinking she was just making a fuss. Her gut folded with guilt. It was a new perspective for her, an admission that employing Lorraine had not been in her mother's best interests. This, coupled with her mum's suggestion that Emma live her own life and not meddle so much in hers, was certainly food for thought.

She turned the ignition and was preparing to head home when her phone rang, and she closed her eyes, wondering which one of her family needed to bend her ear now.

'Mum, can I get a camera?'

Alex sounded hyped up and excited.

'A camera?' She wondered where this idea had come from, as she turned up the heat to clear the windows.

'For the ski trip!'

'Of course, for the ski trip.' *The bloody ski trip* . . . She could only imagine Brendan's reaction if Alex had asked him something similar.

'I'm going to take loads of pictures, Mum, and then I thought we could have like a movie night, where we get popcorn and things, and Dad can put the big screen up in the lounge like he did when we watched your wedding video from the olden days.'

He made the statement without any hint of humour. *Olden days, indeed* . . . They had married in 1999 – Prince was singing about it while everyone fretted and made doom-laden predictions for what would happen to all the computers in the world, unable to cope with Y2K – she remembered the headlines declaring that planes would surely drop from the sky! All data ever gathered about everything, ever would be lost! The new millennium had, however, arrived with a boring yet welcome lack of drama. How she wished she could say the same for her life.

Alex continued, his volume rising in direct proportion to his excitement for the event he was proposing, 'And we can turn the lights down, and I can tell you all about my trip and show you the pictures!'

'Well, that sounds like a plan.' Knowing Brendan would reprimand her later, it felt easier to go along with the idea, encourage the situation, when her son sounded beside himself with the joy of planning. 'Anyway, I'm heading home now, see you in a sec.'

'Love you, Mum.'

'And I love you, little one.' And she really did. As she clicked her seat belt on, she saw the movement of Mr Blundesthorpe's net curtain and wondered if he had been checking on her again. Probably. And no doubt curious as to whether she was going to start swearing loudly about cake or fall asleep at the wheel. She couldn't wait to tell Roz all about it and just this thought was enough to remind her again that not only had they rowed, but that one day her friend might not be here to tell. The realisation took all the air from her lungs and left her panting.

Winding down the window, she took a moment, slowly breathing in the cold night air and trying to summon the energy to drive home, feeling at some level that she'd rather curl up and hide. At least for a while.

CHAPTER EIGHTEEN

THURSTON

It had been a long day for Thurston Brancher.

Standing at the kitchen window as he ran his teacup under the tap, he stared at the big stone barn, which was to be the final place his earthly feet would walk. He decided to have a recce of the place where he would come to rest. With Rhubarb trotting alongside, he flicked on the outside light and ventured out into the cool dark night.

The heavy wooden barn door, with its ancient metal hinges, gave its familiar creak as he hefted it open. A door that he could see would benefit from a good drink of wood preservative. The corner of his mouth lifted in a wry smile; only six weeks left on the earth and still this was of concern.

He took a moment, staring up into the grand, high space with open eaves that carried right up to the apex. Appropriately cathedral-like, with exposed beams, a concrete floor his dad and granddad had poured in the 1970s, and rough tacked blackened nails holding old wood panels, placed by his forefathers. A vintage hoe and plough chain had been put up on one of the walls, the sight of which made him nostalgic for those boyhood days when he'd watch his kin toil the earth. His childhood, when heavy horses breathed hard into the morning air, the sweet smell of fresh-cut crops filled the air, women carrying drinks and bulky sandwiches out to the fields laughed gaily, and the men retired as they lost the light, with tan faces and forearms, sweat on their brows and the expression of those who knew the satisfaction of a good day's graft. *Busy.* He thought of his conversation with Emma earlier. It was a curious thing how their meeting had briefly lifted his mood, how he felt connected to the girl, based on no more than shared emotion.

Standing now in the middle of the space, he looked up at the wide beam. How would he reach it? The rickety tall ladder that had once been used to reach the old hayloft would do the trick. And rope? He had a whole range in the tool shed, deciding to make his selection when it came to it. Rhubarb whined. Dropping down, Thurston gathered his dog into his arms and held him tightly.

'Thing is, Barb, they don't tell you about how much life is going to hurt sometimes. They say take care of your health, look after those you love, save for rainy days, be kind. And you do all of that as if you've cracked the code, as if you are getting life right, and then bam! Something comes along and knocks you off your feet and it hurts so bad it taints all the good stuff that you've had up until that point. Makes you question everything. I'm in pain, my heart hurts, and this is how I make it all go away. You'll be okay, little fella; Nancy will take good care of you. I know it. Just think about all them sausages!'

The dog rested his narrow muzzle on his shoulder, and it was as close to a hug that his four-legged son could give him. Thurston felt the love in it and closed his eyes, feeling Rhubarb's heart beat against his chest.

What had Emma said? 'I don't think we fully understand the devastation and hurt we cause when we leave those behind who love us, do we?' He knew this was certainly true when it came to losing Mary, but how would Rhubarb fare at his departure, and June, Loftus, Nancy . . . ? It was easier not to think of the impact.

'Come on, boy.' He carried his dog back into the safe space of home.

Tiredness encouraged his muscles to pull on his bones, his limbs were heavy, as he placed Rhubarb carefully in his basket. He could barely look at his pup, wary of giving away his intention and alarming the little dog. Six weeks, that was all they had left together, just six weeks. His heart flexed at the thought. He decided not to rail against his fatigue, but instead to call a halt to the day and go to bed at this early evening hour when most were considering what to have for supper. Not for the first time in recent weeks, he had no appetite.

Having clicked off the lamps in the sitting room and clicked his fingers so that Rhubarb knew it was time for bed, the old man's hips clicked accordingly as he climbed the stairs slowly, taking one at a time.

The floor creaked beneath his tread as he ambled the length of the long corridor towards the bedroom, and, without putting on the light, he sat on the edge of the bed.

'I'll try and make the most of every day I have left, and then I'm coming for you, Mary,' he whispered into the darkness.

He was a little winded by the lack of response to such a monumental phrase, a decision that would alter the course of the Branchers, the family who had farmed and lived on this soil for nearly two hundred years. Of course, this was nonsense, as he was the last Brancher on this land. He pictured the sturdy beam of the big barn . . .

The very last Brancher.

The silence hummed around him.

The quiet resonated like a string plucked in advance of music, a precursor, a warning to listen as the orchestra took up position and breath was held in anticipation of the composition that would follow.

There in the darkness, he lifted his head in recognition of the sound. The humming silence and the quiet shivering in the air was indeed music he recognised, but this brought him no comfort. It was instead distressing to realise that what he heard, the sound that echoed through the big old farmhouse full of redundant floral prints, ancient ornaments where dust gathered and rugs that would never feel the tread of her small foot, was the symphony of loneliness.

And it played loudly.

He thought again about his exchange with Emma Fountain, her children, her poorly friend, her husband. How he envied her the knotty ball of worry that filled her thoughts and occupied her time, *too busy*.

The knock on the front door was jarring, drawing him from thought. He ambled down the stairs with obvious irritation and flicked on the hall lamp before opening it. Rhubarb the guard dog, he noted, slept soundly.

The irony wasn't lost on him, as he prayed it wasn't the Reverend Dunster come for a rematch. Despite not wanting to see the man, he had been feeling regret over his sarcasm towards the vicar. It didn't mean he approved or forgave the man's blatancy and lack of tact, but Thurston knew that the whole exchange had been unsatisfactory, in the way it was when someone said something cutting and you could only think of perfect responses hours later when there was no chance of retort.

It was instead his sister and her two leggy dogs, who crept out of the shadows to stand in the porch light.

'I've come to collect the Thermos I gave you earlier. If I don't keep tabs on things, they get lost.' She spoke as she marched straight past him into the kitchen and threw on the light. Rhubarb hid his eyes behind his paws. She plucked the Thermos from the kitchen table and rinsed it under the hot tap, sluicing the stewed tea remnants down the plughole. 'And I wanted to say thank you for taking Nancy to work. Andrew offered to do it tomorrow, he's decided he's well enough to drive after all, but Nancy said she'd rather you did it. Likes your chat apparently. Good to know you chat to someone.' She let this linger. 'Andrew's also sorted the recycling and swept the yard, all without asking, can you believe it? Nancy's walking around with a grin like a Cheshire cat, or one that's got the cream, whichever.'

Thurston was happy to hear this. It boded well. Maybe that bum-shaped spud had done the trick.

'Anyway, I've got my flask, and don't forget to set your alarm.'

'I won't.'

She dried her hands on the tea towel that hung on the Aga door. 'Christmas in a few weeks then.'

He felt his face colour. December the twenty-second ringed on his calendar and in his mind. The day his world, his pain would end.

'Yep.' He feigned indifference.

His sister made the observation with about as much enthusiasm as one might discover a fungal infection. So very different from Mary, who would right about now start singing carols, wearing jumpers with a bit of sparkle in the wool and dropping hints as to what she might like to find under the tree. Never anything extravagant, but always a little quirky. He recalled having to scavenge the shops in search of a heart-shaped cookie cutter, a hot-water bottle cover with a stag on it, pink furry ear muffs and new laces for her walking boots, in rainbows. He smiled, certain that she did indeed want these things, but also that she rather liked the idea of setting him the challenge. June continued, pulling him from the memory.

'I've got my dried fruit steeping in brandy ready for the cakes and puddings. So that's one job done.'

She made it sound like a chore. The tradition had been going on as far back as he could remember, recalling his mother and grandmother pouring bottles of brandy into their vast copper jam pans, which his sister still used to this day. The smell had been intoxicating, quite literally, filling this very room on fruit-steeping day. In his humble opinion, June, staring at him now with her thin mouth, clearly hadn't sniffed or sampled nearly enough. 'Chef's perks!' his mum used to shout as she took a snifter, tucked her pinny up into her waistband, dancing gaily around the very table by which they now stood.

The thought of Mary not being around to prettify their house with garlands of pine cones and red berries, tartan ribbons tied here and there, was more than he could bear. His intention to check out before then was no coincidence. His wife had taken the festivities seriously, and always placed a small but full tree on the round table in the hallway. That little tree was visible from every room if you left the doors open and was always bedecked with clusters of warm white lights that sparkled, giving their evenings a little bit of magic. Even he, the old cynic, felt a bit giddy when he first saw the tree all lit and full of promise of what the Christmas season might hold. They'd sit of an evening and nibble from fancy boxes of chocolates, as they sipped sherry. Mary always got first pick of the confections, leaving him anything with orange or coffee in them as these she favoured the least. Not that he minded. Sitting on their old sofa with Rhubarb on the rug at their feet, legs touching, holding hands sometimes, it had been his happy place, his happy time. The happiest.

June pulled him into the present. 'Reason I mention it is that Loftus has invited us up to Cumbria. And I'm thinking of going. What do you think?'

'I think . . .' He considered how best to respond, knowing he wouldn't be here to celebrate and doubting his sister would be able to make the drive in the twilight of his passing. The truth was, however, that even if he hadn't planned on his exit, there would still be no way he'd want to go and spend the festive season with his younger brother and his loud wife on their hill farm. Not that it wasn't kind of Loftus to reach out; it was. This in itself a prompt for Thurston to tackle the letters he would leave.

'That's kind of him to ask, but I think this year, I'd prefer to stay close to home.'

'I already told him you'd say that, you old stick-in-the-mud.'

'Well, there we go then. At least I'm predictable.' How was it his sibling had the ability to annoy him like no other human on earth? It had always been her knack.

'I told him I'd go, if that's okay with you. I quite like the idea of the drive up there.'

'Well, of course, now you've got that fancy old gas guzzler.' He did his best to mask dark thoughts with the quip.

She ignored him.

'And I can't pretend the thought of someone else doing all the cooking for once is not unattractive. Plus, I thought it might do Nancy and that lump of a husband of hers some good to have some space from me, the old witch of a mother-in-law.'

'You'll not hear me disagree.' He winked at her, the old witch. 'But I think you need to cut Andrew a bit of slack. Nancy said he'd been through a lot, and if she has faith in him, maybe we should too?'

'If you say so, Thurston.'

'I do.'

June folded her arms. 'Christmas Day then, will you be okay? 'Cos you only have to say the word and I'll stay here and cook for us both.'

He was struck by her kindness, her message that she was not going anywhere, that she considered him. It meant a lot.

'No, no. You go, June. I'm planning on giving the whole thing a miss this year.' *And next year, and the one after that . . .*

'I told Loftus you'd say that too.'

And for some reason this made him laugh out loud, a natural laugh, a timely reminder that small pockets of joy still lurked in the most unexpected places, and this was how it would be for those he left behind who loved him. June stared at him with a look that left him admonished, as she whistled Fern and Flora to heel and disappeared back into the dark of night.

Using the landline in the kitchen, he dialled Nancy's number.

'Uncle Thurston, everything okay?' She sounded a little sleepy and he hoped he'd not disturbed her.

'Yes, yes, all fine. I was just wondering, do you think Andrew would mind giving me a hand to paint the old barn doors? They need a coat of protection and it's more than my old shoulder can manage.'

'Oh, I'm sure he would!' The lift in her voice was unmistakable.

'Righto, I'll order the stuff in and give him a shout.'

'Thank you,' she whispered into the phone. 'Thank you!'

'Night then, Nancy. See you in the morning.'

'Yes, see you in the morning. Night night.'

CHAPTER NINETEEN

EMMA

'Hello!' Having made it home from her mother's, Emma called out as she put her keys in the bowl and hung up her lightweight blue fleece on the newel post, taking a moment to steady herself.

'Martha called,' Brendan smiled from the sofa as she popped her head into the lounge, 'to say don't forget—'

'If your next words are anything to do with plates then save it!' With her hand raised like an irate traffic warden, she headed for the kitchen. She could not hear one more piece of negativity, bad news, or another demand on her time.

'Okay, nice reunion and so loving!' he teased, jumping up to follow her. She shot him a withering look. 'So, who's shat in your glitter?' Her husband leaned on the door frame as she grabbed a box of fish fingers from the freezer and turned on the grill.

They both knew this phrase usually made her chuckle, but not today. 'I can't laugh right now, Bren. I just can't.' Her body shook.

He walked over and took the fish fingers from her hands. 'That's okay, little love, you don't have to laugh. You don't have to do anything. I can do supper. Let me make you a cup of tea. Sit down and talk to me. You look wiped out.'

He pointed to the high leather stool at the breakfast bar.

'I can make supper. I'll be okay in a bit.' Reaching for the grill pan, she placed it on the countertop.

'Em, listen to me.' He spoke forcefully. 'Please, please just sit down, let me help you. Just stop!'

Irked by his tone, yet somehow grateful for his insistence, she did as instructed and reluctantly took a seat, wary of being still, of not keeping distracted. She watched as he filled the kettle and set it to boil before arranging fish fingers with uniform precision in the grill pan she'd abandoned. Her fingers twitched with the desire to turn up the grill a little higher, to check he'd flicked the kettle on and to fetch the ketchup from the larder cupboard.

'Chips or sandwiches?' he asked, hesitating as he stood between the freezer and the bread bin.

'Sandwiches.' It was an easy decision as this would be quicker, and the thought of a fish-finger sandwich doused in salad cream was just what the doctor ordered.

'Are you thinking about Roz?' he asked softly as he pulled a mug from the cupboard and put a teabag into it before hoisting the farmhouse loaf from the bread bin and placing it on the breadboard ready to be cut thickly.

Always, always . . . every minute, every second . . .

'Yes. I spoke to her earlier, Bren, and she told me . . .' It was an effort to force out the words that still tasted bitter on her tongue. Her voice broke. 'She told me she's not going to have any treatment.'

'What? Why? I don't understand.'

'That makes two of us. She says it's because she's too poorly. And thinks there's little point and because of how bad it made her feel and how horrible it was. She more or less said that whatever time she has—' She stopped to swallow her croak, as her stomach rolled with her impending loss. 'Whatever time she has left, she doesn't want to spend it having invasive procedures or drugs that will spoil her days. I'm scared, Bren. I'm really scared.'

Abandoning the bread, he held her close to him with her head resting under his chin. 'It'll be okay, Em. I promise you. Whatever happens, it will be okay.'

Closing her eyes, gripping his shirt, she breathed against him, hoping, praying he was right.

'What's for tea?' Reggie's voice cut through the moment.

'Er, fish-finger sandwiches.' Brendan leaped into action, grabbing the ketchup and salad cream from the larder cupboard and slicing thick wedges of soft bread with a hard crust.

'Why are you crying, Mum?' Her son stared at her, his concern evident, as she wiped her eyes on the edge of a tea towel.

'You know how sometimes everything feels like it's a bit too much?'

He nodded. And his downward expression told her that he surely did. A reminder that she needed to go gently with him, not pile on any more pressure to find solutions to his issues, but rather to navigate them and learn coping strategies for his future.

'It's that. I have to do a bit more looking after Nanny Marge for a while.'

This caught her husband's attention. 'Oh? What's happened?'

'Lorraine is no longer her carer.' Her jaw twitched.

'Not the Battenberg thing again, is it?' His attempt at humour fell on angry ears.

'She's been horrible to my mum, like really horrible, and I don't know how I'm going to forgive myself. I've just put her to bed, and she has bruised arms and apparently Lorraine has been calling her nasty names.'

Brendan's face flushed red, as it did when he was furious; she used to call him the angry tomato, as it was the only time his face coloured in this way. 'I am not having that.' He put down the breadknife. 'I'm not having that, Em. How dare she do that to an old lady.' He began to pace. 'Tomorrow, I'm talking to the agency she worked for.'

'She told me she was self-employed and that she didn't work for anyone. It was like she found it amusing.'

'Poor Nanny Marge, shall I go and sit with her?'

'Oh, Reggie, that's so sweet of you, kind boy. But she'll be asleep by now.'

'Lorraine might technically be self-employed,' Brendan went on, 'but I will contact the agency and every other in the area and I'll make sure no one touches the nasty cow with a barge pole. I'll take out an advert if I have to – I'll put a big poster up on the main road with her picture and tell the whole county what she's done and what she's like! I'm fuming.'

'Me too. I'll text Nancy later and explain that I need to go and get Mum up and ready in the morning. I can make the hours up.'

They shared a lingering look, both silently acknowledging the extra work, the extra worry.

Her phone pinged. It was a text from Martha with two links to two different dinner services that apparently she 'didn't hate'. One was by a designer Emma had never heard of and came with a hefty price tag and the other was, in her opinion, ornate and ugly. There was no way she could picture serving fish-finger sandwiches on either of them.

'I'm starving!' Alex glided into the kitchen in his stockinged feet, with his arms in a kind of arabesque pose. It was a trick of his, kicking off his shoes, getting a run-up in the hallway and then sliding along the smooth tiled floor like it was an ice rink. He made them all laugh, her jumping bean of a boy.

'Two minutes!' Brendan turned the fish fingers and they all sat at the counter.

'I spoke to Martha today.' Emma's tone told them that what came next required their full attention, and hush fell over the room. 'She gave very strict instructions.'

'Course she did.' Reggie, her troubled, insightful teen, tutted.

'When *Sergio*' – she emphasised his name, as much as a reminder to herself than anyone else – 'comes for supper on Friday, we are to be on good behaviour. No fart jokes. No cutlery licking and no saying how good my lasagne is and questioning why we are not having it when that's the meal I envisaged and have bought the ingredients for. Okay?'

The boys exchanged a look, and she knew they would never have any intention of discussing the absence of her average lasagne.

'And just so you are up to speed, Alex, I'll be helping out a bit more with Nanny Marge, and so Dad might be dropping you off in the mornings, stuff like that. Little changes, just while we find her a new carer or whatever happens.'

'I could walk to school, two miles there and two miles back. I don't mind!' She wondered why he was so appeasing, seeming to have suspiciously recovered from the fact that his dad's transport was less than fashionable; or maybe that was her being mean.

'Thank you, Alex.' She meant it. 'Maybe once in a while if it makes life easier and it's not raining or anything, then you can.' She shared a lingering look with Brendan. It felt like quite the development for their youngest. For her too, letting her little one find his feet, a bit of independence.

'Dad, can you show me how to use your camera?'

'My camera? Not sure it still works, haven't used it for yonks. But sure. I'll dig it out for you.'

'I want to practise on yours until I get my own so that I know how to use it properly on the ski trip,' Alex explained, unaware of how each mention of the trip made her gut jump with anxiety at how they were either going to a) afford it, or b) let him down . . .

'Your own camera?' Emma's husband stared at her.

'Yes, Mum said.'

'Did she now?' He tutted, and she looked away, in no mood for that talk right now.

'I didn't, not quite, and besides, I didn't think you kids would bother with a fancy camera nowadays.' Not that there was anything fancy about their old point-and-shoot, thought Emma.

'I'll dig the old camera out, for sure, and if you go on your trip or any other, it will do you just fine.' Brendan spoke with authority. 'You don't need a new one.'

'Dimitri and Piers are taking proper cameras so I thought I would too. We're going to join camera club at school!'

Camera club. Of course.

Brendan pulled the golden-crumbed fish fingers from under the grill. They were well done, just the way she liked them. Expertly, he placed four slices of bread on the breadboard and laid four fish fingers along each, before liberally applying ketchup and the top slice of bread, cutting them in half and handing one to each of the boys. Hers he laced with salad cream before cutting it in half. Her mouth watered as she tried to recall when and if she had eaten that day. As she pulled the plate towards her, her phone rang.

'All okay, Mum?'

'I . . . I don't want to make a fuss, but I can hear a noise, Emma.'

'What kind of noise?' She looked at her husband, almost able to predict that she was not going to have the luxury of eating her sandwich while it was hot.

'I don't know. Like a, like a knocking kind of noise. And I know it sounds stupid, but I was worried that Lorraine has come back. Did you take her key? That's all I really wanted to ask – does she still have a key to my house?'

Shit!

186

No, in her rather flustered expulsion, Emma had not thought to take the key she had to her mother's front door.

'Yes, I took her key.' This, she decided, was the best way to give her mother peace of mind. She'd sort the key situation tomorrow, knowing tonight she had to go and speak to Roz, make things good between them. What was it Thurston had said? *Don't waste a second of this little life . . .* It was good advice. 'She won't be coming back, don't worry. But if you want me to, if anything bothers you later, I can be there in no time at all. Just holler.'

'No need for that, I'm quite capable, don't need you rushing over every five minutes, but thanks, love.'

Brendan took huge bites of his sandwich, which she knew meant he too forwent the delight of eating it, rushing as he did to get it down his neck.

She put the phone down and reached for her supper, trying to heed her mother's words and not 'rush over every five minutes . . .'

'Are you not going over?' Brendan stared at her, wide-eyed.

'No.'

'Flippin' 'eck, Em! I'd have made a bet that you'd jump in the car quicker than I could say "Let me know how your mum is" but there'd be no point, as we've already eaten all the Magnums.'

'And you'd have lost.' She pushed the sandwich away from her, no longer in the mood to eat.

'Yes.' He looked at her with smiling eyes. 'I'm proud of you, Emma Fountain.'

◆ ◆ ◆

Emma listened again to Roz's answerphone message and decided not to leave a third message. It would be enough that her friend would see her missed calls and no doubt Mrs Lineacre, her nosy neighbour, would fill her in on how Emma had banged on the front door to no avail, only for the woman to lean out of her bedroom window to explain how she'd seen Roz '. . . jump into a car with a young man wearing very high heels'.

'Blimey.' Emma had stared up at her from the pavement. 'Hope he can drive safely in them.'

The exchange had made her laugh on the way home. First, because it was that or sob at how heartsick she was not to have seen her friend, her beloved friend who was living her end of days . . . what would it be like when she could no longer see her, visit her, call her, because she was gone for ever? And second, it felt good to be slightly sarcastic to Mrs Lineacre, the sticky beak, and also because Thurston was right, it was important not to waste a second of this little life . . . and Roz could certainly never be accused of that.

Arriving home, the kitchen was quiet. Her rather sorry-looking half-sandwich was sitting on top of the microwave. Bruce gave her a dirty look and placed his head on his paws as he curled into his basket.

'Did I abandon you, Brucie?' She bent down to smooth his head and rub his back. 'I love you. Nice big walk tomorrow with me, I promise.'

With her trainers paired and shoved in the cupboard under the stairs, she made her way up to bed. The boys' rooms were in shadow, and she decided not to risk waking them with a goodnight. Brendan was in bed with the TV on, its blue light filling their room.

'Did you see Roz?'

'Nope.' She kept her tears at bay, just. It didn't feel good to be going to bed without seeing her mate, the situation unresolved.

'Is that you, Mum?' Alex called out.

'Yes, love, all okay?' she hollered into the hallway.

'Yep, night night.'

'Night, Alex, see you in the morning.'

'I think he likes to know you're home,' her husband whispered.

'Bless him. How was Reggie?'

'Same, a little quiet. A little thoughtful. He'll be okay, Em. Don't worry.'

With her jeans and long-sleeved T-shirt balled and lobbed into the laundry basket, she delighted in the relief that was removing her bra at the end of a busy day and reached for the pjs that lived under her pillow.

'Everyone keeps saying that to me, Bren, telling me that things will be okay, but no one can tell me how or when. And no one can help Roz, can they?' Her heart lurched at this truth.

Pulling back the corner of the duvet, he revealed the white sheet and the space next to him that was hers. She almost fell into the bed, and he pulled her to him, scooping his arm under her body and rolling against her until she lay with her head on his chest. It was warm and she felt safe and just for a second able to forget all that lapped at her heels.

'I say that because I believe it. And I want you to believe it too. Bad things happen, that's true, but we always come out the other side.'

'I know you're right.'

'I invariably am.' He squeezed her hard and she laughed. 'I remember when my dad left—'

'Shacked up with Big Shirl from the pub,' she interjected with the now familiar phrase that even her children could recite.

'The very same.' She could sense him smiling. 'My mum was so broken, devastated – "The shame of it," she used to say in her Irish accent, always that, "The shame of it!" And as much as I hated him for leaving, hated him for abandoning us, I hated him just as much for making my brilliant mum feel shame for something that was nothing to do with her. It was shit.'

'I bet.' What *she* hated was that her lovely man had had to endure something so fundamentally life changing at such a young age.

'And we not only lost our dad, and our mum lost her sparkle for a while, but we also lost his income and things went from bad to worse, but we got through it. Cormac and I got closer, and we figured it out and it taught me that no matter what, you just have to keep putting one foot in front of the other and you keep going, and one day you'll look up and it's behind you. You might never be the same again or you might be changed, but it'll be behind you.'

'You are wise.'

'That sounded really sarcastic.' He kissed her head.

'I didn't mean it to. You do, you sound wise.'

'Dumbledore-wise?'

'No, don't be ridiculous.' Playfully, she shot him down. They lay quietly for a moment, letting the calm of night settle around them, erasing some of the chaos of the day. 'I sometimes feel like I have so much to think and worry about, I don't know how to process it all or which way to turn.'

'Yep, today we were picking up the slabs for that patio job over on Coburg Road and all I could think about was that the job would barely cover Alex's desired ski trip. The one you've given him the green light for.' His tone was clipped.

She felt the flare of tension in her muscles, didn't need reminding that it was her who had created the pressure, after Brendan had said no.

'I know . . . I know . . .' She closed her eyes, too fatigued to deal with the irritation that flared in her veins. 'Do you ever wonder, Bren, how you get to be those people? How you get to have all the options, all the bells and whistles? I mean, we work hard, we're quite smart, we pay our taxes, we do our best but it's just . . .'

'It's just what?'

'It's just bloody hard to keep our heads above water sometimes.' She sighed.

'Tell me about it.'

'And I can't see it getting any easier. I mean, what happens when we get older and we can't work as much? I worry not only about the money, but your job is so physical, I know you already twinge and ache.'

'Mate, I've been twingeing and aching since I started the job in my teens. But it's nothing a nice back rub wouldn't sort out . . .'

'Nice try, but I'm knackered.' She poured cold water on his advances, the second time she'd said no in one evening and it felt . . . good!

'I suppose if we look at it practically, and I know it's not nice, but the fact is that Marge won't live forever.'

Emma wriggled free of his grip and pulled away to face him. 'So that's it, is it? Wait until my mother dies? She is our pension plan?'

'No, I . . .'

'You're answering far too slowly for me to think that I am anything other than correct!'

Brendan sat up. 'Well, what did you think – that I have a secret offshore account we can tap into? That I might finally have to sell my gold reserves?'

'I don't know what I thought, but she's my mum and no matter how skint we are I would rather have her here.'

He spoke softly now. 'Of course! Of course we would rather have Marge around for as long as possible, you know that. But maybe . . . maybe if you're intent on Alex jetting off to far-flung places, we could use some of the money in her savings account for Alex's trip?'

'We can't do that! It's not ours. It's what she lives on and what pays her carer.'

'Yes, but if you're her carer for a while . . .'

'No, Brendan, it doesn't work like that. I'll be happy to do it, and we don't know how much she'll need in the future, for residential care or whatever is needed when the time comes. Not that she'd like the idea of that.'

'Okay, okay, calm down, Em! It was just a suggestion. I'm trying to find solutions and we're on the same side.'

She too sat up and hugged her knees, now wide awake with her heart thumping and the beginnings of a headache. Brendan leaned over to the bedside table and switched the lamp off, plunging them into darkness. She felt him move on the mattress until he was horizontal, head on pillow, pulling the quilt up over his shoulder.

'I'm going to start doing the lottery.' This she addressed to the shadow of his form.

'Why didn't I think of that? Why hasn't anyone thought of that?'

Slipping under the duvet, she spooned against him and with her nose and mouth against his back, inhaled the tea-tree and mint scent of his shower gel. It never felt good to bicker.

'I know you're thinking I'm an arsehole too. Roz has already told me that.'

'You're not an arsehole, you just have a lot on. But I wish you'd think a bit sometimes.' His tone was conciliatorily, a reminder of his kindness.

'God, Bren, the problem is I can't stop thinking!' She closed her eyes and let this land. 'I met a very nice man today.' She pictured the kindly face of Nancy's uncle as they'd chatted in the cab of his truck.

'Should I be worried? Do I need to polish my duelling pistols?'

'No. His name is Thurston. He's in his eighties, he seemed really lovely. He's just lost his wife and I got the impression he's a bit lost.'

'I can't imagine losing you.'

'I love you, Bren.' His nature was and always would be the thing she found most attractive about him.

'But not enough to make sexy time?'

'How about tomorrow? After . . .' She yawned loudly. 'After Martha and Carlos have left.'

'That sounds like a plan.' He nestled into the pillow, and she fell back on hers. Sleep felt imminent and how she welcomed it . . .

'You mean Sergio, of course.' Brendan's voice cut through the quiet and roused her once again.

'What did I say?' she whispered.

'Carlos. You said Carlos.'

'Did I?'

'You definitely did.'

Emma screwed her eyes shut tightly.

Shit!

CHAPTER TWENTY

Thurston

It had got Thurston thinking, all the talk about steeping dried fruit in brandy for the Christmas cake and the memory of his mother a little merry. Wonderful days. He had once felt such joy, and how far he had fallen into a pit of despair.

He eyed the bottle of scrumpy that nestled on the larder shelf. What would be the harm? If these were to be his last few weeks, the least he deserved was a final drink. The brown glass bottle was a little dusty. By his reckoning it had sat there undisturbed for at least two years, a gift from Loftus on one of his infrequent visits. Thurston vaguely remembered remarking that if he was going to come bearing such a gift, he should come more often. Highlighting, they both knew, how infrequently they got together. His tongue salivated and his mouth lifted at the prospect of the flat dry cider. A quick glance at the kitchen clock confirmed it was indeed five o'clock somewhere, and he grabbed the bottle.

Mary would have insisted on him pouring his grog into a tankard or glass, this at least giving the rough cider some air of respectability. Today, however, he couldn't have cared less what any-one thought or said, and he carried it like a precious thing to the kitchen table. Having levered out the stopper with the flat of his thumbs, he lifted the glass to his lips and simultaneously revelled in the taste and scent of his favoured tipple. Unable to recall the last time he'd drunk alcohol, it felt illicit and lovely all at the same time.

He drank and drank some more, delighting as each sip pushed him further and further off the path of grief, steering him instead on to the track of recall that led to somewhere very close to happiness; no matter how temporary the state, it was a pleasant place to reside, as the fog of drunkenness dulled the sharp edges of his old friend sorrow.

Rhubarb came to rest beneath the kitchen table, a little furry guardian, while Thurston welcomed the haze the booze provided to the clarity of his sadness. He welcomed it all. Quickly, however, as he consumed more, this turned to something close to melancholy, as if that darned sadness was determined to make itself felt one way or another. Not even a good glug of scrumpy could erase it completely.

'I'm going to miss you, fella,' he spoke aloud, 'but the truth is there's no point to it all, Barb.' The little dog didn't answer and this in itself was a disappointment. 'I mean it,' – Thurston raised his voice – 'no point to anything without her. She was why I worked the fields; she was why I wanted to wake up each morning, she was Christmas, summer, snow, she was my whole world!' He banged the table and closed his eyes, letting the thickening of his throat settle. 'I miss her. I miss her so badly. It's like, it's like that feeling when you walk into a room, and you can't for the life of you remember what you've gone into it for. It's like that every waking minute, like I've forgotten something or mislaid something. Stepping into the barn earlier to look at that sturdy old beam . . .' He let this trail. 'I'd never thought about leaving this world, Rhubarb, not ever, until I lost her, but I can't do this without her.'

He took a long, slow swig from the bottle before pushing the chair away from the table; the sound of it scraping made Rhubarb skedaddle into his basket. Thurston opened the middle drawer on the dresser and carefully took out a spiral-bound notepad, in which Mary liked to jot her lists, and a biro. Taking his time, he thought about who to write to first, and in his spidery script, he wrote:

For Nancy,

Where to begin . . . this is a letter I never thought I'd write and it's only the first, I still have to put pen to paper for your mother and Loftus too.

First, I meant what I said, you deserve the best life, Nancy, you need friends, and to have fun! I'm glad you and Andrew are happy – life's too short not to live happily, this much I do know.

And that's why I've decided to say my goodbyes and to leave on my terms. By the time you read this, I will be gone.

I can take this step knowing you are going to care for Barbie and will do so well. He is a gentle soul, a good son. I can hardly look him in the eye and it's as if he knows . . . my little shadow . . .

I want to disappear from the face of the earth, if there is even the smallest chance I might get to see her, be with her . . .

I want to sleep

I want peace

I want escape

As the booze began to sedate, his hand drifted across the page and with his balance a little off and his breathing slow, Thurston felt the familiar creep of tears. Abandoning his task, he stood on unsteady legs and made his way up the stairs. Taking one step at a time, he bumped along the corridor, leaning on the walls, before he reached his marital bed and fell on to it face down with his chest heaving and his heart heavy. The room spun until he closed his eyes. Rhubarb hopped up beside him and that's how they spent the night, Thurston snoring off his booze intake and Rhubarb close by, keeping watch . . .

CHAPTER TWENTY-ONE

Emma

Brendan was taking the boys to school, freeing Emma up to go and get her mother out of bed, showered, dressed and into her chair, where she could serve her breakfast. She'd put an early call in to Nancy, explaining her late start today, and her boss could not have been nicer, laughing and explaining how her own morning had not been without its own hiccups as her lift to work had failed to materialise. Emma wondered if that lift was from Thurston and wondered if he was okay. It felt a little intrusive to ask.

'I don't really like you having to do this, Emma.'

Her mum spoke firmly as Emma helped her up awkwardly on to unsteady legs to make it to the bathroom, arms around her narrow back, heads uncomfortably close together, skin touching skin. Her mother wasn't too heavy for her to lift, but there was stiffness in her movement that made Emma wary and a hesitancy in her actions that spoke of their mutual embarrassment.

'I know you don't, but we'll figure it out, Mum.'

'I didn't like *that Lorraine*, not from the get-go, but at least it felt less personal to have her haul me around. And don't think I'm not grateful to you, I am, but having someone professional here was better for me.'

'I get that.' Her mum's words only echoed her own thoughts. 'I've left a message with a new agency to see if they have anyone available and we'll do as we did before, you can meet them and see what you think . . .' She let this hang. It hadn't been a foolproof system when 'that Lorraine', who had been great during her interview, had turned out to be anything but. Emma felt the flame of guilt at how she'd abandoned her mother to her care. 'Brendan is coming to sit with you this afternoon, make you a cuppa, be here while you go to the loo and stuff. I know you can manage to walk from your chair to the loo, but if you could hang on for him, I'll worry less, knowing he's on hand in case you stumble or anything. Reggie offered to come and sit with you after school, thought you might like the company.'

'Don't fuss. I'm fine.'

'Course you are.' Emma bit the thumbnail of her right hand and tore it between her teeth. Her mother spent half her time telling her how poorly she was and the other half telling her that she was fine and not to make a fuss.

'And it will be lovely to see Reggie *if* he's up to it. Maybe next week, on a less busy day.'

Emma ignored the dig, feeling proud that her teenage boy was so thoughtful.

'Plus, I'm very much looking forward to tonight.' Her mother changed the subject.

'Tonight?' Emma stared at her – what in the world was her mother up to on a Friday night? Silent disco? Underground rave? Dinner with a handsome suitor? *Maybe all three . . .* she certainly hoped so!

'Meeting Martha's new boyfriend, of course! She called me and said she thinks I'm going to like this one. Said it might be the real thing.'

Martha had seen fit to invite her mum over for supper! Jesus! Wasn't she under enough pressure to get the evening right without worrying about the collection and drop-off of her mother, and the fact that her mum was always so . . . honest with her sometimes less than savoury views? Not to mention the plate situation.

'Sorry?' Emma had been miles away.

'For our supper, what are we having?' she enunciated, as if Emma was deaf.

'Well, I'd been planning on lasagne.'

'You can't give the boy lasagne! He's Italian! You can't do that.'

'Apparently not.' She bit the nail of the little finger on her left hand, ripping at the white tip with her teeth and nibbling until there was the briefest flash of pain telling her that she had done minor damage. 'So, I'm thinking chilli, a nice hot chilli! I would have made it last night had the timings worked out, but instead I'll have to do it after work. I'm sure it'll be fine.'

'Can I have mine not so hot? It plays havoc with my indigestion.'

'Sure, I'll make you a separate one.' She tried to make it sound like the extra hassle was no problem at all.

'And what's for pudding?' Her mother's eyes twinkled.

'Martha is bringing pudding, but I think she said brownies and ice cream.'

'Oh, smashing! Such a clever girl.'

'She is that. Must take after her father,' she joked. Her mother only nodded, as if this was gospel.

Roz would love this in the retelling . . . *Oh Roz* . . . remembering in that second that they had rowed, and recalling the reason made her heart drop. Her friend had not replied to her six voice messages and matching texts. Emma decided in that moment to go round again after work and hammer on the door. It would just be too bad if she upset Mrs Lineacre.

With her mother's lunch wrapped under cling film and within reach and not a crumb of Battenberg in sight, she started her car, keen to get to work. It was as she looked up, preparing to indicate, that she saw her best friend on the pavement.

Her heart lifted at the very sight of her, and she felt the tears of joy and relief that gathered at the back of her nose, almost a visceral reaction. Killing the engine, she watched Roz walk around and jump into the passenger seat.

'Dickhead said you'd be here,' she announced as she pulled down the sun visor and checked her scarlet lipstick in the small mirror. 'He was just about to take the boys to school.'

'Did you knock on the front door, or did you chat to him while he was in the bath?'

'Urgh, what a horrible thought!' Her friend visibly shuddered. 'That stinky mutt of yours made a beeline for my cream boots.'

'You're his favourite.'

'Well, he's certainly not mine!' She screwed up her face.

'I think he might be a bit.' She nudged her. It felt good to be in such close proximity, talking naturally. As if in that moment the monster that lurked around the corner was kept at bay.

'Nope. Not even a bit.'

'How was your date in your very high heels?'

'Yes, Mrs Lineacre said you'd been trying to break the door down.'

'Nosy cow.' She smiled at her friend. 'Mum's just informed me that Martha's asked her over for tea tonight when we get to meet the new man.'

'That'll be fun. "Have you been affected by Brexit, Sergio? What with you being a foreigner and all?"'

Roz's impression of her mother was uncanny and even though her giggling was shot through with guilt, giggle she did.

Their laughter subsided and the car felt weighted with quiet. It was hard to know where to begin with so much to talk about and the horrible feeling that they were on a timer.

'I'm sorry I called you an arsehole.' Emma spoke directly.

'Don't be. I am an arsehole, but so are you. That's why we love each other.' Roz shifted to face her and took her hand inside her own, their fingers entwined.

'We do love each other, don't we?' Emma whispered, hating the distress that threatened.

'We do.' Roz swallowed hard. 'And that's why this is difficult.'

'It's worse than difficult, it's horrific!' Finally, her tears broke their banks.

'You're such an ugly crier, always have been.'

'I know.' Emma wiped her face on her sleeve.

Roz pinched her nose. 'The reason I didn't tell you straight away was that I knew *this* would happen, I knew you would fall apart a bit.'

'I'm not falling apart!' Emma screeched through a mouth twisted with distress as her tears and nose ran and her eyes went bloodshot, and her breath came in stuttered bursts, as she shrugged her hand free and banged the steering wheel.

'You're right, you actually look very, very together. What on earth was I worried about?' Roz locked eyes with her. 'I needed to make sure I'd processed it so that I could remain upright. I knew that if we both fell at the same time, we might not get up. This way, it's like a shift, a rota – we take turns in being strong so the other can lean on whoever needs it most.'

'You shouldn't be worrying about me while you are going through this.' The thought alone made her feel terrible.

'Well yes, that's true, but I have a lot of experience. Do you remember on the way home from Brownies, when I nearly sliced right through my thumb on that barbed-wire fence running from those raging bulls, and you saw the blood and nearly fainted and the lady at the bus stop sat rubbing your back and giving you sips of water to quell your light-headedness while we waited for your dad to pick us up, and it turned out I needed fourteen stitches?'

'I do remember that, and it turned out they were only cows anyway.'

'Yep, and then there was the time I got food poisoning and was sick and the sight of me *being* sick made you sick and that bloke came out of the pub and offered you his jacket while I was shitting in a bin behind the chicken shop and vomiting in the alley?'

'I do remember that too. And in my defence, I told you that kebab smelled dodgy, but you ate it anyway.'

'I did. That's true.' Roz sighed. 'Anyway, I think I've made my point. That's why I kept it to myself.'

'I'm angry with you. Angry with you for not at least trying.'

'And I'm angry with the universe for giving me this shitty disease, but what can we do?' Roz shrugged.

'What we can do is take drugs, grab whatever they offer and do whatever the specialist suggests!'

'Not this time, love.' Roz swallowed. 'I've done my homework.'

'Is your mind made up, no treatment?' she almost whispered.

Roz took her time in forming her response. 'It is, mate. It really is.'

'I don't want you to die.' It felt disgusting to use the word, surreal and violent, and she hated it. 'I really don't.'

'I know.' Roz reached for her hand. 'But I also know that we're not going to do this. We are not going to sit in cars crying and feeling sad. Promise me that we're going to carry on as normal, that we're going to ignore it for as long as we can.'

'I . . . I promise.' She spoke the words she hoped she could deliver.

'Good. Good.' Her friend exhaled. 'We're going to drink tea and slate everyone on reality TV with better bodies than us and secretly eat sweets and hide the wrappers down the back of the sofa, and dance in the kitchen to Kris Kross.'

'Don't you want to do extraordinary things while you can?'

'What exactly did you have in mind?' Roz looked a little perplexed.

'I don't know . . .' She thought on the spot. 'Like go to Disneyland or snog Dave Grohl?'

'Urgh, I definitely do not want to go to Disneyland, all that obligatory fun and enforced happiness is my idea of hell, but if you do have Dave Grohl's number then I wouldn't mind taking it off you.'

'I don't have his number.' She pulled a wide-eyed face.

'Could you get it, do you think?'

Emma squeezed her hand. 'I do love you. I really do.'

'And I love you. Are you off to work?'

'Yes.' Emma looked at the clock; she was, as ever, running late.

'One final thing.'

'What?' She wiped her face and sniffed, getting ready to face Nancy and Paddy and a whole big pile of fruit and veg.

'It's a request, really.'

'What kind of request?' She was curious.

'I want you to make friends with Mackenzie McTeeth.'

Emma sprayed her laughter. 'You are joking?'

'I'm not joking.' Roz held her gaze. 'You could do with another friend, and she fits the bill.'

'In what way could she ever fit the bloody bill?' The whole idea was preposterous.

'Because she knows us both, shares our history, kind of, and I think she's okay.'

'You said she's an arsehole!' Emma reminded her.

'Yes, but we're arseholes too, remember?'

Emma stared out of the window, just as Mr Blundesthorpe opened his gate. He caught sight of her in the car and hesitated, looking at her as if unable to predict her next move. And while she was entirely flummoxed by the concept of making friends with Mackenzie McTeeth, his assumption that she was a loose cannon she entirely understood.

'I'll think about it,' she conceded before Roz jumped out of the car, and off she set for work.

'What time do you call this?' Paddy yelled from the back of the shop as she reached for the tabard hanging on the hook by the staff loo and popped it over her head.

'Morning, Nancy. Thank you for being so understanding on such short notice.' She meant it. The woman's kindness had, this morning, made everything possible.

'Not a problem. Paddy and I held the fort, didn't we, Paddy?'

'We did.' He stared at Emma with his eyes crossed. This, she knew, was designed to make her laugh in front of their boss. He was a rotten tease.

Nancy was decidedly more upbeat than she had been of late and seemed more at ease, less uptight, as she retook her seat at the till and bagged up leggy broccoli stems and a punnet of plums for a customer.

'You're a nightmare, Paddy! And I need nothing but kindness at the moment. I've got a lot going on.'

'Like what?' He paused in sorting out boxes of mushrooms to be shipped to the shop floor.

She avoided giving her colleague the true horror of what she faced, knowing that if he was in the know, his daily questioning and well-meant sympathy would mean the reality invaded her working day, and right now it was the one place she could paint on a happy face, pretend and carry on.

'I've got to make a fabulous chilli tonight – Martha's bringing her new boyfriend home for supper.'

'Another new boyfriend? How do you remember their names?'

'Don't even!' She held up her hands. 'I can't joke about it. I'm worried sick about getting his name wrong. At least a nice decent bowl of chilli might make him more forgiving if I do.'

'I know just the thing!' He clicked his fingers. 'We've got some Armageddons in! Nancy doesn't sell them, they're my own personal stash!'

'What's an Armageddon?'

'It's a super-hot chilli with enough kick to fire up your supper! And talking of boyfriends, yours got a mention this morning.' Paddy threw a mouldy mushroom at her, which she caught.

'My boyfriend?' She wasn't following.

'Nancy's uncle, what was his name? Thurrock! Something like that.'

'Thurston.' She laughed. 'Thurrock, isn't that a service station in Essex?'

'Possibly.' He raised his palms to show his indifference. 'Nancy, who was late for work, mentioned how well you two had got on.'

'We actually did. We shared a moment.' The man had been in her thoughts.

'Oh please! Don't you go all Hallmark Channel on me!' Paddy tutted. 'And I still think the bloke might be a psycho, hanging around in the dark, enticing you into the cab of his muddy truck – who knows what might have happened if I hadn't come to the rescue?'

'Everything okay, Paddy?'

They swung around to face Nancy, who must have heard every word.

'Yes, fine, thanks.' Paddy spoke sweetly, as if butter wouldn't melt.

'Emma, there's a lady to see you.' She pointed towards the shop.

'A lady? To see me?' she repeated, despite having heard perfectly.

'Yes.' Nancy stood back to give her a clear view and there was none other than Mackenzie McTeeth, hovering near the organic avocados. Of course she was.

'Bloody Roz!' she muttered under her breath as her heart flexed, understanding her best and beloved friend's intention. 'Sorry, Nancy, first I miss the start of my shift—'

'An hour and a half of your shift, to be precise.' Paddy gave the exact measure and she glared at him.

'And now I've got a visitor.'

'That's okay. Paddy and I can manage and if not, I can always call my Uncle Thurrock, if he's not too busy hanging around in the dark, trying to entice unsuspecting women into the muddy cab of his truck. I mean, the fact that he's in his eighties with a broken heart and a dicky hip is neither here nor there.' She smiled. Emma watched Paddy shrink and knew that she had never liked her boss more. This more confident version of Nancy who was joining in was a wonderful thing to see.

Emma walked out to the shop and folded her arms as she approached the girl who had been in her class throughout school.

'Hi, Emma.' Mackenzie seemed a little ill at ease as she clutched her hessian tote to her gut with one hand and tucked her neat blonde hair behind her ear with the other.

'Hi, Mackenzie.' She did her best to sound welcoming, to sound . . . nice. They had never gelled. By the time Mackenzie joined their class, they were a year into school. Already having established a friendship that meant it was her and Roz against the world, a dynamic duo that left little room for other girlfriends, a hard habit to break.

'Roz called, said you wanted to see me?'

'She did?'

'Yes.' Mackenzie wrinkled her nose as if wondering what was going on. She wasn't the only one.

'Oh, yes!' *Think fast, Em* . . . 'I was just wondering if you fancied a coffee or a . . . a tea, sometime.' She spoke with as much enthusiasm as she could muster, one more chore in an already busy life and not something she would choose. But anything for her Roz right now . . .

Mackenzie stared at her. And she stared back.

'Are you being serious?' The woman's eyes crinkled in disbelief.

'Yes. I thought, why don't I go for a coffee with Mackenzie, and here we are.' She tried out a smile.

Mackenzie said nothing until an awkward amount of time had passed. Emma felt the blush of embarrassment spread over her neck.

'How long have we known each other, Emma?'

'Erm, a long time.'

'Wrong.' Mackenzie shook her head. 'We were first introduced at primary school when we were seven. Where we sat only one table apart. And we were in the same sets at secondary school.'

'Yes, as I said, a long time, forty-odd years or thereabouts.' She sighed at the horror of how quickly life was speeding by. Forty years? It barely felt possible.

'Yes, and my point is that we don't *know* each other, do we?' Mackenzie took a step closer, and Emma could smell her delicious perfume, expensive and crisp. She took in her neatness: the rollneck sweater, subtle jewellery, lip gloss, still decent gnashers . . .

'I guess not, but there's still time to do that, right?' She thought of Roz's request and was doing her best. She had never been anti Mackenzie; rather she was simply one of the background characters to their youth, a girl in their class, a person from school in the pub, someone they knew to wave to in the street, an extra in the great friendship that was the Emma and Roz show.

'No, Emma. There is not still time. Because you have, for my whole life, been a bit of a bitch.'

'What?' She was aware that her voice had gone up an octave. Had they not been in her place of work, she might have demanded examples, which she was fully prepared to defend.

'You heard me. You and Roz have always found me amusing. Do you think I'm stupid? Do you think I didn't know that you went on about my teeth?'

Emma opened her mouth, but no decent retort came forth and she closed it.

'Julia Phillips told me.'

'Julia Phillips! Whatever happened to her?' She pictured the girl who had joined the school at eleven and left a year or two after. Emma had not given her a thought from that day to this.

'Her dad went to work on the oil rigs and the family moved to Aberdeen.'

'Didn't she have a brother? Quite good-looking, blond, played hockey. What was his name? I want to say Carl?'

'No, it was erm . . .' Mackenzie clicked her fingers and closed her eyes. 'Chris!'

'Yes, Chris!' Emma sighed at the thought of the blond teen who had looked a bit like the blond guy from *Dawson's Creek*. Both women laughed.

'So, yes.' Mackenzie sobered and straightened, re-tucking her hair as if it had worked loose. 'Julia told me that you two had been doing impressions of me, saying my new teeth were too white, too shiny, and God only knows what else!'

'We didn't mean anything by it. We were kids and we were just jealous! You had those amazing, beautiful teeth, and we were queuing up for grey fillings! They're still amazing!'

'The reasons behind why you said what you said don't matter, Emma. It still felt like shit.'

'I think we thought we were being funny and that you'd never know,' she confessed, feeling her face flush with shame.

'It wasn't funny, and I did know. I've always known.' Mackenzie held her eyeline.

Emma was aware of customers gathering at the till and knew she had to get back to work. Glancing at the big sky beyond the rooftops opposite, she considered running somewhere wide and open, somewhere away from everyone, where no chores awaited her, her phone was beyond signal and she could breathe.

'So, are we going for a coffee then or what?' she asked, cloaked with shame and mortified not only at the words they had used, the thing they had thought was funny, but also that this woman had carried it for all this time. It was indeed shit.

'I don't think so,' Mackenzie breathed.

'What did you come in for then?' Emma was confused.

'Because Roz said you wanted to speak to me and for one stupid moment, I thought you wanted to apologise for your behaviour towards me for all these years.'

'Asking you for a coffee is the same as apologising!' This was how it worked in her house. Brendan and she might spar but a cup of tea and a slice of cake were enough to mark reconciliation. The same with the kids; any petty argument or moment of discord could be tamed with the provision of supper – assuming they didn't get the green plate, of course.

'Is it, Emma? I don't think so.' Mackenzie took a step towards her. 'And just for the record, I wouldn't go for a coffee with you if you were the last woman on earth. You're an arsehole, and so's your mate.'

'I know we are, but what are you?' She hollered the retort that put them right back in the playground, knowing it would make Roz laugh, but Mackenzie didn't laugh. Instead, she turned on her block-heeled boot and left the greengrocer's.

'Mackenzie!' Emma called her back with words gathering on her tongue as to how she could make amends, but Mackenzie kept on walking.

A man walked into the shop; catching sight of him only in her peripheral vision, it wasn't until he was next to her and speaking that she realised it was Thurston.

'Is everything okay, Emma?' His concerned tone and expression were enough to jolt her core with guilt.

'Thurston . . .' There was something about his presence that calmed her. She also felt a wave of embarrassment, similar to when her dad caught her swearing. 'I don't know if everything is okay actually.' The room suddenly felt a little claustrophobic. She pulled at the neck of her hoodie, whether to let off steam or let in air, she wasn't sure.

'What's the matter? Or is that a stupid question, after our chat yesterday?' He folded his lips into his mouth in a knowing smile.

'Yes, same old.' She swallowed, not wanting to give him the details of her and Mackenzie's exchange; the word 'bitch' was a horrible one to use, even if it was only in the retelling. 'It's just one of those days, although in fairness nearly every day is one of those days at the moment! I'm thinking of running away.' Again, it struck her how easy it was to talk to him. This man who was unconnected to her worries, who had spoken openly to her and did so without judgement.

'Don't do that, Emma. It wouldn't solve anything; everything would still be waiting for you when you came home. Although what do I know.' He looked a little troubled and it bothered her. 'I often feel like running away, disappearing altogether. I hit the grog for the first time in decades and overslept. I forgot to take Nancy to work. Slept right through.' He shook his head as if mortified. 'Hope she's still talking to me!' He looked towards the storeroom, as if trying to seek out his niece.

'That kind of sleep'll do you good.' She hoped she wasn't patronising the old man.

'Maybe. Not sure about this headache though.' He rubbed his forehead and pinched the bridge of his nose. 'And you can run away to Merrydown anytime. I find a good stomp around the fields can help clear your thoughts. There's plenty of space to roam. I can always put the kettle on.'

'As long as I don't get there too early, as you don't go in the kitchen.' She spoke softly.

'Good point.' He grinned widely and it lit his whole demeanour.

'I will come and visit, Thurston, that'd be lovely sometime.'

'Of course!' The twinkle to his eye told her he too relished the prospect. 'Mary was the sociable one, issuing invites and cooking supper – I'm a bit clueless about it all really.'

'Does that make it lonely?' She hoped it wasn't an overstep.

'Yes, it does,' he answered without hesitation.

She smiled at the man who had the knack of turning up when she was in need of anchoring.

'And remember, Emma . . .'

She looked up at him, wanting to hear his words of wisdom, wanting some of her worry to fall away . . .

'You can't do everything, and you can't fix everything. Sometimes, you need to ask for help.'

'I'll try.' It felt like the best she could offer.

◆　◆　◆

A bit of a bitch . . . Emma wrestled with the fact that someone thought of her in this way. It was galling and so very far from how she wanted to be viewed and how she viewed herself. The whole encounter bothered her, and she wondered if it were possible to make amends with Mackenzie – this quickly followed by the question of whether she wanted to befriend the woman at all.

Her car sat in traffic and her leg jumped as the queue crawled along. She was desperate to get home, get the table set, let Bruce out into the back garden for a quick wee and to get the chilli simmering. The bag of Armageddon chillies sat in a plastic bag on the front seat. She wondered how many to use?

Her phone rang and the hands-free Bluetooth answered it.

'Mum?'

'Yes, Reggie, all okay, love?'

Please don't ask me to pick you up . . . please don't ask me to pick you up . . . please don't ask me to pick you up . . .

'Can you pick me up?'

'Right now?' She closed her eyes.

'Yeah.' He sounded a little quiet, a little hesitant.

'I can, love, of course, but don't you finish in an hour or so anyway? You don't fancy waiting and jumping on the school bus?'

Please . . . please . . . please . . .

'I just . . .' Reggie went quiet, and she tried to quell her impatience. 'I just . . .' Again that deep, deep sigh. 'I don't want to be here.'

Her gut jumped – was he saying he didn't want to be in school or didn't want to be here, *here* . . . here on the planet? It was enough to jolt her into action.

'Rightio, hold tight, my love! I'll be there as soon as I can.'

'Kaymum,' he mumbled, and was gone. The traffic was at a standstill and yet the quickest way to get to Reggie's school was to keep going down to the mini roundabout, make a U-turn and head back in the opposite direction. A quick glance at the clock and the futility of the last twenty minutes threatened to weaken her, especially as she was about to turn around and sit in it again – only this time heading back to where she had come from. The chillies taunted her from the seat. They were beautiful, a fiery red that made them almost glow.

Her phone rang. It was Martha.

'Hiya!'

'Hello, darling.' A nerve just under her eye twitched in anticipation of her daughter's latest list of instructions.

'All set?'

'Yep!' she lied. 'All set!'

Because lying was easier than confessing to the reality, as she pictured the mince on the shelf in the fridge, the bare dining table, the spare chair still in the hallway that would need carrying through. The carpets that needed vacuuming. Her hair that needed washing. A quick debrief for the boys, reminding them again not to fart or mention farts. The fact that her mother, who required a separate chilli-less chilli, needed fetching. She had been humiliated by Mackenzie ~~McTeeth~~, just Mackenzie, and Roz was not going to get any better. Oh, and now she was heading in the wrong direction to fetch Reggie, who may or may not be about to jump . . .

'Great!' She heard her daughter's sigh of relief. 'We've decided to go and meet Layla and her new man at the pub after supper and so would it be okay if we stayed over? I know you always hate it when I leave, so if it's okay with you, we'll stay over and have a nice breakfast with you all tomorrow and then head into Bristol about lunchtime. We're happy to stay in my old room, of course, but could you just shove all the teddies into the bottom of the wardrobe and there's an old rugby shirt on my bed that I wore last time I was home . . .' Her daughter began whispering. 'It's Rico's! He left it by mistake, and I hung on to it. I'd hate Sergio to see it, so if you could shove that in the wardrobe too, that'd be great.'

'Sure.'

She made a mental note of the tasks, adding them to the list: *hide teddies in wardrobe and get rid of Rico's rugby shirt. Shit!* Remembering also that Bruce had thrown up on Martha's bedroom carpet and while she had speedily cleaned it up, she had fully intended to go back and give it a proper scrub. It seemed now was the time to do that.

'Can't wait to see you guys!' Martha squealed.

'Me too!' Emma dug deep to find an energetic response as the clock ticked and the traffic failed to move.

CHAPTER TWENTY-TWO

THURSTON

Thurston was relieved that Nancy had seemed quite unperturbed at having been stood up by him. Chatting gaily as she served customers, she'd explained how her mother had apparently done the honours and run her into town, moaning for the duration of the journey about the inconvenience of it all. It didn't feel good to know he'd gone back on his word, caused friction. But it had been good to see Emma again.

Returning home, he'd only intended to sit in the armchair for a moment, to rest his weary eyes a short while, and try to restore the feelings of normality that his hangover had temporarily erased. He was of course completely sober, but it was as if his eyes and stomach were still righting themselves. The midday sun filtered through the living-room window.

He still felt a little embarrassed to have woken in a heap that morning, knowing it would take more than a nap to shake it off. The day had seemed too bright, offensive almost. Never would he have confessed to having opened one eye slowly, unable to remember the last time he'd fallen asleep in his clothes. His mouth dry, tongue coated, his breath unpleasant and with a hammer striking his skull with regularity. He had been in dire need of a trip to the bathroom, a glass of water and a shower, and not necessarily in that order. The feeling had put him off drinking for sure.

This stolen nap in the chair felt both restorative and necessary . . . providing blissful escape for a whole thirty minutes. He woke with a fancy for a cup of tea and, with his dog hot on his heels, made his way along the hallway. His body jolted at the sight of June sitting at the kitchen table. Having thought he was alone, it wasn't only her presence that shocked him, but more so the fact that it had been decades since he had seen his sister crying – and not the delicate eye-dabbing he'd witnessed once or twice, but there she sat with tears streaking her face and a look of utter, utter despair. His heart jumped – what had happened? What *could* have happened to cause such a reaction? He could only think of Nancy . . . but he'd seen her within the last hour, and she was fine, what else . . . ? It was as he racked his brain, opened his mouth to ask what the matter was, that his sister shouted, making him jump.

'You, Thurston, are a fucking idiot!'

'I beg your pardon!' He was unable to recall ever being spoken to like that and had never, in his eighty-odd years on the planet, heard his sister use such language. It was as shocking as it was uncomfortable!

'You heard me.' Her tears came once more and her shoulders heaved. 'How dare you think about fucking suicide!' She banged her hand on the notepad, sitting where he had left it. 'How dare you think of doing something like that!'

At once he remembered scrawling something on the top sheet of the pad that now sat in front of his sister, although the exact words he'd be hard pushed to recall.

'I just, I wasn't, not really.' He couldn't think how to justify it, how to explain it, his mouth now dry with fear. 'I was having a low moment, I—'

'Low? *Low?* She narrowed her eyes at him, her mouth twisted. 'You think I've never been low, you moron! You think after Melvin died I didn't want to curl up and disappear, you think I never eyed the stash of drugs he'd left in the medicine cabinet, all those tempting little bottles with bright-coloured pills, wondering which and how many I'd need to take?'

'Did you?' He was surprised by the admission.

'Of course I did! But never did I mean it, or write it down, or make a plan, but this fucking suicide note!'

'It's not a suicide note, I'd had a drink, it's . . .' He looked at the floor, unable to face her and lie. His words might offer some excuse, but his intention when writing had not been quite so casual.

Much to his shame, and admonishment, his sister began to read aloud: '*Where to begin . . . this is a letter I never thought I'd write and it's only the first, I still have to put pen to paper for your mother and Loftus too . . .*' She broke away, staring at him so intently he had to look away. '*Blah, blah, blah, that's why I've decided to say my goodbyes and to leave on my terms. By the time you read this, I will be gone.* That's what you've put right here!' She jabbed at the page.

'It's a process, I was—' He thought about his conversation with Emma, how easy it was to advise her to ask for help, while the idea of doing the same was mortifying.

June cut him short, shaking the pad before beginning in a faltering voice, '*I want to disappear from the face of the earth, if there is even the smallest chance I might get to see her, be with her . . .*'

Her words fired a bolt of sadness that lanced his chest; to hear his private sentiment so plainly expressed, his innermost thoughts laid bare, was like peeling away his skin. He felt the pain of the exposure. June paused only briefly, and continued, 'Even the dog gets a fucking mention!'

'Your language is terrible! Honestly, terrible!' He wished she'd stop shouting as his head was thumping.

'If ever a situation has required bad language, it's . . . it's this one!' she hiccupped.

'What would Mother say if she heard you swearing?'

'I don't care what she'd say! I'm seventy-three and I can say what I like! Fuck it! Fuckity fuck it!'

Thurston stared at her like she had lost her reason, acting crazy! He wondered, mournfully, what his passing might unleash and felt the pain of it.

'Have you finished?' he asked calmly.

'No, I haven't! Don't you dare, dare ever think of leaving me! You can't leave me. You're all I have left, Thurston. Nancy is smitten with that lump of a husband of hers, I've lost my mum, my dad, my friend Mary, my husband, all of them gone! You're my, my big brother. Loftus is a million miles away and an idiot, married to that plank of a wife of his! You're all I have left,' she sobbed, and it tore at his heart, unused to this level of emotion from his sister, especially directed at him. 'And I've watched you wilt in the months of her illness, and it's torn my heart in two. You used to sing! You used to sing loudly! Your voice a gift, that's what Mary always said, your voice is a gift. But now, *sing*? The idea is laughable. You barely talk! At least, not to me.'

He knew this to be true; he had lost his voice, in every sense. His sister took a sharp breath. '*Now* I've fucking finished.'

Thurston sat down hard at the kitchen table, feeling a little unsteady on his feet.

This was the first time he had heard such sentiment from his sister, and guilt swirled in his gut. He lowered his gaze.

'I'm not going anywhere right now, June.' This was the truth. 'Not going anywhere until I reach the end of the road.' Again he chose his words, lying by omission, speaking carefully, blinking away the image of the sturdy beam that spanned the barn and careful not to talk dishonestly. 'It was the scrumpy talking. You can blame Loftus, the idiot.'

The two sat at the table in silence until the little dog scratched at the back door to be let out.

Thurston stood and walked slowly over to let his boy outside to run free in the yard.

'And that's another thing!' June suddenly yelled again, shattering the peace that had briefly prevailed. 'You say that *life's too short not to live happily* – what do you think? That everyone is perpetually happy, full of bloody joy? Because let me tell you, they're not! Life is hard, life is challenging, life is a mountainous climb, sometimes we stop and look at the view and it fills us up, other times we are so knackered we barely have time to breathe. But that is life! And you talk about this right to happiness as if it's a given and with total disregard for the utter sadness your death would bring us all! What about me, Thurston? What about your sister! Your sister!' She pointed at her chest. 'There's more concern for Rhubarb than anything in this letter!'

'Good Lord, I thought you'd finished! Is there any more to come?'

It was a conversation so bizarre that Thurston started to laugh and so did June and there they sat, snorting, giggling and wheezing, with the notepad abandoned on the tabletop. Letting the absurdity of the situation settle. It felt good to laugh, very good.

When he thought about standing in the barn as the winter wind drifted in through the open door, he felt the smallest fissure in his resolution. There would be no harm in having one last Christmas. He'd erase December the twenty-second from his diary and go for some time in the New Year. That might be easier for them all.

'A fucking dog!' June boomed as she leaned forward, smacking the table and near hysterics.

'You have to stop swearing. You really do.' He tried to scowl through his laughter.

'I know, but I'm quite liking it. Please don't tell Nancy,' she implored, as she calmed and wiped away her tears.

'I won't,' he said. 'She doesn't need to know her mother has a potty mouth.'

'She certainly doesn't,' June agreed. 'She'd go fucking spare.'

And just like that, their laughter again burst from them.

CHAPTER TWENTY-THREE

EMMA

'Right, Reggie.' Kicking the front door shut behind them, Emma raced ahead into the kitchen. 'I need some help. Martha and Sergio will be here in an hour or so. Please go and grab all of the soft toys off Martha's bed and put them in her wardrobe and apparently there's a rugby shirt on her bed, get rid of that too!'

'Why do I have to do it?' he mumbled, as she opened the back door and whistled for Bruce to leave the comfort of his fluffy bed and go pee.

Thurston's advice came to mind. She took a deep breath. 'Because Dad and Alex aren't here yet and because I'm asking you for help. Because when you ask me for help, like coming to pick you up from school, I do it. And right now, I'm in an emerging situation where time is running away with me. So, I'm asking for something in return. Please, Reggie.'

'Okay! No need to shout at me!'

'I wasn't shouting at you!' she shouted.

He twisted his mouth in smug justification.

'I just need to get something to eat and then I'll do it.'

Barging past him to get to the fridge, she grabbed the packets of beef mince and lobbed them on to the countertop, along with onions, tomato puree, garlic, Paddy's bag of chillies, tins of chopped tomatoes and kidney beans and a whole array of herbs and spices, from onion salt to smoked paprika. Finally, she was getting the chilli underway, deciding first to go poke her head into the dining room and think about setting the table. Her theory being that even if the food was a little delayed, everyone could sit up and enjoy the flicker of candlelight and a glass of cold plonk, while she dished up the sour cream dip to go with the main event and arranged nachos in sharing bowls.

The thought of that glass of cold plonk did much to ease her flustered mind. Not that her mother would approve, and not that she wanted Sergio to think she liked to hit the bottle in times of stress . . . ha! She had an idea of such brilliance it made her smile: she'd pop wine in a Diet Coke can so no one would be any the wiser. Was that the road to ruin? She'd seen men cluttering up the park benches, swigging out of lemonade bottles, the contents of which looked nothing like lemonade.

'Don't be daft, Em,' she self-reprimanded, 'one secret Coke can filled with wine is not a gateway activity that ends with you on a park bench.'

The smile, however, was quickly wiped from her face when she stepped into the dining room, as fury licked her patience. On the table, Lego sprawled. Not only was it sprawled, but it had most certainly multiplied since she'd last looked. Piles of it lay sorted into tiny bricks, interspersed with structures in various stages of completion and which were hard to identify. Open Lego boxes with lids askew had been dumped on the dining chairs, and at least three pairs of socks, clearly peeled off and flung by Alex as he sat down to immerse himself in his hobby, were scattered around the room. And if the sight of her son's Lego wasn't disappointing and angst-inducing enough, Brendan's fishing gear was still leaning up against the wall. Rods, nets, a stinky holdall full of crispy dried wet-weather gear, and even a folded chair. The room smelled like a hamster cage, if that hamster cage had a rotting fish in it. Emma felt the rise of a volcanic eruption in her gut, knowing that if time allowed, she'd go a little crazy. Instead, a sweary montage of disappointment ran through her mind as she threw the curtains wide and opened the windows despite the less than clement temperature.

'Fckinlittlbstardarsholesafterallidohowhardisittojusthelpme outthelittelfckers! Illfkingkillthem . . .'

'I'm going up now to do that stuff you asked. What was it again?'

She turned to face Reggie, who, with his free hand, pointed upwards and in the other held a doorstep of a sandwich that bulged with ham and what looked like crisps.

'Removetheteddiesfromthebed puttheminthewardrobe, getridoftherugbyshirt.' She was on double speak, quick time.

'Kay.' He nodded.

His vagueness didn't fill her with any confidence, but she dared not push it. 'Great.'

'I'll eat this then do Martha's room.'

'Thanks, and if you could run the Hoover over as well, that would also be great.'

'Where's the Hoover?'

How could he not know that the Hoover, which had lived in the cupboard under the stairs since before he was born, was located? Was this her fault, always keen to jump in and do the chore herself? A large blob of mayonnaise left the side of his sandwich and plopped on to the floor.

'It's up my bum, Reggie. The Hoover is up my bum.'

'Well, I'm not touching it then. Definitely not.'

She watched as he walked away, treading in the blob of mayonnaise and trailing it across the floor and all the way up the stairs.

The phone in the hallway rang.

'Hello?' She reached it, having navigated the mayonnaise-free sections of the floor like a kid playing lava.

'What time are you picking me up?'

'Hi, Mum.' She rubbed her brow. 'I'm just cooking and trying to get the house straight, so Brendan will come and get you. I think he'll be there in about an hour.' She craned her neck, trying to see the clock in the kitchen, but failed.

'What time is that exactly? I like to be ready to go.'

Emma bit the nail of her index finger on her right hand, refraining from shouting, YOU ARE IN YOUR CHAIR WATCHING SHITE ON THE TELLY, WHO CARES WHEN BRENDAN ARRIVES TO PICK YOU UP? BE READY AND WHEN HE GETS THERE, LET HIM HELP YOU INTO THE CAR BUT WHAT IN GOD'S NAME DOES IT MATTER IF HE'S THERE IN TWENTY MINUTES OR SIXTY? GIVE ME A BREAK!

'I think' – she drew breath – 'that whatever the time is now, and I can't quite see a clock, erm, add sixty minutes and that's when he'll be there. Okay, got to dash, Mum! Looking forward to seeing you in a bit.'

'Have you made my separate chilli, because I don't like it too hot!'

'Yes,' she lied. At this rate, they'd be eating at midnight. 'See you in a bit!' she sang and put the phone down.

Back in the dining room, she was staring at the table like it was a complex problem that maybe staring might help her solve when she heard the front door.

'Oi! Oi!' Brendan hollered and his joviality in the face of her stress sent a flicker of fury rippling through her.

'Can you please, please move your fishing gear!' She met him in the hallway.

'Oh yes it's lovely to see you too darling. My day?' Her husband scratched his chin. 'Well thank you for asking, yes it was a little frantic as I had to fit in looking after your mother while doing my actual job and hauling patio slabs around. But no matter, here we are!'

'I asked you to move it ages ago! But it's still there! Up against the bloody wall and it stinks!' She pointed towards the dining room.

'I'll do it now. I'll do it right now.' Her husband more or less sulked as he sloped past her.

'And Alex, your Lego. Move it! Put it away! I told you too, ages ago! Why does no one do as I ask them? It's infuriating.'

'Where shall I put it?' He stared at her through his glasses.

'Anywhere! Literally anywhere! Do it right now!'

'There's no need to shout at him,' Brendan offered unhelpfully as he emerged from the dining room with fishing gear balanced from his arms and around his neck.

'Everyone tells me not to shout when I get to shouting stage, but I beg to differ, because asking politely has got me nowhere and so now I have to resort to shouting to get things done. You think I like shouting? Because I don't, I don't like shouting!' she shouted. 'And when you've put your fishing gear away, Bren, can you please go and fetch my mum and bring her here for supper.'

'Yes, dearest, anything else?' His mockery wasn't lost on her.

'Get wine, get lots of wine,' she breathed as her chest heaved with the effort of all it tried to contain. This evening was going to be stressful enough and that before she gave in to the desperate sadness she felt about Roz. All she wanted to do was sit with her, hold her . . .

He held her eyeline, the tension palpable. 'We'll get through tonight, we'll get through everything, but just take a minute. And please let me help you.'

'What I asked was that you clear away your bloody fishing gear. And FYI, I don't have a minute to take.' She picked at the skin around her cuticle and tugged.

'You do. You do, Em. No one will mind about the odd stray Lego brick, and if they do then they can sod off.'

'Is it a crime that I wanted everything to be perfect and I wanted to look nice, and I wanted to make a good impression for Martha, and instead it's going to be like every other time when I try to make an effort – a last-minute rush and a bloody disaster?'

'Not a crime, no, but it's bloody unbearable every time you set an unrealistic expectation and go into crazy mode, which changes nothing but just makes the whole run-up really unpleasant.'

'That's so helpful!' She gave a double thumbs-up. 'Thank you.'

He took a beat, closing his eyes and breathing through his nose. 'It won't be a disaster. It will be great; it will all be great. Everyone will have a nice time; Sergio will remember our wit and repartee and he won't care if the house isn't immaculate. Trust me.'

He was right, of course he was right. Her pulse slowed a little.

Alerted by an almighty rumble, they both turned towards the dining room, from where Alex emerged, holding the tablecloth like an enormous Dick Whittington-style bundle with the ends pinched together under his chin, and inside the cloth thousands of little bricks bulged in blocks, definable by their shape.

'Oh Alex! You've muddled them all together!'

'It doesn't matter, Mum. I need to sort it all out again anyway, it's going to be my project, but I'll start when Martha and Sergio have gone home.'

'Sorry I snapped at you, little mate.' The way he had done as she asked and now beamed up at her through his glasses did nothing to abate her guilt. Alex scurried past her and up the stairs, treading a thin seam of mayonnaise in his wake as he did so.

'I understand, Mum. It's probably your hormones. We've been learning about the menopause in Biology.'

Keeping her eyeline on Brendan as their youngest slipped past, she took a deep, slow breath. 'Don't forget the wine.'

Working like a whirling dervish, she chopped tomatoes, onions and Paddy's Armageddon chillies, browning the mince and layering it with generous shakes of the various seasonings and the thick sauce before transferring it all to the large stockpot to simmer on the range. Reggie appeared and inhaled the air in the kitchen.

'That smells nice!'

Brightened by his compliment, she felt the beginnings of relief at the prospect of the evening ahead. The table was finally laid, Lego free and with six white plates and one green, which she would have, of course, and just hope that Sergio didn't notice. But at this late hour, the plate situation was just too much for her to consider or rectify. And the slight smell of muddy riverbank had almost disappeared.

'Would you like to taste it?' He had loved to cook before preferring to lie in his bed.

'Sure!' His mouth lifted, eyes wide as his face beamed in the way it used to, and just this glimmer of joy beneath the mask of anxiety made her heart swell. With her trusty cloth, she pulled the lid from the simmering chilli and took a spoonful, which she handed to Reggie, who blew on it until the steam subsided. Gingerly at first, he tasted and smacked his lips, before tasting again and licking the spoon clean. *Thank God*, she thought, *that Martha wasn't here to witness him licking the cutlery.*

'It's nice, very tomatoey, good seasoning, and I can taste the herbs, but it needs to be hotter, Mum. It needs much more heat. Otherwise, it's just fancy mince.'

'Ooh, we don't want fancy mince!' She pulled a face that made him laugh. 'That'd be the worst!'

'I agree. This is definitely too mild, but the flavour is good! And you get the char from where you've cooked the meat. I like it. But more chillies.'

He looked and sounded confident; it was a revelation. His tone, stance and the light in his eyes spoke of confidence. It was a glimpse of the old Reggie, the boy who had been bold in the kitchen and joined in! She did her best to quell her enthusiasm, lest to him it felt like a pressure. *Eat your heart out, Jamie Oliver.*

'Okay then, more heat. Thank you, Reg. You have a good palate. Can I leave you to make the necessary adjustments? Work your magic?'

'And finish the chilli? Really?'

'Yes, really.' She nodded at the pot.

'Sure!'

She noted the way he stood tall at her suggestion. It was great to see him leap into action without excuse or hesitation. She wanted him to know that both his talent and his opinion were valid and prayed that this might translate into something more. This was her constant riddle: trying to figure out how to boost his confidence, encourage any interests and let him know that he was the most wonderful human with a lovely future if only he could see through the fog and hold on.

He might not know where they kept the Hoover, but she watched as he grabbed the bag of Paddy's chillies from the fridge and placed one on the little chopping board. Using a small sharp knife, he turned it into tiny squares before adding it to the meat.

Leaving him to it, she reached into the bits and bobs drawer for the matchbox, deciding to give Reggie the space to create, while she went to light the candles in the dining room. The place looked a little better with the flickering candlelight to draw attention from the dust on the wall lights. She shifted the placemats and cutlery until it was all as symmetrical as it could be, like that might make the difference.

Reggie stood in the door.

'What do you reckon?' She stared at her boy.

'Looks good!' he smiled. 'I've added the chillies, given it a quick stir and put it back on the hob.'

'Fantastic, Reg, thanks.'

'No worries!' He walked with more purpose than she'd seen in a while towards the stairs. It boded well.

With one eye on the time, Emma rinsed the chopping board and knife, which were stained red; she noted too how the chilli colour was under her fingernails. That wouldn't do, didn't want Sergio to think she was grubby.

'See you in a bit, just off to grab your mum,' Brendan called.

She heard the front door close and felt the simmer of guilt that she'd been short with him.

A quick glance at the clock told her she would have to forgo the bath and hair wash she had been longing for all day. Instead, she raced up the stairs, taking two at a time, before generously spraying her armpits with deodorant and applying a liberal spritz of perfume. Leaning stiff armed on the basin, she felt like the floor was falling away from her as she thought about her friend's illness. Heartsick. It was like hearing the news for the first time as it thumped her hard in the chest. Breathing slowly in and out helped to steady her.

A quick look and the soft denim shirt was the only item in her wardrobe that was freshly ironed and so, by default, was selected as her outfit of choice to meet Martha's new man. She added a long string of multicoloured beads but then removed them, then put them on again but wound them into two smaller strands, then removed them and shoved them in a drawer. There was no time for frippery or beads or worrying about what *Sergio*, *Sergio*, *Sergio*, definitely not *Carlos*, might think of her taste in fashion and accessories.

Grabbing a tissue from the box on her dressing table, she wiped at the smudge of mascara that liked to gather under her lower lashes at the end of the day. It would have to do.

As she made her way down the stairs, hollering to the boys as she did so, 'They'll be here any minute, guys!', she felt the start of a tingling sensation in her left eye, which very quickly developed into burning.

'Ouch!' She blinked and rubbed at it, only feeling the heat rise and the sting increase, before she realised what was the cause of her discomfort: *chillies!* 'Bloody hell, that hurts!'

'You okay, Mum?' Reggie called from his room.

'Yes, just got something in my eye!' She tried to strike the balance between worrying her son and the full-blown panic that threatened. 'Make sure you wash your hands thoroughly, Reg!'

'Way ahead of you, already have, and didn't actually touch inside the chillies!'

'Smart!' she blinked, as her eye wept.

In a mad dash to the downstairs loo, she crouched low over the small basin and ran the cold tap. Making a shallow cup out of her palm, caring little that she doused her hair and shirt in the process, Emma repeatedly filled and sloshed her eye until the stinging subsided a little. Pushing the hand towel into her eye and holding her breath brought further relief.

Aware of how time was marching on, she hurried to the kitchen and popped the rice into water to bring to the boil, before ripping open bags of nachos and depositing them into the four brightly coloured ceramic bowls they'd picked up at a market in Benalmádena one holiday, and which only saw the light of day on the rarest of occasions. Next she opened a can of Diet Coke and swigged some before hurling the rest down the sink. There was a half-bottle of red in the fridge, much of which she poured into the empty Coke can. This she could sip merrily as the evening unfolded. The sneakiness of her genius made her laugh, a moment of lightness in the storm.

Her phone rang.

'Save me some pudding.' Roz, she could tell, was yawning. Was she tired? Sicker? Weak? It took all of her strength not to bombard her with questions that threatened to smother. But they had agreed, *I can only deal with this and talk to you because you are an arsehole who isn't going to sob and suggest I go for an aromatherapy massage or take up Tai Chi. I need normal life.* Normal life, yes, this was what they had agreed. Emma closed her eyes and found a smile.

'Pudding? At this rate, they'll be lucky to get their first course. Anyway, Martha's bringing pudding. Chocolate brownies and vanilla ice cream.'

'Oooh lush, not sure which I fancy.'

'You can have both.' At this stage, Roz could literally live her life however she chose. And just like that, another thunderbolt of realisation that her friend was dying threatened to leave her winded.

'No, I don't like to dilute the taste of either,' Roz explained. 'I could have both, but it'd have to be in separate bowls.'

'I'd forgotten how fussy you are. In fact, you sound like my mother. Oh shit!'

'What have you done now?' There was the vague hint of amusement in her question.

'I was supposed to make Mum a mild chilli. No more than mince really, with the odd kidney bean lurking in it. But I was running late—'

'*Quelle surprise!*'

Emma ignored her. 'And I lobbed all the ingredients into the pot without thinking, and Reggie finished it off. I'll have to do her something different. There's fish fingers in the freezer.' She thought aloud. There were always fish fingers in the freezer.

'Why are you breathing like that?' Roz asked.

'Like what?'

'Like you're breathing in through your teeth, the way you do when you're in pain, giving birth or you're trying to be nice about Mackenzie, but you don't really mean it.'

'I've got something that stings in my eye, and yes, thanks for reminding me – about Mackenzie, fancy saying I wanted to see her!' She was about to launch into a mini tirade, detailing the woman's rudeness and the more than awkward encounter, when she heard the sound of a car on the driveway. 'It'll have to wait! Got to rush! Come later for pudding if you want! Love you!' She spoke quickly and ended the call.

Running back into the kitchen, she shoved four fish fingers under the grill and put the radio on, wanting Sergio to think they were a cool family who regularly danced in the kitchen to nineties vibes. The kind of family you saw on holiday adverts where they were all friends and went on great sunny vacations together. The kind of holiday where they laughed loudly, played fun games with a beach ball and were never covered in wet sand, arguing, trawling the streets with rumbling tums because they couldn't agree on what they wanted for supper or had neglected to book a table, and never did they have to ask their other half to dab aloe on their burnt bits. The kind of family with the kind of mother who never breathed a sigh of relief when the holiday was over and she could get back to the predictable mayhem of life at home and the stinky washing mountain that was an inevitable consequence of said disappointing break.

Brendan, however, managed to thwart her plans from afar and had tuned the radio into some heavy rock station, where the sound of screeching, a frantic drumbeat and the unpleasant twang of a guitar set her teeth on edge. She switched it off immediately; this was not the impression she wanted to give Martha's new man.

'Home!' Brendan called from the hallway.

'Just going to spend a penny, save me getting up later!' her mum yelled.

'Good idea! Don't lock the door!' her reply, as ever worried about any falls or emergencies. She heard the downstairs cloakroom door close and the sound of Brendan running up the stairs, no doubt to spray his pits and grab a clean shirt as she had done earlier.

The rice bubbled nicely on the range. After grabbing a couple of grains with a teaspoon, she bit into them, confirming they were not too firm, not too soft, not chalky and were actually fluffy! Quite possibly the best rice she had ever cooked! With her trusty tea towel, she lifted the heavy pot from the range and hoisted it over to the sink, tipping the rice awkwardly, and only when steam rose and the pot was empty did Emma realise that she had, in her distracted state, neglected to put the colander beneath the rice, which now sat in a white pillowy mountain on the base of the sink.

Shit!

A quick look over her shoulder, knowing she had only seconds to make the decision . . . and with no one around, she made it, using her hands to scoop the hot rice at the top of the pile back into the saucepan, blowing on and waving her toasty palms and leaving the thin layer of rice that was in actual contact with the surface of the sink where it lay.

'It'll be fine.' She whispered her self-justification. 'Five-second rule and all that. Plus, the sink is clean, haven't bleached it for a while, and I've only rescued rice that was on the top – and my hands aren't dirty. It'll be fine.' She placed a clean tea towel over the rice and set it to one side. At the sound of the flush, she went to retrieve her mother, who now loitered in the doorway of the loo.

'Something smells nice!' Her mother inhaled as Emma took her crooked arm into her own and guided her towards the sitting room, where the lamps were on, cushions plumped and her multi-wick candle flickered on the side table, providing a delicious scent, a bit of ambience, and it also meant that, along with the lamps, the lighting was low enough that Sergio might not notice the mayhem and clutter lurking behind the sofa and under the coffee table. 'I'm looking forward to my chilli!'

'Ah, about that.' She was about to explain her mess-up when she heard the key in the door. *Martha . . .*

And just this one sound, enough for all her doubts and worries over Lego, dust, rice, the lingering scent of fish in the dining room, even whether she'd remember the name of her daughter's new bloke – all of it gone, because that one sound meant Martha was home, her little girl back where she belonged, under their roof. There was nothing like having all her children in the same place, it was a particular joy! Having tucked her hair behind her ears, she pulled her shoulders back and walked confidently and not too quickly into the hallway. There was only a second between her taking in her pretty daughter with a bulky cool box, the tall, athletic frame of the handsome boy who held a bottle of wine and her daughter turning to face her before she heard Martha's rather alarmed scream.

'Sweet Jesus, Mother, what on earth!' she shouted. Loudly enough to alert Reggie and Alex, who came running down the stairs, Brendan too, who appeared in his denim shirt. If she hadn't been so distracted by Martha's yell, she'd have asked him to go and change, sincerely hoping Sergio would understand that theirs was an accidental twinning and not some weird middle-aged thing where couples slowly morphed into each other and went full matchy-matchy.

'What's the matter?' Emma stared at the faces of her family, who all stared back at her.

'Mum! What have you done to your face?' Martha looked horrified and repulsed in equal measure, touching her own eye to indicate where the problem lay as her mouth drooped with something close to disgust.

Quickly making her way into the downstairs cloakroom, Emma switched on the light and gasped at the sight that greeted her. Her shirt was sodden on one shoulder and down one side; her left eye was swollen, blotchy, red, and looked like she'd gone a couple of rounds with Rocky. Her hair was soaking wet and stuck flat to her head. Remnants of mascara on the other eye were smudged and sat in a racoon-like mask.

'Shall I get you some antihistamines?' Brendan crowded behind her.

'Yes, yes please, Brendan. That would be lovely.' Keeping as calm as she was able, she touched the outside of her eye and the sting pulsed. *Bloody Paddy!* She'd give him Armageddon when she next saw him.

It was as Emma further dabbed her eye with wet loo roll that she heard Martha say to her guest, 'Sorry about the mess.' And her heart squeezed.

Brendan was chattering in the way he did when he knew he had to hold the fort, make conversation, but was a little nervous.

'Good journey? Roads not too bad, I hope.'

'It was fine, Dad. I need to get this ice cream in the freezer.'

'I'll do it!' Alex the little keener piped up, and she knew this one action would simultaneously please Martha and irritate his big brother. Job done.

'Great to meet you, son. Better go get the wife's drugs!'

Emma closed her eyes briefly – had Brendan just called her *the wife*? And even higher on the cringe scale, had he just called

Martha's boyfriend *son?* Oh dear, that was what was known as committing too soon, jumping without looking to see what he might land on, and she thought *Alex* was a keener. She'd need to be a little cooler, restore the balance. Aware that she couldn't hide in the loo with her swollen face and soggy shirt for the whole evening, Emma painted on the most positive expression she could muster and went into the hallway to greet Martha and her guest properly.

With her arms open, forgetting all thoughts of coolness, she walked towards Sergio. 'Hello, love, welcome! I must say, we are not always in this kind of chaos.'

Reggie snickered behind her. She ignored him.

'Usually Friday nights are quite calm, but welcome nonetheless.'

'That's all right! Is just life innit?' The boy was sweet, bouncy even, and with the unmistakeable twang of an Essex accent.

'Your English is incredible!' It really was.

'Oh thanks!' the handsome boy beamed.

'Where are you from?' Emma enunciated, curious as to how he had become so fluent and swallowing the thought that she was a little disappointed not to hear the glorious rolling Italian accent she loved. Brendan appeared with a glass of water and two little white antihistamines, which she necked like a pro, realising in that moment that there'd be no wine for her tonight, not on top of these bad boys.

'Romford.' The boy handed her the bottle of wine, a crisp New Zealand white, according to the label.

'Thank you, Sergio, that's really kind.' She glanced at Martha, courting her attention, wanting some sort of recognition for getting his name right.

'Smashing.' Brendan relieved her of the bottle. 'This looks like a fruity little number.' He nodded sagely. Emma did her best to avoid Martha's eyeline.

'So, Romford?' She was a little confused, but also glad of the diversion. 'You moved there from Italy?'

Sergio's laugh was loud, hearty and endearing. 'Italy? No, I was born there, only ever lived in Romford until I moved to Bristol and that's where I met Marfs.'

Marfs . . .

'His family are Italian!' Martha cut in. 'Aren't they, Serge?'

'Well, yes, my great nan, way back. But I've never been. Not yet. It's on my list.'

'So, no sitting at the knee of your nonna learning how to make the best pasta in the world?' Emma gave a short laugh that verged on the hysterical.

'No.' The boy shook his head, clearly without the first clue about what she rambled, but obviously too polite to say so. 'My nan was more of a ready meal kind of cook. Or tacos. She made banging tacos!'

'Tacos. I see.' Again, she glanced at *Marfs . . .*

'Whose family are Italian?' Nanny Marge called from the sitting room.

'Better go and say hello to your nan.' Emma smiled sweetly at her daughter, just as the smoke alarm started pipping and the acrid smell of burnt fish fingers filled the hallway . . .

'Reggie, love,' she called over the din, as she made her way into the kitchen with some degree of urgency, plonking the wine on the side, 'can I borrow you?'

She pointed at the smoke alarm and her tall son reached up and grappled with the device, trying to press the button, as she pulled the blackened fish fingers from under the grill and dumped the whole tray, burnt grub and all, into the sink, where it landed with a clatter and made a sizzling noise as it stuck to the thin layer of rice beneath it.

Perfect.

Next she opened the windows and the back door, out of which Bruce darted, as if keen to escape, and some small part of Emma wished she could follow him. The halting of the alarm was most welcome. Wafting the tea towel towards the back door to dispel the smoke, she stared at Reggie. 'I hope we haven't gone overboard with the chillies.' She pulled a face. 'Don't want to injure anyone with our cooking. How many did you put in?'

'Erm, like, the whole bag . . .' Reggie pulled a wide-mouthed look of horror.

Her heart sank. 'Shall we open the pot and have a look?' Aware that her voice had taken on a reed-like quality, a forerunner to hysteria.

'Do you want me to taste it?' He looked almost gleeful in anticipation.

'That's probably a good idea.' Slowly, as she and Reggie gathered around the pot, and with great caution, she lifted the lid. Both shot backwards as the noxious fumes reached their noses and made them both splutter. 'Oh Reggie!' she gasped.

'What have we done?' He coughed and gripped his throat.

Emma laid her hand on his arm. 'I think the question should be, what on earth are we going to do?'

A mere forty minutes later and with appetites stoked by the wait, the whole family, along with their guest from Essex, sat around the dining-room table, each with a big bag of fish and chips spread out in front of them, reaching for the bottle of tomato ketchup and salt and vinegar as the usual hubbub and conversation flowed, just like any other Friday night.

Brendan beamed at her from the other end of the table, and she wondered if, like her, he'd been rattled at the expense of the takeaway, albeit a lovely treat. They still, after all, had a car to fix and a ski trip to fund. She also wondered if he, like her, noticed how Martha and Sergio held hands briefly under the table when the chance allowed, swapping long, lingering glances. There was a tenderness in it that made her feel quite emotional; maybe this time it *was* different, maybe Sergio was going to be sticking around. She hoped so, knowing that Martha deserved to find the same happiness she had.

'I like that I got the green plate, is it special or something? I noticed it's the only one, so I guessed it was like the VIP plate!' Sergio looked chuffed.

Emma deliberately ignored Martha's stare boring into the side of her swollen face. 'It absolutely *is* the VIP plate and you, Sergio, are most welcome.'

'So, you two are heading out tonight?' Brendan asked.

'Yep, I'm taking Serge to meet Layla and her bloke up the pub.'

Emma knew it would be important for her daughter to show off her new boy to her school friend. Her thoughts went to Roz, thinking of when they were the same age and going to the pub was everything, and all the adventures that had followed. The rise of tears in her throat she swallowed with a big gulp of water, not wanting here and now to be when she broke the news to her daughter that her beloved Auntie Roz was poorly again. More than poorly . . .

'I'm looking forward to it,' the boy enthused. 'You've got a good chippy!' He shoved a chip into his mouth.

'I had intended to cook for you.' She coughed to clear her throat.

'But luckily that went belly up and here we are!' Brendan lifted his glass of wine in a toast.

The boys laughed. Even Martha raised a smile.

Emma sipped her water, thankful that the swelling on her eye seemed to have gone down a little. Despite a slightly rocky start, the evening seemed to be going well. Her mother tucked into her cod, which Emma had cut up for her.

'How long have you been Martha's boyfriend?' Alex asked and Emma's heart skipped, wondering where he might be heading with this line of questioning.

'Three months.' Sergio responded with energy, as if this was some achievement, and she liked him even more.

'And do you think,' Alex began, 'that you'll still—'

'Alexander, please,' she cut in, trying to halt whatever might have been coming out of her younger son's mouth next. 'Can we let Sergio eat without being given the third degree? Why don't you tell him about your ski trip?'

Brendan pulled a face, indicating a) that she must be desperate to change the topic if that was her subject of choice and b) that he was still not overly pleased about her condoning the trip they could not afford. Her jaw tensed.

Reggie put his fork down. 'Oh please, not the ski trip again! "I'm going skiing with the other idiots at my very expensive school."' He mimicked his brother's well-spoken voice.

Alex's cheeks flamed. 'Shut up, Reggie! You think you're so clever, but it wasn't me who got catfished by a hairy Slovakian who asked for a photograph of my bollocks!'

'Language, please, Alex. Say sorry to your nan.' Her heart jumped. Surely it wasn't true?

'Sorry, Nan,' Alex mumbled.

Nanny Marge took a sip of her drink. 'I don't know if you can say "hairy Slovakian" – is that racist? I never know nowadays. It's all changed since my day, not sure what's allowed and what isn't.'

It left Emma speechless – this from her mother, who was not typically concerned with what was politically correct.

Brendan sat up straight. 'I think saying hairy Slovakian is okay. But to be honest, I'm more interested in Reggie's bollocks.'

'Eeuuw, Dad! Nasty!' Martha pulled a face.

'You know what your dad means.' She was glad he was raising it, as her pulse quickened at the thought that Reggie might be involved in something so ghastly.

'You're such a prick, Alex!'

'Language, please, Reggie. Say sorry to your nan!' she barked, making a face of wide-eyed apology to Sergio, who seemed to be stifling laughter.

'Sorry, Nan,' Reggie murmured from the side of his mouth.

'You haven't sent photos like that, have you, Reg?' she asked tenderly, knowing that if he had, they needed to tread gently.

Her son shrugged and muttered 'No', which was not quite the strong denial she had been quietly praying for.

'Thank God for that!' Martha shook her head.

'And Alex thinks he's so clever, but it's not me who lies to his friends about where we live. I heard him tell them we were on the other side of town, up near the church.'

'Why would you lie about where we live?' Emma was perplexed.

Alex toyed with a chip.

And then with a flash of anger it dawned on her: this wasn't the first time her son had shown such disdain for their hard-won life. Brendan, she noted, sat tall in his chair, as if he could have called this. 'I'm happy that you have the chance to go to Reynard's College, Alex, I really am.' Emma hoped he knew this. 'I want you to fly! I want you to become all the things that you are capable of, and I want you to be happy. But let me be clear – if you ever, ever lie to your mates about where we live, how we live or who we are, then I will whip you out of that fancy blazer quicker than you can say "Anyone for lacrosse?" Do you understand me?'

Alex nodded, and instantly she regretted speaking so plainly in front of Sergio.

'Are you ashamed of us?' Brendan asked for them both. It seemed he too had forgotten that they were supposed to be on their best behaviour, or at least a little guarded in front of their guest.

Alex stared at the tabletop.

'What's going on, mate?' her husband pushed, and she felt a little sorry for her youngest, even though it was her who had started the boulder rolling.

Alex spoke up. 'I just know that Dimitri and Piers have really big houses and stuff. And our house is shitty.'

Emma looked around their dining room with the clutch of ornaments and knick-knacks on the shelves and windowsills, given to her by the kids over the years. Martha put her fork down; it seemed Sergio was getting the full Fountain family experience, whether he wanted it or not.

'Our house might be small, but it's not shitty. There's more to a home than the number of bricks in it. This is a happy house, a house full of love and a place you can be safe, and that's everything.' Brendan spoke eloquently.

'I get that, Dad, it's just that I'd really like a big garden and a hot tub and a games room.'

'Did you not hear a single word your dad said?' Emma cut in, wanting to support Brendan as well as set Alex straight.

'Yes, but—'

'No buts, Alex! Bloody games room! I'm sure your mother would like a washing machine that doesn't break down every five minutes and a cupboard just for coats, so you don't have to pile them up on the floor, and a spare bra! Bloody games room!' Having spoken her mind, Nanny Marge put her can of drink down before stifling a belch. '*You* once made out we were Catholic and went to that youth club over at St Dunstan's.' The latter she addressed directly to Emma.

'That was because I fancied someone who went there. And Roz said it was the easiest way to get to know him.' She glanced awkwardly at Sergio, and then Brendan. 'I was thirteen!'

'Was it that Henderson boy from swimming? I thought you liked him!' Nanny Marge was on form.

'No, Mum. It was Father Sean. I'd just read *The Thorn Birds* and he set me all of a dither.'

'I'd have been a bit less worried if I'd known it was him you had eyes for.'

'Well, you shouldn't have been less worried. He ran off with Janey Unite, who was two years above me. They now live out Weston-super-Mare way and have four kids. I saw him in Tesco. Didn't look half as alluring in a zip-up cardi.'

'Your dad liked a zip-up cardi.' Nanny Marge smiled fondly.

Her mum picked up her fork as Martha reached over and squeezed her nan's arm affectionately.

Emma stared at Sergio, wondering if he might make his excuses and bolt. She was certain this was not what he'd had in mind when Martha sold him the idea of a quiet family dinner.

An awkward silence descended over the table while Nanny Marge smacked her lips together, again devouring her battered cod with relish. Emma and Brendan exchanged a knowing look; she guessed that, like her, he was worried about Reggie's love interest and Alex's dim view of their family achievements. They'd deal with them calmly, later, the way they did most things. No matter what else was going on, the kids unified their thoughts.

It was her mother who broke the silence.

'I don't understand about cats and fishing, but I know when your dad was away at sea for long spells, it was hard for us both.'

Emma nodded, hoping to reassure her mother but also to give her the hint that maybe such a maudlin topic might not be the best for Sergio in his first introduction to a family supper. The poor lad had already had to deal with her swollen eye, Reggie's bollocks, the dodgy plate and a distinct lack of home-cooked food.

'Yes, he was, Mum. Doing his bit. Keeping us all safe.'

Her mother took a glug from her can. 'I used to send him pictures of me in my knickers, to keep him going like.'

Brendan put his cutlery down. 'For the love of God! If that hasn't put me off my chips . . .'

'That's nice, Mum. Eat your tea!' She nodded at her mother through gritted teeth.

'I didn't send the pictures. And anyway,' Reggie piped up, speaking through a mouth full of ketchup-covered chip, 'he wasn't Slovakian, he was Bulgarian. And he said his name was Katie and that he lived in Wolverhampton.'

'And if you'd gone to an expensive school like mine, full of idiots, you might have known that it was a catfish!'

Emma hated not only that her kids were bickering, the topic familiar, but also that both of her boys were aware of this phenomenon. Again she took surreptitious glances at Martha and Sergio, still ridiculously concerned with how the evening was panning out, while mortified that her son had nearly got mixed up in such a thing.

'Yes, you're right, Alex, that's the issue here,' Reggie railed, 'that I'm just too stupid to realise that of course any girl that shows an interest in me must be a hairy bloke trying to blackmail me, because what girl in their right mind would want to get to know me? You're right, Alex, I must be an idiot!'

'That's not what Alex was saying, I'm sure.' She gave her youngest a stare of laser-like intensity, knowing that yet again they would have the conversation about him being mean to his big brother and how it just wasn't funny. 'Plenty of girls will want to get to know you, love.' She thought she was saying the right thing, but no sooner had the words left her mouth than Reggie pushed his plate away and stormed from the room.

Brendan lifted his hand, indicating for her to stay put, as if able to predict that her first thought was to rush up the stairs to try and placate their boy. Smiling briefly at the assembled, he abandoned his supper and followed Reggie. Martha grabbed Sergio's hand and held it tight.

'I made him promise,' Emma's mum stated loudly, 'I made him promise not to show his crew mates the pictures. Can you imagine' – she laughed loudly, banging the table with the flat of her palm – 'if I'd met the ossifer . . . ossifer . . .' She tried and failed twice to say the word correctly. 'The man in charge – at a works do, and all the time he'd seen me in my slinkies!'

'Nan, are you *drunk*?' Martha asked the direct question Emma had been wondering how best to voice. Her pulse raced and she felt a swarmy heat rise up over her chest.

'How dare you!' Nanny Marge boomed. 'I have not touched a drop since Charles and Diana's wedding! It was a fairy tale of magnisifent proportions. Long live the King!' The way her mother lifted her can and listed in her chair suggested otherwise.

It was in that moment that realisation dawned, and Emma grabbed her mother's can of Diet Coke. One quick sniff confirmed that she'd necked the equivalent of just under half a bottle of red, which for a dab hand like herself would not be that disastrous, especially if she spread it out over an evening, but for her mother, who was not and never had been a regular drinker, it was another matter entirely.

'Oh, Mum!' Emma felt a wave of guilt wash over her.

'Matron, make mine a toasted teacake! And go fetch the horses!' her mother shouted for no apparent reason, which sent Alex into paroxysms of laughter.

Sergio, she noted, held his fork aloft, loaded up with food, but he was seemingly unsure of whether it was the polite thing to keep eating while the pantomime that was their family life raged around him.

Emma pictured the big skies, fresh air and peace and quiet where her new friend Thurston lived and tried to imagine being away from the chaos. As a proposition, it was, in that moment, more than tempting.

Twenty minutes later, taking refuge in the downstairs loo, hiding as was her MO, she picked up her phone, deciding to text her friend, seeking what? Advice? Comfort? To initiate contact? All three, probably . . .

CHAPTER TWENTY-FOUR

THURSTON

Thurston had a gnawing feeling deep in the pit of his stomach and a jump in his veins. The impact of his drunken scribblings on his sister had certainly affected him, but enough to change his mind entirely about taking his life? He wasn't sure, still thinking that the stay of execution might be best, but no more than a delay. Of one thing he was certain – this feeling of agitation was down to unfinished business knocking on his conscience. It had been the same when Loftus once accused their dad, who had missed a school rugby match in which Loftus had a starring role, of putting profit before family life. It was Thurston who had, across all seasons, watched the man work like a dog, and who had seen his dad nearly weep for all he missed while putting in the hours. Yet he'd bitten his tongue and said nothing, not wanting to upset his little brother or cause friction in the family.

After a month of feeling similar to how he felt now, as if his integrity and moral compass were uncomfortably misaligned, he had felt obligated to speak out. And speak out he had, detailing across the dinner table how he felt his brother had been wrong to say such things and why . . . shortly before the two had rolled around on the ground in the front yard, and after Loftus had tried to punch his older brother on the nose. Regardless of the sore, split lip and the bruised elbow and ego that Thurston sported the next morning, not to mention the ire of their mother, who threatened to 'box your ears and smack you both around the head with the old frying skillet if you ever resort to violence again', the irony of her threat not lost on them either, the gnawing feeling in his gut and jittery blood flow disappeared immediately. This, he knew, was the feeling that came with doing and saying the right thing, of making sure he was true to himself, his own man, who spoke plainly and could hold his head up. With this in mind, he grabbed his car keys and set off.

'Shan't be long, Barb.'

Parking in front of the vicarage, he pulled on the handbrake and walked briskly to the front door. He knocked and stood back. His mouth felt a little dry. The vicar's welcome was lukewarm; clearly he too had not forgotten their last meeting, when he'd left Merrydown Farm with empty pockets and no promise of a fat cheque towards his trip to Brazil.

'Mr Brancher, good evening.' Thurston noted the invoking of his surname and took this as a sign that they were on less than cordial terms, which was fine with him.

'Vicar.'

'How can I help you?' The man's clipped tone bothered him as much as the words of their last conversation. It spoke of petulance, and when the reason for that petulance was a lack of incoming cash, it bothered him even more.

'Thought it best to come and see you, as I've got things on my mind.'

'I see.' The man rocked on his heels.

'Do you know that feeling when something feels unresolved, and it hovers in your thoughts and stops you nodding off at night, and sneaks up on your brain at different times, but enough to be an annoyance, like a small pebble in your shoe?'

'I think I do, yes.' The vicar tilted his head, whether curious or impatient it was hard to tell.

'Good. I have three things that I'd like to say. Need to say.'

'Do you want to come inside? I have a fire in the study.' He stood back as if to allow Thurston to pass.

'That's very kind, but no. I can say what I need to right here.' Thurston swallowed, his bravado wavered, but he dug deep and forged ahead. 'First thing: don't get drunk at someone's funeral. I didn't like to see you knocking back whisky and then port, filling your small mouth with savoury fancies, Scotch egg dropping down your cassock, when you were there to officiate and offer comfort to your flock. It felt wrong somehow to see you on the wrong side of sober.'

'I most certainly was not—'

'The second thing . . .' Thurston cut him short, holding up his index finger, keen not to give him a chance to refute his claims. 'The second thing is that I didn't take kindly to you asking for cash, a contribution of money, when my wife, Mary, who loved your bloody church faithfully, is barely cold. I thought it was the most disrespectful thing imaginable. And I shan't forget it. Not ever.'

'I didn't mean to cause offence, I . . . I simply thought because Mary—'

'And finally . . .' Again Thurston interrupted the man, whose face coloured red, whether with anger or shame, he really didn't care. He did his best to keep his voice steady. 'I loved my wife, and she loved me. Very, very much. And I am shattered, completely destroyed by her passing. I'm lost, so lost and lonely. You talk about faith, and you talk about everlasting life, and you talk all kinds of things, but I know, I *know*' – he raised his shaking fist – 'that if there was any way that woman, who was by my side for sixty-two years, could let me know she was okay, could give me a hint that we'd be together again one day, she would. She absolutely would!' He took a moment to calm his breathing. 'But she hasn't, not a whisper in my ear, not a hand on my cheek, not so much as a wave from the bedroom window! Nothing! Why is that? Why? If life is everlasting and she is not gone, as you say, why has she not done that? Because I'm telling you, vicar, we were one heart, one spirit, and if she could, in any way, let me know she was okay, give me that wave, she bloody well would! Do you understand me? And so, I don't want to hear another mention of it. Have I made myself clear?'

The vicar nodded as his feet shifted on the step, his look one of concern as he watched Thurston climb into the cab of his truck and drive away. Despite the tremble to his limbs, he noted that for the first time since the vicar's visit, his thoughts seemed a little calmer.

The exchange had left him almost jubilant, fired up! It had stoked the embers of life. Taking a seat at the kitchen table, he placed his hands flat on the tabletop. Rhubarb lay across his foot.

'Good boy, Barbie.' Picturing the wide beam of the barn and the plan that he had formed, the date looming, left him feeling a little torn. The exchange with the vicar was a reminder of the force of life, the power of living, and yet he'd never wanted the peace of escape so badly! This, combined with June's reaction, added a new layer of complexity, guilt to the idea.

The euphoria he had previously felt at the thought of escape was replaced with a judder of doubt.

His mobile phone, charging on the countertop, beeped. A rarely used item that his wife had insisted he carry when out and about, but one he'd never really got the hang of. Thank goodness it wasn't one of those button-free, smooth-faced objects he found hard to grip, let alone the newfangled technology that was all swipes and taps. He had previously watched Nancy's thumbs flying over an invisible keyboard with such dexterity it had made him feel very old; just another facet of how the world had left him behind.

The little envelope in the corner told him he had received a text. This in itself a rarity. A text from Emma, no less!

He held the little screen at arm's length and squinted, to better make out the words as he read aloud:

'Hello Thurston, been thinking about what you said about being lonely. I hope you know that you can pick up the phone any time if you want a chat.'

He meant to reply via text, decided to have a bash at forming words – figuring out the three letters that were stamped on each button, how hard could it be? He knew Mary would be proud of his efforts, given he'd never been at ease with technology. His square finger pushed a button, and it was as he stared at the screen, trying to work out what came next, that he heard a small voice asking, 'Hello? Hello? Are you there, Thurston?'

'Emma!' With the phone now at his ear, he could hear clearly and cringed. It was as if he'd called in response to her message saying he *could* call. 'I've just received your text message! I was trying to tap out a reply, but it seems I've called you. That wasn't my intention at all!'

'That's fine, Thurston. I meant it, call any time!'

'Well, that's very kind, but I don't want you to think I've called too keenly.' He found it hard to voice his embarrassment, aware he might actually be making the situation worse.

'I think we might be overthinking this.'

'We might be. Anyway, it was lovely to hear from you, to get your text.' And it was. 'How did you get my number?'

'Nancy! Hope that was okay?'

'Yes, of course.'

'Hope it's not too late.' She sounded a little flustered. 'I do that, fire off texts and calls without thinking. I always assume that if I'm up and running around then the rest of the world must be too.'

He smiled. 'I'm not exactly running around, but I'm certainly awake. The curse of a busy mind and a quiet evening.'

'God, Thurston, I would've given anything for a quiet evening, it's been . . .'

She sounded a little mournful.

'Are you okay, Emma?'

'Well, I'm thoughtful, hiding in the downstairs loo if you must know, while my mum searches for her coat so I can run her home. My mum who is a little sloshed, to put it mildly. The kids have bickered and shown the real us, warts and all, to my daughter Martha's new boyfriend, who I so wanted to impress. Martha and her new man have now escaped to the pub, not that I blame them. I cooked inedible food, and we ended up going to the chippy, so I guess I am okay, but it certainly wasn't the evening I pictured. And all that while smiling so hard my cheeks hurt when what I really wanted to do was howl, beat my fists and cling on to Roz while I can. My beautiful friend . . .'

It was painful for him to hear her voice break.

'Sorry, Thurston, don't know why I find it so easy to offload on to you, but I do.'

'Don't be sorry, I'm quite honoured.'

'It's like . . . it's like I have a picture of Roz behind my eyelids and every time I blink, I see her telling me the news and my heart twists with hurt.'

He closed his eyes and mirrored her action, seeing his wife and hearing the nurse whispering in his ear, *You can let go of her hand now, Mr Brancher . . . she's gone . . .*

'I more than understand that,' he mused. 'I'm thoughtful too.'

'What's at the top of your thoughts?'

He liked her direct manner. It encouraged him to reply in kind without sanitising or overthinking his reply; the words shot from his mouth without a care for the consequences. 'I've been weighing up whether to leave or whether to stay.'

'Leave where?' She sounded perplexed.

His hesitation in replying indicated to Emma that perhaps he had not heard and so she repeated, 'Leave where, Thurston?'

The reality of discussing something so pertinent left him foundering. *The planet . . . the earth . . . this life . . .* He tested the response in his head and thought better of it; Emma was, after all, a relative stranger, no matter how good a listener, plus he didn't want to put this maudlin thought into his new friend's already busy mind.

'Whether to leave Merrydown Farm and move into one of those fancy clean apartments for old people.' He closed his eyes as he lied.

'Oh, like The Maltings on the other side of the town?'

'Yes.'

'Well, I think they look lovely. My mother, however, is not so keen, calls places like that death's waiting room . . .' She stopped short, clearly aware, as was he, that death was a topic very close to their hearts. His, more than she knew. She rallied. 'It might be hard to give up all that space and fresh air.'

'It might,' he conceded. 'I suppose I find it harder than I let on, being here, just being,' he whispered.

'Just being can be hard, too hard sometimes.' She spoke softly, understanding.

There was a beat of silence that crackled between them as he struggled to follow up on his admission, which had come out of nowhere.

'Anyway, best let you get on, you can't hide in the loo all night.' He closed his eyes.

'Sadly, you're right!'

She made him laugh, a pocket of joy in which he could rest awhile.

'Night, Thurston.'

'Yes, night night.'

He sat in the darkened kitchen and let their conversation settle.

'Is it that you're a coward, Thurston?' he asked aloud. 'Don't have the mettle to see it through?' It was a real question to which he didn't know the answer. 'I don't know, Mary. I just want to get to you, see you, to know you're okay, that's all. I need to know you'll be there for me . . . my sweet, sweet love.'

Rhubarb, seemingly in tune with his master's emotional wrangling, pawed at Thurston's leg, a reminder that he was there, his four-legged boy.

CHAPTER TWENTY-FIVE

Emma

With her mother successfully dropped home, it was nearing bed-time when Emma let herself back into the house and stood in the kitchen. Brendan was scraping leftover chips into the food recycling bin and lobbing small bits of fish into Brucie's mouth when he thought no one was looking. It was quite standard; he couldn't resist the lure of those puppy-dog eyes. She put the lid tightly on the chocolate brownies. It was a shame that after all Martha's efforts, not only in the cooking but also the transportation of the puddings, the whole gang had been too full of fish and chips to even consider dessert. Sergio promised to tuck in when he got back from the pub, and she had no doubt that the kids would polish off the brownies over the course of the weekend. With the evening firmly behind her and all that could have gone wrong, gone wrong, she took her foot off the mental gas pedal. With the calm that followed, her thoughts, as they did during any gap in her hectic schedule, turned to Roz. So many end-of-evening chats after dinner parties, so many plans to meet up the day after to debrief. The quiet of the room was now a reminder that this was how it would be without her, and Emma's heart felt shredded.

'How's your mum doing, the old lush!'

Emma tried to match Brendan's jovial tone, to join in.

'She sang loudly all the way back to her house and even yelled up to Mr Blundesthorpe's bedroom window that the night was young, while I wrestled her into the house.'

'Oh no.' She could tell by his expression he didn't know whether to laugh or commiserate.

'I feel really bad, Bren. I got my mother drunk!'

'Well, not exactly. It's not like you force-fed her vodka – she picked up the wrong can.'

'Yes, but I'm still responsible. She takes tablets, it could have been dangerous.'

'Is it dangerous?' The look on his face told her he hadn't considered this less than comedic angle.

'No, not really. I asked Roz, who nearly wet herself laughing. She said it's not to be recommended and that she might be a bit fuzzy-headed in the morning, but no harm done. I also reminded her that she was going to pop in for pudding. I just want to see her, all the time.' She let this settle, feeling the turn of her stomach at the thought of not having her friend around to pop in. 'She said she might, but it was late and that I needed to worry less.' *Easy said* . . .

'Well, there you go. And for the record, I think your mum's had the time of her life, love.' He put the VIP green plate on the work surface and came over to wrap her in his arms.

'Mmm, not sure she'll see it that way tomorrow when I have to explain what happened. Just praying her hangover isn't too much. Poor old thing.'

'What's your plan for tomorrow?'

'I think I might nip over and drop a couple of puzzles off to my new farmer friend.' She yawned. 'He's lonely, Bren, struggling, and I can't stand it. Mum likes the odd jigsaw, so I thought I'd pass on ones she's completed. I'll go get her up and settled for the day, maybe take the boys, then head over. We won't stay or anything, but I just want him to know he has us, as well as his family. He's lovely, Bren. I feel drawn to him.' She recalled their brief chat earlier.

'Drawn to him, eh?' He mock-scowled at her. 'At least you'll have the boys with you if he starts any funny business.'

'Funny business?' She pulled away and looked into the face of her man, unsure if he was joking. 'He's a hundred and four!'

'I hope I've still got fire in my veins at one hundred and four.' She admired his optimism as he nuzzled her neck. 'Mind you, that won't be too difficult if I'm married to a firecracker like you.'

This a welcome moment of reconnection. An apology for the tension, the sniping, the fishing gear abandoned in the dining room, all now behind them, a chance to move forward into calmer waters. It was their way.

'Firecracker? I am at best, right now, a damp squib. A damp squib with a slightly swollen face.'

'You're still beautiful.'

'Oh, stop it!' She never did handle compliments well, especially when she could see they were more than likely just a ploy to achieve sex, which they were already on track for, so he could cut the schmooze.

'No, I won't stop it. You're my wife and I don't tell you enough. I love being married to you and you are beautiful.'

Wondering if her cynicism was a little misplaced, she relaxed against him.

'Plus, Martha's out, the boys are asleep . . .'

Her conversation with Roz about scheduling sex came to mind, no topic off limits, her best, best friend. How she would miss her!

'Do you ever think about how it was before we had kids, when we had more free time, more free cash . . .' She hated to bring up money at a time like this, but it was on her mind.

'I love our life. I wouldn't swap one thing. Not one. We have a great time really, Em, even with all our ups and downs.'

'Tonight was a bit of both.' She laughed. 'Can't believe we served Sergio fish and chips!'

'I like him. I really do.' Her husband's thoughts mirrored her own. 'But right now, I don't want to talk about the kids or anything else, for that matter. I just want you.'

Their kissing was passionate and exciting, in the way it always was at rare moments like this when time and planets aligned, giving them this glorious opportunity for reconnection.

'I love you, Bren.'

'I love you.'

Gripping her hand, he trod the stairs with the perfect mixture of urgency and stealth, so as not to wake the kids, nor waste a second more. Weirdly, in her state of concern over all that ailed her and with a heart broken by her beloved Roz's illness, she wanted the escape of the pure physical act that bound them. Happy to slip into another world where her body led the dance, just for a while.

The bedroom was dark. Tonight, in their haste, there was none of the usual ritual around bedtime, no cleaning of teeth, no putting on of pyjamas, no brushing of hair or the removal of make-up. No turning back the duvet, no double-checking the locks and windows, no letting Bruce out to do his business; all of this, she knew, would happen after. *After* . . . and it was what came next that made her heart race in anticipation. It felt like a glorious gift to still desire him in this way after all this time.

Emma shrugged off her denim shirt and hopped on to the mattress. Brendan did the same, and the two fell giggling into a lovely jumble, where the scent and feel of him was familiar and very welcome as the perfect distraction from the busiest of weeks. All chores and worries slipped from her mind as she allowed herself to get lost in the moment. She'd missed him. Missed this.

It was as their kissing intensified, and her hand roamed, a precursor for what would follow, that she felt her husband's arms stiffen and his torso grow rigid beneath her chest. This accompanied by an unwelcome and uncharacteristic silence . . .

What happened next had not been in her plan. Not at all.

With all his strength, Brendan shoved her forcefully away from him, a move that sent her flying into the headboard, before he crashed across the bed and reached for the lamp, which he knocked to the floor. She caught her breath, her brain taking a second longer than her body to understand the physical rejection. It was an act as out of character as it was jarring. Her thoughts raced, unable to make sense of what had just happened. Thankfully, the boys didn't stir. Jumping up, she switched on the big light and retrieved her shirt from the floor, slipping her arms into it.

Brendan looked . . . odd. His face red, his mouth twisted, and when he spoke it seemed to take supreme effort to get the words out.

'What's going on? What's the matter? Speak to me!' She tried to whisper, loudly, no mean feat, understanding now that there was something unfathomable and odd going on.

His response was no more than a faint whimpering, before he stood and she watched him hop from foot to foot, fanning his body, or rather his groin, with his hand.

'What in the name of God have you done to me? Have you pulled it off?' He stared ahead, as if unable to take a glance at the area of his body where pain clearly emanated.

'What? No! Of course not! What are you talking about?' Realization dawned as she asked the question, watching as he tried to form words with tears gathering in his eyes.

'Sweet mother of Betsy, it's burning!'

'Oh shit! Oh Brendan, it'll be the chillies! The Armageddons!'

'Armageddons? Well, there's a bloody clue in the title if ever we needed one!'

'Come into the bathroom, quickly. I'll wash your willy.'

Brendan grabbed his dressing gown from the back of the door and she bundled him along the landing into the bathroom. With the cold tap running, she cupped water into her hands as her husband stared at her.

'How the hell am I supposed to get my bits and pieces under the cold tap? What am I, a contortionist?'

A quick look at the logistics and she understood that this was not possible. Not one to give up, however, she threw the dribble of water in her palm in the general direction of the affected area.

'Oh my God!' he shouted, and she felt his pain; this, and she was worried about the boys coming to investigate.

'I'll run a cold bath!' She wished they'd sped up the bathroom renovations and had that shower put in.

'That'll take too long! Jesus, Em! It's killing me! Do something!' His eyes were streaming.

'I'm thinking! Shall I get Roz?'

'I'm not showing Roz my willy! No way!' he winced and simultaneously barked.

'Don't be daft, she's a nurse, she's seen lots of willies. Plus, even if she wasn't a nurse – she's seen lots of willies!'

Brendan, whether in fear of her plan or taking action, hobbled down the stairs.

'Ice!' he murmured. 'I need ice!'

Following him quickly, she arrived to find him staring into the freezer.

'We've got no ice!' he cried, his tone now quite desperate.

She clicked her fingers. 'Frozen peas! Yes, frozen peas are the answer!'

Watching as he limped slowly from foot to foot, still fanning his nether regions like that might offer relief, she urgently scanned the shelves.

'I can't see any peas!' She glanced at Brendan, who was decidedly red in the face.

'Sweetcorn? Anything? Jesus, Em!'

'Erm . . . sweetcorn?' It was as if her mind went blank as she stared at the boxes of pizzas, leftover suppers wrapped in foil, blocks of butter and a whole set of empty lolly moulds. 'Brendan, I don't know what to do!'

Barging her out of the way in his need to get somewhere cold, he grabbed the first plastic box he could reach and whipped off the lid.

And it was at this exact moment that Martha and Sergio walked in via the back door, only to find Emma with her shirt undone. And Brendan, the man of the house, with one leg up on a kitchen chair, red-faced and with his willy and associated dangly bits plunged deep into the tub of vanilla soft scoop, lovingly crafted and transported with such care by their daughter.

'What in the name of God?' Martha shouted, which of course woke Reggie and Alex, who came running down the stairs and into the kitchen.

Brandan crouched as far as he was able out of view.

'Sorry, Martha, it's the first thing I reached. It's helping.'

Martha's mouth moved but no words came out and this seemed to be the state for the similarly stunned boys, who stared open-mouthed at the spectacle.

It was Sergio who spoke, breaking the silence and providing a little light relief.

'Thinking about it, Marfs, I've changed my mind. Don't think I fancy pudding after all.'

And if her husband hadn't been so incapacitated and the whole situation so bloody awful, Emma might just have kissed the boy.

◆ ◆ ◆

With antihistamines administered and a compress of a towel soaked in cold water offering relief, she and Brendan both agreed it was time for bed. It had been a long, long day.

'I'm so sorry, love. I feel awful.'

'We'll laugh about it one day.' He took her hand. 'But not today.'

'No.' She squeezed his fingers inside her own before letting Bruce out for his final pee.

Taking a moment to look up at the dark sky, she tried to imagine what Sergio might tell his family about Martha's insane relatives and their antics. What was it Thurston had said? *You can't do everything, and you can't fix everything. Sometimes, you need to ask for help.*

Emma wondered if she was part of the problem, trying to hold on so tightly, to steer the ship. Was the answer to loosen her grip a little, and let things be . . .

With the house locked up, they made their way up the stairs, reaching the top landing just as Martha stormed out of her room, closely followed by her beau.

'This family is the worst!' she screamed. 'Why do I bother coming home at all? Everything is a disaster! And all I wanted was one nice evening to show Sergio how normal we are, but we aren't! We aren't normal!'

Her daughter's words were cutting, considering how hard Emma had tried to pull everything together at the eleventh hour, the worry she had wasted on making a plan.

Brendan slipped into the bathroom, whether to avoid Martha's rant or tend to business in his nether regions, it was hard to tell.

'Speak for yourself!' Reggie replied through his bedroom door.

'Urgh!' Martha looked fit to burst.

'Take a deep breath, Martha,' Emma began.

'Take a deep breath?' she screeched. 'We had fish and chips for tea when you promised you'd cook something decent, Nan got sloshed, and then we come home to find Dad with his knob in the pudding and now this! What is *wrong* with you people?' Martha began crying on the landing, her shoulders heaving in great sobs.

It tore at Emma's heart; she understood more than most the need for everything to be neat, organised, and for her vision to come to fruition, and the inevitable disappointment that flared when it didn't. It was a pressure she could see was as unnecessary as it was hard to achieve, this laced with guilt that Martha might only be emulating her own unachievable quest to control everything.

'Don't cry. Please don't cry!' Sergio rubbed her back. 'It doesn't matter.'

'Doesn't matter?' Martha sniffed. 'One nice evening so you guys could get to know each other, just one!' She turned to face Emma. 'And you couldn't even be bothered to get a white plate!' Her tears fell down her cheeks, fat and clear and leaving her eyes bloodshot.

'What's going on?' Reggie came out on to the landing wearing none other than Rico's rugby shirt, which only encouraged Martha to cry harder.

'Is this your idea of a joke too, Reggie?' She pointed at the shirt. 'Because it's not funny! None of it is!'

'I've no idea what you're talking about, you silly cow!' Reggie yelled.

'Don't talk to your sister like that, Reggie, please, you're not helping!' Emma did her best to calm the situation.

'Who did that to my bed, who?' Martha shouted now, and Alex, who had appeared on the crowded landing with hair mussed and squinting without his glasses, looked a little sheepish.

'Who did what to your bed, Martha?' Emma was finding it hard to figure out exactly what offence had been committed.

Brendan suddenly wailed from the bathroom, 'What the bloody hell?'

Emma, Martha and the boys chose to ignore his cries for fear of what they might witness next.

'This!' Martha marched to her bedroom and threw open the door, to reveal her bed with the quilt pulled back and the mattress covered with Lego in various shapes and sizes.

Emma stared at her youngest, feeling a little beaten and wishing that everyone would do a bit more to make her life, and theirs, easier. Part of her new resolution to loosen her grip and not try so hard was definitely to train her kids better, make them more self-sufficient and not so bloody inconsiderate.

'You said get rid of it till they'd gone! You said put it anywhere! You said hide it, so I did!'

Brendan opened the door and ran across the landing with a towel around his waist, quickly followed by Roz, who it seemed had a fancy for that pudding after all.

'Honestly, Bren, I don't know what you're so flustered about, it's nothing I haven't seen before, or at least one very like it!' She turned to the assembled on the landing. 'Hello, Marthamoo – oh!' She stepped forward. 'You must be Sergio! Lovely to meet you.'

'Were you hiding in the bathroom with my dad?' Martha looked ready to bawl again.

'No, love, just arrived on a ladder. Didn't realise he was examining his bits and pieces with your mum's make-up mirror. Not sure who was more shocked, him or me!'

Despite the unfolding drama, and the beat of fatigue, Emma's heart lifted at the sight of her mate, who had obviously arrived in her less than orthodox manner. Sergio, Emma noted, looked from one family member to another, and she wondered if he was going to bolt.

Martha did indeed burst into tears.

'Don't cry, baby girl!' Roz cooed.

'It's her hormones!' Sergio explained with a deep sigh, as he pulled her close.

'Is she going through the menopause?' Alex asked. 'I've been learning about it in school.'

Emma and Roz laughed at each other in the way they did when it verged on hysteria; that and to hear the little one even say the word 'menopause' was funny. And with her laughter, Emma felt any remaining angst slip from her bones. This was the answer: to laugh more, care less, to let go! Because she could not fix everything.

'Good for you, bud! Learning about that! Super proud!' Emma meant it, but still she giggled a little with Roz.

Sergio clicked his fingers and looked skyward, as if that was where the right words might be lurking. 'No, no, not menopause, different hormones, I guess, because she's pregnant. Marfs is pregnant. She's twelve weeks pregnant.'

And as all gathered on the landing fell silent, Brendan stuck his head out of the bedroom door, his face now quite ashen.

Emma stopped laughing.

CHAPTER TWENTY-SIX

THURSTON

Freshly shaved but still in his pyjama bottoms, Thurston was tired, having chased his thoughts around for much of the night, writing a mental list with two columns – one with all the reasons to stay, and one with the only two reasons to go: to find peace and the possibility of reunion with Mary, that was it. The 'stay' list, however, having grown from the smallest seed, had started to sprout and was a little more extensive than he might have thought. It was a shock, although a pleasing one, the idea of maybe being around to turn the page on the calendar and not having to keep his appointment in the barn. However, when Mary's face filled his mind, that tiny list of reasons to go shone brightly, lit like neon in his thoughts – it might only be two things, finding peace and reunion with his love, but to him they were, in fact, everything.

Mary, I'm coming, my love . . .

In that moment, with the new day ahead, he felt a flood of warmth at the prospect of seeing her again, holding her again, tempered of course by the devastation he would leave in his wake, and nearly all of it heaped on to his sister's shoulders. Plus there was still the tricky issue of finding the courage. Staring now at the raised bumpy veins and liver spots on the back of his hands, he considered the fact that he was in his eighties and could quite feasibly croak any time soon. That alone made the whole prospect of his suicide hullaballoo feel a little redundant; it would certainly save him the bother. He could only hope.

The telephone in the hallway rang. He raced, as far as he was able, down the stairs.

'Morning, Thurston!' Nancy's husband, his voice a surprise, someone who rarely called.

'Morning, Andrew. Good to hear from you.' Judging from the man's demeanour, Nancy had succeeded in cheering him up.

'Thought I'd pop over – Nancy says you need a hand with painting some barn doors?'

'I do indeed. Not sure today is a good painting day, too cold, but by all means come and size up the job.'

'Yes, I will. Good, good.' Andrew took a deep breath. 'I just wanted to say that I've been feeling a little' – he paused – 'off colour, but back in the saddle now and erm, yes, I'd like to help.'

'That's fantastic, Andrew.' Hoping that whatever had perked the man up was more than just a hiatus.

'So we'll see you later?'

'Yes, no rush, lad, whenever is good for you.'

'Great, and thanks for asking me. I'm excited!'

'Good for you!' Thurston ended the call. 'Well, how about that, Barbie?' He spoke to the dog, who ignored him as he loped back up the stairs to get dressed. He wondered what Mary would make of the change in Andrew. She was always so much better at deciphering the human condition than he. He'd found it pretty much impossible to talk to Nancy until she became a teenager. It was only with Mary as their interpreter that he was able to make her laugh over the supper table or chat about the dogs when they walked the fields. She'd been there when Rhubarb had arrived as a pup, and Thurston had been given the ultimate honour of walking her down the aisle after her own father, Melvin, had sadly lost his life in a car accident only eighteen months before the wedding. Dark times for Nancy and darker times for his sister, June.

The loss of her husband had changed her. June had always been formidable and fearless, but after the accident she'd put up a shield, a hardened shell, as if this was how she thought it best to repel all future hurt and keep herself together. It made her a little cool, a little remote, verging on hostile when the mood took her. Mary liked to remind Thurston of the need to be tolerant and not to take her sometimes frosty manner to heart. June, she explained, was a little bit angry at the world, hiding hurt that ran deep, nursing grief that had changed the shape of her. It wasn't really until Mary herself had died that he fully understood just what she meant, and he had seen a softening of June's shell when she happened upon his notepad jottings. He decided to be more tolerant of his sister, a little kinder, and again these thoughts shaded his plan to take his life with doubt, knowing his passing would cause her grief and greater loneliness; it was the very opposite of kindness.

'A grief that changed the shape of her . . .'

This he whispered into the mirror above the dressing table and knew that it was a sad way to live, for him and for June. In the immediate aftermath of his wife's passing, his grief had capsized him, weighted him, with the power to pull down his shoulders, his mouth and his legs. He had been stooped, unsmiling and with a heaviness to his gait that no happy man could emulate. And as for his spirit . . . it had curled up, shrivelled, and admitted defeat. And this was how it stayed, sitting in a tight ball in the base of his gut, destroying his appetite and making all movement tricky.

But in recent days, with June's expressions of love and the hand of friendship offered by Emma, he had righted himself a little, or at least could feel the beginnings of it. He recognised this feeling as hope, something he had thought was lost entirely. Not that it was enough to sway him from the task ahead.

Opening his wardrobe door, he ran his fingers over the shirts his wife had laundered. He was loath to wear a fresh one, knowing that each time a shirt got dirty and he balled it into the laundry basket, he was one step further away from their old life, where she washed and ironed them and did so with love. Their old life, where he rushed home at the end of a long day in the fields to rub her feet and join her on the sofa . . . There were five left. Five pristine shirts, two white and three in the country check he and all his peers favoured. A uniform of sorts, to be spotted at county fairs, point-to-points and on market day.

Just five . . .

He rummaged in the chest of drawers, settling on a thermal vest and a thick-knit jersey over the top of that. Nothing fancy; it was good enough. After all, it wasn't as if he was trying to impress anyone, one of the perks of being in his eighties. Not that he'd ever been a dandy. He smiled briefly at the idea; what would Mary – or June, for that matter – think if he'd come down one morning with a silk cravat, a bright jacket and hair oil?

'They'd think you were puggled, Thurston!' He spoke aloud, his voice splintering the silence. His spirit lifted at the thought of Andrew coming over to help him with the barn doors. People, noise, life . . . helping him mark the days until his exit.

Walking slowly into the kitchen, he put the lamp on. He had to admit that even this was getting a little easier; the discovery of her absence no longer made his heart drop to his boots, as if there was the tiniest possibility that when he woke and trod the stairs, he would open the door and find her standing at the Aga – and that the whole thing had been the very worst kind of nightmare. But no, here he was in the quiet kitchen, taking in the morning, running his hand over the oven glove, the cup handle and the breadboard where her fingers had lingered.

His wife, he noted, had declined to answer his call of prayer. There had been no sign, no communication, no otherworldly activity to soothe his soul and give him hope. Nothing. This only added to his feelings of foolishness that he had allowed himself to think otherwise.

It was surely his imagination, but even his cup of tea tasted different. The fuel that had seen him ready to face the world for as long as he could remember, thawing him out in the winter, cooling him down in the summer, and a warm flask of the stuff never more appreciated when working on the furthest reaches of a field in the rain. Tea, poured by his grandmother's and mother's hand . . . yes, even his tea, in the weeks since Mary's death, had tasted flat, never the right temperature and not quite hitting the mark. How could that be? *Tea!* The currency of friendship in a rural community and yet even this, his daily drink, tainted by the bitter tang of loss.

He heard the crunch of tyres on the gravel and looked out of the window to see a blue Ford Focus pull into the yard. A car he didn't instantly recognise until he saw young Emma at the wheel! A surprise to say the least, although not an unwelcome one. He watched, noting two passengers – boys, one in the front seat and one in the back – as she ran her hand over her face and tucked her hair behind her ears in the way someone might when trying to wake up or look their best.

'Thurston!' She waved as she spied him at the kitchen window. Hopping out of the car, she made her way to the boot, where, curiously, she retrieved two large flat boxes.

He wondered whether he had done the right thing in suggesting she could pop in whenever; he did, after all, know very little about her. Nancy had of course known her for a few years now, but still he felt the vaguest hint of regret at saying anything at all; what had he been thinking? They'd only chatted for the briefest of times, and he'd felt sorry for the girl. He had been trying to be more like Mary – kind and inclusive, the sort of thing she'd have said: *Oh, come on up to the farm, dear, bring the kids, I'll pop the kettle on!*

Taking a deep breath, he went outside to welcome his visitor.

'Heel, Barb!' he called to the little Jack Russell who stood by his side, thinking it best to keep him close until he knew if she was comfortable around dogs.

'Good morning, Thurston! Don't worry, we're not staying, don't want to intrude or anything, but thought you might like these!'

He walked forward to see that the large flat boxes contained jigsaw puzzles. The one on top, a detailed picture of a greenhouse chockful of plants.

'Well, that's very kind.' Having never had the patience for such a hobby, he wondered if he might give it a go. Rhubarb barked loudly at the side of the car until out lumbered a large teenager, and a smaller boy emerged from the back seat, slight in build and wearing specs that Thurston would guess were a little too big for his narrow face.

'Thought I told you two to stay in the car!' Emma yelled.

The kids ignored her.

'Aaaw!' The younger boy dropped to his knees, not caring less that his tracksuit bottoms were going to be in direct contact with the cobbles of the yard where numerous kinds of animal waste had been spread, dropped and spilled over the years. 'Come on, girl! Come on!' the lad called, and Rhubarb tootled over, coming to rest by the boy's knees, where, with his head cocked to one side, the little hound seemed to enjoy the ear rubs and tummy tickles that were being freely dished.

'He's called Rhubarb.' It was nice to see their little pup getting so much attention, the kind he must be missing since Mary was no longer around to spoil him rotten, feeding him meat scraps and the corner of a biscuit when she thought he wasn't watching.

'I think he's made a friend!' Emma pointed and giggled as she walked towards him, and again he was reminded of her easy-going nature, although closer inspection revealed a face etched with the fatigue of worry.

'It seems there's no such thing as loyalty when it comes to another human with a snack, or a tummy rub.'

'It's definitely my philosophy. I will literally drop everything and everyone for a chocolate Hobnob.' She pulled a face.

He liked her sense of humour, wondering if he ought to invite them in, and if he did, what he had to offer by way of refreshment.

'My sister's dropped off some homemade parkin.' June had delivered the warm cake the day before, leaving it on the doorstep in a plastic box. Mary used to comment that his sister was, in her opinion, always a little heavy with the powdered ginger. It used to make him chuckle, the two women in his life, friends for sure, good friends, yet always harbouring this fierce competitiveness over cake-making and cooking in general. Never was he able to mention his wife's royally approved jam-making – knowing that might just have sent his sister off the deep end. Not that this stopped Mary bringing it up during many a family event.

He said my jam was delicious and didn't just say delicious, but you know when someone really enjoys something, and they say deeeelishus! He said it just like that!

'If you fancy a cup of tea?'

'That sounds lovely, Thurston. But we won't stay, I really don't want to intrude, just thought you might like these.' She held the boxes up. He took the offering from her. 'As I mentioned last night, we have quite a lot going on at home.' He guessed it was nerves that made her gabble. 'This is Reggie, my oldest.' The boy, whose background he was aware of, seemed hesitant, with a nervousness that his frame and presence belied, a young boy unaware of his physicality, or hyper-aware of it. It was hard to tell, but certainly someone of his build could have made their mark at a place like Reynard's College, on and off the rugby field. In his day, it was the smaller boys who felt the needle of intimidation and displayed the same shrinking manner as Reggie in that moment.

'Hello.' The boy spoke softly, doing his best to avoid eye contact and looking up from beneath a heavy fringe only occasionally.

'And that young scamp is Alex.'

The younger of the two jumped up from where he petted Rhubarb, wiped his hands on his tracksuit bottoms and came over to shake Thurston's hand. He jostled the wide boxes under his left arm.

'How do you do?' The boy surprised him.

It took him right back, remembering how they had to practise this very greeting on the way in and out of chapel each morning. The praepostors would line up along the quad and all the little prep kids, like himself, had to shake hands with them in turn and say, 'How do you do?'

Even now, he could recall the instruction given termly by his housemaster: *The handshake must be neither too firm nor too weak. Maintain eye contact without being boorish. Keep voice levels steady, not booming nor meek. We want to hear rounded, neutral vowels delivered fluidly. The correct amount of pressure from the palm and the longevity of the shake will become instinctive, don't overthink it . . .*

And when he got it right, the 'praep' would give a single nod, indicating he had done a good job. Anything less than the nod was cause not only for mortification, but for public humiliation too. Thurston gave a single nod at the boy and saw his face light up.

'So, you attend Reynard's College?'

'Yes, sir.' Alex stood tall, his pride evident. Thurston remembered this too, the feeling that he was someone special, selected to put on that blazer every day.

'What house are you in?' Thurston's next question.

'Martindale House.'

'Martindale?' He was unfamiliar with the name.

'Named after Louisa Martindale. She was a surgeon and suffragist who carried out over seven thousand operations at a time when it was considered a job for men.'

'Well I never!' Again, the boy's confidence and knowledge were impressive.

'It used to be Fleming House – named after Alexander Fleming, who discovered penicillin, but three of the houses were renamed in 2020 to be more inclusive.'

'Makes sense. I was in De Ganier.'

'Still called De Ganier. I think they helped build the school.'

'They certainly did.'

He became aware of Reggie and Emma standing on the sidelines, as if unable to contribute, and he walked over.

'So, Reggie, what do you like most about school?'

'The coming home, the weekends, breaktime and the holidays.' The boy answered without hesitation and neither his tone nor expression suggested humour. He heard Emma catch her breath.

'It's . . . it's not really his thing, is it, love?'

The older boy shrugged, suggesting he wasn't really sure what his thing was.

'I didn't like school either. I mean yes, the buildings were lovely, and I did like playing cricket, but I could never see the point of it.' Reggie looked up; this had seemingly caught his attention, whereas Alex's shoulders seemed to fall a little. 'All I wanted was to get home here and get out on the tractor. I knew that was how I was going to spend my life. Everything else seemed like a daft distraction.'

Reggie nodded and kicked at the cobbles with the toe of his trainer.

'But then when I had left school, further down the line, after my father had died and I was running the farm – which is after all only a business, no matter that we deal with animals and grain and not widgets or thingamajigs – I wished I'd paid a little more attention to the subjects that would have helped me.'

'What kind of things?' Alex asked.

'Let me think . . .' Thurston did just that. 'Maths, to help with the quantities ordered, to understand prices and percentages better at market, not to mention the balancing of the books. I used to think maths was boring, but I can see that it was setting me up for life. Teaching me things I never knew I might need.' He decided to keep his love of poetry and singing to himself, something he and Mary had shared, a secret.

'I think I might like to work as a chef.' Reggie's features softened as he spoke, as if he'd given this some thought, and it might be where his happiness lay.

'That would really be something, Reg!' Emma's expression was one of delight.

The boy nodded a little sheepishly.

'Will you be making chilli?' She turned to him. 'That's our running joke, Thurston, we both managed to derail supper last night!'

The boy smiled.

'The restaurant game is hard work, I know. My brother Loftus, who lives up in Cumbria, his son Peter is a chef, works all hours. But I believe if you have a passion for something, whatever it is, following it brings you joy.'

'I think that too,' Reggie acknowledged. 'Last night was a disaster though. Mum let me help out and we ended up having fish and chips.' The boy's face creased in agony that smacked of failure.

'Can't beat a bit of fish and chips!' Thurston enthused.

'I think I might have said, my daughter Martha brought her boyfriend home to meet us for the first time.' Thurston heard the catch in her voice.

'Martha's having a baby!' Alex yelled and he jumped on the spot, clearly unable to contain his delight at the fact.

'Yes, Martha is having a baby,' Emma repeated, her eyes staring into the middle distance. 'Big news!'

'Well, that is something to celebrate!' Thurston was more than aware that it was always the news he and Mary had longed for.

'I think . . .' Emma looked close to tears, and he didn't know what to do or say next, feeling a veil of awkwardness descend over them all. 'I think it's still sinking in. It's funny, isn't it? You think you can plan for your future, paint a picture, do the right things to make it all come true or at least make sure that you're heading in the right direction and then, pow!' She splayed her fingers to mimic an explosion. 'Little hand grenades are lobbed in, and they change everything.'

He looked up towards the farmhouse and the empty windows, devoid of his wife's presence. She often liked to go up to their bedroom and watch him in the fields, waving from the window when she knew he was in sight, and he liked to stare back at her silhouette, knowing that reunion was imminent and sweet.

'I think that's just life, isn't it? The trick is making the most of those times when no hand grenades are being lobbed and learning to steel yourself for when they are.'

'I think you're right.' She rallied a little. 'Anyway, Thurston, we are disturbing your morning. Come on, kids!' She clapped. 'Let's leave Mr Brancher in peace!'

'You're not disturbing me at all. In fact, I was just about to take the dog for a quick run up the field, you're welcome to join me. I'll pop these inside – and thank you for thinking of me.' He meant it.

'Would you like that, boys, a walk around the fields?'

'Yes!' Alex jumped up and down on the spot, as Reggie nodded and fell into step beside his brother.

Thurston walked to the back of the house with a spring in his step before placing the puzzles on the counter in the boot room, all doubt over inviting her up to Merrydown now gone. He whistled to Rhubarb, who began to trot by his side, and the troupe headed off out of the yard.

'This is so beautiful.' Emma shielded her eyes and let her gaze sweep the wide green horizon.

'I must admit, even though I've only ever lived here, I never get fed up of the view.'

'I bet.' She closed her eyes briefly, letting the autumn sun glance her face. 'It feels good to be outside.'

'I always think so.' He began the walk up the field, keeping to the footpath that was set to the left-hand side, running along the incline of the field, proud to share this land, this experience with Emma and her family.

'This is like the biggest garden in the world!' Alex observed.

'Yes. In fact, we only have a relatively small garden around the farmhouse – a flowerbed border, really, with some grass. But then we have the large paddock right in front, just the other side of the yard.' He thought of their dream, looking out of the bedroom window to see a large family gathered in the field, old and young, playing sport, cricket maybe, having a picnic . . . Not to be. 'Truth was, I didn't feel like mowing grass and tending plants when I was doing just that in the fields all day.'

'Not much of a day off!' Emma laughed.

'Day off? What's that then?' He smiled. 'Not that I'd swap it for the world. When I said farming is just like any other business, that's not strictly true. It's one of those odd occupations where your job and your life are one and the same. Hard to separate the work and my heritage.'

Reggie dropped to the ground, picked up a small conker that had fallen from the spreading horse chestnut tree that grew on the border of the fields and ran his thumb over its flawless mahogany surface.

'Funny to think, isn't it, that if you treated that conker right, you'd get a great big tree like the one it came from and then another from a similar seed and then another. It doesn't matter how long I've been planting things and watching them grow, I still find the process fascinating. A miracle, really.' He watched the boy lean back to take in the full majesty of the tree.

Alex scampered on the ground with Rhubarb in hot pursuit, gathering and holding conkers up for scrutiny, deciding which to discard and which to place in pockets that quickly bulged with his haul.

'I'd like to grow something and then eat it. I think that'd be really cool,' Reggie offered, his face colouring as if even to make the confession was a big deal and like he didn't really think himself capable.

'Then you'll be a farmer!' Thurston tried to encourage the lad.

'I don't think I'd like to be a farmer, but I'd like to erm, I'd like to . . .' Reggie paused and when he spoke it was a little more confident, more direct. 'I'd like to be a chef, but a chef that has all his own food to go and pick or use within reach. Home-grown produce.'

'Like that Hugh Fearnley Whatsisname,' Emma joined in, 'the one with the hair, very posh, goes foraging.'

'Yes, like him, Mum. But not so posh.' Reggie laughed.

'That sounds like a noble plan.' Thurston meant it. In his opinion, anyone who understood that what went on a plate started in the ground, and how important the provenance of food was, shared a farming ethos, whether they fancied farming or not. It was great to see in this young lad. 'If I were you, I'd start with something small, like herbs in pots – you can grow those on any windowsill and herbs are wonderful for transforming even the humblest of ingredients. My wife used to make carrots with thyme and honey, roast them in a hot oven. Goodness me, they were a treat!'

'And any left you could whizz up and add to a good stock, a splash of crème fraîche, maybe some ginger, a little turmeric, and you'd have a great soup.'

'And who doesn't love a good soup?' Thurston warmed to the boy, finding it far easier than he had anticipated to talk to the teenager.

'Don't cry, Mum.' Reggie spoke softly. Thurston turned to look at the woman he didn't really know, amazed and slightly embarrassed by her show of emotion.

'Sorry, Thurston!' she sniffed. 'I'm not normally a crier.'

Me neither, until recently . . .

'But this is the first time I've seen Reggie, so—' She shook her head, as if searching for the right word. 'Engaged!'

'Give it a rest, Mum, it's only herbs!' Thurston and the boy exchanged a look that was knowing and warm.

'Have you ever been skiing?' Alex popped up in front of them on the path, changing the topic entirely. 'I'm going skiing! In France.'

'No, I never have.' Not only had he never had a fancy for all that snow and all that whizzing about but, more crucially, any break he took during their farming years was brief, too brief to travel anywhere remotely suitable for skiing. Holidays were undertaken by him only after much nagging by Mary. And even then he'd pack and travel half-heartedly with his thoughts firmly on how June and her husband would be faring in their caretaking of his beloved land and animals for a couple of days. 'We preferred to stay quite local if ever we got the chance to go away.'

'It's a school trip. I'm going with my friends Dimitri and Piers, and we're taking Haribo and Pringles for the coach and our iPads so we can all watch movies before we go to sleep. We're going to share a room. It'll be like having a sleepover every night!'

'That sounds like a proper adventure. I think we went on a school trip to Stonehenge when I was about your age, and then when I was older we got the train up to Scotland as part of a geography project to look at Hadrian's Wall.'

'So basically, they only took you to look at old rocks?' Reggie found this funny.

'It's true, they did! And we had fun, as much fun in the travelling as the arrival. And that was without the added attraction of Haribo and Pringles. We had squashed warm cheese and tomato sandwiches and an apple on the turn!'

'When Martha's baby is born, I'm going to be an uncle!' Alex announced and he watched as Emma shrank inside her blue waterproof jacket. 'So, when I go skiing, I'm going to find the baby a little present and bring it back.'

'What a lucky baby.' Thurston loosened his thick wool scarf; all this walking in the blue-sky autumn sunshine and he was warming up nicely. This talk of such an event, something to look forward to, chipped away at his icy grief, meaning his heart and spirit were warmed too. 'And that'll make you a grandma?' He looked across the footpath to Emma.

Her response was slow in coming, her tone measured. The boys chased each other up to the top corner of the field.

'It hasn't really registered.' Her joy didn't quite reach her eyes. 'My daughter, Martha . . .' She swallowed. 'Her boyfriend is quite new. He seems very, very nice, he does, but she changes her mind a lot, always thinks the grass is a little greener.' He watched her bite at her thumbnail and rip it with her teeth. A horrible habit, he always thought, remembering being taught in a biology class about all the germs and disease that lurked beneath them. 'But there's no having a change of heart when it comes to having kids, is there? And it's not that I don't think she's capable, I do. I think she's capable of anything she puts her mind to.'

'I sense a but?' It felt forward asking, but this was the odd thing about this woman – they had started off their friendship by engaging on a personal level, and it had kind of set the tone.

'But life can be hard, can't it? And if she and Sergio – that's her boyfriend – if she and Sergio are no more than a fling, then it will be even harder for her, for them both. They seem so young to me, and I wanted her life to be—'

'More stable?'

'No, I was going to say I wanted her life to be easier than mine.'

'I don't think there are ever guarantees, are there? It's that grenade-lobbing thing again.'

'I suppose there aren't.' She shoved her hands in her pockets. 'My friend, the one I told you about, the one who's sick, Roz.'

'Yes.' He looked downwards; a rotten business.

'I found out that she's not going to have any treatment, and I'm so mad at her.'

'Mad at her?' He hadn't expected that.

'Yes, mad at her for not trying, for just accepting that she's going to leave me. For giving up.' The catch in her voice was moving. 'She nipped over last night for pudding when it was bedtime, laughing and chatting like it was any other day, and left about as quickly, popped in as if nothing was amiss, and I wanted to shake her! Beg her not to give up! But I've promised . . .'

'Promised what?'

'That we'll ignore her sickness until we no longer can, that we'll carry on as normal.'

'It's hard for you. I know how it feels.' He pictured Mary lying in the bed at the hospital, gasping, eyes glassy. 'But recently I've been thinking a lot about my wife, and I wonder if she hung on for me, went along with any suggestion made by the medics for *me*.' He swallowed the thought that she might have suffered longer or more because he didn't say, *Go if you want to! Go now! It'll all be okay!* Because he was selfish, greedy for every second he got to spend with her, and the thought of her not being around was then, as it was now, almost more than he could contemplate. 'And I think the best advice I could give you' – she stared at him as if welcoming any advice – 'is not to do anything that you might regret.' She nodded. 'At the end of the day, when the time comes for your friend to pass, it will happen quicker than you are ready for, whether it's in a week or a decade. It's always too soon. Whether you get mad and shake her or not.'

'Yes. I think that's true. You know I lost my dad, and even though he was my dad and older, I didn't really think it would ever happen.' Her eyes pooled with tears.

It was his turn to give a nod of understanding.

'And also, Emma, when people have died, all the little things that might rile you, all the questions or grievances you might have . . . Could the medics have done more? What if I'd pushed her to go to the doc's sooner? Was I kind enough, supportive enough? Is there a cure I don't know about? Something deep in an Amazonian forest that might have fixed her, because without hesitation I'd sell up every brick, every blade of grass and take her there for just one more week . . .' He coughed, remembering that he was not just talking aloud to himself, as had become his MO. 'The truth is, it makes no difference. My wife is still dead. She died and she isn't coming back, no matter how angry or sad I feel, or how much I hate the world in some moments. Nothing will bring her back and so really is no point. I need to try and accept it and live with it. That's it, really.' *To live with it and accept it or try to reach her and find peace in death . . . these are my choices.*

'I know you're right. I need to try and accept it and live with it.' She wiped her eyes on her sleeve.

'Otherwise, there's the risk you could spoil whatever time you do have with feelings of resentment, or worse, not having the fun you should be.' He spoke from experience.

'That's kind of what Roz said.'

'Well, I think Roz is lucky to have a friend like you.' Never really having close friends himself, certainly not since his teenage years, when he and Mary were content to do everything together. Yes, there were farming acquaintances, neighbours and the like, but a best friend, someone he could share his every thought with? That had been Mary. He looked at Emma and thought of how much easier, nicer his life would be with friends like her in it. No substitute, of course, but nice nonetheless.

'I can see for miles!' Alex yelled as he reached the top corner of the field, crouching down to sit again on the ground, something Thurston noted must be the preserve of the young, flopping down wherever they stood. He always sought out a tree stump, log or – even better – a stool or chair. He envied the youngster his lack of consideration of where to sit and the fact he had the joints flexible enough to do so.

Reggie caught up and stood with his hands on his hips. Catching his breath. Thurston felt the creak to his knees and twinge to his hip as he started the final incline – not steep by any stretch of the imagination, but enough to let his old bones know it was a change of angle. Emma forged ahead, her pace quickening as she got into her stride. And just like that, they arrived.

As ever, the view from the top was worth it. Thurston and his guests stood in quiet reverence, each no doubt like him taking in the majesty, the patchwork of verdant growth that spread out before them, 'God's blanket', his father used to call it. And even at this, the end of autumn, russets, golds and reds peppered the view, studding the hedgerows with pops of colour that drew the eye, a reminder of the glorious rainbow that nature had in waiting for the coming months. The thought thrilled him, as it always had; enamoured and fascinated by the shifting seasons, the changing landscapes and the moving palette that were different every single day.

'Are you okay, Thurston?' He felt the light touch of Emma's hand on his arm.

'I think I am.' He smiled at her, knowing it was going to be hard to jump from this world, when there were these crumbs of delight lurking in the most unexpected of places. This beauty that was a privileged sight for the few. But who knew what awaited him at his next destination?

'That's good. Really good.' She spoke sincerely, and in this moment they shared, he realised that the world in all its glory would indeed carry on, whether he were around to see it or not. It was another thread that bound him to this stranger.

'Hello!' They were all drawn by the call as Nancy and her husband Andrew appeared at the bottom of the field.

'It's your boss!' Alex pointed, before Emma batted his hand down.

'Kids!' She pulled a sideways face, which barely masked her slightly nervous air.

The four watched as Nancy and her less than agile husband made the hike, coming to join them in the sunshine on the brow of the hill. Clearly, the man was on the road to recovery.

'Here you are! Wowsers!' Andrew breathed heavily, as if he'd made Everest base camp and not just climbed up the three-acre plot.

'Andrew, this is Emma, Reggie and Alex, and you all know Nancy, of course.'

'This is some view!' Emma smiled at his niece, and he was happy they might form a friendship of sorts outside of the shop.

It was his hope that she might not know the loneliness that had dogged him recently.

'Really is. I love it best when it's snowing. We used to hurtle down here on tea trays when I was little!' Nancy laughed.

'I'd like to do that!' Alex piped up. Thurston liked his spirit.

'Well, I might be a few years away from that, but maybe I'll join you anyway.' Nancy's husband spoke with determination. 'We've been talking about it, my getting out more, good for my body and certainly good for my noggin.' He tapped his head.

'Good for you, Andrew. If you fancy taking Rhubarb out for company, you only have to ask.' In truth, it hadn't occurred to Thurston in the past that part of Andrew's malaise might be mental, and he wanted only to support the man who had made such a declaration.

'I just might. When I'm not painting your barn doors.' The man, it seemed, was making an effort, and that was to be admired. 'In fact, I was wondering if you'd mind if I grabbed any spare timber you might have lying around.'

'Yes, of course. What are you thinking of building?' He was curious.

'Raised vegetable beds.' Andrew smiled falteringly at his wife. 'Nancy's been asking for them for a while and I've never got round to it, but this year' – he rubbed his hands – 'this is the year we go for it. I reckon eight big high boxes.'

'We're going to grow potatoes, not sure what variety.' Nancy smiled at Emma, who laughed, no doubt thinking of the bum-shaped spuds they'd giggled over. 'And onions, salads – it's exciting. And flowers, I'd like one just for flowers too.'

'How lovely!' Emma, he could tell, was thinking of the joy it would bring.

'It's funny, Andrew, this young man here' – he pointed at Reggie – 'was just talking about growing herbs and whatnot to use in his cooking. Do you think you might need a hand?' Thurston stared at his niece's husband, hoping he might take the hint.

'I could always do with a hand.' Andrew turned to Reggie. 'Tell you what . . .' He paused, as if bringing a plan together in his head. 'You help me build the beds, even help tend them, and I'll give you one of your own, to plant as you like, but it'd be down to you.'

'Seriously?' Reggie sounded excited.

'Seriously. You can grow whatever you like.'

'Herbs, definitely,' the boy enthused, 'and maybe spinach and all sorts – I can plan my menu around what's in season.'

'Well, if I *don't* grow spinach and herbs, we can trade produce!' Andrew suggested. 'You'll be supplying Nancy's store before you know it!' he added jovially.

Thurston looked towards Emma, who had turned to face the outer field, eyes averted, but he could tell by the shake to her shoulders that she was a little overwhelmed with emotion. It seemed like the perfect plan to him; something to get Andrew out of the house, with the responsibility of not letting Reggie down, and a hobby that would get the boy out in the fresh air, something to look forward to outside of school. Keeping them both busy.

'Right, who's ready for a cup of tea and a nice bit of parkin?' He looked forward to seeing the kitchen full once again, to hear the noise of chatter and the hiss of the kettle on the stove. Mary would be proud.

It was as they began their descent that Emma's phone rang. '*Sorry!*' she mouthed to the assembled, awkward at having to take a call, not that they minded a jot.

'Oh no! Oh no!' She placed her hand over her mouth and her sons walked over to stand with her, instinctively putting one arm each around her waist. It spoke of closeness that brought quite the lump to his throat. 'Yes, yes, I'm heading back now. I'll . . . I'll meet you there, okay, okay, Bren.'

'What's happened, Mum?' It was Reggie who spoke, taking control and placing his hand on his little brother's shoulder, as if preparing to calm and placate the younger boy should it be needed.

'Erm, Nanny Marge has had a fall. Mr Blundesthorpe called an ambulance. Dad's with her, I said we'd meet them at the hospital.'

'Oh, I am sorry.'

She blinked quickly as her breath came in unstructured gulps, the crease of concern at the top of her nose one he recognised as staring back at him when he sat night after night by Mary's bedside, waiting for the inevitable, wishing, praying he could turn back time.

'Poor Nanny!' Alex's chest heaved. Reggie held him close about the shoulders.

'Is there anything I can do, Emma?' Nancy walked alongside her as the women picked up pace, Emma understandably keen to get where she was needed.

'I don't . . . I don't think so, but thanks, Nancy.'

They made their way as quickly as they were able back down the field, along the path and across the paddock towards the yard where her blue Ford Focus sat.

'Thurston, thank you, we'll come back for that tea and cake.' She spoke with false joviality.

'You'd all be welcome anytime.' He closed the driver's door as she buckled up.

'I'll get your number off my mum, and we can make a plan to get building.' Reggie addressed Andrew as he jumped into the passenger seat, having made sure his little brother was safely ensconced on the back seat.

'Yes!' Andrew rubbed his hands; he seemed keen to crack on, which was progress in itself.

Thurston stood with Nancy and Andrew, ready to wave off their visitors whose trip had been cut short.

Emma put the key in the ignition and they listened to the engine turn over and splutter. She pulled a face, clearly embarrassed and with obvious anxiety as she tried again. This time, like the first, the engine wheezed a little but then died. He watched as her head fell forward on to her chest and she banged the steering wheel with the heel of her hand. Reggie spoke to her – he couldn't hear what he said, but the lad's expression suggested it was something calming, placatory, and again his admiration for the lad rose. Emma nodded, took a deep breath, and tried for the third time.

Nothing.

She opened the door and stared at him with her lip quivering.

'I can't . . . I can't get the car started.'

'Let's have a look.' Thurston spoke softly, hoping to calm her as she climbed from the seat and he lowered himself into the space she'd just vacated. Compared to his off-roader or his old tractor, the Focus was certainly compact but was super comfy and very clean. He turned the key in the ignition and, as he suspected, the petrol warning light came on. The tank was empty. Not just empty, but as his father would have said, 'running on fumes'!

Climbing out, he tried to think how to phrase it, not wanting to embarrass the girl, who was clearly already dealing with a stressful situation.

'I think you might have run out of fuel.' He nodded at the stranded vehicle.

'You're kidding me!' She ran her hand over her face. 'How can I be so stupid?'

'You've got a lot on,' Nancy piped up kindly.

Emma turned three hundred and sixty degrees, as if hoping a petrol station might have popped up behind her. It hadn't.

'I've got diesel in the shed, but no petrol.' Thurston thought aloud.

'I . . . I need to get to, to the hospital.' Her voice was thin, her eyes wide.

'That's okay, I'll take you. I'll go grab the keys and take you in the truck.'

'We'll hang on to the boys.' Nancy smiled, aware that the truck only had one passenger seat. 'At least someone is going to get tea and cake today!'

'Is that, is that all right, Reg? Alex? I'll come back as soon as I can to get you and the car, will you be okay?' She sounded panicked, flustered.

'Course we will.' Reggie, out of the car now, stood next to his brother.

'Give Nanny my love!' Alex piped up.

'Thanks, Nancy.' Emma stared meekly at Thurston's niece.

'My pleasure, don't worry about a thing. Thurston and Mary have an enviable VHS collection, all the James Bond films, *Star Wars*, all taped off the telly and complete with adverts you've long forgotten!'

'I love *Star Wars*!' Alex bounced on the spot.

'Me too!' Andrew grinned.

Thurston grabbed the keys to the truck from the hook by the back door and within minutes they were pulling out of the driveway having watched the boys go into the farmhouse with Nancy and Andrew.

'I don't know how to thank you. Brendan, my husband, would have come and got us, but he's gone to be with Mum and—'

He noted the tremor to her voice, and it saddened him to see her so fraught.

'Don't worry about it, Emma. It's fine. Glad to be of help.'

'Do you know the way to the hospital? Do you know where it is?' She was nervous, babbling again.

Did he know the way . . . What Emma could never have known was that since Mary's passing, he would drive any amount of extra miles to avoid going near or even seeing the building where he had lost his love. With her last moments playing in his head like a movie, the very last thing he wanted was to return to the scene of that horror, to stoke the embers of his distress; but it seemed, in this instance, that he had very little choice.

'I reckon if I set this old truck on the road, it could head there without me steering. It was where Mary was on and off for the last year and then for the last few weeks of her life.'

'Oh gosh, that never occurred to me! Drop me off somewhere close and I can walk the last bit, I didn't think! That's me all over at the moment, not thinking. My mind is a muddle!'

'Not at all. It's only a building, and one in which I've spent enough time for it to feel a bit like home.' This, he hoped, was the truth.

'Oh, my poor old mum, I hope she's okay.'

He decided against offering a clichéd phrase that might make him a liar, having heard enough of them when Mary was ill. Offered by visitors who he was sure meant well, but their words of reassurance when they were without the facts only did a disservice to what he knew deep down to be true.

'I meant what I said, you can all come over any time.'

'Thank you, that means the world. It was lovely to see Reggie so enthused about growing food.'

'It's good for the soul.' This he believed.

'And we all need that,' she sighed, glancing at her watch, and he wished he could get her there quicker. 'I wonder how she fell? God, I hope she's okay. Do you ever feel like your head might explode, Thurston?'

He laughed; her question was a little left-field. 'No. I feel like the quiet might finish me off sometimes, but head exploding? Not really.'

'So much going on. I can't believe my little girl is having a baby!' He could see out of the corner of his eye that she was shaking her head. 'I don't know what to think. I've always said I want her to be happy.'

'And she is?'

'She says she is, but a *baby*? Oh God, I can't think about it! And now my mum's in the hospital and it's all my fault.'

'How is it all your fault? You were miles away.' He didn't understand.

'Because I should have been with her. I got her up this morning, put her in her chair, but I was in a rush. I mean, she can get around, she can manage, but she's a bit wobbly on her legs and instead of sitting with her, I came out to the farm, and also . . .' She took her time. 'I got her drunk last night, not on purpose, and I bet she was feeling fuzzy because of that.'

'We'll be at the hospital in no time, try not to worry,' was the best he could think of. 'I meant what I said to you the day we met, about not having regrets.'

'I remember.' She twisted in her seat to face him.

'We were talking about your friend—'

'Roz.'

'Yes, Roz, but the same applies to your mother. Take it from one who knows. I've spent the last few weeks thinking about my wife and wondering if I did her wrong by not letting her go off and meet someone else with whom she might have had a baby. Was it my fault, did I deny her the chance? I hate to think of it.' He discovered it was easy to talk when you were driving, staring straight ahead, and didn't have to look directly at someone.

'I think there's only happy. There's no caveats to it. You were either happy or you weren't and you're either happy or you're not. And if you were then that's all there is to it. I love Brendan, my husband, love him so much, and my goodness I adore my kids, but if they hadn't come along, we'd have found a different kind of happy. But still happy.'

Thurston liked this thought very much. 'Yes, we were happy and no, I'm not. Not now. Don't know how to be, without her. There are little fragments of happiness that I gather up. Not the same and never as good, but . . .' *good enough for now* . . . This he kept to himself.

'I understand.' And she too stared ahead, and he liked that she didn't offer him a saccharine-covered platitude aimed at healing his broken heart.

He pulled up the truck outside the entrance to the accident and emergency department where Emma's mother had been taken.

'Would you like me to come inside with you, Emma?' He hoped she'd say no, feeling less sure about entering the place than he had made out earlier.

'No, no, but thank you for offering. I'll run and find her. And thank you, Thurston, for running me in and thank you for having the boys. Either Brendan or I will be over as soon as we can to pick up the car and the kids.'

'No rush, they'll be fine!' He raised his hand as she jumped out of the cab before leaning back through the open door.

'Just remember the golden rules: keep them away from bright lights, don't let them get wet and don't feed them after midnight!'

With that, she slammed the door and was gone, disappeared inside the building where a piece of his heart was lodged in the wall of a quiet ward on the top floor.

You can let go of her hand now, Mr Brancher . . . she's gone . . .

The nurse had spoken softly, kindly.

He'd listened to a documentary on the radio about what happens in someone's final hours of life, wanting, if not necessarily to be prepared, then at least to try to understand. He remembered that first to go would be hunger, then thirst, as if death took them piece by piece, closing its icy jaws around its subject and closing slowly. Then speech, followed by vision. The last senses to go, according to the doctor on the radio, were hearing and touch, and so no, he would not be letting go of her hand just yet, nor would he stop whispering to her, *I love you, Mary, I always have and always will, my girl, my girl.*

The car behind beeped, drawing him from the reverie, the man in the driver's seat raising his arms impatiently, and he understood; no one here was without their own story, their own drama. He pulled out of the space meant for drop-off only.

Emma's words replayed in his head – *Keep them away from bright lights, don't let them get wet and don't feed them after midnight* – what a very strange thing to say!

CHAPTER TWENTY-SEVEN

EMMA

Emma had done her level best to keep it together as she travelled to the hospital, careful not to give credence to the rising sense of emergency that flared in her veins. Now that she'd arrived, this need for containment was no longer necessary and she ran into the building, only to be met by a cacophony and an overload of information. Struggling, she tried to take in the overhead signage, which was abundant and confusing, while running at the same time. Her eyes roved the fixed seating where the walking wounded gathered, and the couple of wheelchairs parked in the corridor. None were where Brendan or her mother were sited. She was about to call him, despite the many signs around asking people not to use mobile phones, when she spied the reception with a stony-faced lady behind it.

'Hi there, I'm trying to find my, erm, my mum, Margery Nicholson? She was brought in by ambulance a little while ago?'

'Mar-ger-ee Nich-ol-son . . .' The woman ran her finger down her computer screen. Slowly. Emma's leg jumped against the desk.

Hurry up! Hurry up! 'Yes, here she is.' She looked up and pointed towards the end of the room. 'Go through the double doors on the right, you'll see the nurses' station and someone there will be able to direct you to your mum.'

'Thanks!' She patted the countertop and headed swiftly towards the double doors, walking straight in behind a medic, who held up a key card.

The nurses' station was empty. Emma had been standing for a few seconds, wondering when someone might return, when she looked up along the long corridor, lined with curtained-off cubicles, and out of one stepped Brendan. Her body shivered. Just the sight of him was wonderful, made her feel less alone and that no matter what, they'd meet whatever came next head on. He rushed towards her and gave her a brief squeeze.

'What happened?' She was desperate to know. 'Is she okay?'

'She's okay.' These words enough for her to stop the tremble to her limbs and for her heart rate to slow a little. 'Mr Blundesthorpe found her in his front garden. She'd taken a tumble over the low hedge and hit the path.'

'What was she doing in Mr Blundesthorpe's front garden?'

'I don't know, Emma.' He sounded firm, indicating that he was giving her all the information he had, and she was not to interrupt with further questions. 'But I'm afraid she's broken her collar bone and is a little bruised.'

'Oh no! It's all my fault!' She rubbed the tears from her eyes.

'Well, that took three seconds longer than I thought it would.'

She ignored him and made her way to the cubicle she'd seen him exit.

When she pulled back the flimsy curtain, it was both a relief and a shock to find her mum, sitting very still. Propped up on pillows, she was upright and, distressingly, her face was three-quarters covered in a dark, spreading bruise. She looked old, frail, pitiful and somehow diminished. Emma's heart sank.

'Oh, Mum! Look at you.' She sat in the chair next to her bed and took her mother's free hand into her own, as the emergency shattered the glass wall of hesitation that usually sat between them. Her mother's other arm was in a sling and tightly bound to her chest.

'You should see the other guy!' her mother joked without opening her eyes. 'Only went out to get some air. I felt queasy, and the next thing I know I'd hit the deck and the ambulance was on its way.'

Emma glanced at her husband, this proof enough that it was her fault; her mother felt sick because of how much she'd drunk, no doubt. *Fact.*

'I didn't want to say anything this morning, Mum, you seemed so settled when I left you, but last night—' She looked at Brendan, dreading the prospect of coming clean but knowing she had to. 'I think you picked up a can with wine in it instead of Coke, that's probably why you felt so sick, a little dizzy or whatever. I'd put the wine inside it so I could sneak a drink during the evening. I'm so sorry.'

Her mother began to make a sound, a wheezy kind of laboured breathing that made both her and Brendan lean in – was she struggling to catch her breath? Emma eyed the red cord that dangled temptingly by the wall and her fingers twitched, knowing that in an emergency, that was the thing to pull, while simultaneously hollering with your head outside of the curtain, calling for *help! Help, someone!* She felt the very real beginning of panic, before it became apparent that her mother was not in fact struggling to breathe but was in fact doing her best to suppress her laughter.

'What's so funny?'

The humour in Brendan's tone matched the relief she too felt.

'I'm not stupid, Emma-Jane! I know the difference between the taste of booze and diet soda! I couldn't believe my luck! I had a lovely evening and slept like a baby!'

'Why didn't you say anything?' Emma tried to laugh along with the woman as her breathing struggled to find a normal rhythm.

'Why didn't you?'

Touché.

'I'd had such a nice time last night. My confidence was high when I woke, and I didn't want to sit cooped up in the house, I wanted to see the world, so when I felt a bit icky, I went outside and was just breathing, happily taking in the morning. I suddenly realised I hadn't got my front-door key and panicked that it might close and lock me out. I turned quickly, too quickly, and my foot slipped on the wet leaves. I twisted and went down hard. It happened so fast – one minute I was standing there and the next, *bang!* I hit my shoulder on the edge of the path, and then my cheek. Have I got a shiner?'

Emma stared at her mother's face, which was more bruise than not.

'Little bit, yes. Does it hurt?'

'Little bit, yes.' Her mother, smart as ever, knowingly echoed the lie. 'They've given me something for the pain and I'm trying not to move. They can't set the shoulder, apparently, only strap it up. And I'm okay as long as I sit still like this, keep my eyes closed and don't move.'

'Where are the boys?' Brendan looked over her shoulder, as if they might appear.

'I had to leave them at the farm, my car ran out of petrol. They're with Nancy and her husband. Thurston drove me here, which was very kind.'

'Oh Emma, you ran out of petrol?' He looked and sounded disappointed, and she wanted to punch him. She changed the topic.

'Have you seen Martha and Sergio this morning?'

He shook his head.

'A great-grandma eh, Margery? Who'd have thought it?' Brendan sat in the spare chair on the other side of her mum. He spoke candidly before she had the chance to properly brief him.

'What are you talking about?' Her mother opened one eye slightly to take in her son-in-law.

'Oh, did Emma not tell you this morning?' He pulled a face, aware he'd messed up.

'No, Emma did not.' She filled him in and watched him shrink in the chair. 'Because Martha wanted to tell her nan herself and so was planning on popping over to visit her today!'

'Tell me *what*, for the love of God? I am here, you know! Martha? Having a baby? Are you telling me she's up the duff?'

'Yes, Martha's pregnant. Martha and Sergio are having a baby.' It felt no more real no matter how often or to whom she said the words.

'Well, I didn't see that coming! How far is she?'

'About twelve weeks.' Emma figured they'd waited to tell people until now, got the first trimester out of the way. The first trimester? How was this thought, this language being applied to her little girl? It was surreal.

'I think that's wonderful!' Her mother's response was as welcome as it was surprising.

'You do?' She had fully expected to hear all the reasons their relationship was bound to fail, and all the reasons Emma should be ashamed of her poor parenting, not to mention the doom-laden road that lay ahead . . .

'Yes. Martha is a lovely, strong, healthy woman, early twenties is a good age to have a baby. Sergio seemed sweet, I thought. Kind. He's very nice-looking and didn't bat an eyelid after spending an evening with our crazy family. Yes, I think it's wonderful.'

Her mum, she figured, might benefit from a bang to the head more often.

'And how are you feeling, Bren?' Emma pointed surreptitiously to his crotch.

'Wonderful, thanks. All good.' He gave a sarcastic double thumbs-up.

She gave a sideways smile as images from the disastrous evening and the conjugal chillies encounter flooded her mind. The curtain moved and in stepped a young doctor.

'Can I have a word, Mrs Fountain?'

'Are you going to be talking about me?' her mother interjected. 'Because you can talk to me, you know! I'm bruised, not deaf!'

'I understand that, Mrs Nicholson, and yes, I do want to talk about you with your daughter to get some background information that you don't need to be troubled with. Far more important that you rest.'

Emma looked up and into the face of the diminutive man, who had a clipboard in his hands and a stethoscope around his neck, two accessories guaranteed to make her feel that she absolutely had to take note.

'Yes, of course, we can do that. Back in a sec, Mum. Can I get you anything?'

'Another can of that stuff I drank last night wouldn't go amiss.'

Emma followed the doctor out into the emergency department. She heard Brendan deploying his big voice of distraction, the one he'd used on the kids many times.

'So, Margery, I'm going to be a grandad – any advice? What would Victor say? Because to be honest, I'm absolutely terrified!'

It made her smile as she followed the doctor into an anteroom with a desk against the wall. He leaned back on it, and she faced him.

'My name's Dr Khan. I'm looking after your mum. I've examined her and we've had a good look at her X-rays—'

'Thank you,' she interrupted.

'Shoulders are tricky.' She didn't like the considered tilt to his head, the pose a mechanic might adopt when surveying the damage to your vehicle and about to give you the bad news. Which reminded her that her car was not only out of fuel, but also needed repair. 'They take a while to heal, even when bones are young and healthy, and they greatly impair movement when they don't work.'

'Yes.'

'Your mother lives alone?'

It was her own insecurity, she knew, that made her take this as an accusation. 'Well, she does, but we pop in and she had a carer until recently, who didn't, didn't work out.'

'Falls like this are not uncommon with someone of your mother's age and certainly not someone with her medical history and difficulties in walking. Trouble is, they can often be a bit like a pull on a loose end of wool and the whole thing can unravel.'

'You think my mother is unravelling?'

His smile was fleeting. 'No, but we need to put everything in place to make sure she doesn't. It won't only be about her physical recovery, which could be slow, but she's had quite a fall and that will knock her confidence.'

'Yes, of course.' Her brain whirred with what they'd need to put in place.

'We'll be keeping her in for a couple of days and then we need to look at her care plan once she's discharged, make sure the best arrangements have been made for when she leaves the hospital.'

She nodded her gratitude.

'Has your mother ever considered residential care?'

Her mother's words came to her sharply: *I will not go into a home to sit with a load of elderly pensioners. If you think that, you've*

got another think coming . . . those places are death's waiting room! I
won't go! No way!

'Erm, we have touched on the topic once or twice.'

'Because I think it might be the best option, even if it's only temporarily for some respite care until she's back on her feet and feeling a little stronger. There are some good facilities with open visiting times. I don't know what availability is like, but we can discuss it with your mum and look into it further, if that's something you'd like to explore?'

'My friend said that once they go into a place like that, they rarely come out.'

'That sounds sinister! But it can be true – often it's because life is easier for everyone when a loved one is infirm and the responsibility of caring for them is huge. And often for the person themselves, who might have been struggling alone and has resisted residential care for a whole range of reasons, they find they enjoy the comradery, being waited on, and sometimes, a feeling of increased safety. Many residents, of course, are of an age where health can decline quite quickly, so there are many reasons they stay, and it's usually not because someone is being held against their will.' He flashed a smile.

'She can come and live with us.' Her words were automatic but no less sincere for that. The question was how she broke it to her husband and the kids, particularly the one who would be giving up their bedroom. If she were being honest, she didn't exactly relish the thought. Yes, it was a pain toing and froing from her childhood home and back again for all and every emergency, but it was still more appealing than having her mother permanently under her roof.

'Well, you have a little while to think about it, make arrangements and whatnot. In the meantime, we are still running tests to

302

make sure we have a full health picture. But then I'll find her a place on a ward, and we'll get her transferred, make her comfortable.'

'Thank you.'

As she made her way back to her mother's cubicle, she caught the tail end of the conversation. Her mother spoke plainly. 'So I never saw the point of it. Emma's dad I think would have liked more, but I said to him, we got it so right the first time, she's a smasher, an absolute smasher, why risk having a second or third? And she is, Brendan, isn't she, she really is an amazing person, for which I take all the credit!'

It wasn't that her mother and husband were sharing such a lovely moment that brought a lump to her throat, nor her poor, injured mum's rarely displayed sense of humour, but the fact that she spoke with such fondness, such love for her. Something Emma had not heard directly before. She knew she'd never forget it.

'Ah, that's why we had to have the three,' Brendan countered. 'All we wanted in life was a kid clever enough to get a scholarship to Reynard's College – and sure Martha's pretty, Reggie kind, but it took us three attempts before we got an Alex!' He laughed, and she heard the faint hum of laughter from her mother. 'An actual Alex!' he chuckled.

'They're good kids.'

'They are, Marge, they really are.'

With her emotions running high, Emma decided to check on the boys. Reaching for her phone, she saw a text from Thurston, which suggested this method of communication wasn't his forte . . .

Tryng to text here. No rush. Have fuel. Stpd at ptrl station on way home. Will top up tank. Hope mother good. Thurston Brancher

This too made her heart swell, not only at the man's extraordinary kindness, but also at the sight of his surname, which thank goodness he'd included as, without it, she might have wondered which of the many Thurstons of her acquaintance it was from.

'Here we are then.' She spoke as she entered the cubicle, intimating she had not overheard the touching conversation that she knew was not for her ears. 'Just had a chat with the doctor. They're going to run a few more tests, Mum, and then when there's a bed, they'll get you up to the ward to make you comfortable.'

'Make me comfortable?' Her mother sniffed. 'How's he going to do that then? I need two new hips, a new shoulder, less of a dodgy stomach, legs that work better, something to stop my hands shaking and while he's at it, might as well throw in a facelift? Well, I can't wait!'

And just like that, normal service was resumed.

'I also got a text from Thurston, and he's very kindly put petrol in the tank, so if you give me a lift over there, Bren, I can drive home.'

'Of course. And how nice is that of him!'

'Very.' She felt a slow burn of exhaustion inside her. Relief, no doubt, at the fact that her mother was going to be okay, happy that Thurston had put petrol in her car and the adrenaline over her mother's hospitalisation had started to ebb.

'I'm always suspicious of people doing kind deeds for strangers!' her mother announced, still with her eyes closed. She and Brendan laughed quietly at each other; this, they knew, spoke volumes about the way her mother viewed the world. It was as sad as it was comical.

'There you are!'

All three looked up at the sound of Roz's voice as she rushed towards them. Emma blinked away the tears that threatened. This was what her best friend did; Roz, her fearless defender who turned up, poured oil on troubled waters, appeared when the chips were down, ran towards her in any given situation when others might run away. Over the years, these situations had been many and varied – when Emma was vomiting in the alley at the back of the chicken shop, had the jitters on the night before her wedding, was distressed as those first labour pains had sprung – *Well, it's a bit late to regret it now, love!* her friend's words of solace. And not least when her heart had cleaved open with loss on the day her dad had died. Roz – she was always there. And the mere thought that this would not always be the case . . .

Emma noted the faint shadow of fatigue beneath her friend's eyes that even the carefully applied concealer could not mask. There was also a pale tinge to her full lips and the smallest hint of breathlessness in this gregarious woman, and she knew, she knew she needed to step up, pull up her big girl pants and allow her friend to lean into her sickness with Emma as her support, *her* fearless defender. Their conversation when the horror had first reared its head came to her now:

I knew that if we both fell at the same time, we might not get up. This way, it's like a shift, a rota – we take turns in being strong so the other can lean on whoever needs it most.

It was time. Emma needed to be strong because that was what her darling Rozzie, from here on in, was going to need most.

'I got here as soon as I could, what's happened?'

'Mum had a fall. Broken shoulder and a bit of a bruised face.' Emma indicated a circle on her own face with her index finger, as if the big dark spread, like a purple and yellow cloud over her mum's cheeks, nose and forehead, were not clue enough.

'Well, Mrs Nicholson, you certainly gave us all a scare.'

'Not as much as Mr Blundesthorpe, who I could hear fussing and flapping while the ambulance was trying to get me loaded into the back. Silly old fool. Squawking away like a chicken!'

No one mentioned the fact that Margery's old fool of a neighbour was in fact a few years younger than her.

'Thank goodness he found you!' Brendan joined in. 'You could have been lying in the cold for a while if he hadn't.'

'Oh, Bren, don't, it doesn't bear thinking about.' Emma shuddered nonetheless.

'Mmm.' Margery, it seemed, wasn't giving the old man an inch.

'How did you know we were here?' Emma was glad, however, that she was.

'I popped in to see Martha and her and love's young dream were at the kitchen table drinking tea and talking like grown-ups. Made me feel very old.'

'How do you think I feel?' Emma pulled a face.

'How do you think *I* feel? A great-gran!' Margery hollered.

It was sudden and rare, the way Roz's face crumpled. Her best friend was not a crier, never had been, but it was as if she had been punched in the gut. Folding over, she shuffled backwards out of the cubicle.

'Back in a sec!' Emma shared a lingering look with Bren, who again sat forward in his chair, his concern evident, as he prepared for more small talk.

Emma followed her friend out of the curtain, worry flaring that something was very wrong.

'Roz, are you okay?' she asked, placing one hand across her back.

'Yes, I'm absolute peachy, that's why I'm standing here in the bloody A&E in tears, you arsehole!'

'Good point. What I should have said is, why are you crying, arsehole?' She knew the only way to bring her friend out of this melancholy was to match her, arsehole for arsehole.

It worked. Roz laughed and pulled her sunglasses from her handbag, which looked most incongruous inside the low-ceilinged A&E of the general hospital on this autumn day. Not that either of them gave a fig about that.

'Life, Em! Bloody life! That's why I'm crying.' Her nose ran and she wiped it on her sleeve.

'What can I do or say to make it better?'

'Nothing.' Her friend sniffed and Emma heard her own breathing loud in her ears, the echo of impotence at this truth. 'Nothing. It just gets me sometimes. Small things that cut me to the quick. I mean *Martha*, having a baby . . . *Martha!*'

'I know. I know.'

'One minute you pushed her out of your puppy canal . . .' Emma laughed. She'd forgotten they used to say this. Roz used to tease her, deciding that for how much Emma had always loved her dogs, preferring them to most humans, the only explanation was that she must have given birth to them. 'And when she was born, she was so tiny, and we used to cuddle her till her pips nearly popped, and she was a darling.'

Emma nodded, too overcome to mention the quaver to Roz's words or the fat tear that snaked from beneath the frame of her glasses, but most importantly, concentrating on being a strong and fearless defender so that Roz could lean on her.

'And what happened? We blinked and now that little freckle of a thing is going to be a mother. And I won't—' Roz took her time. 'I won't be here when that little thing grows up. I won't be here, Em!'

Emma let her best friend fall into her and held her tightly. 'I can't even . . .' Words failed her as a wave of grief rolled inside her.

A middle-aged doctor with close-cropped grey hair walked past, his eyes on his phone, pace determined. Roz straightened and watched him pass.

'I've shagged him,' she whispered.

'I see.' Emma shook her head in mock disgust.

'Hi, Roz!' A young doctor, rather bouncy and with a fashionably big beard, waved as he whizzed past with a colleague.

'I've shagged him too.' She nodded after the bearded medic.

'Is there anyone in this department you haven't shagged?'

A heavy-set nurse came out of a storeroom holding a stack of plastic-wrapped tubes, the purpose of which Emma could only guess at.

'I haven't shagged her.' Roz spoke with the vaguest twitch of a smile around her mouth.

'The day's young though,' Emma pointed out.

'True.'

'My mother always said you were a tarty piece. I think she might be right.'

Both women bit their lips to stifle the laughter that threatened to erupt from them, both knowing this was neither the time nor the place for such shenanigans. And both also knowing it was a case of laughing or crying. This felt preferable.

'You feeling a bit better?'

'A little bit.' Roz removed her sunglasses and took a deep breath.

'It'll all be okay. We'll get through whatever comes next.'

'Yep, whatever comes next.' Roz held her eyeline as a current of understanding passed between them, both aware of what would come and the fact that there wasn't a darned thing they could do to prevent it. Emma stood calmly, wanting to howl, wanting to rage at the world; her beloved best friend was going to leave her, and the thought alone cut her to the core.

Brendan emerged from the cubicle and stood close, rubbing her back quite briskly, up and down, up and down, and it irritated her, but she said nothing. Eventually, thankfully, he stopped rubbing and took her hand into his.

'I just wanted to check you guys were okay.'

'We are.' She squeezed his hand.

'Also . . .' He took his time. 'I wondered if you could come back to sit with your mum. I can't think of anything else to say to her. We've kind of run out of chat.'

'You ran out of chat in the mid-nineties, Bren.' Roz's tongue was sharp as ever. 'If it wasn't for me, you'd still be working out how to get her phone number.' She pointed at Emma. 'I was the conduit. If I hadn't acted as messenger, you might be leading a different life right now. One where you're married to someone else and aren't in the A&E on a Saturday afternoon with kids abandoned and your eldest preggers.'

'Thanks for that beautiful summing up of my life, Roz.' He clicked his tongue against the roof of his mouth.

'Not that you'd change a thing, right?' Emma stared at him.

'Not that I'd change a thing.' He kissed her on the cheek.

'Urgh, you guys make me puke.' Roz marched towards the cubicle; the way she wiped her eyes before going through the curtain suggested her words might be a lie. Emma shuffled in, holding her husband's hand.

Margery slowly turned her head on the pillow and spoke as if she wasn't present.

'You know, Rosalind, illness, especially terminal illness, is the worst thing, but if ever there was a character who could not only withstand the challenges but could bear it with dignity, with fortitude, it's you. You've always been so smart. The smartest, and a wonderful friend to Emma. Goodness only knows what kind of merry mess she'd have been without you by her side.'

Emma felt emotion rise in her throat; her mother's words were poignant, beautiful and laced with just the right amount of humour. It was odd that she'd not noticed it before, the similarity between her mother and best friend.

Roz took the chair recently vacated by Brendan.

'You are absolutely right, Mrs Nicholson, she would have been a merry old mess . . . but we kept her on the straight and narrow.'

'Yes.' Her mother yawned. 'We kept her busy, that was the key.'

◆ ◆ ◆

With her mum settled on the ward, tucked into a pristine bed and snoring, the trio made their way slowly out of the hospital. Weariness wrapped Emma's bones as adrenaline subsided, and the weekend and its events caught up with her.

'I need to pick the kids up.' Emma remembered they were stranded at Thurston's farm.

'We can do that on the way home. If we have to,' Brendan joked.

'And we need to let Martha know that Mum's okay and we're incoming.' She pictured her daughter at home, her pregnant daughter, and to think she'd been worrying that a mismatched plate might put the kibosh on her weekend. Nanny Marge's fall had top-trumped that.

'I'll do that now.' He reached for his phone, and she was glad, happy to hand over the rudder that steered the ship of their family life.

'She looked small, didn't she, my mum, lying in that bed, small and old.' Emma felt a little floored by the reminder of her vulnerability, her demise. Her mother's demeanour having shrunk in the short window between supper last night and her admittance to hospital.

'Did you want to sit with her for a little while longer? I'm happy to go pick up the boys.' Roz spoke in a caring voice that was, she guessed, one she saved for work, and in any other situation would have invited mimicry or scorn, but not today.

'Thanks, doll, but I'll let her sleep. I'll come back later for visiting time.'

'There's enough of us to put a plan together, share the load.' Brendan sounded firm. 'You don't have to be there for every visiting hour, every day.'

'That's true,' she agreed, feeling a small amount of relief that this was the case, with only a fleeting dart of guilt. 'It's a good idea, we can share the load.'

Brendan stopped suddenly and turned to her. 'Where is my wife and what have you done with her? Good God, I fully expected you to give me a thousand reasons why you might have to chain yourself to her hospital bed and be there at her beck and call!'

'Me too!' It was rare and comical for Roz to agree with him. The two high-fived over her head.

'You guys can mock, but the simple truth is that you're right, I can't do everything, and I can't fix everything. Sometimes, I need to ask for help.'

'Are you concussed? Drunk?' Roz stared at her with her top lip curled as she twirled her car keys in her hand.

'No, it's my new philosophy. Although getting drunk sounds quite attractive after the weekend we've had.'

'Shall I see if your mum has any of that Diet Coke left?' Brendan chuckled.

'You're not funny!' she snapped, while laughing hard at her husband, the idiot.

CHAPTER TWENTY-EIGHT

THURSTON

Thurston had found it funny at first, Andrew's suggestion that Emma had done a runner and was probably right at that very moment on a flight to Acapulco and he was in fact now responsible for the two boys, who had eaten more food than he managed in a whole day – for lunch! As the hours ticked by, however, he began to worry about what he might feed them for supper should they still be here. Such appetites!

He tried to remember being of a similar age, when there were sandwiches during breaks in the field, eaten leaning on a fence or sitting in the cab of his dad's battered Landy, doors open, muddied boots resting on the inside of the door, flasks of hot tea. Taking in the view, not saying much. He was certain it was a better dining experience, more memorable and delicious, than he'd have got at any of the fancy Michelin-starred restaurants he and Mary watched snippets of on the telly. His mother insisted they had home-made cake with tea in the afternoon and a hearty supper, which was always meat and spuds in any number of variants with seasonal vegetables. This was her most brilliant and constant contribution to farm life, but these lads had already put away three rounds of wide sandwiches, fist-sized chunks of parkin and enough blackcurrant squash to keep him rushing to the bathroom all night, had he consumed the same. Not that he was complaining; to have company, to feel the house alive with life, was a tonic that lifted his spirit.

It was mid-afternoon when he heard the sound of wheels on gravel; at the same time, Rhubarb began to bark towards the window. The pup's ears far more attuned than his own.

'That'll probably be your mother.' Thurston stood from the armchair.

'Noooooh!' Alex slapped his head with the flat of his palm and Thurston felt a flare of delight that the lad was happy with no more than a real fire, which seemed to hold a fascination, the soft sofa in which to sink next to his brother, a ready supply of grub and an old video of *The Magnificent Seven*. 'I want to watch the end of the film!'

'Well, I'm sure you can come again, if your mother says it's okay.'

'I'll be back in the week anyway, as Andy and I are going to start building the raised vegetable beds,' Reggie asserted.

Andy? Thurston had never seen the man as an Andy . . . He knew this would have made Mary laugh.

'You know where you're siting them?'

There had been much pacing and much toing and froing with a tape measure, and it had made him chuckle on the inside while simultaneously pleasing him. He and Nancy had shared a look, understanding that it was most definitely a case of the blind leading the blind, but there was no doubting their enthusiasm for the project and that was to be lauded. She had looked a little elated, a little relieved that her husband was up and about, involved, motivated, *busy.*

313

'Yes, we've marked out our plots at the back of the yard behind the tool barn and next we're going to get the wood, measure it up.' Reggie spoke with authority.

'Hello?' Emma's voice called from the kitchen door. He walked out to meet her and was surprised to see her standing outside, with who he assumed was her husband by her side, a tall chap who looked like Reggie. At Merrydown Farm, man and boy, he'd only ever known visitors to arrive and walk straight in. He reminded himself that this was only the third time he'd met Emma and she was not actually one of the fold who had peppered his memories for decades.

'Come in! Come in!' he urged. And they did just that, standing by the scrubbed table, whose round legs had worn shallow dips in the flagstones where dog hair and stray crumbs liked to gather.

He noted her slightly hesitant manner and hoped that they'd not had bad news, the worst.

You can let go of her hand now, Mr Brancher . . . she's gone . . .

'Thurston, I am so sorry we've been this long, what a disaster of a day it's been.' She caught her breath. 'This is my husband, Brendan.'

The lanky man stepped forward and shook Thurston's hand. His eye contact was a little off, his head tilt awkward, his grip a little weak, the contact too brief. Definitely not worthy of a solemn nod from the praepostor.

'Good to meet you. Thank you for making such a tricky day easier.' Brendan's genuine smile, warm manner and easy tone, however, more than made up for it. He was likeable and for that alone, Thurston gave him the nod.

'Likewise, Brendan, good to meet you.'

'Did you get my text?' Emma wrung her hands, as if hoping he did and that maybe it might contain information that was important.

'No!' He scanned the countertop and tabletop, wondering where he'd left his phone. And as for receiving a text, he'd only managed to send one with Nancy's patient instruction. 'I'm not very good with the phone. Had it for years and am only just starting to figure it out. I much prefer the landline.' He remembered when mobile phones first arrived, saying to Mary, 'They'll never catch on, why would anyone need to call anyone when they were out and about – what could be so important that can't wait until you get home? I mean, even in an emergency there's phone boxes on every corner!'

'You must have thought we'd done a runner and left you with the reprobates!' Brendan made an attempt at humour.

'Not at all,' he lied. 'They've been no trouble. Nancy and Andrew only left half an hour ago, they were cooking June a roast. That's my sister,' he explained, declining to mention that he too was invited, his attendance entirely dependent on when they arrived to collect the boys. He smiled now to think of a lovely rich gravy that might await him if he got a wiggle on.

'How's your mother?' he asked softly, aware that this might be a sensitive topic, but equally aware that not to ask, considering their dash to the emergency room, would be odd.

'She could be a lot worse,' Brendan whispered and Emma closed her eyes, head down, as if giving thanks. Something he could relate to. 'A broken shoulder and a lot of bruising. They've kept her in, and she was snoring like a sailor when we left.'

'Well, I'm truly glad to hear that.' Only able to think about his own experience and the drive back to Merrydown alone on that fateful day, knowing his wife would never again step over the threshold. Even the prospect of being around fresh grief was enough to lift the lid on the pot of sorrow that he carried in his gut, and he felt his throat tighten. 'Happy she's on the mend. And it's a wonderful hospital. Really is.'

'Thank you, Thurston.' Her warmth and sincerity tore at his heart.

'Hi, Mum!' Reggie loped into the kitchen. 'Andy and I are going to start building this week, and we already have a fair idea of what we're planting.'

'That sounds great. I was telling your dad about your plans.'

'It sounds amazing!' the boy's father enthused, and Thurston felt a flare of envy; what a wonderful honour it was to guide a young life in this way.

'Come on, love, in the car.' Emma clapped, like she was herding geese. 'And Thurston, how much do I owe you for fuel? That was so very kind of you.'

'No, not at all! Nothing, you owe me nothing.' He held up his hand. 'My absolute pleasure.' It felt good to do something nice for this young couple who had had a trying day.

'Thank you. Thank you for everything.' She walked forward and gave him the warmest hug. He found the contact profoundly moving. The last person to hold him like this had been his wife, quite a long time ago now, and in that instant he recalled the comfort in it and his heart ached a little at the loss of it. Emma was a wonder, her physical ease with him a reminder that if he let others get close there was still happiness and even love to be found in this world that for him had turned a little grey. Not romantic love, never that again for him, who at his age had lost his one and only, but maybe with people like Emma as a friend, June relying on him and even Nancy popping in, his final years, if he decided to stick around, might not be as bleak as he had first envisaged. Would that be so bad?

'Thurston, I look forward to seeing you again and yes, what Em said, thank you for everything.' Brendan looked him squarely in the eye. 'Come on, Alex!' he called through the open kitchen door.

The boys traipsed reluctantly out of the house and into the cold evening air.

◆ ◆ ◆

He watched from the kitchen window as the family jumped into cars and prepared to head home, Reggie with his dad and Alex travelling with his mum. The boys' general demeanour spoke of a day well spent and it pleased him; it would have felt rotten if they'd hated their trip.

The phone on the kitchen wall rang.

'Your dinner's on the table!' June barked and put the phone down.

'Righto,' he replied to the dull tone of disconnection. 'Come on, Rhubarb, we are off for a good gravy.'

The dog wagged his tail in obvious delight and Thurston knew if he had one, he'd probably wag it too.

CHAPTER
TWENTY-NINE

Emma

'How's Nan?' Martha asked the moment they walked inside the house. It was hard to see her little face twisted in anguish. Sergio, she noted, stood close to her, his hand on her lower back. Supportive, in anticipation of whatever the news might be, and yes, kind. It was nice to see.

'She's okay, love, going to be fine. Did you not get Dad's text?' He had, she knew, already conveyed the good news, wanting to put her girl out of her misery.

'No!' Martha's chest heaved, her emotions clearly hovering very close to the surface.

'Don't fret, lovely, it's all good, I promise. Let's go sit in the lounge.'

Despite her fatigue, Emma did her best to raise a smile while Brendan shepherded the kids into the room where they liked to gather. Brendan sat on the arm of the big chair, and she lowered herself into it. Her three kids were lined up on the sofa and they all looked so young, even Martha, the expectant mum. Sergio sat by her feet with Bruce on his lap. The dog was fussy about who he plonked his bottom on, so this boded very well.

'Nanny Marge is doing okay,' she began, pausing.

'Is she going to die?' Alex cut in with the question.

'One day, we all are,' Brendan answered, and the air in the room gained weight. She could feel it on her shoulders and head.

'Way to go, buzzkill!' Reggie rolled his eyes. His confidence, despite the dire topic, she found exciting, hoping it signified the start of something.

Martha began to cry. 'I thought we were going to lose her today, I thought that was what had happened when Dad said she was going to hospital!'

Emma, acting on instinct, jostled forward, preparing to take her child in her arms, but in that moment she watched as Sergio turned and did just that, sandwiching Bruce between the two of them. This boy, the father of her first grandchild, the man who owned her daughter's heart, held her close and brushed her hair with the flat of his palm. Brendan ran his arm across Emma's shoulders and let it rest there. Was this how her parents had felt when she'd brought Brendan home and suddenly they faded a little, became less distinct in her thoughts as her love for this man eroded their hold on her heart? She still loved them, of course she did, but to hold Brendan's hand, to walk with Brendan, talk to Brendan, lie with Brendan . . . he was all she could see and think about. Her parents were relegated, and she now understood the pain of it. With this pain, however, was the understanding that there were other people holding the corners of the safety net, if and when her loved ones fell. Thurston was right, she didn't need to do it all.

'What, what happened then, how did she get hurt?' Martha managed, pulling away from Sergio to blot her eyes and nose with her sleeve.

'She tripped in her neighbour's garden, turned suddenly and down she went.' She gave the paltry explanation that seemed to be a bit of a catch-all today.

'And she broke her bones?' Alex asked with more glee than any of them thought was appropriate.

'Not all of them, her collar bone, and she's got some nasty bruises.' Brendan, she could feel, was trying to silence their son with no more than a hard stare over her head.

'You're such a div,' Reggie snapped at his brother, and she was without the energy or inclination to reprimand him.

'Why was she in her neighbour's garden?' Martha asked, and Emma wondered this too.

'I don't know, love. But what I do know is that Nanny Marge is in good hands, nice and comfy in the hospital, so you don't have to worry. We can all visit her.'

'I don't think I'll go to school on Monday,' Reggie stated, and she felt Brendan's grip on her shoulder. They could have predicted this.

'How long will they keep her in, Mum? Should we go back to Bristol or stay here?' Martha went into planning mode.

We . . .

'I don't know, love, but it could be a few days, a week maybe,' she guessed, 'so go back to Bristol, there's nothing you can do here really. You can speak to her on the phone, of course, and visit her soon. You need to look after yourself, Martha.'

'She will,' Sergio interjected. 'I'll make sure. I've got her all the right vitamins and I cook for her from scratch every night.'

'She's lucky to have you, Sergio.' No matter how much her instinct was to be wary of this fast-moving lad who'd swooped in when Carlo's seat was still warm and got her child pregnant, every time he opened his darned mouth, she liked him a little bit more.

'I'm lucky to have her.' And the way he held her eyeline filled her with optimism.

'I've got a question.' Alex sat forward and pushed his glasses up on to his nose.

'What is it, lovey?'

'Can we get a new house now?'

'A new house?' She was a little confused; this was not what she had expected, although it was Alex doing the asking and he was never predictable.

He nodded. 'I was thinking that because our house is a bit rubbish and now that Nanny's in hospital and will have to go into an old people's home, we can take the money from her house and sell our house and get a really nice house, like Piers and Dimitri's houses. Piers has a games room and Dimitri has a swimming pool.'

Sergio let out a burst of laughter and she didn't blame him, knowing that if she hadn't been the mother of the boy born without a verbal filter and an as yet poorly developed moral compass, she might have found it funny too.

'For the love of God, Alex!' Brendan spoke despairingly on her behalf.

'What?' He looked close to tears. 'What have I done now?'

'The fact that you don't know shows you're not as clever as you like to think you are,' Reggie countered.

'All right, enough!' It was unusual for Brendan to raise his voice. Even Sergio jumped. 'Nanny Marge is only going to be in hospital for a little while and when she comes out, she will need taking care of and that will cost a lot of money. Old people's homes, as you call them, cost an arm and a leg. This certainly isn't the time to be thinking about what might make your life better. It's about helping her and helping your mum.' He addressed Alex.

Emma knew this was the time to mention her chat with Dr Khan; she would have done so sooner had Roz not had a meltdown, the poor love.

'Actually, when Nanny Marge comes out of hospital, she'll be coming to live with us for a bit, just so we can keep an eye on her until she gets back on her feet and things are put in place.'

She felt the collective eyes of her family on her.

'Where will she sleep?' Alex asked.

'Well.' She swallowed. 'I was going to ask one of you to give up your room for a bit.'

'She can have my room, I'm away most of time.' Martha the first to speak.

Emma drew on her strength. 'That's sweet of you, love, thank you, but your room is tiny. I was thinking maybe one of you boys could hop into Martha's room and let Nanny—'

'Jesus!' Reggie jumped up from the sofa, interrupting her. 'I'm not moving! No way! It's my room! Alex can go.'

'I have all my books and my desk for studying!' Alex pleaded his case.

Emma's heart sank to hear the fracas emerging.

'Enough!' Brendan shouted. The room fell silent. Even Sergio looked a little sheepish. 'I have just explained that your mum and Nanny Marge in particular need your kindness, your support. This is the opposite of that, boys!'

'Sorry, Dad.' Reggie kicked at the floor.

'I'm sorry, Dad, but I still think Nan would be happier in Reggie's room.'

Reggie reached out to grab his little brother as Alex leaped up. Reggie chased him from the room and up the stairs.

'I'm going to make a cup of tea.' Emma found solace in the chore and liked the quiet of her lovely kitchen, still her favourite room in the house.

Brendan crept in and leaned on the countertop. She felt a little nervous, knowing the conversation they were going to have. 'That was a nice announcement you made. Didn't you think to let me know in advance your mum was moving in, or at least ask?' He shook his head and snorted his frustration, as if she wasn't already aware of his underlying hurt.

'This was the first moment I've had to—'

'No, Em, no it isn't. You and I both know you preferred to wait till you had an audience, avoid the debate alone with me. And for the record, for any family and life-altering event, I would always, always okay it with you first. Because I'm considerate. And what bugs me most is that I would of course agree in a heartbeat, of course I would!'

Her mood flared with embarrassment masquerading as anger. 'Okay, what do you want, an apology?'

'No, I want you to not shut me out or make me feel like an outsider, like it's the Emma show and I have to just go along with the plan. I want to shape the plan, to help *you* shape the plan!'

'What bloody plan?' She stared at him, one hand rubbing her face, her eyes itchy. 'We don't have a plan, we coast along by the seat of our pants and deal with shite when we step in it.'

'That's how most people live, Emma – what, do you think everyone has some grand strategy? That most people aren't just dodging puddles of shite?'

'Actually, that's right, now I do remember your strategy – wasn't it you who suggested my mother's death was our pension plan?' She filled the kettle with trembling hands.

'What?' He stared at her as if he had misheard.

'You know what I'm talking about.' Reaching for two mugs, she banged them down on the countertop. It was as if she'd got on this anger train and couldn't jump off, even if she knew it was misdirected.

'Emma,' he began, 'I love you and know that today is a tough one, we have a lot going on, but don't treat me like something you can kick when things are difficult. That demeans us both. I know you're stressed, tired, upset; I am too. So please try to remember that we are on the same side.'

To hear his calm and accurate reasoning was enough to remove the dam that had kept her tears at bay. Her sob was loud and forceful, causing her to catch her breath and cling to the countertop while she bent forward.

'It has been a bit of a day, Bren!' Roz's tears, her distress at the inevitability of her illness hit her fully in the chest. This bookended with guilt that her mum had ended up falling while she had been absent.

'I know.' He stood close, ready for a hug, whatever she might need.

'I just wanted a bit of fresh air, a walk in a field, but my mother ends up in A&E, Roz is falling apart and Martha's having a baby! It's a lot,' she sobbed, her face wet with snot and tears. 'And I guess I was wary of mentioning her coming to stay here because the truth is, the truth is . . .'

'What, love?' he coaxed.

'I don't want her to come and live here, even for a short while! I don't want to disrupt the kids. I love my mum, I like seeing her, but I also like it when she goes home!' She sniffed. 'I like it when she goes home very much. I'm trying hard to be less controlling, give up things, share the load and then bam! She'll be here twenty-four/seven! Am I a bad person?' she asked, looking up at him.

'No.' He spoke softly. 'Just a tired one, who's dodging puddles of shite, like us all. You're wonderful to your mum, and you were a good daughter to your dad, a really, really good and attentive daughter, and so you can't waste a day feeling misplaced guilt. You can't, and neither of them would want you to.'

His words helped, a little.

'Seeing Roz so distressed today and not having any answers for her, it's made me think about her end, her funeral . . .'

'Just don't, Em.' He sighed. 'Please can we deal with one tragedy at a time. One day at a time.'

Easier said than done . . . She grabbed a square of kitchen roll from the counter and wiped her eyes and blew her nose. 'I'm going to nip over to Mum's and make sure it's all locked up, everything switched off and stuff. I don't even know if the windows are open, or if the oven's on. I won't settle until I've given it the once-over.'

'I'll come with you.'

'No – thanks, love, but I want to go on my own. I'll probably sit and have a little cry and grab some of her things.'

'Are you sure you don't want me to come with you?' She loved his sweetness.

'I'm sure. But you can shove oven chips in the oven if you feel up to it, I'll do egg and chips when I get back. I expect the boys are hungry, don't know if they've eaten.'

'Course I will. It'll all be all right, you know, all of it.'

'Yep.' She forced a smile and grabbed her car keys.

It occurred to her, as she pulled into the road, that there would be no need for her to make this trip thrice daily anymore with her mum living under her own roof. It had become such a major part of her routine, a habit. To get that time back would, she figured, be nice. A silver lining and all that.

No sooner had she parked the car than her mother's neighbour came running out into his front garden.

Oh, please no . . . this was the last thing she needed. He started calling out before her feet had touched the pavement.

'Emma! Hello, Emma! Is there any news? Are they keeping her in? I've . . . I've been waiting all day.' He seemed highly agitated. 'I didn't want to disturb you, but I was wondering how your mum was and what the visiting arrangements are? I've picked some late-blooming chrysanthemums; I know she likes them. A proper riot of colour! They'll brighten any dreary ward and if she's not allowed flowers then I'll take them in to show her and then bring them home again and pop them in a vase for when she's discharged.'

Her dread in the face of his kindness ladled guilt over her thoughts.

'Oh, Mr Blundesthorpe, that's so kind of you. Yes, yes' – she swallowed – 'thank you for helping my mum out today, for calling the ambulance and everything.'

'Of course, my pleasure!' He beamed at her.

'She's broken her collar bone and is very bruised. They're keeping her in for a few days at least and we'll go from there.'

It would have been hard to express what she might have expected from her mother's neighbour, but what she wouldn't have foreseen was the way he leaned on the wall, his body folded, racked by loud and unsightly crying.

'Oh no! No! Mr Blundesthorpe, whatever is the matter?' Emma stared at the man, unsure of what to do or say next. 'Can I, can I get you a chair or a glass of water?'

He shook his head and reached into the pocket of his trousers for an ironed white handkerchief, with which he wiped his eyes and nose.

'I've been so worried. I thought I might have lost her, the longer there was no news, my mind ran riot. I called my niece and said I feared the worst. One minute Margery was dancing on the path to make me laugh, twirling she was like a teen, and we were chuckling, the next thing I knew she tripped over her feet and bang! Down she went.' The man dried his eyes and coughed to clear his throat. His relief evident.

She took a moment to process his words. There was much that she needed to sense-check – the image of her often cranky mother twirling like a teen was one – but also his phrase 'I thought I might have lost her . . .' This was not the muted response to a neighbour having a fall. Her mouth ran dry as she mentally joined the dots, unable to accept the picture she was painting, surely not . . .

'Relief doesn't come close, Emma. The whole thing has knocked the wind right out of my sails, I don't mind telling you.' He sniffed and took some deep breaths.

'Yes.' She had to admit to feeling a little bit embarrassed by his display. It was one thing to be neighbourly, to deliver spare courgettes and tomatoes when you had a bumper harvest, even to call an ambulance when that neighbour was in need, but his distress was . . . surprising. Yes, that was the word. But not as surprising as what came next. Confirmation that her dot-joining was in fact on point. 'So you and my mother are . . .'

'We are company for each other, good company. Friends. No more than that. Courting, I suppose the word is.'

'You and my *mother*?' She needed clarification. 'Courting?' Her face twitched as the desire to laugh at the absurdity and cry at the shock of it battled in her mind.

'She doesn't want you to know. But we make sense. It's easy.' He gazed into the middle distance, as if picturing the woman he was courting. 'I lost Sylvia, and then of course your dad passed away, and Margery and I have known each other since we first moved here, before you were born.'

'A long time,' she echoed.

'A lifetime! A whole lifetime.' He stared up at his own house. 'At first we'd talk over the fence, keep each other company of an evening, and it developed from there.'

'Developed how?' Shoving her fingers into her jeans pockets, instantly she regretted asking. Did she really want to know whatever it was he had to say about him and her mother? The facts just would not sink in.

'We are . . .' He took his time, and she was grateful, knowing his choice of words would make all the difference when she analysed this later and when she told Brendan and Roz. 'We are companions.'

Companions. Yes, that would do.

'I wonder why she's never said, doesn't want me to know.' This both perplexed and saddened her.

'Well, she knows how desperately cut up you are over losing your dad, as was she. And she thought it might be too much for you, to think I might be on the scene. Don't know how she'll feel about me letting the cat out of the bag, but I can't say I'm not relieved about this too.'

'But I've never seen you together!' she blurted, not wanting to cast doubt on his claim but more interested in how this was so.

'We're very careful. She bangs on the wall when you leave, I watch you drive off and then nip in when you've disappeared around the corner, and once or twice when you've arrived at the front door, I've had to leg it out of the back door a bit sharpish!' This explained his constant curtain twitching, the feeling that he was watching her now confirmed. 'I think it's part of the appeal for your mum at least, the skullduggery of it all.' He wheezed as he chuckled. She couldn't imagine the octogenarian legging it anywhere. 'We make each other laugh, Emma, and that's very important.'

'It is.' The image of the man waiting for her mother's signal made her smile, yet she also felt a little hurt that her mum felt she couldn't talk to her about this relationship. She was glad that her mum had found laughter with her companion. She deserved nothing less. It was, however, going to take a while for the discovery to percolate. A conversation with her mother came to her now.

I mean it, Emma, I'm fine! But if you are going to come then do come when you say you are. Being late or just popping in upsets my routine, messes with my plans . . .

She had tutted, believing her mother to have a routine that was dull, fixed and certainly without any plans to speak of. And when her mother had called about pick-up time for dinner with Martha, Emma had found it irritating.

What time is that exactly? I like to be ready to go.

But maybe her mum wasn't being pedantic, but rather making sure her fancy man was out of sight! It was a thought as amusing as it was jarring.

'I think we're friends, Emma, aren't we?' It was close to asking for her approval and she was delighted by it, knowing that neither he nor her mother required any such thing.

'We are, Mr Blundesthorpe.'

'Good. Good.' He let out a deep sigh, as if he'd been holding his breath.

'I'm just going to go into the house and make sure everything is properly locked up and give it the once-over.'

She pointed towards the front door through which she'd been walking her whole life, understanding that this was another step change, her mother moving on romantically. Swallowing tears of nostalgia at the memory of her mum calling her in.

Emma-Jane, your tea's ready!

Emma-Jane, what time do you call this?

Emma-Jane, take off your shoes, I've just scrubbed the hall floor!

Emma-Jane, is that you? I thought I heard a noise . . .

'Would you like me to come in with you?' His question pulled her from the memory.

'No thank you, Mr Blundesthorpe. But thanks for offering.'

'I think it's time you stopped calling me Mr Blundesthorpe, don't you?'

'I guess so. I don't actually know what your name is.' She laughed to mask her embarrassment.

Mr Blundesthorpe laughed too. 'My name is Gordon.'

Emma bit the inside of her cheek, quashing the inexplicable desire to laugh. 'Gordon. Right then.'

She wondered what in the world Roz was going to make of this little gem of news . . .

CHAPTER THIRTY

THURSTON

'Thank you for dropping me home, June.' He spoke as the wide wheels of her Range Rover crunched over the cobbles in the front yard. 'That was quite some roast. I've not had much of an appetite of late, but I did enjoy that.' He felt the ache of his stomach against the waistband of his ancient moleskins.

'You're welcome, Thurston. It was nice to see you and nice to see Nancy and Andrew as well. They seem . . .' She tapped the steering wheel as if the right word evaded her and he nodded.

'Yes, they do.' He could only agree, having noticed they were a lot more touchy-feely than he'd ever seen before.

'He sounds highly motivated about his raised vegetable beds.'

He detected the merest hint of mockery in her tone.

'I think it's good he has a project, no matter what it is. And good he's roping in young Reggie, feels like they can both only benefit. Who knows where it might lead for the man, an interest in farming?'

'Yes, yes,' she conceded. 'I'm all for it. Not that I can see him getting stuck in the way you and Dad always have.'

'I think it needs to be in your blood.' He'd long thought this. 'Spending time with Emma and her family and then with my own tonight, it's made me think—'

'Think about what?' she asked with the faintest whiff of impatience, as if pre-empting what he might be about to say.

'About how I want to spend the rest of the time I have left on the planet.'

'Oh God, I knew it! Don't go all maudlin on me again. I can't stand it!' She rolled her eyes.

'I'm not, but I look at this big old house, this land, and I wonder how I'll manage.'

'You'll manage because you shall have help, we'll all help you. We'll all help each other. That's how it works.'

He took comfort from this, his heart warmed. 'I wonder if it might be wise to sell the farm . . .' He spoke as the thought occurred, the words slipping from his tongue without any forethought, yet not the first time he had considered it. But whether he was going to die or whether he was going to live, wouldn't it be easier not to have Merrydown to worry about?

'What do you mean, *sell* the farm?' his sister snapped.

'What do you think it means?' She was so irritating. 'And I was only voicing a thought, that maybe it might make sense to get rid of the lot and move somewhere smaller, a manageable house like the new ones they've built at the end of the lane.'

'Don't be so ridiculous!' she shouted, loudly enough that Rhubarb in the footwell jumped up on to his lap.

'It's not ridiculous, June. As I say, it was just a thought, no more, and it might be the most practical outcome.'

'Well, that's just grief talking, you don't mean it! *Sell the farm* . . .' She tutted.

'Yes, it is grief talking, grief that shapes my thoughts and my worries right now. And it's no bad thing to make provision, to look towards the future.' He hated how he had to justify everything to the woman who had been bossing him around since she was five years old.

'You think we don't all have those crazy thoughts when in the first stages of loss? You think I didn't spend hours on Rightmove looking at apartments in Fuerteventura where I thought I could make out I was on holiday for the rest of my days, drink sangria, swim in the sea and not have to climb into a bed without Melvin in it? Of course I did! Everyone thinks it when they are suffering, it's universal, that dream of packing a little bag and running far away.'

'Have you ever been to Fuerteventura?'

'That's not the point, Thurston!'

He stared at her, thinking this was exactly the point.

'This isn't just a house. Merrydown is our life, our heritage, where all our memories are. You can't just pack up and go. Pass it on to strangers! It's Brancher blood that runs through the soil, our sweat that built the place, every stone, every blade of grass, it's Great-grandpa, Pops, our own dad and now you. The tools that have been handed down, the old tractor, the leaky tin roofs and the stone walls that mark our boundaries. Old and solid. Our *land*, Thurston, our *land* . . . a tiny part of God's green earth that we are the custodians of. It's . . . so much more than an address!' Her tone was panicked, her chest heaving.

'It's precisely because of all those memories that I think I might want to be somewhere else.'

The thought of not having to run the gauntlet of the kitchen every morning was a welcome one, not to sob at the sight of a lick of gravy on the dining room wall where Mary had once tripped and splashed the wallpaper. He knew it was indeed 'ridiculous', but even the sight of this drip on the anaglypta was enough for him to feel the pull of tears.

June shook her head. 'Maybe now. But in a short while you'll be glad they're all around you. They'll keep you warm. They're like little spots of glitter, they turn up in the most unexpected of places, they're hard to get rid of, and when you find one, it gladdens your heart.'

He felt the shiver along his limbs and knew that if it were true, he couldn't wait for that day.

June turned towards the wall that ran along the back of the big barn, the big barn where he planned to end his days.

'Look, Thurston.' She pointed at little dark holes in the stone, now filled with dust, muck and cobwebs. 'All those round dents, that's where Father and Uncle Banbury took potshots with an air rifle after one too many snowballs at Christmas the year war broke out. And inside that barn, if you look behind the old bread oven door, you'll see the name of the boy I wanted to marry, written on the wall when I was fourteen. *Fourteen!* My friend Hetty Walbridge said if you wrote it or carved it somewhere, it might come true. Our history, our heritage.'

'Well, I need to go and have a look now. Whose name did you write?' He was curious and tried to imagine who his fourteen-year-old sister had had her eye on. This another revelation, an insight into her life, a chapter she had kept closed.

'You don't need to go and look, Thurston.' He watched as she ran her thumb over the thin gold band on the third finger of her left hand. 'It says Melvin Armitage. It was always him.'

Instinctively, he reached out and held her hand in his own, this kind of contact rare, yet necessary, as he recognised the depth of grief that had altered his sister as something similar to his own. Squeezing his fingers with her head averted, he knew she took comfort from it.

Having watched her car disappear down the driveway, he whistled for Rhubarb and made his way inside. It had been nice to have people at Merrydown today, their presence in the sitting room and the chatter bouncing off the walls. The kitchen was now warm, welcoming almost, as he walked over to the Aga where Mary had spent many an hour and ran his hand over the long rail on the front of which she used to hang dishcloths and even socks to dry.

'Little spots of glitter.' He spoke aloud.

His sister's words had certainly provided food for thought.

'If only you could let me know I *will* see you again, my love. Maybe I could hold on, wait out my days with the love around me and new friends and things to look forward to . . .'

In that moment, recovery, even if only partial, felt possible and just as much of a revelation was the fact that he didn't wholly hate the idea. Previously, he had decided that he had so loved his wife that it felt only fitting to be altered, encumbered by the loss of her. His physical stance proof that his capacity for joy, to love, indeed all his appetites had been scythed to stubs. But not right now.

It was with some kind of relief that he questioned whether, no matter how much he longed for reunion with his sweet wife, he was prepared to create the devastation and hurt to those he'd leave behind. Emma's words again stood bold in his thoughts. Whatever the future held and however long he had left, could he find a new way to live, embracing all that this beautiful world had to offer, but doing so with a Band-Aid running right across his broken heart?

He truly did not know the answer. But maybe he didn't need contact from the other side, a whisper in his ear, a hand on his cheek, or even that wave from the bedroom window; maybe Mary was in fact all around him, if he just knew where to look . . .

CHAPTER
THIRTY-ONE

EMMA

Nanny Marge resolutely refused to leave her home and move into Reggie's bedroom. She was quite insistent that now she and Gordon had gone public, there was no need for her to go anywhere. The man who was once a friendly neighbour now spent more time in Emma's childhood home than he did his own, tending to the impatient patient's varying needs and welcoming the community nurse twice daily. Not that Emma was complaining.

'I was just thinking about you and, erm . . .' She sat in front of her mother in the open-plan kitchen/dining room.

'Spit it out, Emma!' Margery tucked the blanket around her legs. 'You look like you have words queuing up to jump off your tongue.'

'I guess . . .' She took her time, not entirely sure what she wanted to say or indeed how to say it. 'I guess I'm still a little bit surprised that you and Gordon are . . .'

'An item?'

'Yup.' She nodded.

'Surprised because you think I should be content to wallow in my aged years without friendship, without love?'

'You *love* him?' For some reason this she found most jarring of all, the idea that her dad could in some way be supplanted.

'Yes.' Her mother held her gaze, unflinching. 'In my own way I do, and surely I don't need to explain to you, a grown woman, how it's possible to love many people in your life, and to love them differently.'

'You don't.' Emma stared back. 'I guess I'm still getting my head around it. It feels like you went from lonely widow to part of a couple very quickly.'

'First, Emma-Jane, it was not quick, and I resent that suggestion and all its implications.' She felt suitably admonished and had to admit it was a mean and petty thing to say and did them both a disservice. 'Second, it's only ever been you who has seen me as a lonely widow! Coming and sitting by my side every spare second, force-feeding me lunch, good God it was smothering! I told you time and again, there was no need to come and sit with me. I'm perfectly capable of eating my lunch alone as and when I feel like it. But it was like—' Her mother paused.

'Like what?' She braced herself.

'Like you didn't want to move on from grief, didn't want to stop talking about Dad, didn't want to let him go, not finally, not properly, not in the way you need to when someone dies. Not forget him, not stop loving him, of course not, not ever, but letting him go is vital so you and I can move on. Go forward. Carry on living.'

Upon hearing this truth, Emma's tears were hot and cathartic as her mother voiced with such ease all that she'd fought hard to hide.

'I don't say it often enough and I know that you and I are maybe not so good at the mushy stuff, but I do, I do love you, Mum,' she hiccupped.

'Thank you.' Her mother picked at a loose thread on the blanket.

'And I know you love me, I heard what you said to Brendan – that you and Dad got it so right the first time, that I was a smasher, an absolute smasher . . . an amazing person. That's what you said!'

'Did I?' Her mother feigned ignorance. 'Must have been that bump on the head.'

'If you say so.' She liked this ease with which they chatted; it was far more akin to how she and her dad had interacted.

'So, I'm assuming you'd rather not call Gordon "Dad" or "Daddy"?'

'Are you fucking kidding me?' She took the bait, hook, line and sinker.

'I *am* kidding you,' her mother chortled. 'Too easy, Emma-Jane, too easy. And please let's have no more of that language.'

It was now a month since her mother had been released from hospital. One month that had marked a turning point without the previously tense edge to every encounter, lest Margery's illicit romance be discovered. Emma found her pace of life far less hectic and her thoughts calmer. Her full focus was on Roz. Thurston was right, she could not risk spoiling whatever time they had left. It would indeed be a dire waste not to have the fun that had always shaped their relationship.

Not that Emma didn't, on occasion, go home and howl into her pillow at the injustice of it all or sit in the bath and sob at the prospect of what lay ahead, allowing herself some time to grieve in advance. It helped her accept what was going to happen and removed the naked fear over the prospect.

They were able to pretend for much of the time, like when Roz popped into the greengrocer's and they had chatted to Paddy shortly after the chilli incident, laughing until their tears flowed.

'So, just to get this right,' – Paddy had placed his hand on his chin – 'you ended up with a swollen face and stinging eye and Brendan ended up with a severe pain in his nether regions?' He had stared at her.

'Yes, Paddy, and all because of your little bag of contraband chillies! It's not funny!'

'It's a little bit funny!' Roz had snorted. 'I can't even tell you what I witnessed on that night, but my eyes will never be the same!'

'I understand that, and I'm not laughing!' Looking skyward, Paddy stroked his stubble. 'But what I'm trying to work out is what you were *doing* to cause both injuries. The mind boggles, Emma. It really does. And to think I had you pegged as a goody two-shoes!'

He swept from the room, grabbing a tray of fennel as he went, leaving her lost for words. What on earth was he imagining? And actually, that wasn't the point!

'See, I told you you were a goody two-shoes!' Roz squealed.

'Mew mew mew mew mew-mew mew mew mew!' Emma imitated her friend with this childish repeat. It made them both laugh.

'Ready, love?' Brendan called from the hallway, pulling her from thoughts of that day. A quick glance through the open doorway revealed the weather to be cold, blustery and with once-vibrant leaves now turned copper, clustering in the kerb and on the pathways. A fine reminder that everything wintered, withered and returned to the earth. The natural order of things. Certainly the natural order of things for her dad. Her dad who had chosen her as the person to receive his last phone call, on whom to gift his last words on earth. A most precious thing. Maybe he'd called that day to say goodbye or to make sure she knew how proud he was of her; either way, she was glad he'd done so. Very glad.

Today, they were off to Reggie's school carol concert at St Stephen's. An annual tradition, and family attendance was mandatory. She loved to see her little gang in their finery, all singing together the words of Christmas celebration. It took her right back to those nativity plays when her kids managed their one line with aplomb.

The boys stood side by side in the hallway, best buddies for once, unified in their dislike of having to wear smart clothes on a Sunday. Martha too, clutching Sergio's hand, and now, at sixteen weeks pregnant, she had started to rub her tummy in the way that felt natural when you were nurturing something so treasured. Emma was immensely proud of her girl and was very much enjoying the perusing of baby clothes online.

A granny! A privilege indeed.

Sergio stood with Martha's handbag on his shoulder while she sorted the collar of her shirt. Emma watched the boy closely, sensing he was going to be a good partner, the kind of man who'd hold Martha's handbag while she went to the bathroom or stopped to tie her laces or had to vomit in the kerb, the kind of man who'd just have that bag hanging on his shoulder without a second thought . . .

'Come on then, let's get this over with.' Roz, noticeably losing weight from her already slender frame, and with her breathing a little more laboured, came in to the hallway and took a moment, exchanging a knowing look with her best friend. 'What?'

'It's supposed to be fun! A pretty church, candles, singing and Jesus stuff.' Emma adjusted the collar of her navy-blue shirt. 'You're supposed to be looking forward to it! I find it very emotional.'

'Do you know me at all?' Roz took her arm and with Brendan on the other side, the three stepped out into the afternoon winter sun. 'I am not into Jesus stuff, and I don't find it emotional, I find it irritating. Think of all the things I could be doing instead of spending the day with your horrible children.'

'I heard that!' Alex piped up.

'Good!' Roz curled her lip at him, followed with a wink.

'I could be flirting with doctors right now . . .' Roz whispered. 'Finding my next heart to break.'

'I thought you'd already slept with every doctor at the General?' Emma thought it only prudent to point out.

'True, but I was thinking of the cottage hospital outside of town, new hunting ground.'

'Tarty piece.' Emma tutted.

It occurred to her that the reason for her friend's hesitance in visiting the church might be that, like her, Roz was thinking about the wintering and returning to the earth of all things. Squeezing her arm, she took a deep breath and stood tall, forcing herself to blink away funereal thoughts. Brendan was right: one tragedy at a time.

◆ ◆ ◆

The church was packed, as it always was for this annual event. Having ushered her gang into a long pew, Emma gripped the order of service and scanned the crowd in front of her, spotting one or two faces that were familiar: mums, dads and grandparents from the school, a couple of customers from the greengrocer's, her hairdresser JoJo, and Gloria from the bank. There were neighbours she recognised from the street she had grown up on, who had known her family for decades and who would of course now be aware that Mrs Nicholson and Mr Blundesthorpe were shacked up. There was old Mrs Tate, supported by her son, and a couple of rows ahead sat her mother's fancy piece himself, Mr Blundesthorpe, *Gordon* . . . Gordon. Gordon, her mother's neighbour, companion, beau . . . she wasn't sure she'd ever get used to calling the man by his first name or the fact that he and her mother were *friends*. Her mum had declined the invitation, pointing out that it would do her wobbly legs no good at all to be standing in a cold church for hours on end . . . Emma wasn't so convinced.

She vaguely recognised the woman standing by Gordon's side but couldn't quite place her. The Blundesthorpes only had one son, Michael, who now lived in Australia – but this woman, Emma knew her face from somewhere. It would no doubt come to her.

The organ struck a long, low note as the sound of shuffling feet filled the air. All stood in the blond wood pews with lyric sheets poised and anticipation in their bellies. Emma looked up at the roof of the modern church. The music was slow and moving. 'Staring at your shoes' music, she'd once heard someone describe it as, and she got it – not sure where to look, and so she stared at the toes of her smart navy loafers, peeping out from beneath the overly long grey linen trousers that were slightly flared.

She wasn't fond of it, the music, disliked how the sound manipulated her. It was always an emotionally charged service. Listening carefully now, she closed her eyes, quite lost to the low, slow note of the mournful oboe, the sorrowful pull of a bow over the strings of a cello and the clarinet, heralding loss with every note. It made her want to give in to the pull of melancholy that she fought hard to keep at bay.

And so she did. Previously, the thought of public crying in a quiet setting like this had made her nervous in case she was unable to control all that she held in, fearful of the noise alone. But right now her tears felt fitting and were exacerbated by the fact that her darling Roz, in just a few short weeks, was no longer able to climb the ladder and break into her bathroom. Instead, she had to knock on the front door like a normal person, which of course she wasn't, not even close. Who stuffs their mouth with tiny plastic dinosaurs, and why?

Emma sang the first carol with as much gusto as she could muster and retook her seat ready to hear what the vicar might have to say, no doubt a rehash of last year's verbal highlight reel and a thousand reasons why we should feel thankful. Sitting next to her beloved best friend, it felt easier, safer, to study the roof, which reminded her of an upturned hull, wide planks of honey-coloured wood with obvious nuts and bolts securing it. The curve beautiful, and streamlined, enough for her to imagine it righting itself and carrying them all off across the waves . . . A quick look around the room at the congregation, and she decided this would be horrific. Imagine being stranded on an ocean in a bobbing church with her entire family, Mr Blundesthorpe, Mrs Tate and Gloria from the bank, among others. And just as she tried to imagine this very thing, she looked to her right and caught sight of Mackenzie Baverstock. What was *she* doing here? Her kids hadn't even gone to Reggie's school! It bothered her that Mackenzie was in attendance, knowing that to face her was going to be awkward after their embarrassing display in the greengrocer's a few weeks ago. Mackenzie caught her eye and gave her a closed-mouth smile of acknowledgement. Emma looked straight ahead.

'And now, Year Seven will come to the front of the church to sing "I Saw Three Ships!"' the vicar boomed.

'Kill me now!' Roz whispered in her ear.

Emma ignored her, as ever quite taken by the communal singing, the feeling of togetherness and the voices of little ones. Not for the first time that day, she cried.

With carols sung, good cheer doled out in abundance, candles held aloft and a Christmas poem poorly delivered by a lisping sixth former, the service ended.

'Just nipping to the loo,' Emma informed Brendan as he corralled the family, ready for the walk home.

She pushed on a cubicle door and it flew open. Emma took a seat on the loo, breathing heavily with her face in her hands.

The next time I come into a church, it could be to say goodbye to my best friend . . . I will never, ever be ready for that . . .

'Em?' Roz called.

'I'm in here!' She dropped to the floor, leaned forward and wiggled her hand under the gap at the bottom of the door.

'Why don't you just open the door?'

'Because I've got my trousers and pants around my ankles,' she explained.

'Right.' Roz slunk down and spoke to the door, and Emma sat back against the cistern. It was certainly easier to chat when you didn't have to look directly at someone.

'I'm just having a moment.' She closed her eyes.

'I know.'

'And—' she started, not knowing how to finish.

'And what, Em?' Roz's voice was encouraging.

'And I don't want to think about your funeral but being in a church . . .' She felt the tight pull of sadness in her throat.

'That's funny, because I've been thinking about it a lot.'

'You have?' She was surprised. Coming from the super-positive Roz, it sounded a lot like defeat, made her dire prognosis real, and it tore at her heart.

'I've decided I want an Abba-themed funeral.'

Emma sprayed her laughter. 'You do?'

'Yes. I want "Dancing Queen" blaring far and wide and the whole congregation in flares and sequins. I want laughter and I want you to know that' – her friend's voice cracked – 'I want you to know that I will miss you. I will miss watching you getting older and fatter, which I think is inevitable. I will miss watching your awful kids turn into awful adults.' Emma could tell she was smiling; it helped plug the chasm of sadness that Roz's words opened inside her. 'And I will even miss seeing your dickhead husband lose his hair, which is already sparse, and I fully expect him to sport a paunch and whistling dentures. I shall miss all of it. All of it.'

'I love you, Roz.' She did her best to speak through a mouth twisted with distress, her friend's words like glass lodged in her throat.

'And I love you. My soul will miss you.'

'And mine yours. Forever.'

There was a beat of silence as the solemnity of their exchange filled the space around them.

'It will be terrible at first, Em, almost unbearable, just like when you lost your dad, but you know it gets easier. It does.'

Emma nodded, listening to her friend on the other side of the door.

'And you've got Bren.'

'Roz, I love Bren, I really do, but compared to you he's a bit rubbish.'

'That's very true.' Roz laughed. 'But I know you'll be okay, because even when the chips are down, you're loved and your life is mad, chaotic and hectic with not one minute to yourself, but I know you wouldn't have it any other way, would you?'

'I wouldn't have it any other way,' she confessed. 'I'm lucky, Roz. I know, so very, very lucky.' She shifted on the seat and slipped a little. 'Oh God! I've just wee'd on my trousers!'

'Jesus, Em, they're *my* trousers!'

She snorted her laughter and wiped her tears. They were both rather shocked, rendered silent by the sound of a loo along the row, flushing.

She had, quite obviously, assumed they were alone.

Rushing out of the cubicle with her dignity and trousers restored, as Roz scrambled to her feet, they were a little taken aback as Mackenzie stepped out of a stall.

'Don't look at me like that, I didn't know what to do.' The woman walked calmly to the taps to wash her hands. 'I was going to yell out that I was here, but then you started crying and I kind of missed the moment and then I thought it might be easier just to stay quiet, hoping you'd leave. And here we are.' She dried her manicured hands on a paper towel and stared at them.

'I didn't know you were coming, Mackenzie.' Emma washed her hands.

'Yes, I'm a governor.'

'Of course you are.' She couldn't help herself.

Roz pulled a face. 'For the record, Mackenzie, it was me who tried to make you two go out for a coffee,' she confessed. 'Emma had nothing to do with it. I just said she did.'

'Why?' the woman asked.

'Because I'm dying and you're lonely and I think you'd be good for each other. She's going to need someone, and I thought you might like the job.' Roz folded her arms across her chest.

Emma could only stare at Mackenzie as she felt the chill in her blood, unable to look Roz in the eye. Her friend's words made the whole prospect of her death real and her limbs shook accordingly.

'I am sorry, Mackenzie, for what we said when we were younger, about the whole Julia Phillips thing and your . . .' She touched her own mouth, wary that the nickname might slip from her lips.

Mackenzie tucked her hair behind her ears, ran her tongue over her pearly whites and addressed them both.

'I had to get new, immaculate teeth because, erm, because . . .' She took a deep breath. 'My stepdad. He erm . . .' She took her time, suggesting whatever it was she wanted to say wasn't easy. 'I got home one day, and he was hitting my mum.'

'Mackenzie!' Emma stepped forward and the woman took a step back.

'It wasn't unusual. He hit her a lot; I thought it was normal. And then one day, I came home and she was bleeding quite heavily and I tried to intervene, tried to protect her and he . . . he hit me. He knocked my front tooth out.'

'Shit!' Roz's succinct summary.

'Yes, shit.' Mackenzie coughed. 'He was loaded, and so I was whisked to a private dentist, who fixed my gnashers!' She beamed, showing off her immaculate smile.

'I feel like an arsehole.' Emma felt the hot lance of shame in her gut.

'Because you are an arsehole.' Mackenzie spoke with the beginnings of a smile around her mouth.

'She really is.' Roz went and stood by Mackenzie.

The bathroom door opened and in walked Mr Blundesthorpe's guest. The moment she saw her close up, Emma knew where she'd seen her before.

'Oh my God!' She put her hand over her mouth. 'You're the woman from the Ikea car park! When I reversed into the bollard!'

'Bollard!' Roz snickered.

'That was you?' The woman squinted.

'Yes. That was me.' Emma felt her face colour, recalling what she had said in her moment of stress.

'I was gobsmacked! I literally gave Uncle Gordon a lift to Ikea, and—'

'Uncle Gordon?' she interjected.

'Yes, I'm his niece. I picked up some plants and bits and bobs for my new flat—'

'Your new flat?' Roz asked.

'Yes, in one of the new builds on Merrydown Lane?'

'I know it.' Emma glanced at Roz, who twisted her mouth in the way she did pre-laughter.

'And what you never let me finish because you started yelling at me, and all I wanted to say, was that I saw the whole thing and a child could have been standing by the post or an old lady and they'd have been totally squished. And if you looked there was a whole bunch of paint on the bollard—'

Roz again tittered.

Car park police woman stared at her for a beat before continuing, clearly expecting more titters. '—and so it must have happened before and therefore it wasn't really your fault, the car park people should make the thing more obvious. It's dangerous and I was trying to help.'

'Oh.' Emma felt more than a little foolish. 'If it's any consolation, I would have come back and apologised but I had to get back to pick up kids and get my mum her lunch. Or at least, I thought I did.'

'Uncle Gordon has just explained to me that your mother and he are . . .' Car park police woman looked nervous. 'Close?'

'They sure are,' Emma acknowledged.

'They're shagging!' Roz pulled a face.

'For God's sake, Roz, we don't know that!' Emma yelled, as her face coloured with embarrassment.

'They are,' Roz giggled, 'one hundred per cent!'

Gordon's niece stood, dumbfounded.

'Well, this is a fun chat!' Mackenzie piped up. 'I'll leave you ladies to it!'

'Not so fast, Mackenzie!' Roz blocked the door.

'And what did you mean by "I ought to do more pub quizzes" – what was that all about?' The woman would not let it drop.

'Sorry, what's your name?' Emma knew she couldn't keep calling her car park police woman.

'Flick.'

'Flick!' Roz snorted. 'Sorry.' As if aware that this was not the time or place.

'I'm Emma, this is Roz and Mackenzie.'

'Hi!' Flick smiled and waved at them all.

'Flick, I honestly don't know why I said that. I was under a lot of stress. I think I was trying to be funny or cutting or cool, but I've never in my life done a pub quiz so I'm not sure where it came from.'

'I thought about it,' Flick confessed. 'I've just got divorced, actually, and I don't know anyone here, and I thought about what you said, "pub quiz". It sowed a seed, and I thought it might be a good way to make friends.'

'We could form a team!' Roz spoke like an excited teen in a way that was so out of character it made Emma laugh.

'Yay! Pub quiz team!' she offered, a little more sarcastically than she'd intended.

'I think it's a good idea.' Roz held her eyeline and nodded and Emma read between the lines. Her best friend turned to Flick. 'I'm actually looking for a friend for Emma, who is going to miss me, a lot.'

'Why, where are you going?' Flick asked in all innocence.

'Not sure really . . .' Roz twisted her mouth. 'But I hope that when I get there, I find eligible young men, cheap wine and peanut butter. They're the things I'm going to miss the most.'

'I thought being Emma's new friend was my new role?' Mackenzie asked with mock affront.

'How about a job share?' Roz suggested.

Flick looked from one to the other and there was an atmosphere in the bathroom that was warm, nice.

'I hope you don't mind me saying' – Flick stared at Mackenzie's mouth – 'but you have incredible teeth!'

'Thanks.' She smiled widely and said nothing.

'What shall we call our pub quiz team?' Emma was starting to come around to the idea.

'How about "The Arseholes"?' Roz's brilliant suggestion.

'I like it.' Mackenzie nodded her approval. 'The Arseholes.'

'Me too.' Flick beamed.

'Right, back to mine for sandwiches and cake, if anyone is interested. We should probably talk quiz strategy.'

Roz put her arms around Emma and rocked her. 'A bit of cake and a cup of tea, does it get any better than that?'

'I have to agree, I think cake makes everything better!' Flick enthused. 'Especially Battenberg, that's my very favourite.'

Emma groaned loudly.

'What did I say?' Flick asked, as she followed her fellow arseholes out of the bathroom . . .

A fortnight later, Emma said goodbye to Nancy and finished up at work, yawning as she climbed into her car. It had been a crazy run-up to Christmas and they were all a little exhausted. Not that she had to worry about supper; Reggie, with his reawakened passion for cooking, was taking care of that.

Her phone rang.

'What're you up to?' This was how Roz began their calls.

'Nothing, just leaving work.'

'Don't forget we're at the Rose and Crown tomorrow – festive pub quiz night! I've learned the names of Santa's reindeer!'

'It bothers me how excited you get,' she admitted.

'I'm grabbing life while I can, Em, squeezing every last drop out of it, remember?'

I never forget . . . 'Yep. I told you Thurston is joining us, didn't I, and Nancy?'

'What are their specialist subjects?' Roz sounded demanding.

'What are your specialist subjects?' she countered.

'Mew mew, mew mew mew!' her friend squeaked.

'Whatever. Shut up.' Emma yawned again.

'And as we're talking about the forbidden topic of my demise . . .' Emma steeled herself as she did when the topic was raised, but now understood that Roz had a need to talk about it and her job was to listen. 'I've decided to give you advice, words of wisdom that you can lock away and use in the future, things to help you be less of an arsehole.'

'We'd have to change our pub quiz name.' She pointed out the obvious.

'A small price to pay.' Her friend broke away to catch her breath and Emma closed her eyes, to better listen. 'First bit of advice is that you need to wear less blue.'

'Less blue? Where has this come from?'

'I've been waiting for the right time, but seriously, girl, every-thing in your closet is blue. Your trainers, your jacket, your hoodie, shirts, everything! You walk around like Papa Smurf.'

She looked down at her blue ensemble and her jeans.

'I like blue!'

'Yes, but it doesn't like you! You look washed out, it's dull, cold and flat – you need to wear orange, grass green and hot pink! Colours that spark joy! Tones that will lift your skin tone and your spirit! Happy colours!'

'Okay, got it, happy colours.' She made a snorting noise of dissent. 'Anything else?'

'Stop biting your nails. It's disgusting.'

'I'm not aware I do it.' She examined her fingers where, in lieu of lovely nails, ripped strips of pink sat close to the cuticle. Roz was right, disgusting. 'Right, nails, got it, I'll try. Anything else?'

'Yes. I'm leaving your kids my house, my money, the lot.' Roz spoke as casually as she had been when discussing jumper colours.

'You're what?' She didn't know what to make of it. It was a generous and kind act of love that meant her kids would have an easier start to life than her and Brendan, better able to dodge those darned grenades when they struck, choices . . . it was a life-changing gift that left her almost speechless.

'You heard. I'm leaving them everything. Martha can use the house until they're all older and decide what to do. She's having a baby and she'll need somewhere to live, to start her family, her own story, and she'll need her mum close by, and . . . she's my daughter, isn't she? And Reggie and Alex, they're . . . they're my sons.' Roz's voice faltered.

Emma felt the familiar sting of tears. 'Yes.' She could barely speak, her voice no more than a whisper. 'She is your daughter, darling. And the boys are your sons.'

'The only caveat is that she's not to let that stinky hound of yours on to the sofa! I'll be watching!'

'But Brucie loves his Auntie Roz.' She smiled through her tears.

'Well, I don't love him, not a bit.'

Emma didn't believe her for a second. 'I can't believe you'd do that for the children.' It was news so big, she couldn't process it.

'Family,' Roz breathed, 'family. Not that I want to discuss the detail until I have to and not that Martha should plan on moving in just yet. I've got some living left to do.'

'Yeah, you have!' Her joyous tone a reminder that life was wonderful and the people in it the only things that mattered, because who knew what was around the corner?

'Oh, hang on, Roz.' It was rubbish timing. 'There's another call coming, can we speak later?'

'You bet.'

Emma answered the incoming call. It was Reggie.

352

'Hi, Mum!'

'Hello, love.' She tried to pick up on his underlying mood, judge his tone from those two small words. 'Don't tell me you need picking up sooner! And please don't tell me you've changed your mind about cooking supper!'

'Ha! No, I called to remind you to take the chops out of the fridge, they cook better from room temperature, is that okay?'

'Of course, and you know the deal, I'll come and get you whenever you need me to.'

'Thanks, Mum, but not till after school, I've got double maths. I think Thurston's right, I need to learn stuff that will help me run my restaurant.' If Thurston had been in front of her, she would, she knew, have kissed him. 'And then after supper, can you drop me at Merrydown? Andy and I have got the membrane to put down, to stop weeds coming up through the soil. It's going to be epic!'

'It is, my darling.' Her heart soared to hear his enthusiasm. 'It's going to be epic.' Her phone beeped in her ear. 'Oh, got to go, Reggie, Alex is trying to get through, see you later!' She pressed the button and took the call from her youngest. 'Hello, love!'

'Mum, I've forgotten my swimming kit, can you bring it up to Marton Weir? If I forget my kit I lose house points!'

'Well, Alex, looks like you're losing house points, buddy.'

'But Mum—'

'Oops, gotta go, Alex, you're breaking up! Bad signal!' she lied. It was as she sat stunned that a text arrived from Martha.

Sergio driving me crazy. I feel like packing a bag and coming home, like for good. He's so nice to me! I need air! Is this normal? Love you x

Her reply was swift and true.

That kindness is everything, kiddo. Grab it with both hands and hold him tight. Anyway, you can't come home, because that would mean you'd need your bed and where else are we going to store the Lego? Love you too X

Emma arrived home and threw her keys into the bowl on the console that had once lived in her dad's garage, deciding to unstack the dishwasher while the kettle boiled.

Grabbing at plates and clutching at mugs, she rushed, and in her haste the green plate slipped from her fingers and shattered on the floor.

'Oh!'

Sinking down among the shards, she found it hard to explain to herself why she felt such a level of distress at something so ridiculous as a broken plate. The VIP plate, no less! Gathering a small piece, she popped it into a glass bud vase on the windowsill, keeping it for posterity's sake. This small edge of green china a reminder of the chaos of her family life and all those meals and all those squabbles and every emergency dash for forgotten kit, or to pick up or drop off a human who was in the wrong place.

She stared at her reflection in the window of her lovely kitchen, her favourite room in the house, and understood that things and people would come and go, they would get broken, they would no longer be at her fingertips, but as long as she could keep a little piece safe and sound, tucked away in her mind, then they were never really gone. It was in her memory that they would live forever!

She did the mental maths and decided to make a quick dash to Ikea – they were now, if and when Martha and Sergio came for supper, or Thurston or Nancy and Andy, a couple of plates short. It was unthinkable.

The roads were unusually kind, and she pulled into the car park, carefully avoiding any misplaced bollards that might be lurking out of view.

Plates . . . plates . . . plates . . . she held the items in her mind, focusing. How many to get, four, five, six? *Don't go crazy, Emma!*

As she dashed along the squeaky floor, looking at arrows and trying not to get distracted by the fancy displays in small rooms that made her want to redecorate the whole house, she spied a double bed.

She stopped walking. It was a double bed that looked soft, comfortable and inviting. A double bed made with immaculate floral bed linen and not one or two, but *four* fat pillows on which she just wanted to lay her head.

It was like she was on autopilot.

Her fingers reached out to feel the soft duvet, and before she knew it, Emma Fountain had pulled back the quilt and climbed beneath it, letting her body fall against the taut white sheet, letting her head sink into the pillows. It was as if her muscles softened, falling, weighted into the mattress, sinking right into it, and taking comfort from it. All was calm, as the breath left her lips in a soft purr. It was the kind of breathing that only occurs when you slip from that glorious state of dozy into deep and restful sleep, leaving the real world behind . . .

CHAPTER THIRTY-TWO

THURSTON

Thurston took his time, not for want of energy or enthusiasm for the day ahead, but rather that he wanted to savour the morning of this new day. Opening the wardrobe door, he ran his hand over the items that hung there. His fingers lingered over the single shirt that was buttoned up just so, with neat, ironed creases along the arms, and to hold it close to his nose meant he could savour the scent of summer meadows, infused with the fabric softener his wife favoured. He had saved the last of his shirts that Mary had laundered, and chose to wear it today, knowing she would think him a silly old fool for being so sentimental over something as mundane as laundry.

Nevertheless, it was with great care that he eased it from the wooden hanger and slipped his arms inside the sleeves, buttoning up the soft cotton fabric and letting the collar graze his face. If he closed his eyes and willed it so, he was able to detect the faintest hint of his wife's floral perfume. Or maybe not, maybe that was a fabrication from which he took comfort, and why not? He brushed his hair neatly and fastened the brown leather belt around his waist. His beard was trimmed, and he looked smart, even if he did say so himself.

Making his way down the wooden stairs, stepping as he liked to, only on the outside of the carpet strip on the centre of the tread, he stopped in the flagstone hallway and plugged the fairy lights in at the wall. The small but full tree on the table sprang into life, sending out a magical glow that bounced from the ceiling and across the walls, filling the space with its warm glow. He might not have managed all the tartan ribbons and bowers of pine cones that Mary was expert at putting around the place, but he felt fairly certain she'd approve. He had, after all, come a long way in the two months since she had passed away. His heart still hurt, of course it did, and he'd be a liar if he didn't confess to dreaming of her coming to take him home, but here he was, much less constrained by the net of grief that had held him fast and even, at points in the day, able to smile. This was real progress.

Next, he opened all the doors that led from the hallway, enabling him to admire the little tree from every room on the ground floor. Rhubarb stared at him as he popped the kettle on to boil and grabbed a fresh egg, which he'd scramble for his breakfast, becoming quite a dab hand at this old cooking malarky. Well, that wasn't strictly true, nothing tasted nor looked the way his wife's food had, but with his sister's patient instruction, at least it was no longer blackened and acrid, stuff that even Rhubarb, who ate all manner of foul matter he came across on the farm, turned his nose up at.

Thurston sat at the table in the middle of the room and sipped his tea and ate his breakfast, slipping a slice of buttered wholewheat toast beneath his egg and dousing it in more salt than Mary would think healthy.

It was Boxing Day, December the twenty-sixth. December the twenty-second had come and gone, and he had survived his first Christmas Day without his wife. In fact, he had more than survived. Nancy and Andrew had prepared a glorious lunch with all the trimmings and June, having decided she wanted to be closer to home rather than schlep up to their brother Loftus in Cumbria, had provided the pudding. The brandy-steeped fruit had made it perfect.

Eventually, Rhubarb rose from his basket in front of the Aga, sporting his brand-new tartan bow tie that was very natty, and made his way out into the yard.

'I can't help but think on days like this about what we'd be doing, about the years gone by. You with tinsel on your head, Christmas carols on the radio, leftover meat being readied for your Boxing Day pie. I miss it, Mary, I miss all of it. But I want you to know' – he coughed, feeling a little self-conscious that he now chatted with such ease to the air – 'I want you to know that I'm okay.' He paused a moment to allow this truth to percolate. 'I'm all right. And I've been thinking about what you said, about when we first met, and I was all shy and stuttery and we danced at the Young Farmers. I remember every detail – what you were wearing, that sage green dress, and I remember the way you felt, dancing as I held you in my arms. But mostly I remember what you said, that if a marriage was good then you'd be content to have twenty, thirty, forty or fifty years of it, rain or shine, that'd be enough. That's what you said.' He smiled at the memory of that night. 'But we got even luckier, Mary my love, we had sixty-two years. Rain and shine . . . and I would not swap a single day of it, not one.'

Rhubarb began barking loudly, his little guard dog, his buddy. Thurston looked up and smiled, knowing this heralded the arrival of his visitors.

'We're invading!' Emma shouted through the window as she parked her Ford Focus. 'Seriously, Thurston, are you sure you want us mob descending on you? Isn't this supposed to be a day of rest? We bring nothing but carnage!' She stood out to him from the car in her very, very bright pink furry jumper; he had, he realised, only ever seen her wearing blue. This pink suited her.

He chuckled, liking the kind of carnage that came with this large family.

'I'm all prepared! Just let me grab my coat!'

He did just that and emerged seconds later in his old waxed jacket with the shiny arms, the maroon woolly scarf around his neck, and his cap with the repairs on the brim firmly on his head. Reggie and Alex jumped out of the car and grabbed the wheelchair from the boot, opening it like experts. He watched as Alex wheeled it around to the front seat and Emma helped her friend Roz into it before placing a thick blanket over her legs.

'Hope you've got that port ready!' Roz yelled. 'It's the only reason I've agreed to these shenanigans, I was promised Christmas cake and port in very large quantities!'

'And I told you,' Emma sighed, 'that you've got to earn it. We need sound and loud support or you're not getting anything.'

Thurston felt the rise of emotion in his throat. Roz's spirit was admirable.

Brendan arrived in his truck with Martha, who, at a little over eighteen weeks pregnant, sported a neat baby bump. It gladdened his heart to see this miracle and had to admit to feeling a little overwhelmed when she had told him he would be on call to babysit! He couldn't imagine holding something so little and helpless; calves and lambs were for him a doddle, but they were so much sturdier and smarter than human babies, so he'd heard. Martha gripped the hand of her partner, Sergio, and he reminded himself to ask the boy which part of Italy he was from. He and Mary had always wanted to go.

Bruce the terrier jumped out of the truck and made a beeline for Rhubarb's bow tie, sniffing at it madly, whether in approval or mockery it was hard to tell.

June beeped the horn of her fancy car and pulled along the side of the yard. Nancy and Andrew jumped out, wearing matching jumpers with gaudy Christmas pudding designs on the front. June's eyeroll told him all he needed to know about what she thought of this. But what mattered was how happy Nancy looked. Smiling widely, she looked like one of those girls who had the whole world in her hands, and everything was possible!

'Uncle Thurston.' She rushed over and pulled him into a close hug. 'I've got some news.' She kept her voice low, and he understood discretion was required.

'What's that then?' He wondered if they'd finally decided to sell her old car and get something a bit more reliable.

'I wanted to tell you that night in the car when you dropped me off, when I told you that we had a lot to look forward to. I'd only just found out and we decided to wait, to make sure everything was going to be okay.'

'Only just found out what?'

'Andrew and I, we're having a baby! Can you believe it? It couldn't have come at a better time, we are thrilled!' She bit her lip and as her eyes brimmed he felt a flash of affection, not only for his niece, but also this little one, a Brancher baby, almost. Looking up, he found June's eyeline and she grinned knowingly; clearly she approved of the prospect of grannyhood much more than the matching sweaters.

'Well I never, Nancy, that is the most wonderful news imaginable.' He pictured the little nursery room in her cottage, filled with new life! New beginnings! As he accepted the kiss she planted on his cheek. Truly something to look forward to.

'It's like buses, isn't it? None come along for ages, and then both Martha and I, that's two babies at once . . .'

'It is, my lovely, just like buses.'

'And . . .' She hesitated. 'If it's okay with you, if it's a little girl . . .'

'Yes?' He knew what she was going to ask and felt an overwhelming pride rising in his stomach, knowing his wife would have been so honoured.

'We'd like to call her Barbie, after little Rhubarb, who we love so much!'

'Barbie? After the dog?' He needed it confirming.

'Only if that's okay with you.'

'It's . . . great.' He stared at his niece and tried so hard to contain his laughter that his eyes watered.

'Oh, don't get all upset, Uncle Thurston! Do you think Auntie Mary would have approved?'

'I know she would,' he chuckled.

The last guests to arrive were Mr Blundesthorpe, his partner Margery, whom he walked with slowly while carrying a sturdy camping chair, and his niece Flick.

'Is Mackenzie coming?' Roz shouted, looking around the crowd.

'No, she's visiting her son who is at university *in* Oxford, which is categorically not the same as being *at* Oxford.' Emma laughed.

'She's an arsehole!' Roz yelled.

'She *is* an arsehole!' Emma agreed.

Thurston shook his head; he knew no matter how long he spent in the company of these lovely people, he'd never quite understand this term of endearment and was mortified to sit in the pub quiz at the Rose and Crown weekly with this as their team name written on a chalkboard.

'Right,' Brendan boomed, 'let's play ball!' He used a fake American accent that made the kids cringe. 'Thurston, it's only right that as our host you're a team captain, so you get to choose first. Reggie, you're the other captain, so you go second.'

Reggie's face lit up at the announcement.

'How come I can't be captain?' Alex shouted, to the laughter of his parents.

'Next year, Alex!' Emma assured him and Thurston felt the swell of joy, knowing that this was where he would be next year, something else to put in his mental diary, plans for the future.

'Oh! Well, all right then.' Thurston had not expected the honour but looked now at the assembled mishmash of players for this, the inaugural Merrydown Boxing Day Rounders Match. 'This feels like quite the responsibility.' He caught the eye of Mr Blundesthorpe and could see the embarrassment hovering over him like a cloud, knowing that if he were standing there, he'd dread getting picked last.

'I pick Gordon, us old fogeys have to stick together!'

It felt good to hear everyone laugh, gave him confidence. He watched as the man walked slowly over to join him. They shook hands and Gordon leaned in, whispering, 'My plan is to get out as soon as is humanly possible, and with my gammy leg it shouldn't be too difficult.'

'Well, my hip matches your leg and so let's do just that!'

'Oi! No sneaky tactic talks!' Brendan hollered from the pack.

It was Reggie's turn to pick. 'Andy!' he yelled. Of course.

The two had formed a vegetable-growing alliance, the planning of which took up much of their time. Thurston watched as Nancy's husband ran to join his team, giving Reggie a pat on the back that made the lad stand taller.

'Alex!' He figured it was all about balance and with him and Gordon, Alex brought their average age down considerably. Not that the boy looked overly happy about being lumped together with the physically impaired octogenarians.

Thurston bent low and addressed him eye to eye. 'From one Reynard's College boy to another, always remember to congratulate anyone who beats you in any sporting situation, as losing sorely leaves a mark that is more permanent and memorable than a win.'

'We haven't lost yet, Thurston!' Alex whispered, and he could only admire his pluck.

'Martha!' Reggie's next pick.

'Sergio!' Thurston laughed as the young couple reluctantly let go of each other's hands, only to make gestures of threat, their competitive spirit strong. And so it went, until the teams were in position, with Brendan and Emma the last to get chosen and Roz, chief cheerleader, sitting next to Margery on the side of the paddock. Her voice was loud!

'Come on! Move it, June!' Roz hollered, and everyone bar June herself found this hysterical. 'Look at us, Margery! Wrapped up pitch side – couple of old tarts together!'

Margery stared at the girl. 'Chance would be a fine thing, Rosalind.' Her eyes danced with laughter.

With the posts marked out with jumpers, Thurston's maroon scarf and other discarded items of clothing, and the batting square made out of sticks, with bats in hand and a ball being tossed in the air intimidatingly by Andrew, Brendan shouted out, 'Speech, Thurston! Speech!' to a ripple of applause and encouragement.

He stood and took a deep breath, facing the gaggle in front of him, all twitchy fingered and keen to get playing.

'I'll keep it short,' he began, and there were whoops from the noisy rabble. 'This day is a special one for me, surrounded by people, by family, by love. My wife and I—' He coughed to clear the falter to his voice. 'My wife, Mary, and I, we dreamed that one day we'd look out of our bedroom window to see a large family gathered in the field, old and young. To do what, we weren't quite sure – play sport, quite possibly.' He smiled. 'We knew it wouldn't matter what was going on, winning or losing, it was all about being together. We'd imagine it often, the burble of chatter, bursts of laughter, even the ribbing in the way that families do. Life . . . I guess, life right there in our backyard. And here we are.'

He looked up at the sound of sniffing to see Emma and June both wiping beneath their eyes.

'The point is, we should never take days like this for granted, days like this that make us all realise that time together is precious, and we are all so very, very lucky.' He took a deep breath and felt . . . good. Yes, for the first time since he had watched his beloved slip away to tread a path that he could not follow, he felt good.

You can let go of her hand now, Mr Brancher . . . she's gone . . .

Yes, he felt good.

'Now let's play ball!' He too attempted an American accent.

The cheers and laughter were loud, and he knew he would always remember the hugs, high-fives and lingering looks exchanged by his guests, his family, his friends.

Thurston was preparing to take up his position on the field as everyone, with backs towards the house, made their way to their spot in the paddock, when, for no reason he could explain, he no more than glanced towards the bedroom window.

And . . . and . . .

His heart jumped in his chest and his tears flooded his nose and throat, because there in the window was his Mary – *Mary!*

'Sweet Lord!' he whispered.

There she was in her Christmas pinny, smiling at him. And as if the sight of her wasn't the sweetest gift he could ever have wished for, he heard her, oh dear Lord above, once again he *heard* her, loud and clear inside his head!

Hello, my darling. My sweet, sweet man. Never forget, I know all sides of you, Thurston Brancher, I know you're a man prone to silliness when the opportunity allows, a poet, a man who is quite adept at singing, when your throat, tongue and larynx are lubricated with God's golden nectar.

He laughed and she chuckled; her laughter, like every facet of her, something he had so badly missed . . .

And know your voice is a gift, my love, a gift. And know I love you. I loved you then, I love you now and I'll love you always.

And I you, my beloved, I you . . . he replied.

I will wait for you, Thurston; I will wait for you . . .

He watched as she placed the flat of her palms on the window, staring at him through the glass. Her smile, her laughter was light, sweet, and reminded him of spring and all good things ahead.

Wondering if he had succumbed to madness, he looked over his shoulder as Emma and Brendan, arms cast loosely around each other's waists, headed to the paddock, their backs averted. Reggie and Alex were tussling over the rounders ball, Reggie holding it high above his head so his shorter brother couldn't reach it. Martha walked slowly with her head resting on Sergio's shoulder and Nancy and Flick were deep in conversation, as if putting the world to rights. Roz, with Bruce the dog now positioned firmly on her lap, was chatting to Margery, the two laughing loudly, with Gordon and Andrew busy reorganising the bases, as if they had some understanding of the rules.

All this he took in in mere seconds, unable to tear his eyes away from the window at which stood the unmistakable outline of his beloved wife, just as she had so many times before. Her pinny tied tightly over her dress, her hair swept up into a bun with loose tendrils about her pretty, pretty face.

It was only when he felt the touch of something against his hand that he realised June was not only by his side, but that she too was looking up at the house. Her mouth open slightly, her fingers trembling as she took his hand. And for the first time in his life, he saw his sister lost for words. Fat tears fell down her cheeks, ran over her lips and dripped from her chin. It was no more than seconds. Mere seconds in which his beloved wife waved her hands and smiled at him.

The breath caught in his throat; he knew that he could neither explain nor forget the most incredible happening of his whole life. Greater than when they lay together in a boarding house in Lyme Regis, greater than when she told him how she would love him forever and that theirs was the greatest love.

June gasped. He blinked, and just like that, Mary was gone.

'June! Oh June!' He turned to face his sister, but the words wouldn't come. He dared not speak of it in case she had not seen the same thing, although her expression and demeanour told him that she had.

'I think . . .' She paused to collect herself. 'It's time you sang, Thurston,' she sniffed, shrugging her hand free and wiping her nose and eyes on the corner of her head scarf. 'I think it's time you sang out loud!'

Thurston turned from the house, knowing the peace in his heart was not because of his wife's goodbye, for he was in no doubt that that was what it was, but because the very happening itself spoke of hope and of reunion, of things he dared not dream nor believe. Of communication beyond, communication that was eternal, everlasting.

She was waiting for him and that was all he needed to know. All he had ever needed to know.

He looked out over the paddock, where frost lit the tips of the grass, sparkling in farewell as it was taken by the rise of the wintry midday sun and the people around squawked their laughter, squabbled their closeness, and gave their love in abundance.

He took a deep breath, and the sound of his beautiful, flawless pitch filled the space around him, the words of 'I Vow To Thee My Country' carrying far and wide on a gentle breeze that stirred the leaves and ruffled the feathers of the birds with whom he shared his home.

> . . . *the love that asks no questions*
> *The love that stands the test*
> *That lays upon the altar*
> *The dearest and the best . . .*

He sang loud and clear, in a deep voice that Mary used to say made the hairs on the back of her neck stand up.

He sang with his eyes towards the farmhouse, as if in serenade, and equally loud was the silence around him, as if nature itself paid reverence to this pure and holy sound. Everyone stopped, turned and stared, held fast by the man, that sound and the hymn that carried.

Thurston took his time, neither harried nor hurried; he sang slow and low, until he reached the last chorus and everyone, old and young, joined in with the words they knew and loved.

Turning now to face them all, he watched Emma, his lovely friend, saw how she smiled at her family, her wonderful, chaotic family, before locking eyes with her very best friend in the whole wide world, who then buried her face in the fur of Brucie the dog.

He knew that she, like him, was going to be okay, all of them would be, because they had each other. They would be okay because no matter how tough the choices, how difficult the struggle or how deep the hurt of what might come, it was simply life, and they would face it together.

Never, ever forgetting that for every day, every memory and every moment they got to spend on this glorious earth, they would always be so very, very lucky . . .

ABOUT THE AUTHOR

Photo © 2023 Paul Smith @paulsmithpics

Amanda Prowse is an international bestselling author of thirty novels published in dozens of languages. Her chart-topping titles *What Have I Done?*, *Perfect Daughter*, *My Husband's Wife*, *The Coordinates of Loss*, *The Girl in the Corner* and *The Things I Know* have sold millions of copies around the world. Other novels by Amanda Prowse include *A Mother's Story*, which won the coveted Sainsbury's eBook of the Year Award. *Perfect Daughter* was selected as a World Book Night title in 2016, and *The Boy Between* (a memoir written with her son, Josiah Hartley) was selected in 2022. She has been described by the *Daily Mail* as 'the queen of family drama'.

Amanda is one of the most prolific writers of bestselling contemporary fiction in the UK today. Her titles consistently score the highest online review approval ratings across several genres.

A popular TV and radio personality, Amanda is a regular panellist on numerous daytime ITV programmes. She also makes countless guest appearances on national and independent radio stations, including LBC and talkRADIO, where she is well known for her insightful observations and infectious humour.

Amanda's ambition is to create stories that keep people from turning off the bedside lamp at night, that ensure you walk every step with her great characters, and fill your head so you can't possibly read another book until the memory fades . . .

Follow the Author on Amazon

If you enjoyed this book, follow Amanda Prowse on Amazon to be notified when the author releases a new book!

To do this, please follow these instructions:

Desktop:

1) Search for the author's name on Amazon or in the Amazon App.
2) Click on the author's name to arrive on their Amazon page.
3) Click the 'Follow' button.

Mobile and Tablet:

1) Search for the author's name on Amazon or in the Amazon App.
2) Click on one of the author's books.
3) Click on the author's name to arrive on their Amazon page.
4) Click the 'Follow' button.

Kindle eReader and Kindle App:

If you enjoyed this book on a Kindle eReader or in the Kindle App, you will find the author 'Follow' button after the last page.